Praise for Lorie O'Clare's previous novels

"An explosive, fast-paced thrill ride that will leave you hanging on to the edge of your seat to the very end. Having read this at breakneck speed, I eagerly await the next book in the series."—*Once Upon a Romance Review* on *Stay Hungry*

"Another exciting, fast-paced, and very hot read from Lorie O'Clare." —*Sensual Reads* (4 stars) on *Stay Hungry*

"O'Clare does a great job putting tons of action and suspense in each of her books. Yet there is a solid love story going on with interesting characters. Her characters are strong and independent which means when they fall in love, they are going to fall hard."

—*Night Owl Reviews* (5 stars) on *Stay Hungry*

"O'Clare [writes] page-turners filled with well-developed characters, and sparkling, sharp-witted dialogue . . . and attraction so strong you can feel it!"

—*Romantic Times BOOKreviews*

"Gripping." —*A Romance Review*

"Intriguing [and] highly stimulating . . . a fantastic blend of mystery and suspense." —*All About Murder*

"The passion and steamy sensuality are great, as are the action and emotion." —*Romance Reviews Today*

"Sexy . . . I am irrevocably hooked on Lorie O'Clare."

—*Joyfully Reviewed*

Also by Lorie O'Clare

THE BOUNTY HUNTERS

THE FBI SERIES

ANTHOLOGIES

Slow Heat

Lorie O'Clare

St. Martin's Paperbacks

This is a work of fiction. All of the characters, organizations, and events portrayed in this novel are either products of the author's imagination or are used fictitiously.

SLOW HEAT

Copyright © 2012 by Lorie O'Clare.
Excerpt from *Hot Pursuit* copyright © 2012 by Lorie O'Clare.

For information address St. Martin's Press, 175 Fifth Avenue, New York, NY 10010.

ISBN: 978-0-312-53460-8

Printed in the United States of America

St. Martin's Paperbacks edition / December 2012

St. Martin's Paperbacks are published by St. Martin's Press, 175 Fifth Avenue, New York, NY 10010.

10 9 8 7 6 5 4 3 2 1

Chapter One

Micah Jones studied Greg King as he stood at the entrance of KFA, King Fugitive Apprehension. King squinted against the sun, which was hovering just over the horizon and not quite ready to set. King was a good boss—not that Micah had many in his past to compare the man to. But he didn't act like he was better than God.

It hadn't taken long for Micah to see just how good King was. The rumors about his reputation were right. King was an incredible bounty hunter and was clear when it came to explaining how he wanted things done. Micah was cool with cut-and-dry orders. He didn't have a problem going out and doing as he was told. It's what he'd done most of his life.

This wasn't a safe line of work. Micah didn't flinch over potential danger, though. The job was a lot safer than his last, and he was still alive. At twenty-eight, Micah had lived longer than many others in his former line of work.

King walked out of the KFA office with his wife beside him. The man was almost six and a half feet and somewhere around fifty years old. He didn't bark orders. Even when he got pissed, he growled instead of yelling.

But then, why bother raising your voice when your mere presence in a room grabbed everyone's attention? The man stood a few inches taller than Micah. In the three months Micah had been in Los Angeles, he'd grown to respect King. He reminded Micah of his father. There were differences, but both men were careful, levelheaded, and knew what the fuck they were doing.

King looked at Micah as he joined him in the curved driveway where their trucks were parked. Haley King, Greg's wife, remained next to him looking over paperwork.

"You ready to head out?" King asked, and looked over at Ben Mercy, their bounty-hunter-in-training. The kid wasn't licensed yet, and therefore got to do all the grunt work. Mercy never complained.

"Always ready," Micah answered, feeling pumped. Ever since Haley had described their job today, he'd been fired up to chase someone down.

There was a slight smirk on King's face. "You think so?"

"Sure do," Micah grunted, doing his best to keep a tap on his adrenaline. He didn't want to sound too excited about trailing someone again. "Ready when you are."

"Good. Got the trucks gassed up?" King asked Ben.

"Yes, sir," Ben said, straightening to attention. Everyone was laid-back at KFA, but Ben always acted as if he might salute King anytime the man spoke to him. "Ran them all through the car wash earlier this morning, too."

King nodded and glanced at the trucks in his driveway. "Look good," he muttered, his tone changing and sounding less aggressive when he spoke to the kid. "You can go with us on this one, Mercy. Haley will explain what you'll be doing."

Ben looked ready to split with pride.

"Micah, you're in unit two. Ben, you're in three." King thumbed at the two trucks parked behind his as his expression turned serious. "Okay, here is the deal," King continued, and glanced down at paperwork Haley was showing him. "You've already been shown Larry Santinos's stats and picture. Haley has copies of his photograph for both of you. Pin it on your dash so his face is fresh in your head. We're going in under the assumption Santinos is armed and dangerous. You understand the drill, right, Jones?"

"Capture and detain, no kill," Micah recited, and kept his hands relaxed at his sides. He never knew how desperately he craved having a gun back in his hand until he tried not using it. "We haul them in so a court-appointed lawyer can escort them into a courtroom where they are tried and convicted and more of the taxpayers' money is spent daily."

King grinned and Haley looked up from the papers in her hand. She smiled up at her husband. Micah had repeated what King ranted about on a regular basis. King wasn't cynical, but from time to time cases were sent over to them where everyone would be a lot better off if KFA just took out the scumbag once they found him. Micah was all for doing it that way.

Greg studied him with bright blue eyes. "That's right," he said slowly. "We never kill them. We haul them in so our wonderful judicial system can drag them through the system."

Haley was one hot MILF—although Micah would take that thought to his grave. She handed Micah and Ben pictures of Santinos.

"We're resetting the GPSs," she said, picking up where Greg left off. "One of our informants just sent word that Santinos is heading to his club early today. He should be at Club Paradise in about thirty minutes."

She stepped around her husband, then headed over to the three black Avalanches parked in a row outside the King's beachfront home and the KFA office. "It will only take a second to program the GPSs, then we can head out."

"And we stay together on the highway." Greg King looked pointedly at Ben. "I'm lead. No shortcuts."

"At this time of day traffic shouldn't be too bad," Haley added, then climbed into the rear of Ben's truck.

Micah gave up trying to convince Haley he knew how to program the GPS in their trucks. He waited patiently outside the middle truck that he would be driving until Haley finished with Ben's GPS and headed to Micah's truck. Haley was all business as she opened his driver-side door and climbed in, then typed their destination into the small GPS in the dash.

Greg and Haley had two sons who were around Micah's

age. King occasionally reminded Micah of his father, but Haley wasn't anything like the memories he had of his mother, which were vague at best. Micah hadn't seen his mother since he was ten but would bet good money she didn't look anything like Haley. He wisely diverted his eyes from her firm, tan legs when she hopped out of his truck a moment later.

"Once we get there, and before you get out of your trucks, be ready with your phones. Haley will three-way us in, then we take our positions." King stood outside his truck at the lead and pointed a finger at Micah and Ben. "No one jumps the gun on this one. This guy is big-time. We take him down neat and easy. No one gets carried away. Do you hear me?"

Micah gave a swift nod and climbed inside the black Avalanche parked behind King's. KFA had purchased two more trucks identical to the one they already owned right before Micah started working for them. He didn't care about the new-car smell, but having all the latest conveniences on his dash worked for him.

Three black Avalanches made them a bit conspicuous. Micah had spent almost ten years mastering how to be invisible. This wasn't his show, though. He followed King's lead. The man knew what he was doing.

Micah had to admit, when the three trucks drove down the interstate, it was a power trip. They appeared a force to be reckoned with. And they were. Micah had done his research. Greg King's impressive reputation wasn't just talk. KFA was the best bounty-hunting business in the United States. King knew how to arrive near a scene with all three trucks and park so no one noticed them. He also knew when to arrive making a show so their fugitive knew that his or her run was over.

Micah preferred his hunts more reticent. It was how he'd been trained. King had a hell of a lot of knowledge, and Micah would learn a lot from the man. Hunting wasn't the same as killing, and no one would come looking for a man with Micah's very specific qualifications at KFA. But broadening his horizons would only make him more versatile once he returned to his old life. He only had nine more months to wait out until this life was over and his previous life was back in full force.

Micah sat in his truck, driver's-side door open, and watched Greg and Haley talk to each other before she leaned against her giant of a husband and kissed him. Greg swatted her rear when she turned from him for the passenger side of their truck.

There were some things Micah doubted he'd ever learn from his boss. King had a relationship with his wife that was something out of fairy tales. The two of them were best friends, something Micah wouldn't believe possible after so many years of marriage if he weren't witnessing it for himself.

He couldn't remember the last time his dad had mentioned his mom. She'd been out of their lives for so long, it was as if she'd never been part of their small family to begin with. Maybe he'd never been part of a traditional nuclear family like the Kings, but Micah was proud of what he, his dad, and his uncle had accomplished. In circles not quite as public as KFA's, Micah's family had at least as strong a reputation.

"Jones," King called out.

"What's up?" Micah put his past out of his head and focused on King when he walked over to Micah's truck.

"Something about Santinos's MO bugs me." King rested his forearm on the top of the truck door and leaned in to talk to Micah. "Santinos has managed Club Paradise for several years now. The club was a dive and he turned it into a reputable, successful nightclub. The profile we've worked up on Santinos doesn't make him sound like the kind of person who would take a dive and turn it into a gold mine. The man is flashy. He loves his expensive clothes and fast cars. He lives on the edge, tossing money around as if it meant nothing to him. Nothing in his MO suggests he has any type of bookkeeping experience. Nor does it sound like he cares about budgeting."

"Maybe he doesn't."

"I think the man might have a partner."

"Someone under the radar?" Micah was intrigued. A hunt always proved more challenging when the prey was a bit more elusive than usual.

"What I'm thinking."

King's bright blue eyes pinned Micah with a hard look. King knew telling Micah his thoughts would intrigue and grab his interest. Micah waited out the moment, holding the older man's gaze. He'd learned shortly after joining the KFA team that King was really good at reading people, often pinning their qualities and faults down after talking to them for only a few minutes. What impressed Micah more than anything was how the man could also nail a person without even knowing him. It was a trait Micah would love to possess.

"I'm thinking he doesn't have a concept of what it takes to build a business like Club Paradise, and someone else is handing him an allowance to serve as their front man."

"Then nailing Santinos won't end the money laundering. But is that our problem?"

King sighed. He let go of the top of Micah's car door and straightened, cracking his knuckles as he turned and stared toward his truck idling in front of Micah's.

"The bounty is on Santinos," King said slowly. "We'll get him and turn him over to the authorities. That's our job. On our way over, I'm going to put a call into the detective on this case. I know the guy. We go back," he added, giving no indication if he missed the twenty years he'd been a cop for LAPD. Once he retired from the force, he had opened up KFA. King spoke matter-of-factly as he continued. "This is simply a hunch. So when we're there, here is what I want you to do. After our phones are patched together, I'll position everyone around the building. There is a back door to the club, and at this hour, I'm told it's often propped open while the cooks are in the kitchen preparing food for the evening. I want you to head in there and find the office. Find out what they're doing in that office. If I'm right, whoever is back there will be handling the club's real set of books."

King was always right when it came to profiling. It was uncanny.

"So while you are getting our man, you're sending me in to help out the cops?"

Greg King stared at him a moment, his gaze shifting as he appeared to be determining something about Micah. "Yup," he said finally, and pushed away from the truck. "I wouldn't be surprised if Santinos is hardwired. Marketing gurus often like to keep close tabs on their covers. He might tip off whoever is in the office when we take him down."

"I can handle it."

"I wouldn't have assigned this part of the job to you if I thought you couldn't." It was as close to a compliment as King would ever give.

Micah watched his boss return to his truck, climb in, and start it. In that short time, the sun had quit procrastinating and finally dipped below the horizon. Evening shades of pinks and oranges streaked across the sky, making for one hell of a sunset. Micah glanced at the clock on his dash and put the truck in drive, pulling out of the circular drive of the Kings' home and office, then looked in his rearview mirror when Ben pulled out behind him.

Three months wasn't long at all for a bounty hunter. Micah had helped chase down plenty of criminals skipping out on their bail. There had only been a couple of cases that got interesting like this one. Greg and Haley had been profiling this case for a while. Micah had overheard them discussing it, and now he understood why. The information they'd been given on Santinos hadn't added up for them. It was the irony of all ironies that King chose Micah to help out the cops.

Micah never once imagined working like this. Not only was he bringing in men and women who tried bailing on court dates or skipping out on their bonds, but now he was going even farther and searching for a person that the law hadn't found yet. He'd hunted down more people than he could count in his previous life who were guilty of crimes but not yet convicted. Micah had never brought them in; he'd killed them.

That was Micah Mulligan, though, and for now that man was buried so far under the radar, not even Greg King would find him. Micah pulled into traffic as he stayed a car length behind his boss. It felt good to be given a loose rein on this one. He wouldn't let it go to his head, though. Get cocky and take a bullet. Guaranteed.

Micah reached under his shirt for the silver pendant he always wore. The flat coin-shaped pendant had an engraving of Saint Michael on it. His father had given it to him when he was a boy after Micah had killed his first deer.

"Saint Michael protects hunters. You're part of an elite, proud group of men now," Micah's father had told him. Micah had stood tall and proud. That day he had felt like a man, just like his father and uncle. "That doesn't make you invincible. Remember that every time you aim your rifle, son."

Micah thought about his old man and his uncle, hunters in the purest sense. Micah had learned how to hold a shotgun, aim, and fire when he'd barely been taller than the gun was long. Hauling home large game had been a thrill through his teenage years. By the time he'd hit his early twenties, there wasn't a creature on God's earth Micah couldn't take down with a single shot.

Except for one.

When his father and uncle moved just outside Pontoria, Minnesota, a town in the northern part of the state, and beautiful country, Micah had been seventeen. With his mother long gone, and the old man and uncle all he had in the world, he trudged along begrudgingly. Their reason for leaving Evansville, Indiana, the only home he'd remembered up to that point, hadn't been clear to Micah at the time. He had seen Pontoria and the many lakes and wilderness around the town as boredom personified. It wasn't until he was much older that he learned the truth behind the Mulligan brothers' relocation.

Except now, for the following year, he wasn't a Mulligan. He was a Jones.

The pendant warmed between his fingers as Micah silently mumbled words to Saint Michael and rubbed it one last time before slipping it back under his shirt. His grandfather had been the strongest influence when it came to prayer. Micah's dad went through the motions. Micah wasn't sure why he always wore the pendant or said silent prayers. There was no harm in it. If he let go of the traditions his father and grandfather always followed, something bad might happen. Although what had already happened was bad enough.

Micah focused on King's taillights ahead of him as twilight slowly drifted into night. Maybe there was a Mulligan curse. His father, uncle, and Micah had made the best of the curse, or gift, they were born with. For a number of years the three of them handpicked the jobs they took, and made a lot of money as agents hired to kill—assassins. Within a few years the Mulligan reputation grew to the point where they'd moved into some incredibly elite circles. None of them had hesitated when the U.S. government started paying attention to their success record. Maybe they should have. But the money was incredible. The jobs were more than satisfying. The power was addictive.

Micah still firmly believed they'd been set up. They hadn't learned that their target was CIA until after Micah had put a bullet through his heart. His last kill had brought an end to the life they'd led for seven years. Micah's dad and uncle quickly devised a plan. Mulligans didn't go to jail. That same night they learned that Micah's target had been CIA—and that now the elusive branch was inquiring into his death—Micah, his father, and uncle had packed their bags and left their home, each of them going in a different direction. For a full year they wouldn't contact one another. None of them knew where the other two went. Three months of that year had passed. Three months now that he'd been Micah Jones instead of Micah Mulligan.

He signaled to turn when King's blinker began flashing. Their exit was up ahead. He prayed his father and uncle had found new lives that allowed them to satisfy the hunter in them. In nine months Micah would find the man who'd hired him to kill Sylvester Neice. That man would regret the day he ever hired Mulligan's Stew, the code name used when contacting the Mulligans. Once their world was safe for them again, Micah would track down his father and uncle. Micah wasn't the young son in need of protection by his father and uncle any longer. He was the grown man, in his prime, a hunter no one would ever be able to hunt down and kill. His father and uncle were getting older. Micah would see to their protection.

Micah followed King's truck, with Ben behind him. The three trucks slowed as they took the exit and reached the intersection that the street Club Paradise was on. Five minutes later they were pulling into a shopping center across the street from the club. Their trucks were conspicuous, but in the large parking lot with a four-lane, busy street between them and the club, their presence wouldn't be as easily detected. Micah glanced at the digital clock on his dash at the same time his GPS announced he'd arrived at his destination. He'd been so lost in thought all the way here, it was the first time he'd heard the soft female voice speak.

"Good to know," he muttered and parked alongside King. They had an hour before the club opened, plenty of time to nail Santinos.

King hopped out of his truck as Micah and Ben got out of their trucks. Haley hurried around to join them looking as if she'd just hung up her phone.

"Okay, Micah," she said, sounding out of breath. She didn't continue but instead looked at her husband. "We've only got about half an hour. You were right. The minute we explained our theory, they wanted in on the action."

Greg gave his wife a knowing look and nod. "Not surprising. Anyone else isn't our bounty, though. We have to let them in. All we get is Santinos." He looked at Micah and Ben. "Which means we need to hustle."

They took a few minutes to secure bulletproof vests over their shirts and check safeties on their guns. King was inspecting his Glock and slid it into the holster at his waist when he approached Micah again.

"You willing to go into this without the getup?" He nodded at the vest Micah was pulling up his arms. "If I send you around back, I need you looking as inconspicuous as possible." He lowered his voice, although there was no one around but the four of them. "We called in our hunch, and it's no one's surprise that we have police detectives on the way. This isn't their jurisdiction, though, so they have to go through red tape. That means the local jurisdiction will hightail over here, too." King shook his head. "A piece of the action never grows old," he muttered. "Needless to say, before long we'll have a three-ring circus. I want to move in on this now, though. What I want you to do is sniff out the back end of the club undercover, so to speak. You up for this?"

Micah stared at King a moment before letting the vest slide back down his arms. "No problem," he heard himself say and ignored the adrenaline spiking inside him.

King was one of the good guys. He wouldn't set Micah up. Just because he'd been used as a scapegoat to get rid of a crooked CIA agent, then thrown to the wolves when someone needed to be charged with the man's death, didn't mean something like that would happen again. Not in this lifetime at least, which would last another nine months before Micah would return to his old life. Cats might have nine lives, but Mulligans had an infinite number, as long as they lived by the code.

Honor-bound is honor-solid. Find another by the same code and he'll run by your side as true as Mulligan blood runs through your veins. Grandpa Paul had often grabbed Micah by the arms and given him a solid shake as he repeated those words to him. Even after he passed, his father had made him recite the Mulligan code, especially when they were forced to work with others.

Micah felt his Saint Michael's pendant press against his chest as he put the vest back into the side compartment alongside his truck.

"No weapons? Nothing?" he confirmed.

King nodded. "Just your true grit and intuition," King told him, then patted him on the back of his shoulder. "Something tells me you have a lot of both. And this will go down a lot smoother if we have everything wrapped up by the time the men in blue show up."

Micah watched King walk back to his wife. He prayed that was all King sensed about Micah. The next nine months would be hell if anyone learned who he really was.

Maggie O'Malley glanced up from her books when she heard the cook talking to someone out in the kitchen. Max was back there alone and would be for another hour until the club opened. He worked better alone and did an incredible job of setting up all the meal preparation if he didn't have anyone to distract him.

Four other cooks would arrive and clock in within the hour. By then, Max would have all the sauces simmering, vegetables diced and sliced—all the preparations that would be needed for them to serve the dinner listed on the dry-erase board behind the bar for that evening.

When her other cooks clocked in, all they would have to do was prepare the orders once the club opened. It was a good system, one that worked well and kept everyone happy.

Maggie hadn't asked to be kitchen manager along with accountant. When Uncle Larry hired her on as the club's accountant two years ago, right after she'd graduated from UCLA with an accounting degree, she'd considered herself blessed to be doing exactly what she'd wanted to do. The club had been in worse shape than her uncle had described, though. In fact, it had been on the verge of bankruptcy. At first she'd been pissed—furious, in fact, that Uncle Larry had lied to her.

It was her mother who'd convinced her to make a go of it. "Your uncle probably doesn't have a clue how bad off the club is. He doesn't realize the blessing he's been given by hiring you on, sweetheart," her mother had explained in the soft-spoken, matter-of-fact tone she used so often. "God has sent you on this special mission. I just know it. Uncle Larry is a free spirit but a good man. You've got that level head and your feet are grounded, blessings you've been given and can put to good use now. I just know you can turn your uncle's club around for him."

Maggie had done just that. She'd even had to admit that she'd enjoyed the challenge. When her uncle was arrested, for money laundering no less, Maggie had been so livid she'd walked off the job. It took more than a bit of gentle persuading this time for her mother to convince her to ride out the storm. Lucy O'Malley could see no wrong in her younger brother. Maggie wasn't so sure this time that Uncle Larry was innocent. What she didn't know, and could only find out by remaining at work, was where he got the money to launder. It sure as hell wasn't through the club. Maggie's books were squeaky-clean.

Glancing up, she cursed under her breath when Max continued talking to whoever was out in the kitchen with him. Uncle Larry might be an idiot, but she'd sworn more than once that he'd given her this office, right off the kitchen, on purpose. Uncle Larry knew Maggie would jump in and put his kitchen in order once she heard the chaos that occurred there daily. And she had. The kitchen was run like a smooth sailing ship today. It would stay that way, too, damn it!

She pushed her chair back from her desk, eyeing her numbers longingly. They were so much easier to get along with than real people. Numbers were cut and dry. They were black or they were white. There weren't shades of gray the way there was with people.

Not to mention, babysitting wasn't part of her job description. Already Uncle Larry was on her shit list. It was bad enough trying to keep tabs on him day and night. Unlike her mother, Maggie's father continually demanded that she wash her hands of him. Every time he said that, Maggie's mother would show her true Italian blood and start banging pots and pans as she yelled at her husband that a Santinos never turned her back on family and she knew an O'Malley would never do that, either. When Lucy O'Malley started yelling there was nothing to do but let her run through her liturgy, which usually ended with a winded cry to Saint Joseph and Mary and the good Lord Jesus to protect them all from hell.

As she headed around her desk, the mixture of Irish and Italian blood inside her brought Maggie's temper to a quick boil. She would never be like her mother, but a glance at the small statue of the Mother Mary holding baby Jesus, a gift from her parents, brought her pause.

"Saints preserve me," she grumbled under her breath, then crossed herself and blew out an exasperated sigh as she headed out of her office. Max knew he wasn't allowed to have friends in the kitchen while he was working.

"Max," she said, using his name as a warning when she stared at the tall, dark-haired man facing Max from across the large, cutting board counter. She'd put her foot down on anyone showing up and hanging out in the kitchen. The club couldn't afford to hand out free meals to everyone who decided Max was their best friend.

"He showed up at the back door with some questions." Max stuck his chin out stubbornly and turned to stir something that smelled strongly of garlic and oregano. Max was making his famous spaghetti sauce, one of Uncle Larry's favorite food items.

Maggie's stomach almost growled its appreciation. One of the upsides of being the accountant at Club Paradise was Max's incredible cooking. He could have been a four-star chef, but being a felon made it hard for him to find work. They were lucky to have him at Club Paradise. The club's reputation for good food had helped keep them afloat during its rough times.

"Who are you?" Maggie crossed her arms, possibly more as a shield than out of frustration. The man she stared at was incredibly sexy. There was something in his eyes that bothered her, though. They were a soft brown, and his lashes and eyebrows were a thick black. The lashes didn't quite hide the way his eyes appeared doused with danger. "What questions do you have?"

"I'm looking for Larry," the guy said, his deep baritone crisp and a bit too confident.

"Larry isn't back here. This is the kitchen. Larry would be up front. Are you lost?"

She watched something spark in his brown eyes. "And you didn't say your name."

"You're right." He didn't look like a vagrant wanting free food, or in need of a job. He looked healthy, very healthy, and dangerous. "Are you a cook also?" he asked, walking around Max's prep counter then between the stocking shelves.

"I work here and you don't." No matter how big or how muscular this man appeared, Maggie had had her fair share of dealing with bullies. She wasn't easily daunted or intimidated. Coming from a large family, Maggie had learned at an early age to stand her ground, or she'd never get what she wanted. "Tell me your name, why you're here, and what you want—or leave."

He didn't appear interested in anything on the shelves where cooking supplies were stocked but reached the end of the aisle and turned, then stopped when she blocked him.

The top of Maggie's head probably wouldn't have touched this man's nose. He was tall. And muscular, damn! When she stared at him straight on, she got an eyeful of roped muscle pressing against his T-shirt. Where his shirtsleeves ended, corded biceps began. He had a tan and she noticed a couple small puckers, old scars remaining from some previous trauma in his life. She imagined him fighting like a mercenary late at night in some loading dock against bad guys.

"If you want to go out front you can leave the way you came and walk around the building." She again crossed her arms, but this time felt the solid beat of her heart grow stronger against her chest. "The back door is that way." She nodded in the direction of the door, proud of herself for not trembling as adrenaline started pumping through her.

He glanced at her for only a moment before looking over her shoulder. Maggie couldn't physically stop him and wasn't sure touching him would be to her advantage. The way he brushed against her when he walked past suggested he wanted her doing just that.

"Is there a place we can talk?" he asked and took determined steps toward her office.

"Stop, now!" she ordered, hurrying after him and grabbing the door, then damn near skidding in front of him before facing him again.

The amusement in his eyes pissed her off. Who the hell was this guy?

"Anything you want me to do?" Max asked from behind the man. His voice was a lot deeper and meaner than he usually sounded.

"I don't know yet, Max," she said, focusing on the man facing her. She caught him glancing down her body before meeting her gaze. No way would she look away, but she was very grateful for Max being close, just in case. "Who do you think you are prancing in here as if you had a right?"

The man stepped closer, moving into her space, and lowered his head so that when he spoke, his breath tickled her skin. "Because criminals don't have rights. The police are going to be here any minute."

Oh God! This man really was dangerous. The law was looking for him and he had to choose her place to hide. Maggie had to think fast. She hadn't made the deposit yet. No way in hell would he take her and Max hostage. Not if she could outthink him.

"Why are they coming here?" she asked, trying to match his cool, soft tone.

"They're about to make an arrest." Now he looked amused, as if her question were ludicrous.

Maybe it was. Hell, she didn't have a clue how to talk to a criminal.

"Oh really?" she asked, wondering how for-real this man was. "And you sauntered into the back door of my kitchen just to tell me that?"

"Your kitchen? I thought Larry Santinos ran this place."

"He does." She didn't need to explain herself to him, and apparently the look on her face made that clear.

The buzzer next to her desk went off, letting her know someone had just come in the front door. She turned, glancing at it, and shifted her attention to the small box next to her phone. A second later it beeped, letting her know it was Larry who was here.

"Who do they want to arrest?" she asked, trying for a different tactic.

"Is that telling you Larry is here?" the man asked, nodding at the devices on her desk.

"That's enough." She pointed behind him. "Turn around and march out that door. Now."

"I will in a minute."

When he reached for his back pocket, Max moved faster than Maggie had ever seen the man move. For a giant black man, his looks could intimidate. But in the year and a half that he'd been here as their cook, all Maggie had seen was an oversized teddy bear with a heart of gold. At the moment, though, he looked terrifying enough that Maggie took a step backward. Max grabbed the man before he could get his hand to his back pocket.

Max stood over six feet tall, and this man was just as tall. Where Max was very large, Maggie imagined this man would be all steel and packed muscle. Instead of struggling, the stranger stepped to the side, turning to face Max and holding his hands up in surrender. Max looked mean as hell. The stranger didn't look scared. That same annoying, amused look was still on his face.

"Easy now," the man said, holding his hands out in front of him when he slipped out of Max's grasp.

Maggie noticed he was now also in her office.

"I was just taking out my ID to show the lady here who I am," the man said. "Is she your boss? You're a good man to keep an eye on her."

Max grabbed the man. His expression never changed and again he moved so fast a cry escaped Maggie's lips before she could hold it back. Pressing her fingers to her lips, she stepped backward until she leaned against her desk. Did she have time to call 911?

Max flipped the man around, and her office wall shook when he shoved him against it. The man's face was turned to the side, his cheek against her wall, terribly close to the crucifix hanging there. The amused look was gone. He blinked once, twice, and exhaled. Maggie swore she could see his brain working through the expression that changed on his face. He was trying to decide if he should try throwing Max off him or not.

Thick dark brown hair tapered around his face but didn't hide his intense features. This man was doing a really good job of controlling his reaction to Max's sudden attack. And Max, with his back to her, didn't look like the soft and cuddly teddy bear anymore. His large body looked hard as steel, just like the stranger he held. His thick, dark arms were like small tree trunks. And although defined muscle didn't bulge against his black skin, he held the man where he was and didn't appear to be struggling to do so.

"Take it out where I can see it," Max said, his voice a guttural growl.

"I will, man," the guy said, his voice still calm. "Best to let go of me so we don't fight over a piece of ID. I have a feeling your boss wouldn't like her office destroyed if you and I go at it."

"No, I wouldn't." Maggie wished she could say she hadn't seen grown men fight before. But with brothers both older and younger, she'd witnessed them scrap as children and more than once go at each other as adults. Italian and Irish blood was a bad mix, but it was who they were. Nonetheless, her heart pounded in her chest with two huge men standing just inside her office door and testosterone pumping through the air strong enough to slice through with a knife. "Pull out your ID," she managed, speaking softly so she wouldn't start screaming.

Suddenly she understood why her mother always spoke softly, almost whispering when disciplining them. She was trying to maintain control while raising five children and not instantly lose her temper. Maggie was on the verge of screaming at both of them.

Max adjusted his hold on the man, not willing yet to release him, but allowed the man to pull his wallet from his back pocket. The man flipped it open and held it out, his cheek still pressed against the wall. He strained to watch her when Maggie stepped closer.

She glanced at it but stepped back when the stranger applied a bit of strength and turned against Max, forcing him to take a step back as well. Did this stranger really possess the strength to push Max off him?

The man turned slightly, looking at Max. "Just a wallet, my friend." His tone changed just a bit when he added, "It's never smart to carry a gun in your back pocket."

"Hand your ID to me," Maggie instructed, deciding it would be smarter to keep her distance from both of them just in case one of them made a quick move. Another thing she'd learned at a young age. Two boys, or men, fighting worked on blind rage. Get too close and get hurt.

Max dropped his arms, taking his hands off the man, and stepped back until he filled her doorway. He was still so unlike her usual teddy bear cook. Maggie was grateful for him being there. She gave him a quick glance, hoping her look showed as much. There wasn't time to express her gratitude right now, though. She shot her attention back to the man when he turned, faced her, tugged on his T-shirt to straighten it, and gave her an eyeful of richly defined curves and bulges.

Maggie swallowed even though her mouth was too dry and forced composure through her body. Shifting her attention from that virile body to his hand didn't help much. She glanced at the laminated card he held out to her but couldn't read it from their distance. Her legs didn't wobble when she stepped forward and took it, then stared at the picture of the man standing in front of her, then his credentials. Her stomach did a small flip-flop.

"Micah Jones," she read. "Bounty hunter." Then shooting him a pensive glance, she speculated. "You go after people who don't show up for court dates, right?"

"Most of the time." Micah had a gift for not elaborating.

Her mind raced. Uncle Larry had his court date earlier that week. She'd called him that morning to remind him. She remembered talking to him afterward. He hadn't missed it, and there wasn't anyone else here who was involved with the courts. "Why are you here?"

Micah looked over his shoulder at Max.

Her large teddy bear had returned. His eyes opened so wide that white glowed around his black pupils. "Don't look at me," he said, defensively, taking a step backward. "I've never missed a meeting with my parole officer."

Since Maggie kept in touch with Max's parole officer as well, she believed him.

"Would it be okay if I spoke with you a moment, alone?" he stressed, looking pointedly at Max.

Maggie looked at Max, too. It really didn't sound like a good idea being alone with this man, Micah Jones. Probably most bounty hunters were tall and muscular. They would need all that brawn for their job. Her thoughts shifted. Instead of pissed, suddenly she was curious. She was reacting to all that virility like a female cat in heat. God, what would it be like to rub up against a body built like his?

She sighed, hoping she sounded frustrated instead of giving away the fact that warm throbbing sensations suddenly started between her legs. "Go back to work, Max." She smiled to reassure him. "I'll leave my office door open. I know you'll be here in a flash if I need you," she added, for her own sake as well as to remind the man facing her that he'd better not try anything.

What if he did try something while they were alone?

Crap! She'd read too many romance novels. Real men didn't try seducing women they didn't know.

Max hesitated but returned to his work, although not before snarling at Micah. Maggie would cheer him later. She'd rushed out of her office, ready to chew his ass for entertaining and feeding friends while on the clock, and now he was her hero. She moved around her desk on legs that were now shaky and collapsed in her chair. When she looked up, Micah

Jones stood before her desk, filling her small office with his presence. She stared into his eyes for a moment, trying to learn about the man inside the body. His eyes were a dark hazel, a thick, rich green that she had first thought were brown. They were clear, focused, and staring straight at her. She sensed intelligence, a man incredibly determined who took what he did very seriously.

As she stared, she swore his eyes clouded over. She got the oddest sensation that he had just intentionally closed himself off, shut down completely other than what he was doing right there and now. Maggie couldn't help thinking he was a man with many secrets. Remembering the puckered scars she'd seen on his arms, she wondered if those secrets were dark and terrible. Maggie suddenly felt trapped, cornered by a very seductive, yet dangerous man.

She patted the receipts scattered around her logbook for her pencil. Her computer was still open to QuickBooks and she tapped her keyboard, minimizing the screen. Regardless of why this bounty hunter stood in her office, the books for the club were none of his business.

"What's your name?" he asked, causing her to look up again into those shut-down, dark eyes.

For some reason, it was a relief knowing he didn't already know who she was. "Maggie," she offered, not seeing any reason to keep anything from him that was as simple as her name. "Maggie O'Malley." She gave up looking for the pencil she'd had in her hand before she'd gotten up from her desk and pressed her hands in her lap.

"Nice Irish name." His lashes were long and she couldn't be positive, but Maggie thought he was focusing on her breasts and not her face.

"I'll let my Italian mother know you said so."

Micah grinned but had already looked away from her and was taking in the items around her office. She watched his focus shift as he studied the scented candles on the small shelves next to her desk. In between them was a small figurine of an angel, with her wings spread wide and her arms extended. He looked at the top of her filing cabinet at the

Mother Mary with baby Jesus that her mother and father had given her years ago.

"Why are you here, Mr. Jones?" she demanded when he squinted at the picture on her wall of her and her brother and sisters, taken the previous year at their Easter family gathering.

"It's Micah." He took a step toward the picture, studying it a moment longer before returning his attention to her. There was a picture of her parents facing her on her desk. Next to it was a smaller snapshot she'd framed of her two nieces. He glanced at the frames but wouldn't be able to see the pictures from where he stood. "And as I said, the police are on their way."

"Right now?" she asked.

"Yes. Right now."

"Why?"

Micah gave her an appraising look. "You're either very good or very stupid." He cocked an eyebrow while again letting his focus drop below her face. "Are you going to tell me which, or do I make my own conclusions?"

"I'm not stupid at all," she said defensively, hating that amused look on his face when he returned his attention to her face. "And since you won't find out on your own, I'll let you know now. I am very good."

"Is that so?" For a moment the clouds lifted from his eyes. In that brief second that he dropped his guard, Maggie saw raw, unadulterated lust.

Her heart skipped a beat. Instead of that guarded wall returning, he narrowed his gaze, making it harder to see into his eyes. He didn't frown but something shifted, bringing her pause. Micah came across as being a rock, impermeable, yet there was a weakness there and she'd just found it. Her sexual innuendo threw him off. Knowing her adversary's weaknesses was always a plus. Now if she only had a clue what to do with her newfound knowledge.

"So I'm told," she said, lowering her voice just a little, not enough to be obvious but just enough to make him wonder.

"And now that we've established that, assume nothing and tell me why you're here."

"To learn if you're the brains behind this operation." He leaned against her desk, bending over so that his face was closer to hers. His arms were lined with thick, corded muscles that were impossible not to stare at for a moment. His hands were large and his fingers long. When he fisted them and pressed them against the edge of her desk, she felt the piece of furniture lean slightly from his weight.

"We probably only have a few minutes, darling. Do you run Club Paradise?"

"Larry Santinos owns Club Paradise and that's public knowledge if you care to check. Although I'm sure you already know since he's in the system now." Maggie didn't care if an edge of disdain surfaced in her voice. It would be idiotic to sound proud of her uncle's foolishness.

"I didn't ask who owns the club. I asked who runs it. Are you in charge of the books?" He looked pointedly at the ledger and receipts on her desk.

Maggie would welcome an audit at any time. Although bounty hunters didn't audit books. "I do the books, yes. Are you with the IRS, too?"

"Nope. All I'm doing is bringing you in. Although I'm sure the IRS will be involved soon enough."

"My books are squeaky-clean." She straightened, stuck her chin out, and dared him silently to suggest otherwise. Nonetheless, when her heart began pounding against her chest, this time it wasn't because the sexiest man she'd ever laid eyes on was leaning over her desk staring down at her. Her father had argued each time he and her mother fought about this that Maggie needed to get away from the club. If her uncle had fucked up, her father didn't want any of his transgressions affecting Maggie. Up until now, Maggie hadn't been worried. She hadn't broken any laws.

"But you admit that you handle all the books for this place," Micah said, his tone matter-of-fact.

His phone buzzed at the same time the buzzer on her

desk went off, indicating someone else was entering the club. This time the light on the box by her phone didn't flash. Someone had come in the front door of the club. Larry didn't have any appointments. If he did, she would have set them up for him. She glanced at the clock on her wall then shot Micah a side glance as he straightened and pulled his phone free from his belt. He stared at the crucifix on her wall as he tapped his phone's screen with his long fingers.

Micah put it back on his belt and gave her an appraising look. "Would you mind coming up front with me, Miss O'Malley?"

"What's going on?" Her voice cracked as she asked. She hated sounding scared, but Micah was doing a good job of making her feel that way.

Everything about Micah stiffened. He stood straighter and no longer appeared relaxed. His expression hardened, and his dark eyes were almost black. Suddenly he terrified her. A sheen of perspiration broke out over her body. Maggie's shirt clung to her back when she stood. Her legs trembled and she braced herself, pressing her palm to the edge of her desk.

"Let's go, Miss O'Malley."

"I haven't done anything wrong."

"It would be a lot easier if you come with me of your own accord."

She was sure she had to look terrified. "Where?"

She tugged on her shirt, knowing she offered a fair amount of cleavage. Micah didn't glance down this time but kept his eyes pinned on hers.

"If you don't mind," he said, gesturing to the door.

Who had entered the club? They opened in fifteen minutes but usually when Larry got there early, he came straight back to the kitchen, hungry and whining worse than a child. Sometimes he had someone meeting him up front before the club opened for business and he'd make the bartenders work before they were supposed to clock in, waiting on him and whoever he entertained. Ever since his arrest, though, Maggie had made sure she knew who he was meeting with and what the meeting was about. Her uncle, who was ten years older than she was and the youngest of the ten Santinos, too often behaved as if he were ten years younger. He always acted wounded, if not put out, that Maggie continually questioned his behavior. Uncle Larry swore he was innocent and had been framed. Either way, Maggie firmly believed that if he were hanging around good people, none of this would have happened.

Maggie stepped around her desk, moving to the door, but froze when Micah grabbed her ledger book, flipped it shut, and clasped it under one powerful arm.

"You can't take that!" she complained loudly, turning on him and reaching for the book. Her fear dissipated and anger replaced it. It didn't matter how much sex appeal Micah Jones possessed. This had gone too far. "Give that back to me right now," she demanded, extending her hand and staring him down with all the outrage she felt at the moment.

"Actually, I can take it." He took her extended arm and held on to her with a grip strong enough that she couldn't free herself. "Tell your guard dog there is no problem," Micah whispered in her ear when he pulled her up against his virile body. "Unless you want him to see his boss being arrested."

She spun around so fast, Maggie slapped Micah's chest to maintain her balance. If she hadn't seen his relaxed, carefree expression when he'd first entered the building, she wouldn't have believed it existed.

"Arrested?" she gasped, her entire body suddenly trembling. "You don't mean me, no!" she argued. "I haven't done anything wrong."

"Then I'm sure you'll be back to work in no time." Micah held on to her and half dragged, half carried her to the front of the club.

"What's going on?" Max bellowed.

Maggie didn't have a chance to reassure him everything was fine, as Micah had told her to do. She didn't even see him. Micah had her pinned against him, his grip pinching her skin, and her feet barely touching the ground as he headed into the club.

Club Paradise was a large establishment, with over thirty small tables for drinking and dining, a pool hall, and a dance floor complete with an incredibly expensive light system. Freddy, their DJ, was already behind his booth, leaning against it with a sober look on his face as he watched the people in the club. Three of their bartenders were behind the bar, all of them huddled together and shifting their attention quickly to Maggie when she appeared, still in Micah's clutches.

Maggie felt her skin burn, her heart pound so hard in her chest she could barely move, and her legs threaten to turn to jelly. Larry was red-faced, his hands fisted at his sides as he shifted repeatedly from one foot to the other.

"I want my lawyer," he kept repeating, although he was hard to see with the giant men standing around him. "You can't do this," he wailed.

Maggie made inventory of each man, noting one man who was so large he had to be at least six and a half feet tall. There was another man next to him. A short woman spoke softly to Larry. All of them faced her uncle. None of them looked at her when she entered the club. Were they arresting him? Why would Micah suggest she be arrested, too?

"What's happening here?" she asked, glancing up at Micah's stony expression.

He didn't answer her—just looked straight ahead and held on to her until they joined the group.

"This is Maggie O'Malley, the club's accountant." Micah then looked at the man facing him.

An older man with threads of silver going through his short hair nodded at Micah. "You've got the books to the place?"

"Yes, sir." Micah turned over Maggie's ledger book.

The state of shock that had overtaken her when Micah practically dragged her out of her office lifted as she watched her ledger book exchange hands.

"Let go of me, now!" She almost ripped her arm out of its socket when she freed herself from Micah's grip. "I need to see credentials from all of you, right now," she demanded and tried grabbing her ledger book. "And I don't think you can take these without a warrant," she informed the very large man who was at least twice her size.

That's when it dawned on her. This wasn't the first time some part of the Mafia had tried pushing their way into Club Paradise, although she admitted this was the best staged. Maggie grabbed her book and felt it slip from her fingers as the man turned from her, passing the book on to the man next to him.

"Larry Santinos is coming with us. He missed his court date and we're here to take him in." The large man had a stony, almost cruel sound to his voice. "You, Miss O'Malley, will wait right here with us until the police arrive."

"What?" she cried out, jumping behind Micah when the man tried taking her wrist.

Larry started howling for his lawyer again when the really large man pulled his wrists behind his back and pulled out handcuffs.

"You are not putting handcuffs on me." Maggie made a dash for the bar. "Alex, quick, call nine-one-one!" she yelled at her bartender who stood closest to the phone. "Now!" she screamed as she slid around the bar.

Her bartender hesitated for only a second before dashing to the phone. Max busted his way through the swinging doors and froze as he stared at the group of people in the club. At the same time that he froze, a large body pounced on her backside and Maggie slammed against the hard floor.

She started screaming but an arm stronger than steel wrapped around her waist, squeezing all the air out of her lungs so that her scream left her mouth sounding more like a gagged yelp.

"Don't make this worse on yourself," Micah whispered into her ear, holding her against his body, which felt more like a brick wall.

"Who are you people?" she gasped, her mind spinning as everything around her suddenly seemed a bit too surreal. The only thing she was acutely aware of at the moment was the rock-hard body pressed against her backside and the warm, unmovable arm pinning her against it.

"You've already been told who we are." He was still whispering in her ear.

Maggie turned her head and stared into his eyes. Micah didn't blink or let on to any emotion he might be experiencing at the moment. His tone was flat, not reassuring, not hostile, just stating basic facts.

"Why are you doing this to me?" Her voice didn't sound like her own.

"For being way too good of an accountant, sweetheart. I suggest you use some of that extra money you made to get yourself a really good lawyer."

Chapter Two

Micah declined heading out for a beer when he and Ben clocked out several days later.

"You just don't strike me as the clean-cut type," Haley teased, sitting on Greg's lap on one of the couches in the KFA office.

The office, which had once been a screened-in porch, was an extension of the King home. He'd only been inside the rest of the large beachside house once when he'd been interviewed for the job.

"Looks can be deceiving," Micah said, nodding to her, then Greg. Both of them grinned and appeared very relaxed. It amazed the crap out of Micah that couples like Greg and Haley existed. They'd been married forever and still looked as if they were head over heels crazy for each other. "I'm heading home and fixing food," he added, although he doubted they cared.

"What happened with Santinos? Was that chick they busted his brains? God, she was hot!" Ben said, already at the door and holding the doorknob. He dragged his hand across his forehead and blew out a loud breath, then grinned at all of them.

Micah couldn't leave until Ben did since he blocked the door. Although Maggie's confused expression and her shocked reaction to being hauled out of her office had confused Micah for a bit, criminals came in all sizes and shapes. Maggie sure didn't look, or act, guilty. She had been terrified, shaking worse than a leaf in a storm. When she ran to her bartenders and ordered them to call 911, he'd almost believed her innocence.

He agreed with Ben, though. Maggie O'Malley was hot as hell. She wore her auburn hair pulled back with two barrettes, which showed off her high cheekbones and trim, straight nose. Her lips were full and naturally red and had been moist and incredibly distracting the entire time he'd been with her. She'd had bright blue eyes that had flashed with defiance and a rush of other emotions while in her office. Maggie definitely had no training in curbing her emotions or reactions to anything happening around her. She hadn't been guarded. Those bright blue orbs had been open books so easy to read. He hadn't seen her temper seriously rage until they'd joined the others in the club and she'd raced around the bar. Then they'd been a hard, steely cobalt guarded with long, thick dark lashes.

Micah preferred his women with a fair amount of makeup, and tight-fitting clothing that showed off all their curves. For the most part, women who were slutty. When he'd given himself downtime, which hadn't been often, there wasn't time to chase down and seduce a lady. He knew what he wanted and a woman who wanted the same thing, with no strings attached, was always the best catch. He'd indulged in ladies who ran a bit wild since he'd been barely a man.

Maggie O'Malley had been as far from the type of woman Micah sought out as possible. She had dressed rather conservatively, with a sleeveless cream-colored blouse that had a V-neck collar. She'd tugged on it quite a bit, showing off a decent amount of cleavage each time. He'd never found capris to be very attractive. They had always reminded him of clothing that settled-down married women wore. But Maggie had been wearing capris that had fit nicely around her slender hips and full, round ass. She wasn't tanned like most women in LA, but her creamy white, perfect complexion had brought out the blush in her cheeks when she'd noticed him as more than an intrusion to her daily routine. And she'd noticed him more than once—that was, until she realized he'd been there to bust her special form of accounting wide open. Then all sexual curiosity had vanished.

Micah wasn't much on families. His old man and uncle meant the world to him but he'd never considered the three of them anything close to a traditional family. Maggie's pictures in her office revealed a good-sized family. She'd yelled out to her uncle Larry a couple of times during the confusion of Micah trying to restrain her until the police had shown up. For a few minutes there he'd contemplated whether her entire family were corrupt, an Irish Mafia—or possibly Italian, since she'd mentioned her mother was Italian.

Call it intuition, but Maggie didn't fit the profile. Granted, Micah only spent about half an hour with her before two police officers had escorted her and her uncle to patrol cars, but Micah had always trusted his initial gut reaction to people. He seldom read a person wrong. Maggie was either innocent or damn good at what she did. Since her uncle had initially been arrested and not her, Micah was glad the law would determine if she were guilty or innocent. The fiery little sexpot had done a good job of appearing shocked, then outraged, that any of them would consider her a criminal.

"Santinos has been charged with money laundering across state lines, and the country's border." It was Haley who answered. "You two both did a great job with that case," she added. "Micah, you sure had a feisty one on your hands."

"Maybe you'll get a chance to take her down again someday." Greg grinned at him.

Micah frowned. "What's that supposed to mean?" he asked.

"They weren't able to pin charges on her. Maggie O'Malley was released. She does remain a person of interest, however."

"Let me know if you need help with that one," Ben said, punching Micah in the arm before heading out the door. "If I'm off the clock, I'm headed out to play some pool."

"You're both off the clock," Haley told them. "Micah, you're on call tonight."

"No problem," he said. It wouldn't bother him if they needed to capture someone during the night. He had no intention of creating a life for himself while here in LA.

Micah followed Ben out the door, waving over his shoulder as Greg and Haley called out their good-byes for the night. He headed across the driveway to the side of the house where his bike was parked. Greg King also rode a Harley. The garage door was open when Micah reached his bike. He glanced at the shiny chrome on the expensive machine inside. Micah's bike wasn't quite as fancy as Greg's. Micah used it as his only means of transportation. Gas was cheaper on two wheels, and he traveled light; anything he ever needed, he could take with him on the motorcycle. Micah didn't ride to stand out. He rode to blend in, be nondescript, and be able to move out of a situation fast if needed. There might not be anything to worry about right now, but he remained alert. It was the way he was raised and part of his nature.

His ride home didn't take more than twenty minutes. Living in LA was a slight adjustment after small-town life. Micah adjusted to his new surroundings easily enough, though. He'd spent most of his life watching people, their behaviors, and how they lived. For the most part people didn't vary too much from one part of the country to another. But it was smart to put surroundings to memory. If anything, he took learning his way around a new city as a challenge. LA was his home turf now, and he needed to be comfortable here.

By the time he rolled into his narrow driveway and parked his bike in the garage, it was dark. Not that he ever got home from work with it light outside, unless it was because the sun was coming up.

Micah preferred long hours on the job. Creating a personal life would be a very bad idea. He would work for KFA for the rest of the year until things had calmed down enough that no one would suspect him returning and making his kill. The asshole who'd set him up had numbered days. He wouldn't risk trying to find his old man and uncle before whoever set the Mulligans up was no longer breathing.

He entered his small, dilapidated rental house through the back door, flipped on his kitchen light, and locked the door behind him. There were frozen pizzas and a variation of different types of store-bought prepared meals in his freezer. He had juice, milk, bottled water, and beer, along with a dozen eggs, a mixture of different sliced meats and cheeses for sandwiches, and the usual condiments. Mulligans didn't do drive-through fast food. A person was an open target waiting in a fast-food lane.

Dropping his leather gloves on the small table just inside the door, Micah then slipped off his jacket and hung it on the back of the chair pushed under the table. His cell rang and he pulled it off his belt and headed through the house to his bathroom.

"Jones," he grumbled and struggled with his shirt while keeping his phone to the ear.

"You left the house too soon." Haley's good mood was obvious in her tone.

"Why is that?" He pulled his phone from his ear just long enough to yank his shirt off and toss it in his laundry basket.

"She showed up right after you left."

"What?" Micah missed the first part of what Haley said. "Say that again."

"Maggie O'Malley, the young lady we were talking about right before you left. We told you she'd been released since they couldn't charge her with anything. But she's a person of interest," Haley repeated, speaking fast. "She came into the office right after you left. She asked for your number. She wants to hire you to find whoever is framing her for money laundering. Greg and I are starting to think she might actually be innocent. No one who is guilty can act that confused and terrified. I almost felt for the girl," Haley said, the smile still in her voice.

"She wants to hire me?" Micah remained rooted where he stood, trying to make sense of what Haley just said. "To find a money launderer?"

"Yes." Her voice regained its smooth, authoritative calmness. "If you aren't interested, let me know. But we don't have a problem with people we brought in seeking out our professional assistance to confirm their innocence. Sometimes they are innocent, other times they are really good cons until we break through their act and bring them in again. Either way, you have your license. If you want to do some moonlighting on the side and pull off some detective work, that's fine with us."

"I'll let you know."

Maggie wondered for the hundredth time if she was making a really big mistake. Things had barely settled down and returned to normal since she'd come home from the police station after damn near being arrested for something she didn't do. Her mother had practically become hoarse yelling about how the country was shit down a pothole when a good American citizen was guilty until proven innocent.

John O'Malley would turn on his wife, pointing at her with his tobacco pipe that he hadn't smoked in the house since Maggie's older sister, Deidre, had been diagnosed with asthma. He would then bellow his disapproval loud enough for everyone in the house to hear.

"Saints preserve us all, woman!" he'd begin. "I served in two wars that made this country even stronger than it was when our parents came over. If Maggie had been in the old country, only the good Lord above knows how they might have treated her."

If Maggie's mother didn't lighten up after his war comments, her father would throw the deadly retort that would silence the entire household. "If that daughter of mine had listened to her papa, believed for a moment he might have known what he was talking about, and steered clear of that no-good brother of yours, she wouldn't be in trouble right now."

The silence that followed hadn't been a pleasant quiet. John and Lucy O'Malley wouldn't storm to opposite ends of their home and stew about the intolerable nature of their spouse. They would both march into their bedroom, close the door, then sit on the edge of the bed, at the small desk in their room, or stand facing the window, and ignore each other.

Maggie's brother Aiden had once said, "Even when they fight they do it together. They truly are the perfect couple."

Maggie wasn't sure screaming and yelling at each other qualified her parents as couple of the year, but after fifty years they were still married. It was more than many could say.

Either way, it had been several days since she'd come home from the police station. Her temper had cooled as well, and now it was time to do something about it. If the police thought they were being discreet following her everywhere she went, they were really lousy at their jobs. Well, just let them follow her across the city to the bounty-hunting office. See if she cared!

She hadn't discussed hiring the bounty hunter with her parents—or with anyone, for that matter. There was no reason to start the ranting and raving all over again. Maggie had done her research, though. Bounty hunters were required to be licensed private investigators in the state of California. Micah Jones already knew everything about her situation. Hiring him made a lot more sense to her than seeking out a stranger and trying to explain the situation when she barely understood it herself. That is, if he was willing to investigate why anyone would have thought her guilty of a crime in the first place.

Her father had told her enough times that if she wasn't comfortable discussing her actions before doing them, then they probably weren't honorable enough to do. Ignoring her parents' often-repeated dialogue, Maggie went with her gut on this one. There had been something about Micah Jones.

A man his size probably wasn't afraid to do anything. Her brothers Aiden and Bernie were both just over six feet tall, although neither had the bulging muscles that Micah Jones did. Aiden and Bernie weren't afraid of anything. Size had its advantages.

Micah was more than just tall. She'd seen something in his eyes. They weren't exactly green. Maggie remembered flecks of light brown mixed with the green surrounding his focused pupils. She would say they were hazel. Still, it wasn't his eye color that had stuck in her memory as much as the way he'd looked at her. It was as if he'd been able to search deep into her soul and had learned every secret about her in the few minutes he'd talked to her in her office. Of course, if that were actually true, he wouldn't have hauled her out to the front of the club like some common criminal.

Maggie had been impressed with how Micah had handled Max, though. Max was a really large man. She'd never seen him look more dangerous than he had that day when Micah had sauntered in through the back door of the kitchen as if he'd owned the place. She and Max had formed a special bond that day. This entire mess sucked even more now because Max didn't want to work at Club Paradise anymore. He couldn't be associated with criminals through the terms of his parole. Maggie wasn't a criminal, but Uncle Larry was still listed as the owner of Club Paradise.

God help her! This entire ordeal was a serious mess. Part of her wanted to wash her hands of the club, too. But another part of her argued she'd invested too much time and effort to leave Club Paradise, which had been a dive when she'd first started working there and was now a successful nightclub.

If Micah Jones was willing to do some work on the side, she would bet he'd be able to find who was behind making her look guilty of a crime she didn't commit. As much as she loved her uncle Larry, she was starting to believe he had done something terrible involving the club. Maggie might be a good accountant, but she couldn't see anything through her books that showed any illegal money entering the business.

She'd found KFA's business address off paperwork connected to her uncle Larry. She was still livid that he'd lied to her and said he'd kept his court date. If he'd just shown up like he was supposed to, none of this would have happened. But she was just as mad at herself for believing she could keep Uncle Larry out of trouble when trouble had been his middle name for as long as she could remember.

The people at KFA had been willing to give her contact information for Micah Jones. The first step was done. Glancing around as she sat in her driver's seat, she didn't see any nondescript car parked anywhere along the long stretch of road where KFA was located.

Maggie punched in the phone number for Micah Jones. It rang only once before he answered. She barely had time to gather her thoughts.

"Hello, this is Maggie O'Malley," she stumbled. Had the people in the KFA office already warned him she'd be calling? He didn't say anything, so she forged forward. "Earlier this week you . . ." She let her words trail off. What did he do? Maggie bit her lower lip but then decided the heck with it. Why mince words? "Earlier this week you dragged me out of my office so that cops could take me to the police station and question me for twelve hours."

"Okay," he said when she paused.

"I want to hire you to find out who is really guilty."

"I'm a bounty hunter."

"You're required to be a licensed investigator in the state of California in order to be a bounty hunter," she said, reciting the words she'd already rehearsed for when he told her he couldn't do this. Granted, he hadn't said no yet. But she was ready to challenge him so he would say yes. "Which means if you wanted, you could investigate this for me."

He said nothing. Maggie sighed. "May I come over and discuss this with you?"

"That's fine." Micah hung up.

"Fine," she grumbled. "Don't say bye." But she already knew he wasn't blessed with manners. This also meant he knew she had his address, which they'd given her in the KFA office. So he'd already talked to them and knew she'd be calling. "And that tells me he was intentionally rude."

Her stomach twisted into a ball of nerves as she drove through traffic and across the interstate toward Micah's home in Santa Monica. Although raised in LA, this was a town Maggie wasn't overly familiar with. Her friends used to rave about the roller-coaster rides on the beach, and all the shopping they'd done after going to the amusement parks. Maggie had always worked after school, then there was college. Now she worked even harder. No roller-coaster rides for her.

She relied on Google Maps on her phone to make sure she didn't get lost. So when her phone rang, Maggie glanced nervously up and down a strip mall as she pulled off the road and into its parking lot and stopped her car. Over half the shops in the mall had gone under; boards covering windows were spray-painted with bright graffiti. She prayed they weren't gang signs and that she hadn't parked on some gang's turf just so she could answer her phone.

"Hello, Mom," she answered and realized if she told her mother to hurry up because she didn't like where she'd parked, her mother would want to know why. She couldn't exactly tell her that she couldn't read Google Maps on her phone and talk on it at the same time. Her mother would then want to know where she was going.

"Will you be home soon?" her mother asked.

"Sure. Why?"

"Deidre and Bernie are here."

"They are?" Maggie saw her older sister Deidre more often than her other brothers and sisters since she lived the closest. But Bernie, her younger brother, had been on the road with his band for almost a year. "I didn't even know Bernie was in LA."

"We found out earlier today. I just got off the phone with Annalisa."

Maggie's radar went up instantly. "What are you doing, Mom?"

Annalisa never talked to her parents, not since they'd made a scene in front of her boyfriend because he was black. Maggie talked to her baby sister from time to time, but for the most part Annalisa had cut all ties with the family.

"Aiden just showed up. And I'm making my famous sausage meatballs," her mom informed her, neatly avoiding the real meaning behind Maggie's question.

Maggie groaned. She wouldn't set her mom off. Maggie couldn't remember the last time her entire family had been under one roof. There was only one reason why they would all be there on such short notice. "Did you tell everyone the police talked to me, Mom?"

"Everyone is worried about you, sweetheart. As they should be. We're family and we stick together when something bad happens." Her mother lowered her voice as she continued. "And yes, I told your brothers and sisters. Of course, everyone is worried about your Uncle Larry, too."

Suddenly it all made sense. Her mother was doing this for her father. Maggie's dad hated all of his children being so spread apart. If the world rotated on its axis the way John O'Malley would have it, all of his children would be on the same block they lived on and cranking out grandbabies for him to spoil. Her parents had fought terribly after Maggie got home from the police station. It had made Maggie sick. Her mother's health wasn't great in the best of times, and she'd looked seriously run-down the past day or so. But her mother had rounded up the family, not just because they would all want to know about Maggie, but to make her father feel better.

"You'll be here soon?" Her mother barely made it a question.

Well, that would cut into the time she might need to persuade Micah to help her. If she didn't show up at the house soon, her parents would send the O'Malley army out looking for her. After promising not to be long and using the argument that traffic was a nightmare, Maggie got off the phone, confirmed where she was on Google Maps, and drove the last few blocks to Micah's house.

Micah Jones didn't live as extravagantly as the Kings did.

Maggie parked in front of a run-down small house with a
narrow cracked cement driveway leading up to a detached
garage. After confirming it would be a twenty-minute drive,
at least, to her house from Micah's, Maggie got out of her
car and locked it.

"Stay calm," she ordered herself, and did her best to ignore her pounding heart when she walked up the drive to the
front door.

Micah watched Maggie O'Malley walk up to his house
through his partially closed living room curtains. There had
been something about her auburn hair, pulled back from a
face with very little makeup, that at first he'd thought made
her look innocent. Now, watching her as she looked down,
stepping over the cracks in the drive, with her hair today
tucked behind her ears and partially covering her face, he
had a chance to see Maggie in a new light.

Most of the time when people were released because
charges couldn't be pressed, they started living under the
radar, or they ran. Then their name would inevitably pop
back up on the bounty hunter's list. They'd been released.
They'd taken off. The DA or FBI finally had viable evidence
to book them but couldn't find them. Once again, it became
the bounty hunter's job to track them down. Micah was actually starting to like this line of work. At least as a bounty
hunter, he still got to hunt and capture. He just didn't kill.
Money wasn't everything. Peace of mind often proved just
as necessary and desirable.

Maggie wasn't running. Four days ago the police had let
her go. If he were to step outside it wouldn't surprise him if
he found an unmarked car parked somewhere on his street.
They would be watching her. And more than likely right
now they were as confused as he was. If she was guilty, why
would she return to the bounty hunter who very well may be
asked to track her down in the near future?

Maggie walked in front of the window without looking
in his direction and tapped on his door. She was possibly
one cocky bitch. Maybe she believed she could outsmart

him. Micah had no problem tangling with a beautiful young lady.

Or the possibility existed that she truly was innocent.

Micah stared at his front door. Maggie rapped on it several times. He no longer saw her through the window. He waited a breath then unlocked and opened the door.

"Micah Jones." She combed her fingers through her hair, dragging long, thick strands to the back of her head where they fell and draped around her oval-shaped face. It fell as it did in those shampoo commercials, thick, shiny, healthy-looking hair that was tangle-free. She absently tucked one side behind her ear. "We haven't been formally introduced."

That was an understatement. "We already know each other." Micah stood to the side, pulling his front door far enough open for her to enter. Maggie remained standing in the doorway.

He seriously doubted someone who was working in a club that was a cover for money laundering—guilty or not, Maggie had to know that much—was going to stand on propriety and not enter a single man's home without introduction. Maybe she was trying to make an impression. He wasn't going to discuss shit with her while she stood on his front stoop. There was some outstanding spy equipment out there, and LAPD probably had their share of it. Microphones could pick up conversations easily a block away while a couple of bored cops sat in their car and listened.

Micah cleared his throat. "Welcome to my home, Miss O'Malley." He leaned on the doorknob with one hand and stared at her bright blue eyes. "Are you going to stand in the doorway and interview me, or come in?"

Maggie shot him a scathing look. It disappeared quickly and she took a step into his living room. Micah began closing the door, forcing her to enter farther. He watched her look around his place. When she turned and faced him, clasping her hands together, her expression was blank, relaxed, and impressively unreadable.

"Since this is your area of expertise, and not mine, I don't feel there is a need to interview you. I'm here to hire you to find whoever is truly guilty of this money-laundering crime the police believe I committed. How much do you charge?"

Micah hid his smile. Already she was reaching for her purse. If she paid him cash, he'd be obligated to turn the money in and determine if it was part of the cash being laundered. He doubted she could write a check. Micah was pretty sure her accounts had been frozen.

"That all depends on what you want me to do." He closed and locked his front door then moved around her, leaving the living room for his adjoining dining room. There was no dining room table—just two sets of bookshelves and his extra dresser, where he housed clothes he didn't wear as often and other odds and ends he preferred not to be on display if anyone were to come over. Such as his guns, and the knife collection his uncle had given him at his confirmation. "Apparently you believe, as the police do, that Larry Santinos was only a front man and not the brains behind all this."

"Uncle Larry still claims he hasn't done anything wrong," she said from behind him. It wasn't clear by her tone if she believed that or not.

Micah entered his kitchen, flipped on his light, and opened his refrigerator. He would process her slowly. "Do you want a beer?"

"No, thank you." She was still in his living room.

Micah twisted off the cap of one bottle of beer and held another bottle in his hand. He kicked the refrigerator door shut with his boot and sauntered back to his living room. Maggie remained in the middle of the room where he'd left her.

"You sure?" He held up the unopened bottle.

Maggie shook her head. "I know what you're thinking," she began, and looked around his living room. She looked everywhere but at him.

Micah set the unopened bottle of beer on his coffee table then walked around it. He cleared the stack of newspapers from the corner of the couch, dropped them to the floor by his feet, then sat. He wasn't going to take the lead here. Taking a long sip of the cold beer, he studied Maggie O'Malley.

"What am I thinking?" he asked, tilting his head and watching her as she appeared to become more and more uncomfortable. He hadn't asked her over to his place. This was her show, and he'd let her play it out. He didn't see any reason to go out of his way to make her comfortable. Unless, of course, she thought that he was considering how she would look naked. In which case, if she were to oblige and show him, he'd make her very comfortable.

She was thin, but not anorexic like too many women were these days. The straight-cut tan skirt she wore hugged her curvy hips and flat tummy. It showed off long, slender legs that at the moment were pressed tightly together. Her anklebones touched each other and her brown sandal straps draped over slender, small feet. Her toenails and fingernails were both painted pink.

He let his gaze travel back up her in the next moment. Micah had no intention of making her anymore uncomfortable than she was making herself. He didn't have to gawk to appreciate how her sleeveless fluffy-looking sweater had a deep V-shaped collar. It ended just above the middle of her breasts. This was the second time he'd seen her and the second time she'd worn clothes that showed off her cleavage. Her decent-sized boobs were obviously something about herself that she liked. He most definitely appreciated the view.

Micah would never reveal to a soul how many people he'd killed in his life. He'd killed more than one incredibly beautiful woman in cold blood. None of them glowed the way Maggie did. Even as she fidgeted, either waiting for him to say more or choosing her words carefully, he sensed something in her that he didn't often see.

Was it innocence?

He already knew she was a spitfire. She was intelligent enough to manage the books for a nightclub, legitimate or not. Micah knew better than to pass judgment this soon.

Maggie met his gaze with a mixture of awe and fear, and something else, not quite so subtle, but Micah was aware of it nonetheless.

Curiosity. Lust. Sexual awareness.

"If you think I'm guilty, this isn't going to work," Maggie snapped suddenly. If that's what she thought he was thinking, she was way off base. Her eyes narrowed, and her pencil-thin eyebrows closed together. "Tell me that you were simply doing your job earlier this week and we might be able to work together. But, Mr. Jones, if you believe I am guilty of stealing money from my own club, then I want to know right now."

"I honestly don't have an opinion one way or another." *Spitfire* might have been an understatement. Maggie had a serious Irish temper. "Prove to me you're innocent." He leaned back, crossed one leg over the other, and rested his boots on his coffee table.

Maggie watched the act, swallowing slowly, then licked her lips. He could see the bra line through her sweater and as he watched, her nipples grew hard, puckering slightly against the fuzzy material.

"How can I prove my innocence?" she demanded, extending her arms and then dropping them, sighing loudly. Her blue eyes flashed vibrantly, and for the first time her gaze traveled up the length of his body. "I don't even fully understand what they're trying to charge me with."

"You don't?"

Instead of answering, Maggie crossed her arms and met his gaze head-on, glaring at him as if his question were preposterous. All she could possibly know about him was where he worked, where he lived, and that he was easily twice as strong as her and with skills she didn't possess. Skills to chase down, capture, and arrest men and women who had bounties on their heads. Yet she glared at him as if she'd take him on right then and there. He liked that about her. Micah had a sudden desire to stand, move in on her, and test those tempting waters she was showing off to him.

"The cops think Club Paradise is a cover for illegal activity and that it isn't actually making the money it claims to be making." She dropped her purse on his coffee table next to the unopened beer. "Which is absolutely ridiculous," she exclaimed, and began pacing in front of him. "They took my ledger book." She stopped and pointed an accusing finger at Micah. "You took my ledger book. But someone also took my computer. If it weren't for hard-copy backup files, I wouldn't have a clue how to defend myself through all of this."

He would have to check whether the police had searched her house. Micah would pretend he hadn't heard what she just said, at least for right now. "Why is it ridiculous?"

Maggie stopped pacing, faced him, and put her hands on her hips, gaping. "Did you even look at my ledger book after taking it from me?"

"It was evidence." When her expression didn't change, he slowly shook his head. "I don't make a habit of going through evidence. I handed it to my boss. You were there when I did it."

"My uncle is locked up and I can't talk to him."

"Talking to him wouldn't be a good idea."

Again she looked at him as if he had two heads. "Uncle Larry isn't smart enough to use a nightclub as a front to launder money."

Micah stared at her. Did she really not see why she was the likely candidate behind this operation? Maybe she was one of those book-smart people who didn't have a lot of common sense. If that were the case, and she were guilty, the cops would have gotten it out of her.

"Club Paradise is not being used as a front for money laundering," she stressed.

"Do you understand what the charges are against your uncle?" he asked.

She narrowed her gaze on his. "Maybe you are the wrong person for this job. It's not your responsibility to determine guilt or innocence. All you are is the hunting dog."

He'd been called a lot worse. Micah straightened, pulling his feet off his coffee table. "I'm a bounty hunter," he said simply.

"Then why did you come after me, too?"

"What did the police say to you?" he countered.

Maggie began pacing again. "Nothing. They wouldn't answer any of my questions. But they sure had enough of their own."

"What did they ask you?"

"Questions about the ledger, my bookkeeping." When she paused again her smile was cool, with a hint of warped satisfaction. "They wanted to know where the other ledger was," she said, then laughed drily. "Maybe I should be flattered that they thought me such a good bookkeeper. They went through my books, saw how perfectly well kept they were, and couldn't find where all of this supposed illegal money is. Honestly, I'm not sure it exists. But when I asked them that?" She laughed, but there was no humor in it. "Lord, you'd think I'd asked to see the pope."

"Detectives don't usually like the implication that they've done their job wrong."

"And I do?" she countered. But then she pointed her finger at him. "They fucked up big-time," she hissed, that temper of hers flaring again. It made her eyes glow a beautiful dark shade of blue. "Maggie O'Malley doesn't go down without a fight," she announced, pounding her chest. "They think they can just follow me around town and I'll commit some crime that will prove them right. They can't admit they made a mistake. Like I would lead them to whoever is responsible for hiding some enormous amount of illegal money."

"Then why come to me?" Not that he was complaining. At first he hadn't thought Maggie his type. But he'd been wrong. Maggie was beautiful and he was enjoying the hell out of watching her pace back and forth across his small living room.

She spun around, her back to his dining room. Her shoulder-length auburn hair flipped over her shoulder and fanned across her face. She slapped it out of the way and heaved in a deep breath. Micah let his gaze fall to the swell of cleavage visible at the V of her sweater.

"I don't want the police thinking I'm a criminal. I don't want to be followed. I want my computer back. I want my life back!" she yelled. When her attention dropped to the floor, she blew out a breath and visibly deflated. "You don't seem interested in helping me," she mumbled, that Irish temper of hers completely gone. "Maybe it was a mistake coming here. What time is it? Where did I put my purse?"

He pointed to his coffee table where her purse sat next to the unopened beer. "It's after six."

"Crap. I need to get going." She looked at him pointedly. "Will you help me or not? Will you find out who is really laundering money through my club?"

"You said it was ridiculous for anyone to be doing anything illegal in your club."

"It is." She walked over to her purse, pulled her cell phone out, and looked at it. "LAPD wouldn't waste all this manpower if something weren't wrong."

It was the first seriously intelligent thing she'd said since entering his house. Micah studied Maggie. He really did believe she was innocent. None of the telltale signs that she was lying to him were there, such as glancing to the side instead of never making eye contact, mechanical movements that were the result of a rehearsed soliloquy prepared to convince him of her innocence, or speaking too fast, reciting lines previously memorized. Maggie looked at him, concerned, determined, and frightened. There was no pretense, nothing other than a beautiful young woman, proud of her work and shocked it had been labeled faulty.

Maggie didn't know what to do. Something told him coming to him had been her last shot.

"You want me to snoop around, ask questions, do some research and find out why someone like your uncle could be charged with such a sophisticated crime. And what if I find out your uncle isn't as stupid as everyone thinks?" He'd be smart to tell her no. If he helped her, it might draw more attention to him than he could afford. He should stand up, escort her to the door, wish her the best of luck, and send her on her way.

"I think Uncle Larry is guilty of just that," she mumbled, "being stupid."

"I'm not cheap," he said, and his insides tightened when she looked at him quickly, laughing and almost crying at the same time.

"You'll figure out what is really going on here," she choked out, still smiling.

Her eyes were suddenly moist crystals, large blue orbs dancing with happiness. Maggie sincerely believed he could save her. The amount of power she placed in his hands with that look of sincere gratitude did something to him. The protector, the carnal predator that always existed just under Micah's skin surfaced with a ferocity so strong, he almost growled.

Maybe he could do this. It wouldn't be the first time he'd danced around law enforcement without being detected. Maggie didn't have a clue who she'd come to for help. She thought him nothing more than a bounty hunter with a private investigator's license. She'd come to him because he was already familiar with what was going on. He'd have to be careful, incredibly careful. Micah had to admit, after just three months, he was already growing antsy. Helping Maggie out might very well soothe his itch.

"I'll see what I can do."

"Oh my God," she breathed, clapping her hands together and grinning broadly. "Thank you. Thank you so much. I already feel so much better. Now I can go home and spend time with my family and not worry so much." She started to the door.

He wasn't ready for her to leave. There was no reason for her to stay, though. She looked at him over her shoulder, still grinning broadly, then laughed.

"You need my number, right?" she asked, then looked down at herself and her empty hands. "Damn. My purse," she mumbled, and laughed some more.

Her laughter was like a drug seeping into his body, hardening every inch of him. The trained killer was suddenly screaming halt. But the man didn't want to listen. Micah had spent most of his life learning to read himself so he could better track others. In the very few times he allowed himself downtime, he didn't want a relationship, but a woman willing to spend the evening with him, enjoy incredible sex, then go on her way. Suddenly he was in unfamiliar water. If he worked for Maggie, they would be forced to spend time with each other. He doubted the sensations she was pulling out of him would subside the longer he was with her. Maybe this wasn't a good idea.

The intense urge to go to Maggie, stroke her hair, soothe her until she relaxed, letting him take the reins and ensure she would never be in danger, was so strong he barely managed to control it. Micah didn't protect, though. He killed. People needed protection against him. They didn't seek him out for protection.

Micah stood, reaching for the purse before she could and handing it to her. All he had to do was tell her no, send her out the door.

"I'll write my number down for you," she said and shuffled through her purse for pen and paper.

An incredible weight had just been lifted from Maggie's shoulders. She exhaled, feeling giddy, light-headed, and overwhelmed. "Thank you," she mumbled, hating how she looked like a complete idiot in front of him. Micah had no clue how his willingness to help made her feel. She wasn't sure what she'd expected when she'd come over here, but when he'd said okay her life seemed to have returned to its normal state.

She looked at him when he stepped around the coffee table, moving in on her space. He made her nervous with the carnal, almost animalistic look in his eyes as he locked gazes with hers. Suddenly her hands were so sweaty she almost dropped her purse.

This man was dangerous—terrifying, in fact. He was a different breed of man from any she'd ever known. Maybe allowing him into her world, requesting that he search deep into her life and her job to find out what had happened to throw suspicion onto her, was a serious mistake.

Whatever she'd seen when he first entered her office earlier that week was suddenly there again. Dark flecks around his pupils made his hazel eyes turn almost black. It was an emotion she couldn't label. His expression remained relaxed, just as it had when she first met him. Micah didn't react to anything, at least not like other men did. Even when he'd let his gaze travel over her body, when he'd stared at her boobs a moment longer than he should have, he hadn't as much as cracked a smile.

Whatever she saw in his eyes just now was possibly as much emotion as he ever let through. Was it pain? She wasn't sure. There was definitely something simmering just underneath that mask of indifference on his face, and it wasn't good.

She shivered despite herself and dropped her attention to all the muscles rippling under his T-shirt. "Your boss, er bosses, spoke highly of you." Maggie imagined Micah had some damn good abilities. Heat spread inside her at the thought of him fucking her senseless. Lord, she needed to get out of there. "I know you'll be able to fix this entire mess," she said hastily, forcing her attention on her purse in her hands.

"I'll take a closer look at your case."

There was something about the way Micah spoke, as if he were trying to suppress a growl with each word. His raspy baritone scraped across her flesh, igniting relentless need deep inside her. Thank God it would take a good twenty minutes through traffic to get home, and that she'd be bombarded with the entire family once she got there. Quite possibly they would all already be fighting. At least then no one would notice how flustered she might still be.

His dark hair was a bit more tousled than it had been when she first walked in the door. She didn't remember him running his fingers through it and imagined that accepting a case might create some kind of adrenaline rush inside him.

"Thank you," she heard herself mumble. "I don't have a

lot of time but we can lay out the preliminaries right now and go into more detail on Monday."

"You don't work weekends?"

She dug through her purse, pulling everything out until she reached her wallet. Flipping it open, she took what little money she had left. "My mom has the entire family coming home. Most of them are already there. She called me on my way over here. If I can get away—" She broke off her sentence before finishing. She was rambling. Hell of a way to convince this man she was innocent and completely incapable of committing this crime. But then, how did a money launderer behave?

Maggie handed him two hundred dollars. "I hope this is enough to begin our working relationship. Of course, I expect you to log, and keep receipts of, all of your expenses." When he showed no reaction, and didn't make a move to take the money, Maggie tried a reassuring smile. "You'll learn I'm a stickler for numbers and documenting everything. It's the accountant in me." She shrugged, then fought off her frustration when he still didn't accept the cash or say anything. She waved the money at him. "Take this. I have a receipt book in my purse, I think. If it's not enough I have more cash at home." She was pretty sure he already knew her bank accounts and credit cards had been frozen, which still had her pissed as hell.

When Micah moved, Maggie lowered her hand, straightened, and found herself once again staring into his dark hazel eyes. Maggie held her ground, watching him.

"Pay me when I catch whoever has put you in this situation." That growl that had been barely audible before came out clearly this time.

When he placed his hand over hers, closing his fingers around hers, and the cash she held, heat exploded inside her. An unbearable pressure swelled to life between her legs. Shifting her weight only caused it to grow.

"I'll work up a contract," she said, and looked at his hand over hers. "We'll make everything official." It was impossible not to return her attention to those evasive eyes of his.

There was still nothing to read in his dark gaze, but his lips curved slightly. They were nice lips for a man, not too full but not thin, either. A shadow spread across his jawbone, the end-of-the-day whiskers. If he kissed her, she would feel their abrasion against her skin.

What the hell was she thinking? Maggie tried pulling her hand free of his.

Micah's fingers tightened around hers, preventing her freedom. But only for a moment. Her hand seemed colder than the rest of her when he finally let her go and dropped his hand to his side.

"No contracts. No receipts. No records."

"But—"

"No," he said with finality. "Enter into a verbal agreement with me. That will require that you trust my decisions and my actions, always. A piece of paper holds a lot less value."

Maggie almost dropped her wallet. Her skin prickled. There was unleashed, raw lust emanating from his body. If she didn't take the upper hand immediately, he would have her begging him to take off her clothes, ravish her, do what he wanted with her body. She tried for a deep breath. Her reaction to him had to be a result of so much relief that he'd agreed to help her out.

"All right. We'll do this your way. This will be a working relationship," she told him. "I am hiring you. Contract or no, you will report your daily activities to me. I'm paying you for a service and I expect full cooperation and communication from you."

Maggie wasn't prepared when he grabbed her jaw. Micah didn't hurt her, but long, hot fingers embraced her neck, pressed against her jugular, and stroked her chin when he tilted her head back and stared down at her.

"This will be a working relationship. But I am the one who can do this job. You will trust me, cooperate with me fully, and trust that I always have your best interest at heart. I will share with you what I can while doing my research but you will accept that I am doing everything in my power to find whoever it is who is laundering money through Club Paradise. That includes you not questioning my every action."

"Is this how you treat all your clients?" Maggie grabbed his wrist, not that she could pull him off her if she tried. His pulse beat strongly against her fingertips.

"No."

"Why are you treating me this way?"

"Because of the charged lust radiating off you, and me," he said, his voice that low raspy growl again. "It's strong enough to fog both of our thinking. I'm putting it under control right now. I believe that you think you're innocent. I'll find out the truth, and you'll accept that truth once I show it to you."

Denying what he just said would make her a fool. Plus, something told her that if she did, he would prove her a liar. How he might do that caused a powerful throbbing inside her pussy. Moisture pooled as she looked up at him. "I need to know what you're doing," she insisted. Lust or no lust, she was unwilling to lose control.

He searched her face as one of his fingers moved to the edge of her lips. Maggie fought the urge to open her mouth, to taste him.

"I'll get the job done."

He didn't release her. He didn't move but continued staring down at her. Maggie finally stepped backward and was amazed how easily he let her go. He was right about the fog of lust. Shoving her items back in her purse, she clutched it against her side and turned for the door.

"Okay," she muttered, and hurried out of his house.

Micah picked up her car keys she'd left on his coffee table and opened his front door. He watched her almost run to her car. His dick was hard watching her perfectly shaped ass sway as she walked away from him. He'd wanted to grab her hair, feel how soft it was in his fingers, and tug on it until she completely submitted to him.

Maggie hadn't denied his comment about their lust being off the charts. That had made his blood boil through his veins. She desperately wanted control, probably because she had it in her everyday life. That life was gone to her, at least for the time being. He was in charge now, of her, and her future.

She wasn't going anywhere. Micah waited until she reached her car then turned into his house. He endured the pain of walking into his kitchen with a stiff dick. Then, grabbing two business cards from the small stack he kept by his napkins, Micah wrote his number on the back of one of them.

When he was at his front door again, Maggie was standing at her driver's-side door. He couldn't read her expression but waited until she looked up, over the roof of her car, and stared at him. Micah held up her keys. She exhaled noticeably and dropped her head, letting her hair shroud her face.

When he was eighteen, Micah's father had told him there were few men out there who could read another at a fair distance. He said Micah had that gift. Micah wasn't sure if he'd call it a gift, but he detected Maggie's embarrassment as he crossed his yard. She raised her head when he neared the back of her Civic Hybrid.

"Thank you," she said, holding her head high as she reached for her keys. Maggie didn't move from her driver's-side door.

Micah pushed the button on her key holder and unlocked the car. It was new, possibly less than a year old. Maggie dressed well, too. He wasn't sure how much a bookkeeper for a nightclub would normally make, but he intended to find out. He also planned on learning where Maggie lived. If she had a nice house he would definitely say she was living beyond her means, unless somehow those means had been padded. But looks were often deceiving. He wouldn't judge her yet.

Micah stepped into her space, forcing her to take a step backward, and opened her door. "This is my number." He handed her both business cards and still held her keys. "Write your number on the other card for me, unless you have a business card."

"I don't." She pulled a pen from her purse and used the top of her car to write her number on the back of her card. "Do you charge by the hour, by the day?"

"Neither." He took the card, studied her penmanship for a moment, then slipped the card into his pants pocket. "I'll be in touch soon after I look into a few things."

Maggie shoved her hair behind her shoulder and faced him. "Okay, so I've hired you, right? Is this our verbal agreement?"

"Yes." He wasn't sure why he added, "I'm not much into paperwork."

Something shifted in her expression at his comment. It didn't surprise him much that a bookkeeper, legal or illegal, would prefer things in order and documented. Micah had lived a lifetime of not documenting anything. "I'll do some checking around and be in touch with you in a day or so."

"If I don't answer, leave voicemail. I don't know how long I'll be with all of my family." She tilted her head, studying him. "Do you come from a big family?"

"No." He didn't really come from a family at all. His father and uncle had trained him more than raised him.

"Oh," she said, nodding once. There wasn't approval, or disapproval, but she shifted her focus from his face quickly.

Maggie wasn't trying to divert her reaction to him not having much family. They weren't in the confines of his small living room anymore. But even outside with the entire neighborhood, and a huge metropolis beyond that, the sparks of need still clogged the air around them. It was a bit too strong for Micah's liking. The urge to reach out and touch her damn near overwhelmed him.

There was still time to back out of this. Tell her no, go back inside, and continue with life as he had for the past three months.

Her next comment floored him. Micah hadn't pegged Maggie as being so forward. "I'm not going to have sex with you," she said and stared up at him with those sultry bright blue eyes of hers.

Micah was well trained and quick on his toes whether on

a hunt, or dealing with an unpredictable, gorgeous lady. "Is it because I don't have a strong family name?" he countered. "Or because I'm not Catholic?" he added to throw her off. His Saint Michael pendant suddenly seemed heavier around his neck.

"No." Her fingers fluttered around her hair. "No," she repeated. "It's just that you said inside . . ." Her words tapered off. "I mean the way you touched me," she tried again.

Micah took advantage of the moment. Reaching out, he ran his fingers over her silky smooth hair. He managed not to suck in a harsh breath, but Maggie didn't. She gasped, and froze.

"I would never do anything you don't want me to do," he whispered, and handed her the keys.

Chapter Three

Micah walked silently across the Kings' living room to the hallway that led to their kitchen. There were pictures of the Kings' three sons at different ages hanging on the wall. Micah saw these as landmarks to help him know where to go in the house. His father had taught him to be perfectly in tune with his surroundings. It was the only way to stay alive.

"They're all down there." Haley King pointed to an open door off the kitchen. "Enter at your own risk."

He hadn't worked on the weekend so far since he'd been working for the Kings. The environment was completely different than it was during the week. Haley wore a T-shirt and shorts and stood barefoot, holding a bottle of water to her lips. A young woman, an absolutely gorgeous young woman, sat at the kitchen table, smiling at Haley's comment. She didn't say anything and when Micah looked at her, she held on to her friendly expression but didn't give him a second look. He might have said something to her but noticed the wedding ring on her finger. Micah didn't mess with another man's woman.

He went through the door Haley had indicated and descended stairs into a large family room, complete with two pool tables, a bar, a dartboard on the wall, and a foosball table. That was just to his left. As he reached the bottom of the stairs, large couches and comfortable-looking chairs were arranged in a half circle in front of him; to the right, a large flat-screen TV hung on the wall. The Kings sure as hell weren't hurting for money. Speakers were nailed to the wall, enabling surround sound. Micah stepped on to short, firm carpet, which was a dark gray, perfect for hiding stains.

It was highly unlikely the Kings made enough money to live like this from running bounties brought into them by bondsmen. They did run the occasional personal hunt. Micah knew of a few. Even then, ten grand here and ten grand there wouldn't finance this type of lifestyle. Maybe a major hunt, with no kill, paid more than he realized.

Micah could hear the women upstairs in the kitchen chatting quietly. He heard his name mentioned and paused, taking in a couple of large paintings hanging on the walls. He didn't know a lot about art but guessed they were painted by a local artist. When he turned to the right, there was a third painting of the King house. The beach was visible behind it, and a breathtaking sunset made the picture captivating.

He listened to the women while taking in the large room. All he heard was something about him being recently hired, then the conversation shifted to something about handguns. Many might think it odd to overhear two women sipping bottled water in a kitchen while discussing weapons. Micah wasn't surprised. The Kings lived and breathed the hunt. They were a unique family. If his mother had remained with his father, and they'd had more children, he imagined his family might have been very similar to this one.

Where the hell did that come from? His upbringing hadn't been about family. It had been about training Micah to be the perfect assassin.

Taking in the contents of the room one last time, Micah decided it wouldn't hurt to do a bit more research on the Kings. There was only one type of hunt that paid well enough to live like this. In fact, it was that exact line of work that had him here, staying low until things cooled down.

Micah followed the sounds of men's voices and quickly picked up on Greg King and Ben Mercy talking and laughing. He pushed his way through a door and stared at a door frame set up in the middle of the room, held up with boards.

The room was unfinished, looking more like a basement than the rest of the downstairs.

"Hey, Jones," King said, turning and grinning. "Glad you could make it. You're just in time for a reenactment here."

"Reenactment?" Micah remained where he was, not just because both men held guns, but because he was once again taking in his surroundings.

Micah never entered a new environment without knowing all of the exits, and who was in the room as well as what they were doing. His father had drilled that into him by the time he was ten. *The hunter must always know the playing field better than the hunted.*

"Marc's wife took out four security men on the other side of a closed door during a case," Ben explained while running his fingers over the gun in his hand. He looked at Micah with blue eyes almost too bright to be masculine. "King here swears the story is true. All I had to do was doubt him once and the challenge was on," he added, grinning and not looking at all reprimanded for calling their boss on a good story.

"So that's when I decided it would be good for both of you to step in on this little exercise. And it really did happen. I saw them all crumpled in a pile. Granted, she was scared out of her mind and admits she might not ever be able to do it again," he added, chuckling. Then, gesturing at the door set up in the middle of the room, he sauntered over to it. "Let me explain."

Micah had his thoughts on Maggie ever since he'd woken up that morning. Taking a break from mentally analyzing a person often helped put things in perspective. When Haley had called him that morning to find out if Maggie had come by, Micah had simply told her he'd accepted the job. That's when King had gotten on the phone and insisted he come by and run through a drill he'd set up. Micah wasn't going to tell his boss he wasn't in the mood for a drill. Nor did he need drilling on anything pertaining to weapons or killing. He couldn't tell King that either.

"What happened?" he asked. Getting into whatever it was King wanted from him would help get Maggie off his brain. He studied the door, which stood open with the door frame propped up and held in place by two-by-fours.

King gestured for them to follow as he walked to the other side of the cement room and outside through two double doors. His detached garage, where King kept his Harley, was just outside that part of the house. King opened a side door to the garage, and the two men followed. Leaning over, he flipped open a cooler and pulled out two cold, wet bottles of beer.

"Sorry, man," he said to Ben.

"No worries." Ben waved a hand in the air and sounded as if he meant it. He leaned against a workbench and crossed his arms over his chest. "I have no intention of screwing up my probation. My lawyer says everything could be expunged from my record in the next month. Then I won't be a felon anymore. This is the job all men dream of and I am not going to do anything to mess it up."

"Don't blame you." Greg handed one of the beers to Micah and snapped the cap off the other. "Here's what happened."

Greg King was a giant of a man, at least several inches taller than Micah, who stood six foot one. King was muscular as hell, and for a man close to fifty years old, he never moved stiffly or took his time sitting or standing, like Micah's dad and uncle had started doing.

"It was over a year ago and we were having a hell of a time with an insane woman and a drug she was using to control people."

"Slave juice," Ben offered.

Greg shivered intentionally as he nodded. "Nastiest shit I've ever run up against."

Micah forced himself to quit thinking about his father and uncle. They were fine. There were never two tougher old men, and no matter how the heat might have come down, they would all get through it. He also shoved thoughts of Maggie from his head. That hot little number could get him in to more trouble than she realized if Micah didn't stay focused.

"Slave juice?" he asked. This was a new one for him.

"Yup." Greg led the way back to the cement room and paused next to the door in the middle of the room. "It was a drug that robbed you of your ability to control your own actions." He paused, took a drink of his beer. "Depending on how much was injected, you might have thoughts in your head, but you were helpless when it came to following orders. If someone told you to pick up this gun, point it to your head, and pull the trigger, you'd do it."

"Crap," Micah hissed.

"It took over a year to take down the bitch who invented the shit," Greg growled.

"He was telling me the story last week and mentioned that Marc's wife rescued everyone from an underground prison and shot four guards single-handed, with all of them on the other side of the door."

Ben Mercy was a good kid. He had done time for grand theft auto but didn't fit the profile. Apparently he'd been wrongly convicted, but—not having much money—he'd done time before getting out and finally finding a lawyer willing to help him wipe his record clean. King had hired Mercy, seeing something in him, despite the kid not being able to do everything the rest of them could do. Until the felony was off his record, Mercy couldn't get his P.I. license and be an official bounty hunter.

Ben pointed to the door in the middle of the room when they returned to the basement. "Greg surprised me with this. What I get for questioning his story, I guess."

Micah shifted his attention back to the door. That's when he noticed four mannequins stacked against the far wall.

"Never hurts to take on a little exercise," King said, walking across the room. His giant size made the room appear a lot smaller than it was. "Figured I would set up a mock reenactment. Jones, this will be good for you, too." He grinned at Micah and winked. "Will show me just how finely tuned your skills are."

"Oh yeah?" Micah asked. Only when you got paranoid was there anything to be paranoid about. "What are we doing?"

Greg pointed to the ceiling, then lifted the first mannequin. "I've got these life-sized dolls rigged to come at the door. I took the liberty of drawing a bull's-eye on each one of them. It will be sort of like target practice. You can each take a turn trying to take all four of them out before they can make it through the door." He grinned at Micah. "Want to play?"

Micah shrugged. There was no harm in having a bit of fun. And it wouldn't prove a thing if King saw firsthand how well Micah could shoot. "Sure, I'm in."

"When it happened for real, four men were coming down a flight of stairs toward a closed door. Haley wouldn't let me set this up in the family room, though, so instead"—he straightened each mannequin then hooked them to wiring in the ceiling—"the dolls are going to fly toward the door at a fairly good speed. You will open the door and fire, and you must take out all four dolls before you have the door all the way open. In other words, if the mannequins make it through the door, you lose." Then running his hand up the wiring holding one of the mannequins in place, he added drily, "Not to mention, they'll all get tangled up in the door frame."

"Woo hoo!" Ben whooped, rocking up on his heels. "Let the games begin. Mind if I go first?" he asked, and picked up the gun he'd been holding before following King to his garage. He shot a side glance at Micah. "I'll have more confidence if I don't already know the exercise has been mastered."

Micah didn't comment. Ben was pretty good with a gun, and he was coming around as a bounty hunter. The kid just didn't have the same experience under his belt that Micah did. No one did.

King laughed. "No problem. No one likes being shown up." He grinned easily at Micah. The man was one hell of a shot. King had been a cop for quite a few years before retiring and opening his private practice. "I'll get it set up," he said, and continued hooking the mannequins to heavy wires fixed to the ceiling. "This took most of last night and this morning getting this ready to go," he explained, looking at Micah. "Marc, my son, and I messed with this setup for hours before we got it right. Or thought we had it right. London, his wife, came out here once we had all the mannequins moving smoothly and informed us we had the door opening the wrong way."

As he spoke, he finished hooking the wires, which were threaded through holes drilled in the dolls' backs to pulleys on the ceiling. Ben stood on the opposite side of the door with both hands on his gun, pointing it at the floor. He watched the door like a hawk, though, as if the dolls might come to life and fly through it before King finished getting them ready.

It was amazing how full of life the kid was. Ben had been convicted of a crime he didn't commit, had done time for it, and stood in front of Micah grinning, his face lit up as if he'd just been given a brand-new weapon to play with. Ben wasn't bitter. He didn't act betrayed. If anything, it seemed he'd somehow made it through a tragedy unscathed. Most people would be mad at the world for being so terribly wronged.

Ben almost danced from one foot to the other, waiting to take his turn. Micah turned his attention to the setup, which was pretty elaborate. "Are all four of them going toward the door at the same time? Or will they hit the door one at a time?" he asked, and tried to envision it happening for real.

"Nope. See, we had to re-create it just the way it happened, especially once London was on to us and learned we were re-creating something she went through."

"She wasn't going to let you pull off the scene and have it any easier than it was for her."

"You've got it." King adjusted the wiring on the back of one of the dolls then lowered his hands and looked at Micah. "As soon as London got wind of the fact that we were so incredibly impressed about what she'd done that we wanted to see if we could do it ourselves, she went over the setup with a fine-tooth comb."

King backed away and surveyed his work. He looked

toward the door leading into the family room at the sound of people approaching. Micah heard the low baritone of a man speaking as several people came down the stairs. Instinctively he turned so his back was to the cement wall as he faced the open door.

A large man, taller than Micah, suddenly filled the doorway. Micah homed in on a hairline scar that started at the man's jaw and continued down the side of his neck. It wasn't overly visible but the ceiling light was bright enough for it to be noticed. The man had wavy brown hair that tapered around his collar. He wore a short-sleeved button-down blue shirt that matched the color of his eyes. When Micah made eye contact, the man appeared to be studying him as well.

"Marc," Greg said, again smiling. Greg was more relaxed than usual as he sauntered around the door, ignoring Ben, and moved to stand next to the man, who still filled the doorway. "You're just in time."

Micah guessed this was Marc King, the oldest son who was once part of KFA. Micah had spent a lot of time listening to the Kings talk about their sons. He'd also researched Marc and Jake King, Greg and Haley's two sons, when he'd checked out the Kings and KFA before seeking them out for a job. Marc King's reputation as a bounty hunter was as solid as his father's.

Marc entered the cement room, and checked out the setup he and his father had put together. "You must be Micah Jones," he said solemnly, then held out his hand. "I'm Marc."

"Good to know you." Micah shook hands, acknowledging the strong grip and large hand when they shook.

"Are you going to try to pull off the stunt my wife managed when we were in Arizona?"

"Sure." Micah looked away from the man, who was somewhere around Micah's age, and looked at the mannequins that were all in place behind the door.

"Well, you're going to have to do it with the lights off." The young woman who had been sitting at the table in the kitchen with Haley walked through the door and moved to stand behind Marc. "It was pitch black when I shot at the men on the other side of the door. We were in an underground garage and couldn't find light switches on the wall."

"We?" Ben asked.

"Natasha and I," she explained.

"London, this is the new bounty hunter Dad hired," Marc said. "Micah, this is my wife, London."

London was the beautiful woman he'd seen upstairs. Her black eyes matched the color of her hair. Her hair was thick, fell down her back, and was pulled back with a long red scarf. It was the same color as the short, sleeveless dress she wore. Her skin was tan and she was thin with noticeable, large breasts.

Micah guessed her hair was coarser than Maggie's. Although tanner, there was a slightly wary look in her gaze that he'd caught when she'd first entered the room. It was a dark, watchful, and cautious look that faded when she slipped her arm around Marc's back. He pulled her against him and massaged her arm, which seemed to put her at ease. That look vanished as if it had never been there.

Maggie didn't have that same guarded look; at least she hadn't the two times Micah had been with her. If anything, Micah would say Maggie appeared more content with the world around her than London did. There were visible ghosts in this woman's eyes. Maggie didn't have those ghosts. Although she probably would after the case concerning the books at Club Paradise was over. It dawned on him that he was viewing Maggie as innocent, if not a somewhat sheltered woman, which was the exact opposite impression he got from London.

"I have to try and shoot all four of these mannequins when the door opens in the dark?" Ben asked, sounding dubious.

London had a pretty smile. "There was light on the other side of the door. But we were standing in complete darkness. We'd turned off the flashlight and, like I said, we weren't able to find a light switch."

"London fired all the shots that killed the guards to the underground prison," Marc offered, sounding proud. "Natasha fired but her shots went into the wall."

"Natasha would kick your ass for saying that," London said.

Marc shrugged. "Let her try. It's the truth." He was smiling down at his wife and now let his gaze travel over the makeshift re-creation of the deadly moment. "You two are going to have to fire and hit each mannequin in a kill zone. Dad, the lights have got to go. We'll stand here behind the mannequins and use flashlights the moment the door opens. That should work." He looked down at his wife. "Don't you think?"

She nodded slowly. "Do you have a couple of high-beam flashlights?"

Marc rolled his eyes at her. "Of course," he said, then let her go long enough to saunter around the contraption in the middle of the room to shelves where various items were housed. He picked up two heavy-duty flashlights.

"That works," Greg said, and moved to the other side of the mannequins. "Where is Haley?"

"She told me to tell you that you could play down here for another thirty minutes, then you two are running errands." London grinned a broad, toothy smile as she passed on the message to Greg.

"Want to carry my response back to her?" he asked wryly.

"Text her," Marc said, and moved his wife away from the setup. "My wife isn't going to run back and forth for the two of you just so you can try and bully each other."

London laughed, a melodic sound, and ran her hand up her husband's chest. "They'd keep me going all afternoon."

"No, they won't."

"Okay, Ben," Greg said, willing to change the subject. "Are you ready?"

"Ready as I'll ever be." He posed and stood close and to the side of the door. "Where were you standing?" he asked London, suddenly straightening and looking doubtful again.

"We'd driven Marc's Mustang down into the underground garage and parked it, then shut off the headlights and used a flashlight as we walked to the door." She left her husband's side and walked over to Ben. "I'd say we were to the side of the door, and about this far away."

Ben moved to stand where London was. Marc stepped forward, reaching for his wife and pulling her back into his arms. She didn't fight him but leaned back against his chest as he wrapped both arms around her. Micah found it amusing that the man wished to protect his wife from the pending gunfire, yet she'd been the one who had fired the gun and killed four men. London looked as if she could protect herself.

"Everyone put these on." King passed out earmuffs. They weren't exactly what would be used at a shooting range, but they would do the trick.

Marc handed one of the flashlights to his wife. They moved to the other side of the door, and to the side so they wouldn't be in the line of fire. Greg walked around the staged event and placed his hand on the light switch by the door. "Once I turn off the light, London, you flip the switch to make the mannequins move. It's that box on the floor right next to you."

Micah slipped the earmuffs over his head and covered his ears just as the lights went out and the mannequins started moving. They actually moved faster than Micah imagined they would. The door opened toward Ben, blocking his view of the mannequins. They hadn't said, but the men who had once been behind that door had probably been armed. Ben started shooting seconds before the flashlight turned on and flooded a small area with light.

Micah held himself firmly and didn't flinch as shot after shot went off, exploding loudly in the small room. Other than the flashlight, they were shrouded in darkness. Ben growled, then with his fourth shot yelled, letting out a spew of profanities. Micah remained still, keeping the many ghosts at bay that wanted to surface. There were memories, so many memories, of firing shots, watching his target fall and die.

They got to where they weren't people but simply targets. He provided a service. His targets were the perverse deviants of society. He picked and chose his jobs. Mulligan's Stew was always in high demand. Once he had believed he provided a service to society, but it had gotten to where he accepted that he was addicted to the kill. Over the years he'd embraced his life and never given a thought to being a killer.

He had refused to keep count of how many died at his hand. His father had told him it was better that way. And with time, the count no longer mattered. It was all about the kill, which had mattered more to him than the lavish lifestyle, fast cars, faster women, and bankroll that never went dry.

"All right!" Greg said, breaking the dangerous trance that was taking over Micah's brain. "Let's see what we got."

"I'd say he got dead," Marc laughed, coming forward after Greg flipped on the light.

Everyone pulled off their earmuffs and the King men inspected the mannequins. Ben pushed around them and ran his hands over plastic arms and chests and legs. Ben had his moments of being cocky, but he could laugh at himself, a trait that would hopefully keep him sane in this business.

"I'd say I'm a dead man," Ben admitted, chuckling as he placed the gun on the table along the far wall. "Load her up, Jones. See if you can do better." He shook his head, walking away from the mannequins that now had holes in their legs, except for two, which Ben had missed altogether.

Micah loaded the gun, running his fingers over the metal and watching the bullets slide into place. He touched the trigger with the tip of his index finger. A gun was such a small tool, yet capable of ending life with the slightest move of the finger. He ran his fingertip over the concave curve then over the grooves until he circled the end of it. For years he'd refused to use any weapon other than his own. It had to be a sign that he was moving farther away from being the man he once was as he picked up the gun, got a feel of its weight, then gripped it, poising his finger on the trigger.

"You ready, Jones?" Marc asked.

"Line them up." Micah remembered what Marc's wife had said. He pictured her and the other woman alone in the dark garage, approaching the only door and hearing the many men coming after them.

Most people would be terrified in such a situation. Micah didn't doubt London and Natasha had probably been just that. London appeared jaded just enough that she might have a fair amount of a self-defense mechanism built in from something in her past. He already knew that Natasha, Marc and Jake's cousin, had a black belt in karate. That didn't make her street-smart. She'd been the office manager for KFA for several years, until moving to Northern California. Neither was trained to kill. Put in a deadly situation, London either got lucky as hell, or the woman had experience defending herself. His money was on the latter.

He guessed the women would have plotted somewhat, speaking in hushed whispers in the blackness enveloping them. Their fingers would have been sweaty as they held their weapons. Micah gripped his gun with cool confidence. He couldn't completely match the scenario he was supposed to play out as he focused on the door frame, but he would try.

The lights went out. The door in the middle of the room suddenly appeared before him as a looming shadow, a tall, rectangular target.

It was easier imagining the mannequins as guards, hired thugs, working for an insane scientist. Possibly they had that slave juice King had told him about in their system and were blindly following orders. Regardless, with London and Natasha's situation, it had been kill or be killed.

Micah cleared his head. Who they were, or what they'd done, didn't matter. They became nothing more than targets. Just another target. His father and uncle had assigned his targets up until a couple years ago. Micah had started setting up his own jobs, which had been done through a Gmail address. It had always mattered why someone wanted that target dead. If someone contacted Mulligan's Stew they meant business and could pay to ensure it was done.

Micah and his father and uncle were the top assassins in the nation, possibly the world. Micah always researched his target and had never killed someone who didn't deserve to die.

Micah's past life no longer mattered. All of it had been erased. Every bit of it existed only in his memory, and nowhere else. It hadn't been hard to change his birth certificate, his Social Security card, and all other recorded history so there wouldn't be a paper trail, or any other kind of trail. Micah and his father and uncle could disappear better than any U.S. marshal could do the job. At the age of twenty-three, Micah was on his third first and last name. To the best of his knowledge, Micah Mulligan was his real name; not that there was any proof of that anywhere. Nothing about his past could be proved.

"Ready?" Greg asked.

"Bring it on," he said quietly.

Micah shoved his past back in the dark crevices of his brain where it belonged and gripped his gun, caressing the trigger as the whooshing sound of the mannequins coming toward the door grew closer. The door opened.

It was kill or be killed. This reenactment wasn't a gun for hire. This wasn't about ending someone else's life because that person didn't deserve to live. No one had argued that the world would be a better place if these men were killed.

London and Natasha had fought for their lives in that garage. They'd survived. The men who had been shot would have killed them in cold blood. Micah moved into the position as London had described it and watched the light appear from the other side of the door as it opened.

He waited. The gun was hard and solid in his hand. His fingers were wrapped around it. The cool metal was smooth against his fingertips. He remained relaxed. The secret to a quick assassination was not allowing his body to tense. Keep a clear head and never allow the actions around him to become a blur. Precise movement would be needed. If he remained relaxed, it was always a lot easier to leap in whatever direction was needed. Relaxed and focused. So many didn't realize how incredibly easy it was to be a killer.

The door opened farther still. Micah caught a glimpse of the cream-colored plastic of the first mannequin's leg. He leaned forward, aimed, and fired.

It didn't collapse to the ground as a person would. Instead it swung slightly from the impact of the bullet. There were only seconds. Four against one were horrific odds unless he made his mark each time.

Micah hadn't missed a target in ten years.

He fired again, leaning forward. Once the light hit him he was an easy target. But with bodies to trip over, the shock of blood, and the element of surprise in his favor, Micah pictured the mannequins as humans, toppling over one another to their deaths, and continued firing. With each shot he moved into his targets, needing the new angles to hit his next mark.

Bang. Bang. Bang. Bang.

In less than a minute four mannequins were "dead."

The gun didn't have much of a kick but he felt it jerk as he fired. It was enough to send the rush through him that he'd often embraced after eliminating a target. Bloodlust was a terrible distraction. He now saw it as the creeping claws of an addiction, a craving to do it again. *Kill, no catch.*

"You impress the hell out of me," Ben said after all of them had returned to the kitchen. "Did you kill all those men as fast as Micah shot those mannequins?" he asked London.

"I didn't time it." London had a relaxed smile and seemed at ease in the small kitchen with all of them standing around. She remained next to her husband, who gave her shoulder a gentle squeeze when she kept talking. "It's something I hope never to live through again, although you can reenact it all you want. I'm flattered that you think it is worth trying to imitate. All I did was act on instinct. I didn't feel like dying."

"It's a damn good thing you didn't," Marc said, pulling her into his arms.

"I know. I had to rescue all of you."

Greg and Haley laughed along with Marc.

"You didn't rescue me," he told her. When his wife looked up at him, appearing as if she might say more, Marc added, "I got to play in a Jacuzzi with a mad scientist."

London cringed and shivered. "I'm sorry I couldn't rescue you from that."

King and his son began reminiscing over the details of that case that sounded as if it went grossly out of control before the family managed to bring it around and put the madwoman and her accomplices behind bars. Haley and London were quick to add their comments, and within minutes everyone in the kitchen was talking over one another, remembering details of a past hunt.

If Micah could have snuck out the back door he wouldn't have hesitated. He glanced behind him toward the dining room and considered going out the front door. He didn't want to work his way farther into the Kings' personal life. He wasn't working for KFA to make friends.

When the memories surfaced, it was harder to stay on point. How many times had he sat in the living room listening to his father and uncle dissect every previous case they'd had? It had become an after-dinner tradition, and one Micah had anxiously joined in on once he'd been of age and his father and uncle had acknowledged him in the conversation.

They were good memories. When he got older and took over hunting their targets, those after-dinner conversations meant even more to him. He went over every detail, every moment of his hunt with his father and uncle. And they'd listened to everything he had said, which made him feel so important.

Micah remembered when he believed, for the first time, that he truly had his father and uncle's respect and admiration. It had been right after they'd moved to Minnesota and he'd told both of them he was ready for his first target. His father and uncle had thrown a fit, yelled at him that they didn't want this life for him. Micah was in his prime. He was ready to be part of Mulligan's Stew. He'd won the argument. Two weeks later, when he'd returned home, the target eliminated, his father and uncle had sat anxiously, taking in every word as he'd told them how he had hunted and killed his first man.

Once he was done with his story, the three of them broke down every moment of the kill, analyzing the scene until any possible transgressions were identified. Many times during those intimate conversations with his father and uncle, Micah had walked away with new knowledge and insight into the family trade he'd been brought up to take over and master. He was the perfect killer.

Too perfect. Until his last target, which had ended that life for him, and his father and uncle. *You will see them again.*

"I don't know how you do it." Ben jiggled his keys, inching toward the back door.

Micah should get the hell out of there, too. He didn't need to hear their stories. The sooner he left the Kings', the faster he could get his head on straight again. Pulling the trigger and killing, even if it had been plastic, felt too damn good. Goddamn, he missed his life, when the world had known him as Mulligan's Stew, the most notorious assassin in the profession. But that life was now erased, as if it had never happened.

"You'll get there," he said easily and prayed the kid never would.

Ben said his good-byes, and Marc and London followed suit. Micah started toward the door, too.

"Micah, so you agreed to work for Maggie O'Malley?" Haley asked.

He couldn't get out the back door soon enough. He didn't want to discuss Maggie right now, not with his finger still itching and the impression of the gun still strong against his hand. The Kings were perceptive and if either of them detected a ghost of any kind, they would want to talk about that, too. Micah could never be part of their close-knit family.

"She hired me." Micah held on to the door handle. He

could smell the salt from the ocean and was inches from being out of there.

"Technically, since she contacted you through KFA, it's an assignment," Haley pushed, grinning at him. "Fill me in."

Greg King was watching Micah a bit too closely for Micah's satisfaction.

"Let's go outside," King suggested. "You can fill us in on all the details. Something is on your mind, and I seriously doubt it bothers you to shoot four mannequins through the heart. Wouldn't surprise me a bit to find out you're preoccupied by a pretty young lady who has hired you and you couldn't care less about old cases being rehashed." Definitely too perceptive.

"What she looks like has nothing to do with whether she's innocent or guilty," Micah stated, getting his brain on topic. He stepped outside to the screened-in back porch with the ocean as a backdrop.

"It's not healthy to dehumanize your clients. She professed her innocence," Haley prompted, walking around her husband and taking one of the high-back wicker chairs, then leaning forward and lighting a candle that was in the middle of the table. She smiled easily. "And she is very pretty."

"Yes," Micah agreed, watching the flame dance to life.

King sat next to his wife. There were two other chairs but Micah was content to stand, facing both of them.

"She seemed pretty desperate for help," Haley said.

"I agreed to help her."

"Don't make my wife prompt what happened out of you. Sit down and give us the full story," King barked, his tone stern.

Micah complied, not intimidated but deciding it might be a good idea to go over his meeting with Maggie. He took the chair opposite the two of them as Haley smiled and King's expression remained gruff. Talking about Maggie helped clear his head of the ghosts from his past. It only took a couple of minutes to relay everything to both of them, especially when he left out the part about almost seducing Maggie when he detected the raw, untrained lust emanating from her.

"Are you going to charge her?" Haley asked when he was done.

It had never crossed his mind to do the job pro bono. "I've never broken down the price of my services before," he admitted, which was the truth. His father, or uncle, had always handled that side of their business. All Micah ever did was focus on the target.

"Before?" King asked.

Micah needed to get his head out of his past. His heart skipped a beat, but he raised his guard instantly, not even blinking. "It isn't any of my business what you bring in on each case. I wouldn't know what to charge her until I see what is involved."

"Miss O'Malley made a smart move in hiring you," King said, relaxing in his high-back wicker chair and resting his elbows on the armrests. "I can honestly say I've never seen a better shot."

Micah wasn't going to comment one way or another. He wouldn't bask in the praise nor would he dispute King's claim. "Sounds like your daughter-in-law is a hell of a shot, too," he said. Trying to change the subject might raise suspicion.

"She was fighting for her life. That night she saved all of our lives." Haley tilted her head and studied Micah. "Sounds like you are an amazing shot."

He needed to get the hell out of there. "Thank you."

"All four moving mannequins shot through the heart in the dark. Amazing, Jones. Absolutely amazing." King was relaxed in his chair.

The vast shades of blue, the ocean fading into the sky, added to the tranquil setting around them. Even the breeze, fragranced by the salt water lapping at the beach behind them, was calm. It was truly a serene afternoon.

Micah wasn't relaxed. He wasn't a paranoid man, but the shrewd look in King's eyes had him on his guard.

"I'm a good shot." Micah smiled, and didn't dare look

away from King. "I doubt I'm as good a shot as you are, though. We all have our lucky days."

"That we do," King said, and grinned as well.

Micah managed to leave shortly thereafter. Something told him that he might have sparked too much curiosity about his past. It wasn't a problem. The best bounty hunter in the country wouldn't find a thing if he tried learning more about Micah than what he'd already told him.

Chapter Four

Maggie leaned against the kitchen counter and stared at her half-full cup of coffee. Her mother and Aunt Rebecca were upstairs, arguing over a flower show Aunt Rebecca wanted to go to later that morning. The bus wasn't good enough for Aunt Rebecca, and apparently now, neither was Maggie driving her. Which was fine with her. If one good thing came out of this nightmarish ordeal it would be that her aunt Rebecca now thought Maggie was the devil.

She turned to top off her coffee, having let it get cool while listening to her mom and aunt fight. Hell of a way to start off a Monday. Her father rode the electronic chair up the basement steps, mumbling something about shirts not being ironed.

"Oh crap," she hissed, turning with her steaming cup as her father appeared at the top of the basement stairs with one of his work shirts draped over his arm.

"Oh crap is right. Is there a reason why you didn't get the ironing done?"

She didn't usually complain about the assigned household chores her parents gave her, as if she were still in high school and had too much free time on her hands. Reminding her papa that she lived at home still because her parents were both in failing health didn't sound like a good idea at the moment.

"And would it be so bad for you to go upstairs and save your mother?" Her father gestured with shirt in hand, waving it at the ceiling. "Go tell your aunt Rebecca that you aren't the devil."

"I don't know," Aiden, Maggie's older brother, said, as he stepped into the kitchen and glanced in the direction his father had pointed. "She's got some pretty convincing arguments against Maggie."

Maggie rolled her eyes. "Thanks a lot," she mumbled.

"Anytime." Aiden winked at her.

John O'Malley seldom recited prayers the way their mother did. He went to church every Sunday for their mother. That wasn't a family secret. But when he started calling out to the saints, as children, they had all known to run.

"So now you talk back to your papa?" he asked, lowering his voice in a tone that used to put the fear of God into her as a child.

Aiden moved easily across the kitchen. He'd always been the only one who had seemed immune to their father's yelling. Maggie immediately noticed how much smaller her dad was than Aiden. It seemed only last year they'd been the same size and girth.

"I'll go talk to Aunt Rebecca." Maggie loved her father, who, in truth, was the biggest pushover in the world. Not that she'd ever tell him that. Any more than she'd share her thoughts with him about, once again, wishing she could move out.

She had been on her own for four years after high school, at which time she'd gone to business school. But after graduating, Maggie moved back home and now she paid all the household bills. Thank God the house was paid off. Her parents' Social Security wouldn't have covered their bills if it weren't for her.

"Want some coffee, Dad?" Aiden asked when Maggie started out of the kitchen.

"I want my shirt ironed," he complained, and leaned over the table to look at the morning paper.

There was sudden silence upstairs and Maggie shot her older brother a querying look. Aiden pulled down his father's cup and filled it with coffee.

"Maybe you should iron your father's shirt first," Aiden suggested, looking toward the ceiling.

"Hell of a good idea," her father grumbled. He slid into his chair at the kitchen table, accepted his coffee, then picked up the morning paper. "Then you go get your aunt out of your mother's hair. Hear me?"

"One ironed shirt coming up," she said, trying for cheerful in her voice.

"Then you go talk to your aunt," he reminded her.

"Then I'll go talk to my aunt," she promised.

Maggie embraced the few minutes of solitude she would have while she ironed the shirt. She loved her family. She really did. But there were days, and lately it had been every day, when she really wanted her own place again. Especially now with trumped-up charges looming over her head. It was too much for her. But it was really too much for her mom, which made it hell living with her dad.

Her mother had worked at the hospital in administration as long as Maggie could remember. Her father had been an accountant and owned a third of his business along with his two brothers. All of them were retired now, with Maggie's cousins pretty much running the place. Her father had been heartbroken when Aiden hadn't gone into the family line of work after doing four years with the army straight out of high school. Instead, Aiden got married, had two adorable little boys, and was now divorced. Aiden handled her father's continual complaining a lot better than she did. Her older brother always seemed cheerful when Maggie wanted to scream.

Maggie loved accounting. Her business degree and experience with bookkeeping made her a good candidate for her father's business, but not once had he ever suggested she come work for him. John O'Malley didn't compliment or praise his children often. There were days when she swore the less family she had in her life, the better.

She turned on the iron and draped her father's shirt over the ironing board. With it finally quiet, her thoughts drifted to Micah. She hadn't heard a word from him since she'd gone to his house this past Friday. It bugged her that he hadn't called, but at the same time—though she hated admitting it—relieved she hadn't talked to him again yet. She wasn't sure how much time she needed before she'd be in control of her senses once she was around him.

Possibly *never*?

Good Lord! Micah dripped with a deadly charisma she wouldn't have believed existed in a man. He was overloaded with sensuality and sex appeal that was off the charts. He was taller than most men. But then apparently bounty hunters were required to be giants from what she'd seen of the crew that worked with him.

And his body! Maggie blew out a breath. She'd guess Micah a few years older than she at least, and his body was pure rock-hard muscle . . . everywhere. She wondered if all of him was in such perfect shape.

"Oh man," she whispered, leaning against the ironing board as she imagined Micah naked, his dick as hard as the rest of him was. There was a moment there when she thought she felt his cock pressing against her. With Micah, she imagined sex would be wild, aggressive, and fast. "Crap," she hissed, shaking her head. Maybe she should encourage them to fuck just so she could cool things off between them. Micah wouldn't tell her no. That much she knew.

"And knowledge is hell," Maggie mumbled, then spit on the iron to make sure it was hot.

"Knowledge is hell?" Deidre, her older sister, asked.

"Damn it," Maggie turned on her sister. "You get off sneaking up on people?"

Deidre wrinkled her nose. "I was hardly sneaking. Dad wants his shirt."

"I'm ironing it." Being grouchy helped calm the fire that had ignited just thinking about Micah. Which was messed up. She'd hired him to help get her out of this mess, not so she could jump his bones.

"I see that." Deidre looked pointedly at the shirt and the iron in Maggie's hand.

Maggie pressed the iron to the shirt and began ironing. "It had to warm up."

Deidre always had guys fighting for her attention. Maggie had been the one who buried herself in books. Then when math came so easily to her, numbers had become her best friend. Deidre never cared about school. It was one guy after another. Maggie wondered if she ever cared about any of them.

Deidre shoved her fingers through her dyed-blond hair, which was perfectly long and straight down her back. Maggie would never figure out her sister's secrets for always looking so incredibly beautiful no matter how she dressed or wore her hair.

Deidre ran her finger along the edge of the ironing board. "I'm really sorry," she mumbled.

Maggie glanced up from her task. "It's okay."

"I know you're innocent."

"Me too."

"Hell, Mags, I don't know what to say."

Maggie pushed the iron over the shirt, making quick work of it, then yanked the shirt off the ironing board and faced her older sister. "What would you say if I told you I hired someone to find out why the cops think I was part of some money-laundering scheme?"

Maggie waited out the moment of silence. Her sister stared at her, her expression blank, until a slow smile crossed her face.

"Way to go, little sis," she whispered, her blue eyes lighting up as she spoke. "Is he hot?"

That would be Deidre's first question. Maggie should have been ready for it. Her mouth went dry as she tried thinking of the best way to answer. "Hot doesn't begin to describe Micah," she said, whispering just as her sister had.

"Micah."

Maggie couldn't explain why she didn't like hearing her sister say Micah's name, but a strange possessive darkness filled her. Deidre might get all the guys, but she wouldn't get this one.

"Unusual name," Deidre added. "Is he Catholic?"

"Catholic? Does it matter?" Maggie turned her attention to her father's shirt, although she didn't really check for wrinkles when she held it up.

"Only if you plan on introducing him to Mom and Dad."

"Well, I don't," Maggie snapped.

She glanced at Deidre and wished she hadn't. Her sister was staring at her with a shrewd look. "You were thinking about him when I came down here. You were a million miles away and mumbling to yourself. You've got the hots for him."

Maggie turned off the iron and gripped the shirt as she turned from her sister. "I need to take Dad's shirt to him."

"Wait a minute," Deidre demanded, and her hand was cool when she grabbed Maggie's arm. "Don't go all defensive on me. Tell me about this Micah. You hired him? What does he do? Is he a private dick or something?"

"He's the bounty hunter who grabbed me out of my office and hauled me out to the cops," Maggie informed her and headed to the stairs.

"Holy crap! You're kidding me. Maggie, wait!" Deidre was on her heels when Maggie rushed up the stairs.

Thankfully, she kept her mouth shut when they entered the kitchen and Maggie handed her dad his shirt.

"I'm going to take Aunt Rebecca to her show," Aiden announced, leaning against the counter.

"She's wearing your mother out," Maggie's dad announced.

"I'll go check on Mom," Maggie said and smiled as she turned to leave the kitchen and met Deidre's impatient glare.

"That's my girl," her father said as he stood and slid into his shirt.

"Wait," Deidre whispered, catching up with Maggie before she could get through the living room to the stairs. Once again she grabbed Maggie's arm, this time spinning her around. "You've got to tell me or I'll go nuts. I'll worry about you," she stressed, pulling the older-sister routine as she looked imploringly at Maggie. "How did you hire him?

What's he going to do to help you? Did something happen between you two?" Her last question was barely audible in a hushed whisper.

"Something wrong?" Aiden asked, coming up to both of them and looking from one of his sisters to the other. His shaggy hair showed what was left of his youth. At thirty, Aiden had been divorced now for five years, and worked long hours at his job in San Dimas to help support his sons and their mother as well as himself. It showed in the lines around his eyes as he scrutinized both his sisters. "What's going on?"

"Everything's fine," Maggie said, waving both of them off and hurrying upstairs. She prayed Deidre had the good sense not to tell their brother what she'd just told her.

The house was finally quiet when Maggie left her mom's room, who'd finally drifted off to sleep after sharing several Bible scriptures she'd found that she felt applied to what Maggie was going through right now. Cancer had taken its toll on her mother. Maggie hated how her mom was slowly shrinking away from them. There were good days and bad days. Today was a bad day, with something as slight as Aunt Rebecca arguing with Maggie's mother wearing her out. Lucy O'Malley was a spitfire who could raise holy hell when she was pissed. Maggie had a lump in her throat when she walked out of her parents' bedroom and left her mother sleeping. She missed the spitfire.

She headed to her bedroom for a shower. Hopefully, everyone had headed out. As much as she loved all of her brothers and sisters, when they were all here in the house, it could make her nuts. She reached her bedroom, the room she'd grown up in—except when she'd moved back home, Aiden and Bernie had knocked the wall out between her bedroom and Deidre's to make Maggie's private space a bit larger. She collapsed on her couch inside her room and pulled out her cell phone.

"Deidre," she said the moment her sister answered.

"I didn't tell anyone."

Maggie sighed in relief. She kicked off her shoes and

wiggled her toes as she stared at them. "Good. Thanks. Please don't, okay?"

"You have to tell Aiden."

"Why?"

"Because if you don't, when he finds out, he'll be pissed," her sister said, sounding as if she stated the obvious.

And maybe she did. Maggie would risk it. "*Please* don't tell anyone."

"I won't."

"O'Malley honor."

Deidre laughed. "O'Malley honor, and Mags?"

"Yes?" she asked, dreading the consequences of her sister's willingness to stay quiet.

"Please be careful."

Maggie stared across her bedroom and Micah's powerful body appeared in her mind. He was strong, a bit too aware of her senses, and, yes, dangerous.

"Be careful of what?" she asked, hoping she sounded calm. Her heart was already beating harder than it had been a moment ago.

"I saw you when I went into the basement." Deidre's tone dropped, suddenly sounding concerned. "I know what it feels like when you can't wait to fuck a man."

"Deidre!"

"Don't Deidre me, Mags," her sister snapped. "You were flushed and mumbling under your breath. This Micah person has you flustered already. He hauled you out of your office, manhandled you, then you went to him for help. Doesn't take a rocket scientist."

"God, Deidre, stop already."

"Fine, I'll stop. Just remember. I'm your sister. I know you. You always try to be so logical, and you're buried in your books and numbers. This man sounds out of your league. I just want you to be careful. That's all."

"I'll be careful."

"Okay. And I'm here if you need me."

"Thanks." Maggie sucked in a breath. Her sister was dead-on, and it left Maggie feeling more than a bit unsettled.

But Deidre knew all there was to know about men. "And thanks for keeping all of this quiet."

"I love you, little sis."

"Love you," Maggie said, then hung up, not sure if she felt better after calling her sister. But at least she had her silence.

Maggie technically hadn't been fired from her job. Once she was dressed she would drive over to Club Paradise. Other than Micah, it had bugged her all weekend as to how many times during her interrogation they'd asked her about "the other ledger." There wasn't one. She had told them that so many times it had made her nuts. But now, with her head a bit clearer, Maggie had started to wonder if there might possibly be another set of books for the club.

She was halfway downstairs after showering and choosing which dress to wear when the doorbell rang. Immediately, someone knocked firmly on the front door and tried to turn the doorknob. Her father had made sure the house was locked before he left for the office. Despite retirement, John O'Malley showed up at the office at least a few days each week. He would stay there then head to the corner pub, where he'd spend several hours nursing a few beers and hanging out with most of his buddies, who were also now all retired. Her father, and the rest of his friends, would come home in time for supper, just as if they were getting off work for the day.

Since the police had hauled her in for questioning, he'd made a fuss about locking the house when he left her and her mother alone. He was worried about her, which made Maggie even more upset. When he worried, he yelled and complained about anything out of order. It would send his blood pressure through the roof. She would have locked herself in the house, though, even if her father hadn't insisted. Someone was letting her take the fall for their crime. What else might they do to her?

Maggie glanced through the living room window before easing her way to the door.

"Annalisa!" she cried out as she opened the door and rushed to her baby sister. "Oh my God! You're here!"

"You don't have to announce it to the world," Annalisa told her, grinning. Her smile looked sincere as she stepped back to arm's length and dropped her arms. Annalisa was thinner than she'd been the last time Maggie had seen her, but otherwise she looked happy and her blue eyes glowed as she stared at Maggie.

A really good O'Malley-sized meal wouldn't hurt her little sister a bit. God, she was thinking just like her mother. Maggie gave herself a mental shake. "Dad's not here. Mom's upstairs asleep." She took Annalisa's hand and guided her to the porch swing. "I'm so glad you're here. I didn't think you would show up. Oh honey, I'm so glad you did," she said, her eyes welling up with tears as she sat next to her sister and hugged her fiercely.

Annalisa, the youngest O'Malley, had just turned twenty-one. She had attempted telling her parents, right after breaking up with the only boyfriend she'd ever had, that she had a girlfriend and was a lesbian. Despite John and Lucy O'Malley insisting it was a stage, and nothing a few hundred Hail Marys wouldn't cure, Annalisa continued insisting that this was who she was. Just over a year ago, Annalisa had come home with a fiery redhead, a cute girl, barely nineteen, and head over heels for Maggie's baby sister. They had been adorable together, or at least for the hour the two of them had been at the house for Thanksgiving celebration. When it had come time to go to church, Lucy O'Malley had announced her youngest daughter couldn't attend Thanksgiving mass with the entire family as long as she squandered her life in sin. Annalisa had run from the house, crying her eyes out, and hadn't returned.

Until today. Maggie continued hugging her fiercely. "I can't believe you're here," she whispered into her sister's hair, which smelled like strawberries. Tears welled in her eyes too quickly to stop them from spilling down her cheeks. Maggie swatted at them as she leaned back against their porch swing and smiled.

"Mom's voicemail sounded scary," Annalisa admitted,

speaking just above a whisper. Her pale blue eyes were crystal clear and her auburn hair just a bit shorter than Maggie's. She grinned and searched Maggie's face. "Julie heard it first and just about shit. She couldn't believe Mom was calling me. She texted me and I was still in class. Goddamn, Maggie, in the middle of my psych final of all things," she stressed and rolled her eyes as she shook her head. "I had one more final on Friday or I would have called you, or something. I couldn't even concentrate." She shot a wary glance toward the large living room window.

Annalisa didn't look at all as if she wanted to confront Mom. But she was here. That was what mattered. "And at first I was going to blow it off," she admitted.

"But you came," she prompted and was tempted to tell Annalisa that Mom's health was getting worse. She worried that her baby sister would run from the house once again, possibly thinking her presence would make Mom even worse.

"Yeah," Annalisa said, and sucked in her lower lip. "Finals are over but I start a job at the mercantile off campus here in a few days."

"So you're doing okay?" Maggie wanted to stroke Annalisa's cheek and comb her short hair with her fingers, just as she had when they were younger.

"Fuck an egg, Mags, this isn't about me. I'm fine. How much trouble are you in?"

"I didn't do anything wrong." It had become Maggie's mantra. She bit her lip not to correct Annalisa's foul mouth. Mom would have a conniption fit over her youngest daughter's language before she even began tearing into Annalisa for having a girlfriend instead of a boyfriend. "Honestly, I don't know if I'm in trouble or not. I'm still here," she said, gesturing at their home. Mrs. Gregor walked past the front of their house, and Maggie and Annalisa stopped talking. Annalisa apparently remembered that waving or calling out a greeting to their next-door neighbor was pointless. Mrs. Gregor and her toy poodle, Ginger, who also didn't look their way or acknowledge any of the O'Malleys at any time, cut off the main sidewalk and down the narrow clay path between their homes. The old woman disappeared into the side door of her house. Maggie didn't want her parents to end up like Mrs. Gregor, alone and bitter. Maggie didn't remember her being that way when Maggie was a child, and the Gregor kids, who were older than the O'Malley children, had all still been at home.

"The cops aren't banging down my door," she said when Annalisa looked away from their neighbor's home. But they were following her. Maggie didn't tell her baby sister that part. "Where are you staying?"

Annalisa shrugged.

"I'll pay for a motel room. Then we can visit without any of us worrying about Mom or Dad going on a rampage."

"Mags, you're still the greatest." And for the first time since they spoke her sister initiated a hug. A relaxed, sincere hug that felt so good. Maggie didn't realize how much she'd missed Annalisa until that moment. Deidre was always there for Maggie to talk to, but with Annalisa, it was different. It was as if Maggie didn't have to worry about anything with her younger sister. With Deidre there had always been competition, although it had been one-sided. Deidre had never had to compete with either of her sisters.

When they let go of each other, Annalisa shot a furtive look toward the front door. "I heard someone," she whispered, and tensed.

"Mom could hear the dead roll over. You know that." Maggie did a quick search on her phone for a nearby motel, then called and made the reservations. "Okay, go," she said, standing with her sister and walking her down the porch stairs to the small truck parked in front of the house. That's when she noticed for the first time that Julie was sitting in the passenger seat looking very nervous. "Promise me you'll call me, Aiden and Deidre right after you're checked in and let us know your room number."

"I promise," Annalisa said, then gave her sister a fierce hug. "I hope you aren't in any trouble, Mags. I really do."

Maggie let her go and ruffled Annalisa's hair. "Love you," she said, hugged her one more time, then watched her leave. When she turned to the house, her mother was standing in the doorway.

"I knew she'd come," her mother said, her voice tender.

Maggie opened the screen door and walked past her. She wasn't about to start a conversation with her mom about Annalisa.

Aiden stood in the middle of the living room, looking out the front window. Maggie and Annalisa hadn't had the private chat they thought they had.

"I've got a lawyer for you," Aiden announced, apparently also deciding against bringing up their youngest sister in front of their mother.

Maggie could have hugged him for offering a new topic, even if it was about the trouble she might, or might not, be in.

Maggie was anxious to hear what a lawyer would say about everything she'd been through. Forty-five minutes later she and Aiden were driving into the city. She stared out the window, wondering what Micah was doing. He would either be working on another case for KFA or be working on her case. She hated that she had a case.

Her phone rang. She dug it out of her purse then stared at the name and number on her screen.

"Who is it?" Aiden asked, shooting her a quick look then cutting into the other lane on I-10.

"Someone else who is helping me sort through this mess." Maggie didn't elaborate, especially since it was difficult to explain Micah. She could give his job title, explain that she'd hired him, and none of that would truly answer who Micah was. Maggie couldn't read the man properly, but something deep in her gut told her that he would be able to help her better than anyone else.

She answered the phone before Aiden could press for more information. "Hello," she said, and ignored the curious look he gave her. So what if she spoke softer when she answered. It didn't mean anything.

"Where are you?" Micah asked in a form of greeting.

"With my brother, heading into the city," she offered.

"Why? Where are you going?"

"To see a lawyer."

"About being arrested?"

"Yes. My brother knows a lawyer and he thinks—"

"Bad idea. No lawyers, Maggie."

"It's a bit late to toss in your opinion," she said, and laughed because it seemed better than snapping at Micah and really sending her brother's radar up.

"If you aren't sitting and talking to the lawyer, it's not too late. Where exactly are you going?"

Maggie looked at Aiden's GPS attached to his dash and rattled off the address to the building where Aiden's lawyer friend worked. "The lawyer is Bob Young. Do you know him?" she asked, wondering why Micah wanted the address.

"You hired me," Micah stated instead of addressing her question. "When I told you that I would get the job done, I meant that. I'll keep you informed on any information I can relay to you."

"Did you find something out?" Maggie's heart was suddenly pounding too hard in her chest.

"I'll meet you at your lawyer's office."

"What? Wait. No," Maggie stammered but it was too late. Micah had hung up.

Something quivered in her stomach, a thread of excitement she couldn't ignore. Knowing she was headed straight to him filled her with anxious anticipation that swelled through her body.

"What was that all about?"

Maggie slowly lowered her phone to her lap. She fought the cloud of lust in her brain. Images of Micah, possible ways of how he might show up, what he might do, wouldn't go away even when she told her imagination that her brother would be there right next to her.

"I hired the man who helped turn me over to the cops to help find whoever was guilty of what they wanted to charge me with."

"What? You hired someone?" Her brother scowled, looking confused for a moment and staring at her as if she were nuts.

"Yes," she stated, not regretting that she had. "There were bounty hunters assigned to the case to find Uncle Larry."

"Bounty hunters? Why the hell would bounty hunters be involved in this mess?" Aiden demanded, his voice rising as he white-knuckled the steering wheel. "Did Uncle Larry miss a court date or something?"

"Apparently he did. Uncle Larry lied to me, Aiden. I don't know why. And I'm starting to think he lied to me about a lot of things. But I can't talk to him. He's in jail and I'm on this list of people who can't see him." Maggie still found it incredibly hard to believe that her uncle would have conspired against her. Uncle Larry just wasn't that conniving. Something told her he'd been set up, too. But without being able to talk to him, she couldn't prove anything. "He was gone for a couple of weeks but not lost. At least I knew where he was. He was on vacation. Larry had only been back a day when the bounty hunters showed up at the club, arrested him, and took me in, too."

"Where was he on vacation?"

"I don't know." She did find it interesting that the day he returned from his vacation, he was arrested. It was as if the bounty hunters knew where he'd been vacationing, and when he'd be back. She could ask Micah about that but she wasn't sure he'd tell her.

"Make sure you tell Bob about all of that."

Aiden was excited for her to see Bob Young, his lawyer friend. He'd gone over everything with her that Bob had said after Aiden talked to him on the phone. Bob was very willing to see her and anticipated that she had a strong lawsuit on her hands.

"I'm not sure I'm up to a lawsuit right now," she said, and watched Aiden's profile. He didn't look at her. "I want answers about all of this first."

"Bob is going to take care of all that, too. He would have to in order to confirm that there is a viable lawsuit. But if there is, little sis, you could walk away a very wealthy woman from this trauma that has been inflicted upon you." I'm not for suing without cause, but Maggie, some detective really screwed up on the job when they tried arresting you."

"Micah is looking into why I was suspected of money laundering."

"Micah?" Aiden glanced at her as he turned into a large parking lot between two buildings. "Who is Micah?"

Her phone rang again. Maggie spotted Micah sitting on a large motorcycle, although it didn't look too large with Micah straddling it. Her insides twisted into a huge, throbbing knot. "Hello?"

"You're with your brother?"

She was staring right at Micah yet didn't see his mouth move. His deep baritone created goose bumps that rushed over her body. It wasn't fair how simply seeing him at a distance while being in the confines of her brother's car still made her want him. "Yes, my brother."

"What?" Aiden asked.

"I need you to come with me."

"Right now?" she asked.

"Your appointment with Bob is in five minutes," Aiden informed her.

"Tell him you're going to be late," Micah said, apparently having heard Aiden through the phone.

Aiden parked the car and Maggie hopped out. She stared over the hood of Aiden's car at Micah, who must have been wearing an earpiece because he wasn't holding a phone to his ear. He looked dangerously sexy straddling his motorcycle.

"Let's go," Micah stressed.

She was anxious to know what he'd learned. "Okay," she said, but then hung up the phone before Micah started instructing her on what to say to her brother.

Aiden was around his car to her side before she could meet him halfway. He frowned at her phone in her hand.

"Was that this Micah character again? What's going on, Maggie?" he demanded.

Aiden wasn't going to just let her walk away with a simple *Can't meet with the lawyer right now, but we'll reschedule real soon.*

"I told you what's going on," she said, staying calm. "Micah is investigating what happened. He is the bounty hunter who helped have me taken in by the police. It's what he does." Maggie hated how Aiden looked at her as she tried explaining. She needed him to understand. "It's what bounty hunters do. I decided since he knew as much about what happened as I did, he was the best man to hire."

Aiden looked at her a moment, his expression blank. He was digesting. "I don't know if that's a good idea," he said under his breath.

Maggie hadn't noticed Micah had moved from his bike until he suddenly appeared next to Aiden. She quit looking at her brother and focused on Micah. With a matter of positioning, Micah had placed himself between the two of them.

Micah only stared at her for a moment. During that moment, it was as if they were alone. His eyes were so dark. Maggie found herself drowning in them, being drawn into a spiral of intense emotions that stole her breath. *Complicated* didn't even begin to explain this man. Maggie swore she saw more demons swirling in his eyes than she'd ever seen in another person.

When he looked away from her, Maggie damn near lost her balance. Her insides quickened and her pulse began racing. What the hell was it that this man did to her every time they were close to each other?

"I'm Micah Jones." He was introducing himself to her brother. "And you are?"

Maggie chewed her lower lip as she watched Aiden clench his teeth together, which always caused a tiny muscle to twitch in his jawbone. It was a dead-on giveaway that he was pissed as hell. Aiden might try sending Micah flying. She wasn't going to find out who would win that round.

"Aiden," she said hurriedly, moving around Micah to stand between the two of them. "This is the bounty hunter I told you about who has agreed to help find out why they accused me of money laundering." She lowered her voice almost to a whisper since they were outside. "Micah, this is my brother, Aiden O'Malley."

Testosterone spiked to dangerous levels as the two men sized each other up. There were no handshakes, no displays of chivalry. Aiden could be the perfect gentleman in the right circles. Maggie couldn't picture Micah ever entering those circles. He would be the man in the shadows, watching while not saying a word. She imagined him being able to nail a bad guy before the guy ever knew anyone was on to his tricks. At the same time, Maggie saw that Aiden didn't view Micah as the kind of man worthy of a handshake, or being in those circles that would merit such manners. That bothered her. But why would it matter if Aiden liked Micah? All that mattered was that Micah proved her innocence.

"What do you want with my sister?" Aiden asked, his voice noticeably lower than it had been when she was talking to him alone a minute ago.

"Aiden," she snapped under her breath and shot him a warning look. Turning to Micah, she started to speak, but he cut her off.

"For right now," Micah began, his voice as low as Aiden's had been, "just a couple minutes of her time. She'll be right back."

Micah didn't wait for Aiden to tell him to go to hell. She wasn't sure why Aiden had obviously not liked Micah. He might simply be playing possessive older brother. Or it could be that he had picked up on the dark demons Maggie had sensed in Micah. Whatever it was, she knew Aiden would give her an earful later.

Micah took her by the arm and started toward his bike.

Where are we going?" Maggie demanded, but when she tried twisting out of his grip, he tightened it until she felt the pinch against her skin.

Micah didn't say anything until they'd reached his bike. Then he spun her around so she faced him. Maggie slapped her hand against his chest to balance herself. At the same time that he released her, she caught him searching their surroundings. She tugged her dress, straightening it and glanced around as well. When she looked back up at him, his attention was on her, or rather her body.

The anger that had quickly flared to life inside her over being manhandled subsided in a rush. With one look into his eyes, at his dark hair falling in waves over his forehead and strong lines and angles outlining his serious expression, desire swelled inside her. She was throbbing between her legs. The smooth flesh there grow damp from a distracting need for him. Knowing it was mutual made it even worse.

"What do you want?" she said, almost snarling. It was annoying as hell not being able to control her physical attraction to him.

The second she asked, Maggie regretted it. She saw a change in those unreadable eyes. It was as if she looked into a mirror image of the need ransacking her body.

"The same thing you do," Micah growled.

And damn it. It was most definitely the sexiest, lowest growl she'd ever heard from a man.

Maggie didn't have time to back up, press her hand against him to resist, or in any way react. Micah wrapped his arms around her, pulled her against his body, and practically bent her over backward as he kissed her.

One hand pressed against her lower back. His long fingers stretched over her spine. His palm was just above her ass. He kept her positioned, pressed firmly against his virile body, while his other hand moved to the back of her head.

She would have thought that that first kiss would be as rough and demanding as his actions and behavior leading up to it were. Instead, his lips were soft, warm, and so incredibly enticing. Their mouths fused together, opening for each other mutually, and moved in a perfect rhythm. None of that first-time-kiss awkwardness was there.

That in itself prevented Maggie from thinking. The pure spontaneity along with how perfectly his mouth moved with hers, stole her ability to resist. Micah was large, muscular, dangerous looking, and he behaved just how he looked like he would. So his kiss should have been punishing, demanding, mind-blowing, and almost bruising. Yet it was none of those. Micah kissed her the way a desperately missed lover would kiss upon returning to the only woman he'd ever cared about.

Chapter Five

There were police sitting across the street. Two other cops in street clothing had just entered the building where Maggie was headed for her meeting with the lawyer. They were on her ass hard and from what Micah had dug up so far, it just didn't jibe. LAPD had followed him here. Already he was on their radar. Micah prayed he wasn't making the biggest mistake of his life.

It took every ounce of restraint he'd ever had to muster up in his life to keep his mind focused and not give in to the passion threatening to rip him apart from kissing Maggie. The pain in not getting a raging hard-on equaled how much it would have hurt if he had. He wanted her more than his next breath.

"What?" she whispered, blinking a few times. Maggie's face was flushed, her lips moist and parted, and she panted as both of her hands remained flat against his chest. "What?" she repeated. "Why did you do that?"

Because I wanted to. Because I've been thinking about kissing you all day. "It was necessary," he said instead, looking down at her as she searched his face for understanding.

Micah barely took a second to scan the parking lot and two adjoining streets beyond it. Maggie's brother remained standing by his car, his arms crossed and looking pissed as hell. Micah didn't have a sister. But if he did, he'd want her kept as far away from a monster like him as he could get her.

The car parked down the street, almost out of sight, still had two cops sitting in it. Micah wouldn't be surprised if they had specially designed audio equipment so they could pick up on anything Micah and Maggie said to each other.

The two plainclothes cops who'd entered the building after watching Maggie and her brother park hadn't come back outside. They were waiting, ready to confirm who it was she would go see inside. Maggie going to a lawyer would confirm the police's suspicions that she had something to hide. There was another reason why his protector's instincts were off the charts. He wasn't sure yet that it was just the cops following her.

Micah knew this game all too well. If anyone else was watching Maggie, they would be less willing to risk a success-hungry defense lawyer getting them off scot-free than contacting Mulligan's Stew. Micah had assassinated guilty people whose crimes needed punishment, yet they hadn't been punished. Then there were times when the judicial process moved too slowly, and compiling evidence too difficult. Those who wanted criminals gone were often willing to go to extremes to make it happen, such as hiring him.

Anyone who tried hurting Maggie would learn quick and fast how unprofessional they actually were as hit men.

"It was necessary?" she repeated, sounding confused. The dazed look was gone. She took her hands off his chest and ran them down the hot little outfit she was wearing. "Why was it necessary?"

"You trust me, right?" he asked, whispering.

"I think so," she said slowly.

"That's all I can ask." He knew she trusted him as a bounty hunter, a professional who would do his job. Maggie was still focused on their kiss. She answered his question and told him she thought she could trust him as a man.

Micah desperately wanted to kiss her again. His brain told him it was a bad idea. He would hurt her. Inevitably she would want what he could never give her. Stability, love, compassion, commitment—those weren't words Micah had grown up hearing. They weren't part of the training he received, starting at an early age before he even knew that he was receiving it. A beautiful woman like Maggie deserved the world, not a trained killer like him.

His body didn't want to listen to his brain. Already he was planning, plotting their next kiss. It wouldn't stop at a kiss, either. He could fuck Maggie. She would let him. Her need for him was not only written all over her face, it emanated from every pore in her body. And Goddamn, he wanted her more than he'd ever wanted another woman. Yet another warning sign that he should wash his hands of her and get under the radar again.

If the cops ran a trace on him, and they probably already had, his clean and rather vague history as Micah Jones might raise suspicion. He hadn't planned on anyone doing a deep investigation on him when he created his new identity. There would have been no reason, if he'd stuck with his plan to not be noticed.

"You absolutely cannot go see that lawyer." Micah kept whispering. "Go over to your brother now, give him a hug, and whisper in his ear that you'll call him in a few minutes and explain why you had to leave. Make sure to tell him you'll be calling from a number he won't know."

"Why would I tell him that?"

"Because you're leaving with me and you'll be calling him from my phone, which isn't tapped."

Her eyes grew wide, and her face noticeably paled. He thought she might turn and bolt on him. Just to be safe, he slinked his arm around her waist and lowered his face to the side of hers. Maggie's hair smelled so good. Its soft silkiness immediately tortured his skin. Micah was acutely aware that this time she didn't collapse against him as she had when he kissed her. Maggie's body was stiff. She was confused and probably already wondered if he weren't a thoughtless bastard. Which was good, very good. Let her hate him. It would make this all so much easier. Already he knew he couldn't hate her. But if he let her see the monster that he was . . . what he wouldn't do to prevent her from seeing that part of him.

"I'm the only one who can keep you out of jail, sweetheart. Do as I say. Talk to your brother, but immediately come back here," he whispered into her ear.

It took him a moment to release her. But when he did, her expression was tight with her confusion, and the anger was back.

"Fine," she said, her lips barely moving as she spoke. "But then you're going to explain why you're behaving this way."

Micah didn't think it would affect him as strongly as it did having Maggie on the back of his bike. She cuddled up against his back. At first her hands rested against his legs, but once he accelerated into traffic, she wrapped her arms around his waist. He would have preferred taking Maggie to his house. Being alone with her right now wouldn't be a good idea, though. He knew her dress was hiked up to her thighs. Her pussy was pressed against his ass. He swore he felt her heat soaking through his jeans.

It was easier to tell he was being followed by staying off the interstate. It made their ride longer, but also allowed him to take turns, zigzag his way through the city, and confirm that the nondescript white Taurus was in fact tailing them.

Micah forced himself to focus on that and not the warm body snuggled against his backside. Maggie didn't try talking to him, but rested the side of her face against his back. He couldn't ignore what she was doing to him. Despite the attention he gave to the roads, making sure he didn't get lost, keeping an eye on the Taurus he couldn't shake, emotions were building inside him he hadn't experienced before.

It was one thing to tell himself that it was normal to feel a strong urge to protect Maggie. After all, she came to him in need, entering his home and asking for his help getting out of a dire situation. Micah wasn't sure that what he felt was normal, though. If someone else approached him asking for the same thing, he doubted he'd be experiencing the strong urges that he was now. More than likely he would have told them to go to hell.

It was probably because now he believed she was innocent. But after that kiss. Goddamn! What the hell had he been thinking?

At the time, making a show to the cops that Maggie was coming to him for personal reasons, not professional, sounded like a solid plan. He still agreed with his reasoning on that one. Micah had seriously thought he could kiss Maggie and not be affected by it.

That kiss had screwed up his equilibrium. It had taken everything he had to show Maggie it was a kiss for show, and nothing else. The way she'd reacted when he had looked indifferent afterward created a painful knot deep in his gut that still hadn't gone away.

It would take nothing on his part to put his hand over hers, caress her soft skin, and let her know he wouldn't let her down, or hurt her, in any way. It fucking sucked that he would be lying—to himself as well as to her.

If anyone knew how to be professional and keep emotions out of the job, it was him. And this was just another job. It was a hell of a lot easier killing someone than doing his damnedest to keep them alive and free. He reminded himself that he'd never taken the easy way before. The bigger the kill, the more he thrived from it. This case would be the same way—except Maggie would live.

Micah slowed and turned off Pacific Coast Highway onto a beachfront road and took it at twenty miles an hour, glancing to his right at a long stretch of beach full of sunbathers, kids running and playing, couples strolling hand in hand as well as vendors lined up in small shacks or under umbrellas selling food and tourist memorabilia. There were as many people splashing in the waves, swimming, and surfing. It was a busy, crowded beach. Perfect.

"Where are we going?" she asked, straightening behind him and letting her hands slide to his legs again.

"I'm looking for a place to park," he told her, knowing it didn't exactly answer her question.

"Why here? The pier is always packed."

"It will be harder to overhear us with so much noise around us."

She didn't ask him to elaborate. Micah guessed she doubted he would. She was wrong, though. He had every intention of explaining why he'd driven here the way he had, and chosen this location for them to stop. Maggie had to know how to lose a tail.

It took a while to find a place to park. Several white Tauruses appeared, then disappeared in the parking lot; he wasn't positive whether their friends were back or not.

Micah slipped off his bike then held his hand out to help Maggie get off. When she swung her leg over, he got a view of a white strip of cotton panties covering her pussy. Once again the hardening inside him grew to the point of distraction. His dick jerked to life and he ordered it to be still. Maggie wasn't looking at him during his moment of internal torment but staring at the ground as she combed her hair out with her fingers.

"So why are we here again?" she asked once she was satisfied with her hair.

Micah loved how the color in her face gave her a vibrant look. Her dress was sleeveless, with a choker-style collar and a belt at her waist. The result was taut material over perky breasts. The blue dress flattered her complexion. It ended halfway down her thighs, and her bare legs were slender, not too muscular, and not very tan. He guessed she'd spent most of her time in that small office off the kitchen of that nightclub. She was absolutely perfect from head to toe. And that was with her clothes on. Micah had spent too much time since meeting her imagining her naked. He knew when he finally had her that way—and already he admitted to himself it would happen—Maggie would blow his mind.

Micah looked away from her. Damn! He'd do a piss-poor job of helping her if he couldn't keep his mind off fucking her. It was so much easier killing and not knowing his target than keeping someone alive and getting to know them.

"I'll explain soon. Let's walk," he told her, and took her hand then headed toward the beach.

She didn't try pulling her hand free. "You didn't answer my question." She looked up at him, studying him with her pretty eyes and long lashes.

"You're being followed, Maggie," he began, and looked at her in time to see her mouth open.

"I know," she said simply. "I'm followed wherever I go. I need you to make them stop following me. They think I know something that I don't."

When they reached the beach Micah guided them around sunbathers and children running and playing. Listening devices would have a hell of a time hearing them now.

"There were four cops at the address where you were going to meet that lawyer. Two were just inside the building and two were in a white Taurus. They knew where you were going. The cops entered the building seconds before you pulled into the parking lot. That's a strong indication that your conversations are being monitored."

"God," she muttered, and looked around them, her blue eyes alert.

"Which is why I need you to trust me," he stressed. "Me, and no one else."

Maggie squinted when she looked up at him. She appeared to take what he said into consideration but didn't comment. Instead she said, "You mentioned it would be harder to overhear us with so much noise around us."

"It's common to use audio equipment, usually a sensitive microphone, to hear a conversation taking place quite a ways away. All the activity would distort our voices, though; the mike would pick up all the noise around us, and make it harder for them to hear what we're saying."

"Hmm," she said, nodding once.

He'd scared her but it had been necessary. Instinctively he squeezed her hand and stopped walking. When he faced her, the look she gave him as she stared up at him did something to his heart. Micah considered it more of a tightening of his chest. For a moment capturing his next breath seemed

a chore. He studied her face and immediately needed to reassure her. Maggie stared up at him with an imploring, desperate look he didn't like seeing on her pretty face.

"It's going to be okay, Maggie." He let go of her hand to
stroke her face. It was a natural act, one he gave little thought
to doing until it was already done. The moment her soft,
creamy flesh seared his fingertips, he dropped his hand.
"I've gathered some information and I'll get this matter
cleared up quickly."

"Do you mean that? What information?" She hugged
herself, looking away from him down the beach. "You make
it hard to trust you," she whispered.

He barely heard her; she'd muttered and wasn't looking at
him. But he knew she was doubting his character, which she
was damn smart to do. Nonetheless, Micah wanted her
trusting him. He wanted her knowing that he'd do anything
to keep her safe. A small part of his brain told him to drop it.
It was smarter for her to know he wasn't capable of caring.
That emotion in him had atrophied at a young age. It was a
necessary evil in making him into the man he was today,
capable of taking on any assignment and seeing it through to
the satisfaction of whoever was paying him.

You didn't take any money from Maggie.

"Maggie," he said, his voice gruff. Micah grabbed her
chin and turned her face upward to his. "Look at me."

She blinked a few times, her thick dark lashes preventing
him from seeing her dark eyes. Her mouth was pressed into
a thin line.

"What?" she demanded, and flashed angry eyes at him.
"Don't tell me, everything will be fine, Micah Jones, unless
you mean it. Deal? Don't do anything unless it's real. I'm not
some stupid woman incapable of taking care of herself, or
handling information unless it's sugarcoated. Do you understand me?"

Maggie stood facing him, her hands crossed over her
chest pressing her breasts together. Micah wisely avoided
noticing how nice they looked under her blue dress. He studied her face, looking down at this spirited young woman. If

she knew half of the truth about him she wouldn't demand anything of him, let alone stand so close to him instructing him on how to behave.

Women like Maggie O'Malley belonged next to men with roots in their community, established jobs, and beautiful homes. Not with a man whose past had been changed so many times there were no roots. There wasn't a community for him, and he doubted he'd ever have a home to call his own. It just wasn't in his chemical makeup.

"Yes, ma'am," he drawled and caressed her chin with the edge of his thumb.

"Don't patronize me."

"I'm not."

"Yes, you are." She backed out of his grip on her face, as if just realizing he still held her face. Then, turning as if she might march away from him, which he wouldn't let her do, she walked a few paces before spinning around and coming at him with her finger pointed at his chest. "Why did you kiss me? You didn't have to kiss me to make a distraction. If agents were watching us a simple hug would have created the same impression you said you wanted. You didn't have to kiss me without even preparing me if you didn't mean it."

Maggie had just given him his out. She'd set the stage to keep their relationship at the working level instead of allowing it to head down a dangerous, spiraling path that would inevitably scar him and leave her battle-wounded. He'd be smart to take it and agree with her.

He didn't battle with emotions. Micah knew pride when his father and uncle praised his work. He was happy when the three of them used to sit at their kitchen table at their house in Minnesota and strategize. Micah had recognized the need to protect his dad and uncle when he'd been set up with the dirty CIA agent. He guessed that was love although none of them ever used that word.

Micah didn't love Maggie. They'd just met. He accepted that he didn't understand the emotion as easily as he accepted that he would never experience the emotion. Therefore, he chalked up his next move as a reaction to a challenge.

That was something he understood. Maggie had definitely just offered up a challenge. But as he looked down at Maggie, her perfect face and body housing a frown and scowl directed at him, he acted on instinct. Except this time his instinct sent him down a path he'd never been down before.

Micah grabbed Maggie, yanking her off her feet. She managed a yelp before Micah wrapped his arms around her and pulled her against him. He didn't hold back. Micah's unleashed desire overrode his ability to think.

The moment he tasted her he wanted to feast. Micah's brain grew thick with fog as he pressed his tongue between her lips and devoured what he'd only had a taste of before.

To an extent, Maggie was right. When he'd kissed her in front of her brother, cops, and likely on tape for others to scrutinize later, it was meant to be an act. It was a bold statement for anyone messing with Maggie to see they would be messing with him, too. She'd called him on his act.

Always loving a good challenge, he was more than willing to show her that he didn't do anything unless it was real. This was definitely a real kiss. When he gripped her ass, crumpling her dress in his hand as he lifted and pressed her against his dick, Maggie cried out into his mouth.

His brain, and body, fed on her emotional outburst. Micah would show Maggie that when he did something, he meant it. He dragged his other hand into her auburn, silky long hair and tangled it in his fingers. Keeping her positioned as he wanted her, Micah feasted. And the more he ate, the more he craved the meal.

Maggie tasted and smelled so wonderful, Micah never wanted to breathe air that didn't hold her scent. He never wanted to touch anything without being able to touch Maggie. As he continued kissing her, the fog in his brain lifted just enough to allow him to hear his own thoughts. Instead of denying them, it dawned on him that he wanted Maggie to see him as a man worth wanting. She would never know about who he was minutes before he kissed her.

The moment he ended the kiss, Micah swore he'd do whatever it took to see that realization through. Maggie's eyes were still closed. Her lips were moist, slightly swollen, and parted as her breathing came hard. He brushed his thumb along her lower lip.

"When I do something, I mean it," he informed her, and captured her gaze the moment she looked up at him. "I've never done anything I didn't want to do."

She didn't say anything but studied his face. Micah knew fear for the first time in his life. He was afraid when he stared into her eyes that he didn't have what it took to meet her expectations.

"Good to know." Maggie looked away first and touched her lips, squinting and staring across the crowded beach.

Micah did the same, taking in their surroundings and searching for anyone who might appear out of place, or seem to have a vested interest in them. A good tracker would fade in and never make eye contact with those he was tracking. But Micah put faces to memory. He would remember if he saw any of them again. Once he got a better look at that white Taurus it wouldn't matter how many of them were in Los Angeles, he would know it if he saw it again, too.

"Let's walk," he decided, turning into the sun. If someone was watching them they would battle the glare of the sun, and it could fuck with any cameras they might be using. "There's a couple of things I need to tell you."

"What?" Maggie's heart was still racing. She'd never been kissed like that before. Not in her wildest dreams had she imagined that rough and dominating would be that hot.

This kiss was what she'd expected the first time he'd kissed her. So what was that passionate and gentle kiss he'd given her in the parking lot in the city? It was as if she'd just been kissed by two different men. What was it about Micah? She thought his first kiss would be punishing, aggressive, dominating all her senses. Instead that first kiss had made her melt right there in the parking lot in front of her older brother, the whole city, God, and everyone. She'd been so sure his curiosity for her was as strong as hers for him. But then he'd told her the kiss was necessary. Necessary? Seriously, necessary?

So she'd called him on it. Because hell, what else could she have done?

Maggie hadn't expected him to respond like this. Her legs were wobbly. Walking on them, especially in the sand, was taking more effort than she was able to pull off at the moment. When she damn near tripped as one of her shoes got sand in it, Micah put his arm around her, holding her close, and guided them across the busy beach.

"I have a connection in the FBI."

"A connection?" she asked.

"Yes." He answered as if everyone had a connection in some government agency.

"Go on," she prompted.

"Right. The FBI have been tracking Santinos for a long time."

"How long?"

"Over ten years," he said, and his hand moved up her back and under her hair. He rubbed the base of her neck before relaxing his hand there and stretching his fingers around her neck. "How well do you know your uncle?"

Maggie shrugged, an uncomfortable feeling settling in her gut. "I guess as well as anyone knows their uncle. I mean"—she shrugged—"he's my uncle."

"You weren't just any employee."

"True," she admitted, and was glad he'd noticed. She was more like a babysitter.

"Santinos has been laundering money in and out of the country most of his adult life." He glanced around them at everyone on the beach, then lowered his voice.

Maggie looked around the crowded beach as well. She didn't notice anyone nearby that she'd seen before on the beach, or at the lawyer's office. Although she was sure people had been walking up and down the street and through the parking lot when she'd been standing there talking to Micah, for the life of her she couldn't remember what any of them looked like.

"Santinos testified against a crime lord when he was in

his early twenties and was put in witness protection at that time."

"My uncle? The witness protection program?" Maggie did the math quickly. Uncle Larry was ten years older than she was, which made him thirty-five. That meant somewhere around fifteen years ago . . . which meant when she was ten. "I wasn't around him that much as a little girl," she concluded.

They found a park bench that wasn't occupied. Maggie sat, gratefully, and quickly emptied the sand out of her shoes. Micah sat next to her and when she straightened, he had his arm stretched across the back of the bench. If she leaned back, his arm would appear to be around her. Was he trying to create something between them, or was this more of his acting because it was "necessary"? She would hate that word for the rest of her life.

"Good thing you weren't." Micah saved her the trouble of trying to decide how to sit. He placed his hand on her shoulder and leaned her back against the bench. Stretching his long, thick muscular legs out in front of them, he forced anyone walking in front of them to take a sharp turn to avoid his legs and large, black boots.

Every inch of the man was virile and intimidating. Maggie swore mothers clutched their children closer as they walked past the two of them. Two fast-paced games of volleyball went on in front of them. A couple of ladies playing still managed to shoot curious looks his way. Women lying out rolled over on their beach towels, deciding it was a good time to switch sides and drool over Micah.

Micah might have noticed; hell, he was probably used to it. He stared down and in her direction, his expression solemn and unreadable and he spoke so only she could hear.

"Your uncle didn't stay in witness protection very long. He bailed in less than six months. "

"Now, why doesn't that surprise me?" she muttered wryly.

Maggie shifted on the bench, turning to face him.

"It's no secret to the family that Uncle Larry has been in and out of trouble," she informed him. "I have no idea how he was able to buy Club Paradise. But as soon as I finished school, he called me and offered me a job keeping books." She chuckled at the memory, although she now questioned if a lot of it had been lies. "He told me with my knowledge of numbers he was sure I could turn his club around. I was up for the challenge."

"He set you up." His hazel eyes were dark, even in the sunlight, and searched her face as he spoke. "From the moment he bought that club he's been using it as a cover for laundering illegal money."

"But I kept the books," she complained.

"Come here."

"Huh?"

Micah reached for a strand of hair alongside her face, then tangled his fingers in it. He brought her face close to his and for a moment she thought he would kiss her again.

"We have to find the real books to the club before the cops do," he whispered into her ear. "Or worse yet, before whoever is setting you up."

Maggie shivered. Despite the warm ocean breeze, she was suddenly cold.

Chapter Six

Micah pulled up to his garage and parked long enough for Maggie to climb off. They'd reached a point in their conversation where they needed guaranteed privacy. The only logical place to bring her was his home. When he'd suggested going there, Maggie had readily agreed. He was getting damn sick of the cops following them; it would have taken nothing to pull his gun and shoot out their tires so they couldn't. That would scare Maggie, though, and he needed her full trust.

He looked at her when her cell rang.

"Who is it?" he asked.

"My brother Aiden."

He'd been able to hear her brother when Maggie had called him on Micah's phone while they'd been at the beach. Her brother hadn't been too impressed with Micah. He was a smart man.

"Don't answer it. You can call him on my phone once we're inside," he told her. Micah left his bike running, which he hoped made it harder for anyone to pick up on what they were saying, then pulled up the garage door. "Come in here," he instructed.

Maggie sent the call to voicemail and continued looking at it as she walked up his driveway into his garage. Micah drove his bike inside then pulled the garage door closed, shrouding them in darkness. He turned around, letting his eyes adjust, then moved in on Maggie, putting his arms on her shoulders and holding off the urge to pull her body against his.

"There's no light in here," he explained. He hadn't been looking for creature comforts when he searched for a simple rental property with a landlord who wouldn't ask a lot of questions. Micah had paid cash to rent the semi-dilapidated house for the full year. His landlord had been very happy and had left him alone since then. Exactly what Micah had wanted.

"I can't see a thing," Maggie said, the slightest edge of nerves audible in her voice.

"I've got you," Micah told her, wrapping his arm around her narrow waist. "I guess this is your test in trusting me." He guided them to the door that led to the narrow, weed-infested path between the garage and the house.

"You give bad tests," she said, and this time she was teasing him.

Because he wanted to, Micah scooped her into his arms. Her dress crept up her soft, round ass as she squealed and clawed at his shoulders.

"My God! Micah!" she cried out, turning into him as she clung to him, wrapping her arms around his neck. "Are you always a brute?"

"I'm seldom a brute," he said, which was the truth. Usually he was pure asshole.

Maggie's laughter lightened his mood. He wanted to keep her laughing. He wanted to carry her straight to his bed. The urge was overwhelming as he managed to unlock his door with her still in his arms. The moment his alarm didn't go off, he froze.

"What?" Maggie asked, when he dropped her then pushed her behind him.

Micah pulled his gun, keeping one hand on her arm and using his body as a shield as he kept her behind him and glanced around his house.

"God damn it," he growled, and pulled Maggie with him as he walked to the side wall where the kitchen light switch was. He used the butt of his gun to turn it on.

"Oh my God," Maggie whispered behind him. "Micah, your house."

"Don't say a word," he ordered, his anger peaking too fast for him to control. He stared at his ransacked home. "And don't move. In fact, sit." He pushed her into his kitchen chair, then slid her into the middle of the room where she wasn't near the window or door. "Don't move," he repeated, then turned, willing whoever had the nerve to do this to still be in his home.

Micah checked his two top dresser drawers in his dining area first. The drawers rattled, proof that whoever had been there had tried tampering with the locks on them. He saw a couple of nicks in the wood around the locks. Someone had started working on opening the drawers. They'd stopped, though.

He tensed, his gaze searching his living room. They'd destroyed the room—not that it had been overly clean before he'd left. A newspaper and the dinner he'd eaten on his couch had been tossed to the floor. Someone had pulled the cushions from the couch then hurriedly tossed them back in place.

Micah gripped his gun, feeling the comfort of the metal become one with his hand as he took in how his coffee table and couch were both at angles. They'd been moved during the search. Someone had been in a rush. There wasn't anything in the house that would reveal him as a Mulligan.

Not that Micah cared. They'd intruded on Micah Jones's space. Someone had made a terrible mistake. He moved down his narrow hallway. There were no pictures on his walls. No pictures of family. No pictures of girlfriends. No snapshots of Micah hanging with friends in bars or at family events. There was nothing anywhere to give anyone any indication of what type of person he was, or any indication about his private life. To a good detective, that would have been a serious red flag.

You're risking everything by helping Maggie.

Micah reached his bathroom first and pushed the door open with his gun. He did the same with his shower curtain, shoving it to the side with the end of his gun.

They've invaded your space because she's with you.

He returned to the hallway and turned the doorknob to the only bedroom in his small house. This time Micah turned on the light. His mattress and box springs hung off the bed frame. The sheets were pulled off. The few pieces of clothing he owned had been pulled out of his closet and tossed on the floor. Micah guessed whoever had been in his house had been pretty pissed off at this point in their search. They'd torn his house apart and hadn't learned a Goddamn thing about him.

He turned at the sound of footsteps in his hallway.

"I told you to stay in that chair," he barked, glaring at Maggie.

"Here," she said, ignoring him, but glancing at the gun in his hand as she held out a small business card. "I spotted this stuck inside the doorknob of your front door."

Micah stared at the LAPD insignia stamped on the business card before taking it from her. "Show me where you found it."

He followed her down the hallway to his living room. Micah sheathed his gun in the holster attached to the back of his jeans and tugged his T-shirt over it. Maggie pointed to his front door.

"It was stuck against the doorknob," she said, pointing.

"Against the doorknob?" Micah moved around her, inspecting the simple doorknob that wouldn't keep a fool out of the place. It was loose enough that the card did fit between it and the wooden door. The dead bolt he'd installed after moving in had been tampered with. Glancing up at the almost invisible wire that was part of his security system, he noticed it had been cut. His fury mounted all over again. Whoever had entered his house had known to cut that one wire as soon as they'd entered. They'd done it fast enough to prevent the signal from being sent to his phone, which was how he'd set it up. "The son of a bitch knew it was there and what they needed to do to turn it off."

"Knew what was there?" Maggie asked.

He pointed to the cut wire. "My security system. The

motherfucker cut that wire within a minute of entering. Otherwise, I would have gotten a notice on my phone that someone had entered my house."

"Wow," she said under her breath.

"It's a bad neighborhood," he offered as explanation. Not that the neighborhood bothered him. Looking at the card, Micah pulled out his phone and paced the length of his living room. He called the number then waited out two rings before a man answered. "I suggest you get your ass back over here right now," Micah growled, then hung up.

"What? Wait? Did you just call that detective?"

Micah spun around, too pissed to respond to Maggie's shocked expression. "No one enters my house," he informed her. Micah tried for a calming breath but fury burned him alive inside. Who the fuck did that detective think he was, tearing his place apart?

He was so pissed it took a few tries to make the small key on his keychain fit into the keyhole in his top dresser drawer.

"What are you doing?" Maggie asked as she picked up newspapers scattered on the floor around them.

"Don't touch anything."

"Huh?" she asked, and stared at the crumpled stack of papers she held in both hands.

Micah pulled out the small cigar box he kept under his Glock. Maggie sucked in a breath at the sight of the larger gun. She might as well get accustomed to seeing guns around him, especially if they were dealing with this type of game playing.

"I'm cleaning house before I clean up," he told her, knowing she wouldn't understand.

"That makes sense."

It took yet another few seconds to get the even smaller key into the cigar box's keyhole. He really needed to get a grip on his anger. No one here knew who he was, nor would they. They thought they were dealing with some paid-by-the-hour bounty hunter who didn't know all the ropes. Micah tried cooling down by reminding himself that he needed to play that part. Well, he would, but if that detective showed

up again, Micah would play that part right after showing the
detective he wasn't a stupid paid-by-the-hour bounty hunter.

He pulled his small debugging equipment out of the box,
then set the box back in his dresser drawer. Then slowly he
began running it over everything in his house, including the
house itself. He started with the papers in Maggie's hands.
Immediately the small handheld debugger, which cost more
than that detective would have made in a month, possibly
several months, began blinking rapidly.

"Put the papers back on the table," he told Maggie.

She did, then moved to stand next to him and watched as
he went through each page until his debugger beeped once.
Micah ran it over the page he was on until he saw the flat
disk stuck in the middle of a Walmart ad.

"Damn," Maggie whispered.

Micah moved quickly and precisely, going through his
entire house, and in less than ten minutes found two more
bugs. He promptly destroyed each one.

"What are you doing?" he asked when he returned to the
living room and Maggie had it practically cleaned.

"What's it look like?" she retorted, keeping her back to
him and continuing to pick items off his floor that had been
tossed there.

"I told you, I can handle this."

"I didn't ask if you could handle it or not."

"Sit down and quit touching things."

She spun around and her bright blue eyes flashed defi-
antly at him before she marched to his trash can and stuffed
more newspapers into it. "Where do these go?" she asked,
holding up two triple-A batteries. "I assume there's a re-
mote, but I don't see it."

"Is there a reason why you aren't listening to me?" he
demanded, then walked over to the dresser in his dining
area. He put the debugger back into the cigar box, locked it,
then slid it back under his guns.

"Several actually," Maggie said, moving to stand next to
him as he made sure everything was in order in the drawer.
Her arm brushed against his as he made quick work of cov-

ering the small picture he had of himself, his grandfather, and his father, taken when he was a child. "What's that?" she asked, and tried reaching for the photo.

"God damn it!" Micah's temper roared to life once again, but this time because his guard had been down. It felt so natural having her standing next to him that he hadn't thought about what she might see in the drawer. Although a small part of his brain pointed out that he was being unreasonable, Micah slammed the door shut, locked it, shoved his keys in his back pocket, then grabbed Maggie. "Why won't you follow orders?"

He lifted her, dropped her in the chair he'd asked her to stay in, and felt all rational thought drain from his brain when she sprang right back out of it. Maggie came at him, finger pointed.

"Because I'm not now, nor will I ever be, yours to order around," she yelled, her hair tousling around her face as her eyes turned a torrential midnight blue. She stabbed his chest several times with her finger and actually went up on tiptoe to bring her face closer to his. "If you want anything to do with me, other than professionally, you'd better get that through your thick skull right now, mister."

When she would have stabbed his chest again, Micah grabbed her hand. She tried yanking free, but he held her close. "Hear me, sweetheart," he growled, trying to whisper but failing. She was pushing every one of his buttons and even now, as he stared into her face, he saw the challenge in her eyes. "Don't think for a second you can take me on."

"Oh, for all the saints in heaven," Maggie muttered, rolling her eyes. She looked pointedly at her hand, almost squished in his tight grip. "Let go of me, now!" she demanded, once again yelling. "I will think for a lot more than a second that I can take you on. Would you like me to prove to you how? It shouldn't take much. I know I've got a lot more brains than you have brawn."

Micah let go of her hand. "I would like for you to believe for one moment that there might be reasoning behind why I'm telling you what to do."

"I already know. You're trying to bully me. Sorry, darling. Submission doesn't run through my bloodline." Maggie spun around, her dress fluttering up against the back of her legs, and grabbed the knob to the kitchen door.

"Where do you think you're going?" he roared, too close to losing it.

"I think I'm leaving. Call me when you're willing to be civilized."

Micah raked his hand through the air. He missed her as she flew out of his house. He damn near yanked the door off its hinges when he ran after her. Maggie moved fast. She was at the street and marching down it, her hot little ass swaying and her nose stuck in the air.

In the time it took him to hurry down his driveway and reach her side, Micah felt his anger replaced with an overwhelming urge to protect that he'd never experienced before meeting Maggie.

Micah glanced behind him before reaching her side, noting each parked car. The ones closest were both cars that had been parked up the block since he'd moved there, not having once moved. That didn't mean someone couldn't sit in them to do a stakeout.

He galloped up alongside her, then slowed to match her pace as he took in their surroundings ahead and alongside them. "Maggie," he said on a sigh. "There are things I know that you don't."

"There are things I know that you don't, too, like manners," she spit out.

"Are you going to walk home?"

"Been taking care of myself for quite a few years now," she stated, and her nose perked up in the air a bit more.

"In this section of LA?"

"I have a cell phone."

"Who are you going to call?"

"I've got a big family."

Something tightened in his gut. "Think they'd allow you anywhere near me if you called for a ride from my home?"

"Better hurry up and apologize then."

"How about this," he said, then grabbed her, tossed her over his shoulder, and turned and marched back to his house, ignoring her outbursts. She was calling him every name in the book and hitting him with her fists with everything she had.

Micah didn't put her down until they were back inside and he'd locked the door. The moment he turned she slapped him hard across the face.

"You son of a bitch," she hissed.

"I've been called a lot worse, and maybe I am," he said. "Keep swinging until you've got it out of your system, darling. There's no point in talking until you do."

She slapped him again. This time it stung. "Don't make out to be the one who is cool and collected here, Micah Jones."

For a brief second, it threw him hearing Jones instead of Mulligan. Micah managed not to blink, though, and looked down at Maggie as she breathed heavily and glared up at him.

"You will not touch me again, at all, is that clear?" She fisted and unfisted her hands at her sides while glaring at him.

"I'm not sure I can make you that promise."

A sensual gleam brightened her pretty blue eyes before she regained control of her anger and continued spewing out her Irish temper at him. "Then maybe I need to find someone else to help me."

Someone knocked on Micah's front door. Maggie yelped and took a step backward, then tripped over the chair pushed up to his table. His hot little Irish vixen wasn't a lit fuse anymore. Whoever it was knocked again, louder and more demanding this time. Maggie's attention shot from the door to him.

He reached for her but restrained himself at the last minute. "Maggie, please, if you never listen to anything I ask of you ever again, this one time go back into my bedroom and stay there." He gestured to the hallway. "Go, now. Don't come out until I say it's safe. All right?"

His cool tone, and possibly years of training enabling

him to rein in his temper under dire circumstances, got her
attention. "Okay," she said, and hurried around him. Halfway down the hallway she turned. "Micah?"

"Yeah."

"Don't get hurt."

When he smiled at her, Micah swore he saw that fiery
temper of hers dissipate into thin air. It took him back. Her
reaction was the last thing he'd expected. The pounding on
the front door returned.

"I won't," he said, since it was the truth, and seemed a
logical answer. "Don't come out."

"I won't." She hurried into his bedroom.

Micah waited until the bedroom door closed before turning to his front door. He already knew who was there. Maggie had been the first person in his home since he'd moved
here. And he'd only invited one person over since.

Micah opened his front door and stepped to the side,
holding on to it as he willed the man facing him to enter.

"I'm Detective James Osborne."

A man about Micah's height and a bit on the thick side
sized Micah up with penetrative brown eyes. He wasn't a
white man but he wasn't a black man, either. He was, as Micah would say—but only in the right company at the risk of
being politically incorrect—a product of the melting pot of
America. Osborne was a good-looking man, at least at the
moment. He wouldn't be when Micah was done with him.

"Come in," Micah invited.

The detective entered Micah's home and looked around,
probably impressed with how quickly it had been put back
in order. Maybe he was disappointed that his work hadn't
been better and therefore taken longer to erase. Micah
closed his front door and turned the padlock. The click of
the lock had the detective turning to face Micah.

Micah didn't hesitate. He lunged at the detective, hitting
him full force. When the detective would have fallen backward into Micah's wall, Micah grabbed him by the shoulders, turned him, and sent the man flying over his coffee
table onto his couch.

The detective was fast. Micah always did appreciate a worthy adversary. His gun was pointed at Micah as he managed to come to a sitting position on the couch. It was as far as he got before Micah's gun was aimed at Osborne.

"You don't want to do that, son," Osborne drawled.

Micah seriously doubted the man was as calm as he sounded. They never were.

"You have no idea how much I do," Micah told him honestly. Then, lunging, Micah grabbed his coffee table and had it turned the long way and hitting Osborne full-body just as the detective's gun went off. It would be the only shot the detective would get.

"Fuck!" the detective howled when his bullet went through the coffee table instead of Micah.

Micah threw the coffee table to the side, its clatter loud enough to distract the detective. Micah howled for good measure when he was fairly certain Maggie screamed in the back room. As he grabbed the detective by the collar of the man's button-down shirt, he told himself it was best if Maggie knew how violent a monster he was before she got herself in too deep. Even in her anger, she'd mentioned more than once something about them having a relationship. Or better yet, about them not having a relationship if he continued acting like a pig.

"This is for trashing my house," Micah informed the detective coolly as he lifted the man off the couch and threw him across the room.

Before Osborne got to his feet, Micah kicked the man's gun out of his hand. It went clattering across the floor. Osborne reached for his collar without trying to stand. Micah already knew how easily wires, almost-invisible two-way radios, or silent alarms could be hidden in the collars of button-down shirts. Some looked like cuff links. Cops seldom walked into a potentially dangerous situation alone. Micah's invitation to return to his home had definitely suggested danger.

Micah didn't care if the man was calling in the National Guard. "And this is for spying on my home and following

Maggie around town," he added, hurling the man across the room once again.

"This is for entering my home without a warrant," he added, grabbing Osborne and bringing him to his feet. As soon as he was standing, Micah let go and punched him in the face once again with his free hand. "Sucks when a guy has to defend himself against LAPD's finest," he added as Osborne slumped to the floor.

This time the person who came to the door didn't knock firmly. It sounded more as if he lunged at the door. Truth be told, Micah was surprised the old wood held up. Instead of testing its strength, Micah unlocked and opened it. His timing was perfect. A man, probably Osborne's partner, stumbled into the house when he'd probably planned on hitting Micah's door once again with the side of his body instead.

"LAPD!" the man yelled, even as he stumbled forward.

Micah grabbed Osborne and shoved him into his partner. "I know who you are," he said coolly. "Before coming home to a destroyed house, I thought we were on the same side."

Then, pointing his gun at both of them, he took a step backward. He hadn't broken a sweat; nor had his heartbeat accelerated. His training had kicked in, which was definitely not good. He took a deep calming breath. He needed to play the duty-bound bounty hunter and not the mechanical killer void of emotion. More than likely, both of these men had torn through his home. They had probably already done a background check on him. Now they would see the man who had no established credit, no recorded history of any kind other than a driver's license, high school diploma, and a P.I. license, and draw their conclusions as to what kind of person he was. He was treading on thin ice.

"Get out of my house."

"You've got this a bit backward, son," Osborne said, holding his arms out, his hands in the air in a show of surrender. "Now put down the gun."

"I'm a bit too old to be your son," Micah drawled. He would have guessed Osborne was in his thirties. "And it's you who have things backward. When you have a crime, there's a suspect, which you have. You have a crime scene, allegedly. My house isn't it, though. You didn't have probable cause, or any other cause for that matter, to enter my home without a warrant; to destroy it trying desperately to find a reason to get a warrant; or," he added, raising his voice, "to bug my fucking house."

"Calm down, *son*," Osborne said. He was noticeably cool, despite his bruised and swelling face. "You don't want the kind of trouble this will bring down on you."

"You destroyed my home. If you'd had probable cause or anything at all to justify what you did, you would have knocked on my door with a warrant. I have a hard time remaining calm when my house is bugged and I'm an innocent, law-abiding man." Micah pointed at his open front door. "I said get out of my house. Both of you."

"Huh-uh." The other detective's badge was clipped to his belt. Micah caught the last name: Holloway. "This is how it goes," he snarled. He was definitely not as cool and collected as Osborne. Holloway's face was red with fury, which accentuated gray streaks in his short brown hair. He was obviously suffering from anger management issues. "Turn around and put your hands against the wall, or I'll make you turn around."

Micah glanced past the gun Holloway pointed at Micah's chest and turned to face Osborne. "You're not getting the message I'm trying to relay here."

If he pushed these men too far, it wouldn't matter that he was trying to show them he was a bounty hunter working on the same case they were. He wouldn't be bullied and sure wouldn't go for the crap they'd pulled off in his home tonight. He couldn't shoot them and wouldn't throw more punches.

Micah had more training and experience than either of these men would manage during the duration of his career. He moved before Holloway could react, grabbed his gun, and tossed it to the floor with Osborne's.

"Jones, more backup is on its way," Osborne said, but shifted his weight so he was outside Micah's arm length by a few inches. "Don't make this harder on you than it already is."

"Hard on me? You have nothing on me and no reason to have destroyed my home. Shall we all have a seat and wait for them to arrive?" Micah suggested. "Or wait, I know, we can all explain to your captain why you destroyed and wired my home, then were cocky enough to leave a calling card."

"All right, we'll leave." Osborne nodded at his and Holloway's guns on the floor. "Are you going to give us back our guns? They're registered to LAPD. They're not worth anything to you."

"Take them." He waved indifferently at the two guns. Then, turning his back on the two detectives, Micah dragged his fingers through his hair.

His fucking temper had blown out of control, and all this to ensure Maggie's innocence? If he'd only been mildly on their radar before, Micah had definitely just put himself at the top of the list. So much for a low profile. Micah rubbed his face with his hands as he turned around to face the detectives.

"I'm not going to apologize for my actions," he began. "You entered my house without a warrant." He looked away from both of them and stared down his hallway, fighting to keep his cool and not throw both of them out of his house. "We're all on the same side. We're all interested in Maggie not going to jail."

Osborne slipped his gun into its holster at his waist. The man would have one hell of a bruise the next day. Already the side of his face was turning shades of blue and green and swelling up.

"The only thing we're interested in is putting the criminals responsible for the amount of money that has illegally gone in and out of Club Paradise for way too many years behind bars." Holloway glared at Micah. "I should haul you downtown, Jones."

"On what charges? What crime is it that I've committed?" Micah leveled his gaze on both of them. He might be new to living in California, but he was pretty sure he had all the state laws down. If either of them tried charging him with battery, he'd cry self-defense. They were in his home.

"I can keep you downtown for questioning for quite a long time," Osborne snarled.

"When you come up with what it is exactly that you want to ask me, I'll be here." Micah suddenly felt drained. He wanted to check on Maggie. It was damn quiet in his house right now.

He raised his arm and both detectives tensed. Micah pointed to the front door. "See yourselves out, gentlemen," he encouraged. "And next time, don't trash or wire my home. Knocking on the door and asking your questions will save all of us a lot of time."

Maggie's brother had called while Micah was beating the crap out of two police officers in his living room. She was still shaking from the horrific sounds she had heard during that fight. Her imagination had conjured up all types of scenes to match the grunts and nasty bashing sounds she'd heard. But then it got quiet. Almost too damn quiet. She thought she heard male voices, low baritones grunting at each other. She would have thought the walls in this small, old house would have been thinner. Maggie hadn't been able to pick up a thing said in the living room. No way was she opening that bedroom door.

When her phone rang a second time, although her volume was turned down, she still damn near jumped out of her skin. If she didn't say so herself, Maggie did one hell of a good job convincing Aiden everything was fine. Like she'd tell him Micah was currently beating the crap out of two police officers while she hid out in a shabby bedroom in a seedy part of town. That would have gone over well. Aiden would have dragged her, kicking and screaming, straight to their priest and probably demanded she be locked away somewhere, with lots of holy water, for her own good.

The visuals on that one had almost made her laugh. Apparently overhearing knuckles crunch against bone had pushed her to the edge of hysteria.

After hanging up with Aiden, she was still clutching her phone in her hand and staring dry-eyed at the door. Occasionally she'd shift her attention to the wall directly in front of her, as if she had X-ray vision and could see straight into the living room. The silence that followed offered a few calming moments. She was finally able to quit white-knuckling her phone.

But then she began worrying. What if the police hauled Micah in? They would check his house and find her back here in Micah's bedroom. They would take her in again. Damn, those fucking detectives would have way too much fun dragging her back in and gloating over how she had obviously lied to them. They would accuse Micah and her of having plotted out some scheme since, after all, he'd hauled her out to them when they captured her uncle. Lord, she would have Micah in so much trouble. He would hate her. And it was already quite clear that he had a temper to match an Irishman.

Maggie directed her attention to the window, the only one in his room. It faced the street. There were no curtains, just dust-covered blinds that were closed. It crossed her mind to leap off the bed, shove those blinds aside, and get the window to open so she could escape. They couldn't haul her in if they couldn't find her.

But then what would she be? A fugitive at large? The only place she'd run was to one of her family members. Maggie would be the easiest person for anyone to track. All of this proved rather simply that trying to leave here would be stupid. For a brief moment, however, imagining Micah hunting her down did something to her equilibrium. A fluttering started in her tummy but quickly moved down between her legs until the pulsing there matched the hard, steady thump of her heartbeat. She was most definitely becoming hysterical. Hell, Micah had hurled her over his shoulder and brought her back in here. That might be hot to

fantasize about but in real life, no sane woman tolerated behavior like that. Micah might be a kick-ass bounty hunter.
He had no problem standing up to cops when he was innocent. But he displayed every sign in the book of very, very
bad boyfriend material.

She damn near shrieked when Micah barged into the
bedroom. He shoved the door open until it slammed against
the wall behind it. Maggie wasn't able to scramble off Micah's bed fast enough. He left the door open and stood at the
center of the end of the bed, just as Maggie made it to her
knees.

There was no way to describe the look on Micah's face.
His skin wasn't pale enough for him to look flushed. He had
a slightly weathered look to him, but definitely not worn-
out. Far from worn-out. Maggie would bet good money that
the tribes of her ancestors from Ireland had quite probably
used the same stance Micah held right now. She imagined
many victorious warriors often returned to their women
with that same fiery, almost-savage look in their eyes.

Before she could crawl to the end of the bed, stand, and
talk to him, Micah put one knee on the bed and grabbed her
arms. "They won't come back," he said, his voice raspy as if
he'd been the one yelling out there.

Maggie was pretty sure that hadn't been the case.

"Okay," she said, nodding, because she sensed he needed
assurance that he'd done the right thing. Maggie had never
seen emotions burning so raw in a person before.

Micah didn't say anything else but crawled onto the
bed. His grip tightened on her arms as he came down on
top of her.

There wasn't time to think, to decide if this was the right
move or not. Micah's mouth was on hers, hungry and demanding. His body pressed hers down into the mattress. She
didn't realize her legs were spread with his body between
them until his arm was on her outer thigh, shoving her dress
up to her waist.

She couldn't think. His mouth was doing crazy wicked
things to hers. Maggie wrapped her arms around his neck,

loving the feel of so much rock-hard muscle pressed against her everywhere. She tangled her fingers into his hair and when she tugged, he growled fiercely into her mouth. At the same time, he lifted himself off her far enough to shove her dress and her bra up her body until her breasts were exposed. The second her nipples were free his hand cupped one breast.

His fingers were long and his fingertips rough. Micah was one of those few specialized men who worked not only with his mind, but also with his hands. He was as intelligent as he was skillful. Just as she began imagining him plotting out how he would hunt a man who'd skipped out on his bond, Micah pulled her back into the moment. Those skilled fingers tweaked her nipple. A charge surged from her breast straight to her pussy with so much energy she howled and bucked off the bed.

Micah's body was over hers, preventing her from going anywhere he didn't want her. But the grumbling in his throat had the sound of pure male satisfaction. Their tongues swirled around each other, doing the dance of lovers, but their bodies moved more aggressively, both anxious to explore and claim. She pulled his hair and didn't realize Micah's hand no longer cupped her breast until both his hands circled her wrists.

"I like my hair in my scalp," he whispered against her lips.

Micah lifted himself off her body, leaving her feeling suddenly incredibly exposed. At the same time he raised her arms until he'd pressed her hands into the pillows on either side of her head. Micah looked at her and froze. He kept her wrists pinned to the bed as he came up to his knees and knelt with the roughness of his jeans rubbing her inner thighs.

For a moment he simply stared down at her without moving. Instead of drooling over her exposed breasts or at how hard her nipples were, Micah gazed deeply into Maggie's eyes.

"Is this a good idea?"

His question shocked the hell out of her. "I know I want you," she answered easily. Maggie then saw visible ghosts swirling in Micah's eyes. They were haunting him, torturing him, and bringing forth uncertainties that Micah probably tried to never let anyone see. "Beyond what we feel right now, Micah, neither of us can predict the future."

"What do we feel? Other than my dick being harder than a rock and a damn near uncontrollable urge to fuck you, what else am I feeling?"

"Do you feel something else?" she whispered and immediately held her breath, unable to retract the question and terrified of what his answer might be. Hadn't Micah just displayed behavior that made him a bad candidate for a boyfriend? Why would she push it?

"I don't know that it's ever mattered so much that I not hurt someone."

"I doubt you'll hurt me," she said in a soft drawl and moved her hips between his legs.

Maggie swore that when Micah growled, it rose from deep in his chest and transformed the man holding her down on his bed into something so much stronger, more powerful, and definitely a hell of a lot more dangerous than any man should be. At the same time, as he lowered his face to hers and nipped at her lip, something glowed in his eyes that could only be described as raw vulnerability. Maggie only had a moment before his face blurred before hers, but she suddenly understood. Her stomach fluttered with uncertainty and excitement when it dawned on her that Micah knew rough and tough but possibly not exposed and vulnerable.

She raised her head off the bed just far enough to scrape his lower lip with her teeth. "I might surprise you. I'm tougher than I look." Maggie tried seeing his expression when their faces were so close.

"No promises."

Maggie grinned. "My grandma used to say a man, or woman, unwilling to make a promise was a loser before he was out of the gate."

"Wise woman, this grandma of yours?"

Maggie's smile broadened. "The wisest."

"Okay then. I promise . . ." Micah faltered for a moment.

Maggie held her breath, anxious to hear what he would say. Her lungs began hurting when she couldn't exhale but simply watched Micah scoot away from her. For a moment her vision was blurred by potential tears. Maggie blinked her eyes dry and was ready to leap off the bed, attack Micah, and make herself clear in no uncertain terms that she was content to fuck now, and talk later. Either way, he was not walking away and leaving her with her body burning up from the inside out. He was going to fuck her.

She'd barely made it to a sitting position and braced her hands behind her to help her maintain the position. Micah had inched to the edge of the bed and stripped off his shirt. She almost cried over the perfect specimen of a man he revealed to her. He stood, undid his jeans, then shoved them down powerful, muscular legs. It took him only a moment to fully undress. Micah paraded before her, showing off sculptured shoulder and arm muscles, ripped abs, a rock-hard stomach, and an even harder cock that was thick and long and jutting forward as he stepped around the bed.

Maggie didn't give a damn if he promised her the moon and stars or a simple pebble off the beach. She rolled to her side, watched him open a narrow wooden drawer in a not-so-sturdy-looking nightstand and pull out a thin box of condoms. It looked as if this might be the first time he'd opened the box. Her pussy ignited with feverish need and she reached for him.

"I want to touch it first," she whispered, with no idea where her sudden wave of confidence came from. Possibly knowing Micah wasn't out sleeping around, which she surmised from the unopened package of condoms, helped. Maybe he'd just bought more, but Maggie didn't dwell on that as much as the realization that either way, he was with her now, and she wasn't going to decide right now how soon she would let him go.

When she reached out, Micah took her hand and held it as she wrapped her fingers around his cock. "Damn it," he whispered.

The sense of power from just watching his entire body tense felt better than she'd ever imagined it would. Maggie brushed her fingertips over the velvety smooth, loose flesh that moved with her touch over his swollen dick.

She tried using her free hand to inch her underwear past her thighs. Micah's breathing was coming hard and when he was ready, she wanted to be ready for him.

"Darling," he rumbled.

For some reason she loved how guttural his voice sounded when she pushed him. As gently as he'd taken her hand and helped wrap her fingers around his shaft, Micah was rough when he shoved her hand away from him. His eyelids had been at half-mast, and suddenly they were wide open. Maggie got the acute sensation the demons that hovered under the surface of Micah's confident exterior had just returned. His look was wild when he stared at her.

She didn't quite yelp when he lifted her by one arm. Maggie hurried to cooperate and assist when Micah turned her, unzipped the short zipper at the back of her dress, then flipped her back to face him. He grabbed the material at both sides, pulled it off her, and tossed it to the side. He was just as rough in removing her underwear. Maggie was on fire. She loved it.

"Come here," she whispered as she collapsed onto her back and reached for him.

Micah came to her but not exactly as she imagined. He positioned himself between her legs, grabbed her thighs, and lifted her rear end off the bed. Adjusting her where he wanted her, his cock pressed into her heat, parting her soaked folds and immediately easing inside her. He lowered his mouth to hers and as greedily as a child would take candy, she took his mouth and kissed him.

"My sweet Maggie, I promise to give you everything I have to offer."

She didn't have time to digest his possible meaning when he buried his dick inside her. He moved deep, filling and stretching her. Micah didn't take his time, or slow down and worry he'd come too soon and not satisfy her. As confident as he was in every other aspect of his life, he was the same when fucking her.

Micah receded and impaled. He took her flames of passion to new heights, satisfying then creating unbearable new urges. Maggie came harder than she'd come before.

It was the first time they'd had sex, but Micah knew exactly how to fuck her. She came, then the second time exploded even harder.

"How do you know?" she demanded, panting so hard she could barely speak.

"Because you tell me."

Micah flicked her nipple with his finger and thumb as he fused their mouths together and kissed away her ability to think. After that she lost track of how many times she came.

Even as she ran her hands over his chest, exhilarated in his coiled chest hair, and lingered over an occasional scar, her brain charged with electrified energy allowing her to think only about how he fucked her. She might have worried that she wouldn't remember every inch of his body, but with the orgasms Micah gave her she didn't care. And when that final release tore through her, and she stared at the flat silver medallion hanging around Micah's neck, Saint Michael the avenger of warriors, Maggie suddenly understood the man inside her.

Chapter Seven

"I just got off the phone with Penelope." Haley sat in the truck next to Micah.

Ben was riding with King. On cases like these, where KFA chased down and hauled in someone intentionally hiding out and trying to dodge them, King had started riding with Ben shotgun. King was teaching the kid the ropes, and his faith in Ben having his felony expunged seemed to generate incredible confidence in the kid.

"I think she's Jorge's aunt. I'm not sure," Haley continued. "But Jorge left her apartment just fifteen minutes ago. He wanted money and she wouldn't give him any."

"He's on foot?" Greg King spoke through the speakerphone on Haley's cell phone, which she held in her hand.

"Yup." Haley held her hand out toward Micah. "Slow down here," she said softly, searching out the window. "There, building fifteen. He's got to be close," she said a bit louder into the phone.

"We park," her husband announced and the truck Ben and King were in pulled to the side of the road in front of them. Tall, square brick apartments, building after building the same, spread over a few blocks. "Jones, you're out with me." King said something to Ben that wasn't quite audible through the phone. More than likely he told the kid to hang tight and that his chance would come soon. Ben was lucky to have a mentor like King.

Micah stopped the truck, shoved it into park, and cut the

engine. Haley was out on her side at the same time he climbed out and shut his door. Meeting her at the front of the truck, Micah searched between the buildings. Jorge couldn't have gotten that far.

"He's five-six, one hundred and thirty pounds, with curly long black hair." Haley pulled out the snapshot they'd been provided of Jorge Gutierrez sent to them by the bonding agency when the man missed two court dates and wasn't showing up for meetings with his parole officer. "Aunt Penelope, our source, says he just left the building right there," she continued after handing the picture of Jorge to Micah. "Fifteen minutes." She turned slowly, looking around them. "He's small and thin. He probably can run pretty fast."

"Only if he has reason to," Micah pointed out.

Haley helped her husband into his bulletproof vest. Micah already had his on. He handed the picture back to Haley then stepped out from in between the two trucks. He squinted against the afternoon sun as he began walking and looking for their guy.

King came up alongside him and remained quiet as the two men left Haley and Ben at the trucks and started moving around the buildings. A shot ricocheted off the side of one of the buildings. King dove to the ground, reaching for Micah and yanking him down next to him.

"Live fire—check in." There was urgency in Haley's voice but she spoke softly through the speakerphone King had attached to his collar.

Instead of confirming he was okay, Micah patted King's arm and pointed through a row of buildings with hedges lining each one. There was someone hunched against the brick building at the end of one of the rows of hedges. Instead of talking, Micah remained on all fours and tapped King's arm again. He gestured that he was heading toward the building. King nodded, gave the go-ahead, then responded to his wife, keeping his voice low.

Micah moved in a crab-like position, hurrying to close in on whoever it was sitting flush with the building. Another shot was fired, and it sounded like an older woman started wailing in Spanish. Micah spoke more languages than he'd admit to anyone. The woman was yelling that someone had just fired a gun. She wasn't hurt.

Someone would call 911, though, if they hadn't already. Micah would be damned if the LAPD got credit for bringing in his man. He moved between two buildings, keeping low, and aware that the man he'd suspected as Gutierrez was no longer sitting on the ground. Micah straightened slowly when he reached the location where the man had been hiding.

Three-story, square brick apartment buildings, all identical, with even the shrubbery and sidewalks around them appearing the same, were spread out in equal distances on both sides of Micah. He stared at the ground, focusing on where it looked like the man's heels had created crescent-shaped indentations. Glancing toward the brick wall, Micah imagined where Gutierrez had leaned against it. He would have pushed forward with his hands, slid his feet back to stand . . .

Micah studied the ground a moment longer, then saw it. A slight impression in the ground, and a dusty footprint on the sidewalk.

"You went this way," he hissed under his breath, and broke into a hard run.

There was another round of gunfire. It wasn't directed at Micah. He slowed, reached the end of the next building, and pressed his back against the rough brick exterior. He heard sirens in the distance.

"Fuck," he hissed, and shot hurried looks to his right and left, trying to guess which way the bastard had run. Gutierrez had a partner in crime, possibly even Aunt Penelope. But Micah had seen the little prick and his ass would be in cuffs before the cops showed up.

He scanned the rows of apartment buildings in either direction. Hunting a man wasn't a guessing game. The most experienced criminals too often made fatal errors. Micah had spent much of his career as an assassin learning what those errors were. He narrowed his focus, staring at the ground just ahead of him.

"Gotcha," he whispered, and eased up against the closest building. Once his back was flush with the brick wall, he slowly raised his head, wishing he'd brought sunglasses. "Gutierrez, you impress me after all," he muttered under his breath.

His gaze traveled up the drainpipe along the corner of the building in front of him. Gutierrez had made it almost to the top of the building but hadn't anticipated the lip right before the roof, blocking his way to the top.

Micah pulled his gun from his holster, relaxed his body against the brick wall behind him, and straightened his arm as he aimed above him. Hard footsteps coming close forced his attention from his target, and at the same time grabbed Gutierrez's focus.

"Don't do it," Micah called out as Gutierrez aimed a gun at King.

King had just rounded the other end of the building where Gutierrez clung to the drainpipe flush with the fourth floor. He skidded to a stop and ducked around the corner just as a bullet slammed into the ground where he'd been standing.

Micah's warning yell gave away his presence and Gutierrez swung on the drainpipe, firing at Micah and sliding down it with skilled agility. The man had to be a gymnast. No one moved that quickly outside a four-story building without some kind of prior training.

"Give it up, Gutierrez," Micah yelled and aimed at the man.

"Shoot, no kill!" King's voice bellowed between the buildings.

Micah adjusted his aim and fired. Gutierrez howled, crumpling, and fell the remaining feet to the ground. King and Micah raced toward him.

"Motherfucker!" Gutierrez snarled as he rolled toward Micah. The asshole fired.

Micah fired at the same time.

Patty, KFA's office manager, stared at Micah from across her desk. She sat with her back straight as a board, her fingers laced together, and her palms flat on her desk in front of her. When he was about to scream for her to quit staring at him, Patty sighed, stood, and walked around her desk. If she came anywhere near him he would tell her exactly where she could stick her drama-queen act, not caring how badly he hurt her feelings.

"You're going to drink some coffee," Patty announced, as if his well-being was truly her concern. "And if you don't let me look at that arm, I swear I'm going to call nine-one-one."

Micah stood, towering over her, and started toward the door to the KFA office. "Let King know I'll be out back when he checks in." He let the office door close behind him, and shut out Patty's protests that he get back inside and let her take care of him.

There wasn't a person on this planet who knew how to take care of Micah—well, maybe there was one. He put some speed into his walk as he rounded the side of the Kings' home, passed their backyard, and finally reached the beach. He tucked his left arm against his chest. Micah didn't have to bother looking to know he had a minor flesh wound that wouldn't slow him down a bit. The level of pain was damn near nonexistent compared with other gunshot wounds and injuries he'd endured over the years. He would be fine.

What would it be like having Maggie cleanse my wounds and take care of me?

It would be ridiculous because he didn't have *wounds,* at least nothing to worry about. It was a fucking flesh wound, a scratch that would burn for a while; then he'd be fine. Nothing to be fussed over. He needed a clear head. Letting Maggie, or anyone for that matter, fuss over him would be a distraction.

If anything, he needed a good lecture for being so damn sloppy. Micah trudged around the backside of the property fence that surrounded the Kings' property. Standing with his back to the fence, he crossed his arms over his chest and refused to wince against the pain. He got what he deserved. King had said shoot, no kill. He hadn't said just scratch the asshole so he could still fire back.

Micah's grandpa used to tell him, "Let a woman get too close and you've got the worst distraction God ever put on this earth." Grandpa Mulligan would stand with his legs spread, his big, burly hands planted firmly on either side of his waist, and Micah used to do his best to imitate the stance.

"You know what distractions cause, right, boy?" his grandpa would demand. "That's right," he would grumble and pat Micah on the head whether he said the answer or not. "Distractions cause death."

Micah understood today that his grandpa probably was trying to steer Micah clear of girls who quickly took an interest in him during his teenage years. He might have been somewhat of a late bloomer but he did his best to make up for lost time once the urge to chase girls kicked in. That's when he took his grandpa's words of wisdom to mean no girls around when he was hunting.

There was a bloodstain on the sleeve of his T-shirt he should probably take care of. Micah looked down at it, tugging on the shirt in order to see how much blood had actually soaked through the fabric. The dark odd-shaped blotch reminded him of an inkblot a psychiatrist might have a patient analyze. It was an odd thought, and he wasn't sure why it had just popped into his mind. His shirt scraped over the fresh wound where Gutierrez's bullet had grazed the top of his arm. At the same time his silver pendant of Saint Michael pressed into his flesh just under his collarbone.

Micah didn't flinch as the pain spiked and fresh blood soaked another part of his shirt. Instead he watched waves ripple and turn to foam as he remembered how Maggie had watched his pendant when it bounced against his chest when he fucked her. He'd been rough, demanding—unrelenting, even—and she'd taken everything he had given her. Not once had a woman drained him the way Maggie had, and left him not only completely sated but with a new knowledge.

He'd entered his bedroom that night needing to release the energy that had sizzled across his flesh after dealing with the detectives. When he'd seen Maggie on his bed, not looking scared but instead appearing as pumped up as he had been, something overpowered Micah. The urge to brand Maggie, somehow make her part of who he was, had been too strong to control.

That was bullshit. He could have controlled it. He'd wanted to make Maggie his woman. It had crossed his mind to hold back as he had with so many women in the past. At first he'd told himself it was something about Maggie. To an extent, it was. Maggie looked at him differently than women in his past had. Whether he picked up a lady in a fancy club and drove to a five-star hotel in a fast car, or found a lady in a dive and took her around back, they'd never stared into his eyes the way Maggie did. He told himself it was hiding out, not knowing where his father or uncle were, being pissed over the investigation into the murder of a dirty CIA agent that made him see things that weren't really there. Micah knew better than to hide the truth behind delusional thinking. The past three months as a bounty hunter instead of as an assassin did challenge his perspective. He didn't know if they had changed his outlook on life. But he did know when he stared into Maggie's pretty blue eyes, he swore she stared back at him as if she understood him.

That was his revelation. It had been the first time they'd had sex yet it hadn't felt like it. When he'd come, he'd left part of himself inside her and now wasn't complete without her by his side. Micah had branded Maggie, but she'd done the same thing to him.

Stalking away from the beach, Micah grabbed a clean T-shirt out of the side pouch on his bike just as the black Avalanche pulled into the circular drive in front of the house. King parked the truck behind the other two, then he and Haley got out.

"Glad you're here," King said when he spotted Micah. "We need to talk."

King sounded stern but Micah didn't give it much thought as he followed the two of them into the office. "Let me change shirts," Micah said to King's back.

The giant man turned around once they were inside. Haley dropped paperwork on Patty's desk. She blocked the girl's view of Micah when she turned around, and her eyes grew wide.

"Oh God, Micah!" she exclaimed. "I didn't know you were hurt that bad. Damn, maybe we should take you to the hospital."

Hospitals were definitely on the off-limits list. Micah wouldn't allow himself to get into their database. Not a good idea. "It's not as bad as it looks. Pulling off the shirt just made it bleed again."

He held up the crumpled T-shirt. "I just need to change."

Micah hadn't seen his mother since he was ten. He hadn't spent a lot of time around other kids and their families while growing up. That didn't mean he didn't understand the look that crossed Haley's face as she walked up to him, her attention fully on the bloodstain on his shirt.

"Come into the kitchen with me." Haley wasn't a tall woman. She didn't appear exceptionally strong. She spoke calmly and gestured for him to follow as she left the office.

Micah knew he was stuck. Haley went into full-fledged mothering mode; even King stepped to the side and allowed his wife to do her thing. And apparently at the moment, her thing was Micah.

"Sit," she ordered as they entered the kitchen. Haley pulled one of the chairs out from under the kitchen table and dragged it to the middle of the room.

Micah didn't look at King. He didn't have to. Haley was in charge at the moment, and Micah had no choice but to do as she said. He sat in the chair.

"Honestly, I'm fine," he assured her but one look at her face and he turned so she could see his arm.

"That's a good grazing," King muttered from behind Micah. "You're one lucky son of a bitch that asshole's aim was off."

"I know." Micah shifted so King was in his peripheral. "It never ceases to amaze me how immune some communities can get to gunfire. That was one huge apartment complex and not a soul came outside when shots started."

"They learn at a young age to stay inside when someone starts shooting. That's how they stay alive," King said.

He pushed away from the counter when Haley left the room with Micah's bloodstained shirt. Micah unfolded his clean T-shirt.

"I wouldn't bother putting that on," King warned, pointing to the shirt. "You aren't getting out of this house until Haley has bandaged you and is satisfied you don't need to go to the hospital."

Micah sighed. "I really am fine." But he dropped his clean shirt in his lap.

"Beer?" King asked.

Haley reappeared in the kitchen, her hands full of cotton balls, gauze, medical tape, and several different types of ointments.

"Looks like you might need it," he added, chuckling.

"Sure," Micah said slowly, watching the medical supplies Haley was now arranging on the kitchen table.

Haley didn't waste any time tending to Micah's arm. He was forced to take his beer with his left hand. Her cool hands gripped his upper arm as she cleaned the area where the bullet had sliced across his skin. Micah did his best to relax in the chair. It was kind of nice having someone else clean the wound, apply antibiotics to keep infection away, then bandage him up.

"I think you'll live," Haley said and smiled at the bandaged arm. "You may now get dressed."

"And then sit back down," King said.

Micah was standing, his hands already through the sleeves of his clean T-shirt when he met King's gaze. It hadn't occurred to him that the man had been standing in the kitchen for any reason other than to be with his wife while she cleaned the wound of another man. King had said he'd wanted to talk, and the scowl on his face made it look serious. Micah pulled the shirt over his head, tugged it down to his waist, then reached for his beer.

"What's up?" he asked.

Haley gathered up her doctoring stuff but didn't look at him. Her pleasant mothering persona had been swapped out for the tough and ready bounty hunter.

"And thank you for cleaning my arm," Micah added, not that he was looking for brownie points from either one of them, but he appreciated her doing it.

"You're very welcome." Her smile appeared sincere. "I'm just glad both of you are okay."

"She can put you back together but I'm about ready to tear you a new one," King snapped.

Haley turned immediately to give her husband her full attention. Instead of putting her medical supplies away, she dumped them on the counter and moved next to him. "This is something I don't know about?" she asked.

"Yup. That phone call on our way home."

"Oh yeah," Haley said, nodding. "One of your old cop friends. What did he say?"

"Micah, care to answer that for my wife?" King grumbled. He appeared to grow larger, and taller, as he continued leaning against the counter, staring at Micah.

Micah had never offered information without it being specifically requested for throughout his life. He stared at King unwilling to say anything without his boss being more specific. Osborne was probably ten years or so older than Micah and possibly had been on the force when King had still been a cop. Holloway, Osborne's partner, was older. He might have called King. There was no way for Micah to know until King told him more.

King sighed. "I like you, Jones. But God damn it! Don't insult my intelligence. You just heard my wife say I got a phone call from one of my old cop friends. Tell both of us right now what you did, and why."

"Are you talking about last night?" he asked. He had a right to clarity.

"I'm talking about you beating the crap out of two LAPD detectives," King snarled, looking fierce as hell. The man was a weapon in himself. Despite being almost twice Micah's age, he would be a formidable contender.

Micah kept his temper at bay, although he had taken a few calming breaths. He might be inclined to outbursts just as any Mulligan was. But yelling at his boss that the men who had illegally entered his house and trashed it couldn't possibly be LAPD's finest wouldn't be to his benefit.

"What do you want me to say?" he asked, extending his arms out in a feeble effort to look as if he surrendered.

"Do you realize the only reason you weren't hauled off to jail on some rather serious charges was because they already knew you worked for me?"

It was on the tip of his tongue to ask what charges. There were no charges. Both detectives knew it. He'd called them on illegal actions on their part to learn more about Micah and Maggie. Not only had they failed, if they'd called King and suggested he try to do their dirty work, that wasn't going to happen, either.

"And it's a great job. I really love working here." Micah remained relaxed, knowing he'd just completely diverted the topic of conversation. He waited to see where King would go with it.

The look on his face didn't indicate he was willing to start talking about their jobs as bounty hunters. "Why did you attack Detective Osborne?" King asked, the low cool tone indicating he was fighting to maintain composure.

Micah didn't share anything about his life with anyone. There were times, though, when good judgment demanded he offer an explanation for his behavior.

"Did the detective say I attacked him?"

King pushed himself off the counter and took a single step to clear the distance between them. Micah took a step backward, making a show of giving King space.

"Here's what is going to happen," King stated, and took another step so he was in Micah's face.

Haley grabbed her husband's arm but didn't say anything. She shot Micah a pensive look but he didn't let his attention stray from King. The man was pissed as hell and at the moment putting Micah in a very dangerous position.

"You're going to tell me every little detail about what

happened from the moment you got home last night to the exact second when Detective Osborne, who is an incredible young man and the son of one of my lifelong best friends, walked out of your front door with a broken nose and cheekbone."

"Oh my God!" Haley gasped, letting go of her husband and covering her mouth with both of her hands. "Jimmy?" she asked. She looked at Micah wide-eyed. "How could you have hurt Jimmy so bad and not be in jail?"

That was the question he wanted to hear. "Two detectives entered my home last night without a warrant, planted listening devices in every room, then destroyed the place." It had to be his dumb luck that one of those detectives was the son of King's friend. It was even worse that Osborne pulled some incredibly stupid moves and Micah had simply taken advantage. He had to word everything carefully, especially with his six-and-a-half-foot, incredibly well-built pissed-off boss glowering down at him. "When I got home, I immediately noticed my security system had been tampered with. No one was there but Osborne left his card so I called and told him to come back. Osborne returned, entered the house, and showed no remorse or indication that his actions were wrong, and illegal."

King looked like he might start breathing fire out of his nose at any moment.

Micah quickly added, "I didn't own much but now I own even less. What's worse is that he never did tell me what he was looking for."

"And that's what happened?"

Micah didn't show surprise but immediately was suspicious. "Were you told a different story?"

King actually roared like a lion. He turned from Micah and slapped the table hard enough that Micah's beer toppled and fell. Haley was quick on her feet, grabbing the bottle as foam spilled off the table to the floor.

"Greg," she said, concern evident in her gentle tone. She touched his arm, and he looked at her. "Let me talk to him."

King looked so furious Micah wasn't sure if he heard his

wife, or even saw her before he turned and faced Micah. "Yes, I was told what happened. The story is so different from yours, it's preposterous. Things aren't adding up, Jones. Not just with last night, but all over the goddamn place. I'd better get some good, solid answers really soon, and I mean the fucking truth! Believe me, Jones, you haven't seen me truly pissed off yet."

"And let's keep it that way." Haley wasn't condescending. There was no fear in her tone. She didn't try pushing her husband away from Micah. Haley just looked up at him, her face lined with concern and worry.

Micah wasn't sure what King would do at that moment. Something was wrong, though. A small voice in the back of his head was getting damn close to screaming red alert. Regardless of any other situation going on here, if King started believing there was more to Micah than what he appeared to be, Micah would need to relocate immediately.

"Take your beer outside. Walk some of your anger off. I'll let you know what he says and we'll take it from there."

Greg looked at his wife, nodded once, and headed out the back door without the beer. Once he'd closed the door behind him, Haley took a sponge from behind the sink and wiped off the table and floor.

"We have a real problem here, Micah. I'm sure you're seeing it, too."

"I told you the truth about what happened last night." He was starting to believe there was a serious problem here, too. But not the same problem the Kings were seeing.

Haley finished cleaning the spilled beer then faced Micah, one hand on the counter and the other on her hip. "Jimmy, I mean Detective Osborne—is the son of a very dear friend of ours. We've known Jimmy pretty much his entire life. He's third-generation LAPD. And before you start thinking it, he *is* one of the good cops."

Micah didn't say anything, although he really wanted to hear the story the detective had told King. Haley had been in the car with her husband when the call came through, but apparently hadn't heard what Osborne had said to King.

"Micah," she said and sighed. "There is too much about you that doesn't add up. Greg and I usually read people pretty well. I will stand by my gut in saying we didn't make a mistake hiring you." She lowered her voice, and that motherly look returned to her face. "Greg definitely agrees with me there. We don't see any bad in you."

Haley crossed her arms over her chest but moved one hand to her mouth. She tapped her finger against her lips and walked the distance of the kitchen, which was a fairly large room. "The good in you sometimes disappears, though."

She had no idea how atrophied the good in him was. Micah's dad and uncle instilled values and morals in him when he was a kid, but not necessarily the way other parents might have with their kids.

"You're easier to read sometimes than you probably want to be." She was still behind him when she chuckled. "I think every man likes to think of himself as unreadable, his natural guard against women. But you've got pretty eyes."

Haley was still tapping her finger to her lips when she paced to the other end of the kitchen. She turned at the refrigerator and faced him. "Greg got pissed when I told him that," she said, smiling at the memory. "I'm not the kind of wife who likes making her husband jealous. So I'll assure you the same way I did Greg."

Haley wagged the index finger at him that had been against her lips. "You've got pretty eyes just the way my sons do."

Micah imagined they'd hired bounty hunters before who had tried hitting on Haley. She was a beautiful woman, definitely MILF material. Micah didn't hit on another man's woman, though. Not to mention, he respected Haley. He would never insult her, or King, by making a pass at her.

"Thank you," he said, and forced himself to calm down and wait for her to elaborate.

"You've got a past that haunts you. Many people do, so that doesn't make you unique. But you're awfully young to have all the demons that we have seen in you during the short time you've been with us. Now, it isn't our concern, or even our business, to know everything about your past. But your past seems to have created certain personality traits in you that might have an impact on your work performance or KFA's reputation."

Micah didn't see that one coming, and he should have. This wasn't about anything they might have stumbled on about him personally. He beat up their friend's son, who happened to be an LAPD detective, and it made KFA look bad. The Kings' business did have an impeccable reputation. KFA would survive one of their bounty hunters hitting a detective but that didn't mean that bounty hunter would remain with KFA.

King was a retired cop, though. When he found out about Osborne, it went to his pride. He would feel terrible for his friend, Osborne's father. Possibly he would have imagined how it would have felt if it had been one of his own boys.

"Haley, I won't say Osborne begged for a fight, but I'm supposed to be fighting the same fight he is, and he destroyed my home. If that wasn't bad enough, he then violated my right to privacy by bugging my home." It was as close to an apology as he could manage.

Haley nodded for Micah to sit. She sat facing him and rested her elbow on the table, then her chin in her hand. Her eyes were a pretty shade of green, and there were laugh lines around her eyes. She had her brown hair pulled back, and the thin streaks of gray didn't make her look old. Micah saw happiness in Haley's eyes, but her expression was guarded. Something about Micah bothered her. If he convinced her everything was okay, she would take care of King.

"I want you to pretend I'm not your boss." Haley spoke softly, and smiled at him. "Imagine we're just two friends chatting. Tell me exactly what happened last night."

"I don't play make-believe very well," he said flatly.

Her smile faded. The tough mom returned. "Micah, what happened?"

"When I got home, the first thing I noticed was my security had been tampered with. It's set up to alert my phone if anyone enters my home when I'm not there." Security systems were often set to notify a security company if there was a burglary. Micah didn't see the point in paying for a service he would never need anyway. "There was a wire cut just above my kitchen door. Whoever entered the home already knew the wire was there before entering. They had less than a minute to cut it before it would have notified me. It was a clean slice, like with scissors. They entered already knowing where the wire was and they had the proper tools to cut it."

Haley wasn't reacting to what Micah was telling her, but she was listening. He kept his tone neutral, aware that despite the facts implicating the detective was working around the rules, the Kings wouldn't side with an employee who'd been with them three months over a cop's son, whom they'd known quite a few years.

"I turned the light on and saw how trashed my place was. And yes, I immediately suspected it had something to do with Maggie O'Malley. I searched the house, found listening devices."

"Do you still have those listening devices?"

Micah blinked. Did they not believe him? Or maybe the Kings already suspected that Osborne was a dirty cop and were using Micah to supply their proof. None of that mattered to him. If Osborne was dirty, though, that mattered where Maggie was concerned. He searched his memory, retracing his steps of the night before in his head. He'd destroyed them and thrown them away. But his trash was still in its trash cans.

"I'll bring them in for you."

Haley had given Micah the rest of the afternoon off. She wanted the bugs he'd found in his house. And she'd told him she'd see him in the morning and not to worry about his job. It was secure. She'd laughed when she'd said, "Unless, of course, we discover you're a serial killer, or something like that."

Micah had given her a confident smile, assured her he

wasn't, and had left. He needed to get to where comments like that didn't make him leery. Paranoia could destroy a man.

He'd sat on his bike at the Kings' house only long enough to check his messages. Micah didn't care if he ran into King. He didn't appreciate the man getting in his face, but Micah had worked under a structured chain of command all his life. His uncle couldn't keep him in line but Micah's dad, Jacob Mulligan, an award-winning big-game hunter who just also happened to be an assassin, had always been able to set Micah straight with a look. King wasn't Micah's father, nor would he ever be, but he was Micah's boss. Micah would never throw the first punch.

There were two voicemail messages, one from Maggie and one from Perry O'Toole.

"How are you doing?" Micah asked when Maggie answered her phone.

There was a smile in her voice and his loins immediately responded to her softly spoken words. "Pretty good, actually. We're kind of having a family reunion," she said, laughing.

Micah didn't get the joke but there was definitely noise in the background. He'd pulled off into the first parking lot off the interstate after leaving the Kings'. So far it didn't appear anyone was following him.

"Definitely sounds like a party. How much time do you need? I have to meet with someone but want to see you afterward."

When Maggie spoke again, the noise behind her was gone. She'd apparently gone to where she could talk to him privately. "I've really needed today, Micah," she said and sighed. "I don't remember the last time I hung out with all of my brothers and sisters. Well, Bernie isn't here but Deidre and Aiden and Annalisa are, and it's just been great. Do you have brothers and sisters?"

Maggie was focusing on building a relationship with him. It was normal for a woman like her to do that after having sex with a man she was interested in. Micah had no problem answering her questions. He'd tell her the truth as much as he could. Relaxing somewhat as he straddled his bike and cast continual glances around him as they spoke, he wondered what it would be like to seriously pursue a relationship with Maggie.

"No brothers or sisters," he told her.

"Seriously? Wow," she said, but pushed forward quickly. "But you're Catholic, right? I mean I guessed you were because of the Saint Michael pendant."

His hand instantly went to the flat silver piece around his neck. He pressed his finger to it through his shirt. "Born Catholic but I don't go to church much."

"I believe that about you," she said, chuckling.

Her honest, yet nonjudgmental view of him turned him on more than it should have. Maggie wanted to know about him but accepted him as he was and didn't appear interested in changing him. He told himself that if he actually was able to be in a long-term relationship with her, it would come in time. All women wanted to mold their men into subservient husbands they could stand to live with for the rest of their lives.

"Where are you and what time do you want me to pick you up?"

"Micah?"

"Yeah?"

"When you come get me, will you come inside and meet my brother and sisters?"

Damn. He should tell her no. He didn't need any more people knowing who he was. Not that anyone would ever know Micah Mulligan.

What the hell was he thinking? He was an assassin. Mulligan's Stew terminated the derelicts of society. He didn't stop in during a happy family reunion.

What kind of life would he have if he actually did meet the family of the girl he was dating?

"How painful will it be?" he asked, and hoped he sounded as cheerful as Maggie did.

Half an hour later, Micah was cruising through suburbia.

He would make his appointment with Perry O'Toole then ride back to Maggie's part of town. Her soft, relaxed-sounding voice still lingered in his mind. He could tell she'd been laughing a lot. Micah could see her, possibly stretched out on one of two twin beds in the motel room where she was hanging out with her brother and sisters. He bet her cheeks were sore from laughing and grinning all day. It sounded as if she were close to her siblings and that—other than her obviously no-good uncle—Maggie had a close, loving family.

Micah didn't bother imagining what it would be like being a sibling in a large family. It would never be his life, but it worked well for Maggie.

He pulled into a wide driveway and wasn't able to park before the two-car garage door opened. Perry stood to the side and gestured for Micah to park. Micah pushed his bike forward and entered the garage, which was just like every other two-car garage on this street. He turned off his bike as Perry closed his door.

"I just pulled some kebabs off the grill. Your timing is perfect." Perry O'Toole, if that even was his last name, didn't exactly fit the definition of geek.

Micah had never seen the man wear anything other than black slacks and a buttondown white shirt. His hair was trimmed short but not quite as short as most government men. To the best of Micah's knowledge, Perry had never held a real job other than the one he had right now. He was an information man. Anything anyone wanted to know about anyone, or anything, O'Toole could provide it, for a very nice price.

"How long has it been?" Perry asked over his shoulder, initiating small talk as he entered his kitchen and went straight to sliding glass doors that led to a cement slab patio.

More than likely every house for at least several blocks had that same cement slab for their deck. Perry firmly believed in fading into the suburbia world and never making waves. Micah couldn't remember Perry ever raising his voice, looking nervous, or even laughing too hard. The man had the perfect environment for what he did. He could fade into the woodwork faster than anyone Micah had ever met, and had even disappeared on Micah before. That had been all the proof Micah had needed to know he would do business with this man. Perry was very good at vanishing, often before anyone suggested it necessary.

"It's been a while." Micah remained inside and leaned against the open doorway. The smell from the grill was appetizing.

"You're going to love these." Perry pulled off four kebabs.

Micah was pretty sure the guy was here alone. When Perry stepped past him with the platter of grilled meat, vegetables, and fruit, and placed it at an oval dining room table, it was already set for two. Not the way a meal would be laid out for two lovers, but in a professional, organized manner. A table setting was at either end of the small table, cloth place mats, matching cloth napkins, with silverware placed on top of them. There was already a tossed salad in a wooden bowl, some kind of vinaigrette in a fancy, ornate bottle, and two glasses of wine, already poured.

"Sit. Let's catch up." Perry was always friendly.

Micah had learned early on in his working relationship with O'Toole that he insisted on formalities and wouldn't do business without them. Micah would sit, have lunch, do the small talk, and bring up what he wanted sometime before the meal was over. If he left without finishing his meal, Perry either wouldn't see him the next time, or would charge him an even more exorbitant rate for bad manners.

Perry served himself first. "I can only eat two. Please take both if you want," he offered, handing two of the remaining kebabs to Micah.

They smelled wonderful and Perry was being sincere. Either he didn't like eating alone or had found this the easiest way to remain very far under anyone's radar while still providing a service that Micah wouldn't be surprised if even the president of the United States used. Perry could get any information, and had never been wrong.

Micah slid the kebabs onto his plate, took a small amount

of salad, then slid a shrimp free from its spear before putting it into his mouth. It was good food.

Perry brought up some issue in local legislation that would require homeowners to put up a certain type of fencing. He knew a lot about the local politics although, more than likely, he didn't own this home. He could, however. For all Micah knew, Perry could own a home in every city across the nation. Micah didn't care as long as he got the information he needed, when he needed it.

"I don't get to the suburbs enough," Micah said, leaning back and realizing he'd finished off the two kebabs in record time. "But I have been curious about our men in blue with LAPD."

"They have several fund-raisers that I donate to every year." Always the perfect host, Perry stood and walked to the refrigerator. Apparently he noticed Micah hadn't touched his wine. He pulled out a longneck bottle of beer and brought it to the table. "Did you know they're the third largest police department in the nation? We have ten thousand men and women in blue helping keep our fair city safe. Have you driven by the new police station for this precinct? I guess it's actually been there a few years now, but I donated substantial contributions to build that station."

That was probably all of the free information he would get. Micah knew Perry's questions were rhetorical. He cut to the chase.

"I came over here concerning an arrest made a week ago, money laundering through a local club, Club Paradise," Micah began.

Perry had sat again but wasn't eating. He leaned back in his chair, arms crossed, and listened as if he found every word Micah said fascinating.

"The police seem fairly certain that Maggie O'Malley might be involved in the money laundering along with her uncle, Larry Santinos. Santinos has been arrested. He's behind bars. They couldn't pin anything to Maggie, though. They let her go."

Perry nodded. "Just because she was sent home after

questioning doesn't mean they don't have a crime to nail on her. Quite possibly there are some loose ends they believe she might be able to tie up for them."

"They're following her around. She insists she's innocent. From what I've seen so far, she might be guilty of gullibility but that's about it."

Again Perry nodded.

"I want to know if Santinos had a known partner who isn't currently behind bars. He might not be in the United States. They've got the man so locked up there isn't any way for me to question him." Micah took a long drink from his beer. He hadn't planned on asking Perry two different questions, but his conversation with Haley had piqued his interest on another matter as well, one he prayed wasn't connected to the first. "I also want you to find out if Detective James Osborne is a dirty cop. If he is, does KFA have anything to do with it?"

"King Fugitive Apprehension?" Perry raised one eyebrow, then a slow smile slithered across his face. "Will do."

Chapter Eight

"So are there still people following you?" Annalisa asked and reached for the last slice of pepperoni.

"They aren't people, they're cops," Deidre said, wagging her eyebrows. "Wish I could have men in uniform on the trail for me."

"The last one I spotted looked as if he could put an entire one of these pizzas away by himself, for a snack," Maggie complained, stressing the last part. "And do we have to talk about this? I was having so much fun."

Annalisa's expression sobered and she scooted to the edge of the bed. "Sorry, Mags," she whispered and stretched her hand out to Maggie, who sat at the desk facing the TV in the motel room they'd been camping out in all afternoon. "I didn't mean to bum you out but I'm really curious. No one has told me anything. I'm not sure I can believe that my goody-goody big sister got in trouble unless I hear it straight from your mouth."

"I'm not goody-goody!"

Annalisa and Deidre gave each other knowing looks. Maggie jumped out of her seat and tried punching both of them at the same time. They successfully dodged her efforts as they laughed loudly.

"And I didn't get in trouble!" She had to yell to be heard over their hysterics.

Aiden's phone rang and he glared at the three of them before heading to the bathroom to be heard.

"He's the goody-goody," Maggie muttered, although light-heartedly. After an afternoon of pizza and her family there wasn't a person on the planet she had ill will toward. This had been exactly what she needed.

"Children, I have to head out," Aiden announced when he came back around the wall that separated the bathroom from the rest of the motel room. "Some of us work for a living."

"That's a low blow." Maggie still felt she should go into her office.

Her father had told her Club Paradise was still closed down with yellow police tape draping the doors. Information he got from his drinking buddies down at the bar was almost always more accurate than that heard anywhere else.

Aiden pulled her into a tight hug without asking. "And she did get in trouble," he announced with his arms wrapped around her.

"What?" Maggie twisted free.

"For leaving with one of the most unruly characters I've ever seen in my life instead of going to the lawyer's office with her older brother as planned."

"Unruly character?" Maggie demanded, laughing. She might have picked on her brother for always insisting everything follow a tight schedule. Aiden hated spontaneity.

Maggie thought about how unruly Micah had been the night before when they'd fucked in his bed. She hoped and prayed that hadn't been a onetime deal. She would absolutely cry if it were. Micah was better in bed than she'd imagined. Then when he'd called her earlier, and easily answered the few personal questions she'd slipped in there, her hopes rose that not only would she fuck him again, but hopefully soon. She hadn't bothered telling him that she didn't need to be picked up from the motel. Her car was in the parking lot. Since Julie had to leave Annalisa at the motel room and go back to campus for a night job she had there, Maggie could leave her car with Annalisa. That way she wouldn't be stuck at the motel room after all of them had to leave.

"You could do a lot better," Aiden told her, then tapped her nose the way their father always did.

Better than what? She didn't ask. If she brought up how few dates she'd had this past year, Aiden would put in his argument for her joining youth ministries over at Holy Name again. Maggie cringed at the thought of finding a date at their church. She definitely would never find anyone like Micah at her church.

Annalisa and Deidre sang their good-byes to Aiden as they made shooing signs with their hands for him to leave. When Aiden let go of Maggie, he reached for Annalisa, gave her a hug, too, and reminded her that she was very much part of the family no matter what happened or was said. He tapped Annalisa's nose, then was out the door. Maggie followed him, then made sure it was shut and locked after he left.

"Time for girl talk!" Deidre knelt in the middle of the bed. "Maggie, tell us everything."

"Huh?" She looked from her older sister, who was on the middle of one bed, to her younger sister, who was draped on her side at the edge of the other. It had never occurred to her before how much they looked alike, despite their differences.

Deidre's hair was dyed light blond and Annalisa's hair was auburn like Maggie's. Deidre wore plenty of makeup and Annalisa didn't wear any. Deidre was all about name brands and Annalisa probably didn't know what brand her clothing was. They were opposites yet so similar, too. Both of her sisters were incredibly pretty. They could stop traffic without realizing they did.

"The unruly character," Deidre said.

"Yes, do tell." Annalisa moved to a sitting position and crossed her legs. "Who is he? Bring me up to speed. I know nothing," she wailed and brought the back of her hand to her forehead.

"Well, being the oldest sister and all," Deidre began and scooted to the edge of her bed so she faced Annalisa, "obviously I am kept up to date on everything."

Annalisa snickered, and accepted that statement because it was true. Deidre had always seemed to know everything about anyone in the family.

Deidre didn't miss a beat. "Aiden informed me that he brought his wayward sister to see the lawyer who had graciously agreed to see her pro bono. But the moment he parked in the parking lot, our once precious Maggie leapt out of his car and raced over to an unruly biker character. Then they made out right there. Our derelict sister didn't even consider how embarrassing and humiliating that was for her older brother."

Maggie crossed her arms and tapped her foot, fighting not to laugh at her sister's flair for dramatics. "Are you having fun?" she accused.

Deidre rubbed her hands together. "I'm just getting warmed up, little sister." She looked pointedly at Annalisa. "Other little sister," she continued, "you would have insisted Maggie be hauled off to the nearest confessional. In fact, maybe we should take her there now."

Both of them looked up at Maggie and simultaneously broke into a fit of giggles. Maggie couldn't help laughing, too. She grabbed the chair she'd been sitting in, scooted it between both beds, then sat. They were all close now. Deidre silently gave Maggie the floor, and she and Annalisa looked at her expectantly.

Maggie sucked in a breath, not sure where to begin.

"Oh my God!" Deidre said and clasped her hand over her mouth.

"What?" Maggie asked.

"What?" Annalisa parroted.

"Look at her," Deidre said and pointed her painted fingernail at Maggie's face. "You've slept with him!" she accused.

Annalisa squinted, and the spray of freckles across her nose was more apparent as she wrinkled it. "Yup. I see it now, too. Now we need *all* the details."

Deidre rubbed her hands together. "Spill it."

Maggie hated that she blushed. She also hated Deidre for her perception, especially when she hadn't decided if she was going to tell them about that, or not. The decision had been made for her, though.

She shook her head and looked down at her hands. She had them clasped in her lap but when she loosened them, she didn't know what to do with them. There was no reason to be nervous, though; these were her sisters.

"Micah is . . . ," she began.

"Micah?" Annalisa questioned. "Oh crap! Is he Jewish?"

Maggie laughed. "Nope. Catholic, although I bet he hasn't been near a church in years."

"Damn," Annalisa said, snapping her fingers. "I thought my mortal sins would be forgiven if you brought around a Jewish guy."

Annalisa laughed easily at her own comment, which made it so Maggie and Deidre could laugh with her. Maggie hated having gone so long without seeing Annalisa. And, despite Mom's narrow-minded way of thinking, she had done a good thing in calling Annalisa about Maggie. It had brought Annalisa home. She probably wouldn't go back to the house, but it wouldn't surprise her if Aiden told Mom and Dad that they were all housed up in this motel room catching up. Her family was quirky; they held grudges and fought way too often, but they all loved one another, too. Maggie couldn't think of any other family she'd rather be part of.

"What's he look like?" Deidre asked, rubbing her hands together. "He must be sinfully gorgeous for Aiden to immediately hate him."

"It might also have had something to do with Micah kissing me in the parking lot when I walked over to him."

Her sisters hooted with laughter. Maggie paraphrased a lot but shared everything that happened to her yesterday. When she got to the part about entering his house and the place being torn apart, neither of her sisters was smiling any longer.

"Shit, Mags," Annalisa whispered. "I didn't realize how terrible all of this really is. You're really in serious danger, huh?"

"That's why she hired Micah," Deidre said, but reached

out and gave Annalisa's hand a quick squeeze when their baby sister continued to look horrified.

"Hired?" Annalisa choked out the word. "You're having sex with a man you hired?"

Maggie was shaking her head before the words came out. If all of this weren't so scary, it would be hilarious. "No. No," she repeated and shook her head harder. "Maybe I should have backed up a few more days and begun the story there."

"You didn't hire him?" Annalisa asked, looking confused.

"Well, I guess I did." Maggie held her hand up when Deidre opened her mouth, looking ready to confuse matters more. "It was the day they raided Club Paradise and brought Uncle Larry in for skipping out on two court dates," Maggie explained, holding up two fingers.

"Now I know Larry was cheating at Monopoly when we were kids. He was getting practice for the major crimes he'd be committing as an adult," Deidre complained, rolling her eyes.

Maggie tried to continue explaining to Annalisa. "That was the same day I was hauled in for questioning. I was so pissed by the time they let me go, I was determined to hire the best there was to help me figure out why anyone would suspect me in the first place."

Someone knocked on the motel room door and all three girls jumped.

"I don't think this motel has room service," Deidre whispered.

Annalisa scrambled from her bed, which was closer to the door, to the other bed. Deidre immediately played older sister and wrapped her arms around her. Maggie caught their horrified expressions and hated that her life had put the fear of God into them. At the same time, her tummy twisted in nervous anticipation.

"Calm down, you two. The only one who knows we're here is Micah."

Deidre's expression transformed immediately. She stood,

thrusting her arm out and blocking Maggie when she started to the door. "I'm the oldest. It's my job to protect you."

"I'm not a kid anymore. Try and take this one and I'll kick your ass," Maggie mumbled.

"Ohh," Annalisa said, grinning. "Let's check this guy out."

Maggie rolled her eyes and glanced at her phone. She hadn't missed any calls. Nor had she told Micah which room they were in. She had told him which motel, though. It would be child's play for him to find her after that. Would he show up unannounced? Maggie almost laughed out loud at her line of thinking. Micah didn't strike her as the type of man who followed any laws of propriety. He adhered only to the laws that would suit him at that moment. Nonetheless, she grabbed Deidre's arm.

"Look through the peephole before you open the door," she told her.

"Yes, Mom," Deidre said. She made a face, then looked in the mirror as she checked her face and hair.

Annalisa started laughing. "Stop it, D. I swear Maggie is growling."

Deidre pulled off her best innocent look then walked to the motel room door, putting an extra sway in her hips. When she got to the door she peeked through the peephole. She pressed her face to the door for a moment before turning around slowly. It dawned on Maggie that Deidre wouldn't know what Micah looked like.

"He is really tall," Maggie began.

Deidre turned around. "And exceptionally good looking. I don't know, Mags. I might have to steal this one away from you." She opened the door and stepped back.

Maggie stared wide-eyed at her father. She hated herself for thinking there wasn't anywhere to run, especially when just a minute before she was so happy to be part of her dysfunctional family. But when John O'Malley entered and Deidre closed the door behind him she mouthed, "He came alone."

Maggie barely had the opportunity to acknowledge the much-appreciated message. Her father wasn't looking at her.

Maggie shifted her attention as well when Deidre covered her mouth with her hand and suddenly looked teary-eyed.

"Daddy?" Annalisa whispered and stepped out from between the two beds.

"My baby Annalisa." Her father's words broke on a sob as he held out his arms.

Annalisa rushed into them, and was the first to start crying. "Oh Daddy. I've missed you so much!"

"Same here, sweetheart."

Maggie stood back, deciding for once it didn't bother her that Aiden had again played the informant to their parents. If he had told Mom, then it was her own stubborn Italian pride preventing her from seeing Annalisa. Maggie was glad Irish pride seemed a bit more sensible at the moment.

Her father held Annalisa tightly. Both of their faces were buried in each other as they continued whispering words of regret for being away from each other so long. When her father finally put his youngest child at arm's length and managed something close to his usual stern but loving look, Maggie and her sisters grew quiet. She wasn't the only one who prayed John O'Malley would make a stand against their mother. He seldom did it. But when he did, it was usually over something serious, and then Lucy O'Malley never opposed him. At least she hadn't to date.

"My three daughters, hiding in a motel room just so they can spend time together." He let a few expletives fly but continued holding Annalisa and rubbing her bare arms with his bony hands. "This is not how the O'Malley family will be!"

Maggie wanted to jump in the air and cheer. *Yay, Dad!*

"Does Mom know I'm here?" Annalisa sounded more timid than she had in years.

Her father nodded. "She saw you on the front porch talking to your sister."

Annalisa shook her head. "I meant here in this motel room. Maggie got it for me. I'm not going back to the house, Dad. Not if she is just going to kick me out again."

John O'Malley scraped his teeth over his bottom lip and

appeared to be choosing his words carefully. He took a moment too long and Annalisa began crying.

"Oh baby," Deidre consoled and rushed to her little sister. She pulled her from her father and held her in her arms. "Dad, it's been a great day here with the three of us. But I put my foot down on Mom messing with Annalisa's head again."

"Same here," Maggie said, and moved in to wrap her arms around both her sisters. "If Mom is going to be like this, it's her actions that are breaking the family up, not anyone else's."

"Your mother is an old woman," he began, holding his arms out. It looked as if he'd do anything to have Annalisa back in them again.

"No," Deidre said firmly. "She might be old, but she's not dead. If she won't open her arms and her heart to Annalisa and accept her for how she is, then you can let her know I'll come back by once Annalisa leaves town."

"That goes for me, too," Maggie said. "I'm staying here with Annalisa. If she isn't welcome home then I don't want to be there, either."

Her father didn't react or say anything, but simply stared at his three daughters. Finally he sighed. "The three of you look just like her. All of you are so incredibly beautiful. You talk just like her. You act just like her. The three of you most definitely have her stubborn bullheaded pride," he finished and raised his eyes to heaven as he mouthed a silent prayer that sounded more like a complaint.

"I miss her." Annalisa spoke so softly she was hard to hear.

All of them did, though.

"That does it," their father said and walked to the motel room door.

Maggie wondered if he was leaving and at the same time wondered how he'd gotten there. She started after him but he reached the door first, opened it, then Maggie understood. It was immediately crowded in the room when Aiden entered.

"I wanted to come in alone first," their father announced.

"And now I've made my decision." He suddenly looked a lot older when he tried stepping around his children to reach Annalisa.

Deidre hopped onto the bed and Maggie did the same, clearing the limited amount of floor space so their father could move easier. Annalisa looked frightened but held her ground. Maggie held her breath. She knew her father wouldn't say anything to hurt his youngest child and remembered the fights after their mom had sent Annalisa packing. She still worried that if Annalisa thought she were tearing the family apart, she'd leave and never come back before openly causing them any more pain.

"The O'Malley family stays together," he said firmly. "None of us is perfect." Their father reached Annalisa and she buried her head against his chest and wrapped her arms around his waist. He turned his head so he could see his other children. "We're all going home together. This reunion belongs there, not in some motel room."

"Hear, hear!" Aiden cheered. "Shall we hit the bar first, Dad?"

"Most definitely."

"I would love to buy you a drink, Dad," Annalisa said.

"I would love you to buy me a drink, Dad," Deidre said.

Then all of them were talking at once, deciding where to go and who would ride with whom. Maggie barely heard her phone when it rang. She did manage to slip around everyone to the bathroom and close the door behind her before answering.

"Hello," she said, and her insides were immediately filled with a different type of excitement.

"Enjoying time with your family still?" Micah asked.

Maggie wanted to tell him everything that had just happened. He might not understand, or care. "Yeah. It's been a pretty good day. My youngest sister has been away for quite a while and we're all glad she's back," she said and decided that would work instead of giving details into their messed-up family. Being an only child, he probably had a quiet and perfect family. Hers was as far from both as it got. "Everyone has just decided to go have a drink. I don't know where yet."

"I'm about fifteen minutes from your motel. Call me back when you know and I'll start that way." He hung up without elaborating.

Would he go with them? Already Maggie knew her sisters wouldn't mind Micah being with them. Her father and Aiden would be a different story. And with Annalisa here, but still on shaky ground, Maggie knew it would be best if Micah didn't go. She wanted to spend time with him, too, though. If he had any news for her about who was really behind the money going in and out of Club Paradise other than her uncle, she wanted to hear that as well.

All eyes were on her when she walked out of the bathroom.

"Who is this young man who steals you from the family during such a special moment?" her father demanded.

Maggie would have flipped her oldest brother off for such a pompous look if her father wouldn't have seen it, too. "It was Micah, Dad," she explained. "He's a bounty hunter. I'm sure Aiden has given you all the details."

"Humph." Her father started toward the door with Annalisa's arm wrapped around his. "Your brother is driving me to the pub. Annalisa is going with us. I assume you two can make it without getting lost."

"Dad," Deidre complained as if she resented being sectioned off with Maggie and considered the bad child, too.

Her father turned his back on Maggie and pointed a finger at Deidre. "You make sure she shows up and doesn't go in the wrong direction."

The wrong direction? Is that what her father thought she was doing? Maggie didn't have time to dwell on her family's opinion of her. As much as that mattered, proving her innocence mattered, too. She sighed, feeling torn in two at the moment. Nothing was more important than her family. Without them, her innocence meant nothing. Somehow she'd clear herself from this mess around Club Paradise and be 100 percent part of her family.

Behind their father's back, Deidre grinned a toothy grin at Maggie and mouthed, "Details." At the same time, Aiden walked alongside Dad and glared at Maggie as if she'd have to answer to him later.

Maggie stopped by the front desk after walking everyone to her brother's car. She sent Deidre on around to the back of the motel where her car was parked but had promised Annalisa she'd make sure Julie would be able to get into the room later if she showed up before Annalisa did.

Annalisa was content to go home and stand up to Mom with everyone backing her. But she appreciated a place to escape afterward. Maggie was almost jealous after Annalisa had whispered in her ear, pleading with her to tend to this one detail. All her life Maggie had relied on her family for support in any matter. It hadn't been until the past few years that she'd grown distant, her own person as an adult. Instead of relying on her parents for support, her parents now relied on her.

But when all the shit hit the fan, it hadn't crossed her mind to run to her family for help. The moment she'd been released from questioning, Maggie had hired Micah. Annalisa faced a different type of problem—and just like Maggie's, it was one that shouldn't exist in the first place. She had someone to run to and, from her urgent whispers, couldn't wait to see Julie later.

Maggie had put Micah in the position of protector. She was running to him with all her problems. But would he ever be there by choice? Maggie hated these thoughts. They tumbled over one another in her brain. If only this were a math problem, then it would be simple to see from the beginning to end. Micah wasn't X and she wasn't Y. Furthermore, Micah probably wouldn't fit anywhere in the equation at all. She'd known from the beginning that he didn't meet any boyfriend criteria and probably never would.

After leaving instructions with the clerk at the desk, Maggie hurried down the first-floor hallway toward the exit to the back parking lot. Deidre was sitting in Maggie's pas-

senger seat staring at her fingernails when Maggie pushed
out of the motel's back door. Deidre glanced up and smiled,
then straightened and apparently she reached for the radio.
At the same time an old car desperately in need of a new
muffler entered the parking lot. Deidre probably turned up
the radio to drown out the sound of the old car.

Maggie glanced down at her phone, curious how much
time had passed since she'd hung up with Micah. Even if
they had to sit and wait, Maggie doubted Deidre would complain about the chance to meet Micah. If Maggie could have
avoided her sister meeting Micah, she would have. Her father was insistent on Deidre riding with Maggie, though—
and suddenly it all made sense. Her dad suspected Micah
would be coming by and he didn't want Maggie to be alone
with him. She was instantly pissed and amused at the same
time. It would serve her father, and Deidre, right if Maggie
started making out with Micah right in front of her.

No matter how far back she went in her memories, Maggie couldn't think of a time when she'd met one of Deidre's
boyfriends and her sister hadn't been completely relaxed
with the introduction. That was probably her sister's secret.
She never came across as caring that much for any of the
guys she dated.

On the other hand, whenever Maggie had dated a guy
and he finally met her older sister, she'd repeatedly lived
with the humiliation of her boyfriend making a fool out of
himself in front of Deidre. He would stammer, act like an
idiot, and turn into this buffoon that Maggie didn't recog-
nize. After Deidre would glide out of the room, seemingly
oblivious as to how she'd turned Maggie's boyfriend into an
imbecile, Maggie would then be forced to listen as the imbecile asked too many questions about Deidre and repeated
more than once how hot she was.

Maggie couldn't see Micah acting like a fool no matter
the situation. He definitely didn't come across as the type of
man who would go out of his way to try to impress anyone.
And at the same time, she reminded herself, he wasn't her
boyfriend. She most definitely had first dibs, though. And

second dibs, and third dibs. So what if he wasn't boyfriend material? He was the best sex she ever had and something about him seriously intrigued her. Wait a minute, make that everything about him seriously intrigued her.

"Maggie!" Deidre screamed as if she were hurt.

Maggie jerked her head up as the old car that had just rumbled into the parking lot came at her at full speed. For the first time in her life, she truly understood the meaning of the expression *deer caught in the headlights*. She stared at the car as it came straight at her and she either forgot how to move or was simply too stupefied to put her body into action.

Her survival skills were getting a good workout lately. As much as she didn't want to be accused of a crime she didn't commit, or to be followed around by the police, or to have someone she knew have his home trashed and bugs planted because of her, she had been forced to endure all of the above. Now she needed to move! Maggie most definitely did not want to die.

But when she darted as fast as she could to the other side of the parking lot, the mufflerless car veered and came closer. She stopped running, the end of the motel building behind her and hedges lining the edge of the lot running alongside her. If she had superpowers maybe she could simply jump straight up in the air and the car would hit the building.

Maggie raced back the way she came, keeping to the edge of the parking lot. The car drove past her and slid to a stop. Its tires spun and the smell of rubber filled the parking lot as it turned around and started at her again.

"Deidre!" she screamed, breaking into a full sprint.

"Maggie!" Deidre yelled over the sound of squealing tires.

The vehicle squealed to a stop between her and her car. Maggie stared into the cold menacing eyes of the driver and passenger. She'd never seen either one of them before.

When two shots were fired, Maggie's heart leapt in her throat. She looked around frantically, searching for Micah. But then Deidre was running straight for her.

"Come on! Let's go!" Deidre yelled, grabbing Maggie's

hand and damn near yanking it out of her socket as she broke into a run.

Maggie worried she'd stumble but fright put speed in her feet. She ran as fast as she could. "Over there!" she pointed.

"The Dumpster?"

"They're trying to kill us!" Maggie yelled and suddenly she was the one pulling. She and her sister were about the same size and weight. Maggie tugged Deidre near the Dumpster. The stench made her stomach roil.

"I will not hide behind a huge trash can," Deidre yelled, pulled free of Maggie, and turned to face the car.

Maggie stared in shock at her sister who stood with her legs apart, both hands on her gun and her hair blowing wildly around her.

"Bring it on, motherfucker!" she yelled at the driver.

The car slid into reverse and turned away from them. It drove away as fast as it could with two flat tires. Before it was across the parking lot Deidre started firing again.

"Micah," Maggie whispered and stared past Deidre at the large man on the bike rumbling toward them.

He didn't stop until he was next to Deidre. Maggie rushed at him but Deidre spun and aimed her gun at him.

"Deidre, no," Maggie cried out and grabbed her arm to lower the gun. "It's Micah."

It took Maggie a moment to realize how heavily her sister was breathing, and how tight her fingers were wrapped around the small handgun. Micah left his bike running and climbed off. His stony serious features probably wouldn't convince anyone that he was much safer than the old car that had tried attacking her.

"What's wrong?" Micah asked. Even his voice was low and dangerous sounding.

Maggie pointed, but realized she was shaking. The tremble in her hand spread quickly until she could barely stand on her own two feet.

"That car," she stammered.

Deidre bent over and gripped her knees, still holding her gun in one of her hands. Maggie rested a hand on her back.

She stared at Deidre only a moment then looked at Micah. She'd never seen his eyes so dark.

His mouth barely moved when he spoke. "Tell me what happened."

"We were leaving the motel. Deidre was already at my car. I started toward it and this old car without a muffler pulled into the parking lot and tried to run me over. When I got out of the way, it backed up and tried running me over again."

"It went that way?" Micah shifted and pointed.

Maggie nodded. "With its back tires blown out."

Micah didn't smile or say good shot or even acknowledge her last comment. He turned, climbed on his bike, and was gone.

"What the fuck?" Deidre mumbled. "What the fuck?" she said a bit louder. Then, standing, she arched her back, stared at the sky, and yelled. "What the fuck?"

"I don't know," Maggie said, still watching in the direction Micah had gone.

"You have no idea who those people were?" Deidre demanded. Her face looked wild, like this whole experience had sent her to a crazy, delusional place and she hadn't yet returned.

"How the hell am I supposed to know who they were?" Suddenly she was pissed. "I'm a fucking accountant. People just don't show up and try to run me down in old, shitty cars," she yelled, gesturing wildly in the direction the car, and Micah, had disappeared.

Deidre shot her a side glance. "Do they try to run you down in nice cars?"

O'Malleys were known for their quick tempers. Maggie's had spiked, but one look at her sister's quirky expression and it dissipated.

"Did you cut off someone's tab at the club?" Maggie asked, and shook her head, her expression pinched when she glared in the direction the car had gone. "Where did you get that gun?"

"This gun?" Deidre lifted her hand with the gun in it. "This gun here? You know, it seems to me the question should be, why the hell don't you have a gun?"

"Why would I have a gun?"

Even Deidre's laugh bordered on hysteria. "Oh, I don't know," she drawled, and gestured with the gun still in her hand. "Maybe possibly because *someone is trying to kill you!*" she screamed. "Holy crap, Mags, are you really this pathetic?"

"What?" Maggie pointed at the gun. "Put that thing away."

"Oh, most definitely," Deidre snapped, then marched away from Maggie. She yanked open Maggie's passenger door and bent over for her purse. "God forbid I make you uncomfortable by holding a gun," she bit out, her tone suddenly tight with anger.

Maggie was right behind her when Deidre spun around. "Is that better? Does that put your world back into perfect order?"

Maggie wasn't sure if she should turn around and acknowledge Micah or not when his bike rumbled up behind her. Deidre was out of line and being a bitch, but she'd just had the shit scared out of her. Maggie was scared, too. People didn't try to run her down in a parking lot. Normal people weren't continually worried someone was trying to kill them.

"That's not fair," Maggie said quietly, acutely aware of Micah getting off his bike and moving behind her. "I didn't ask for any of this to happen to me."

"Oh for crap's sake. Get over yourself. And here's a news flash from your older sister. Someone is trying to kill you so pull your head out of your ass, quit thinking the world is some perfect place and that everything can be solved by using some geometric formula or something."

"Deidre," Maggie said, her voice cracking.

"No!" Her sister held her finger up in the air as her eyes flashed with outrage. "You're going to get killed."

"What? Stop it."

"I will not stop it," Deidre roared, fisting her hands at her side. "Today was your wake-up call, darling. But it should have happened the day you were hauled in for questioning. This won't ever happen again."

"I know—"

"You don't know shit," her sister exploded and lunged for Maggie.

Instinctively Maggie backed up, raising her hands to protect herself. Deidre reached for her and suddenly Micah was there, blocking her sister's path. Maggie blinked and there were bulging muscles in her direct line of vision. Good God! He was protecting her from her own sister.

"It's okay, Micah," she began, putting her hand on his arm as she stepped around him.

"I'll get to you next!" Deidre was furious. Her voice was dangerously cool.

Maggie stepped around Micah just in time to see Deidre stab him in the chest with her finger. It was apparent how outraged she was when she didn't make some lewd comment about his chest being a brick wall. Instead she glared up at him.

"Back off," she said in a low dangerous tone.

Maggie didn't dare look into his face. She wasn't sure what she would see. Micah gave Deidre only a quick once-over before setting his dark, brooding stare on Maggie.

"Are you okay?" he asked in his low, smooth baritone.

"She's just peachy," Deidre told him. "Now stay there and don't move." She didn't bother to see if he would listen to her or not when she once again gave Maggie the coldest stare she'd ever seen on her sister. "The reason this is never going to happen again is because you're going to get your head out of your books and learn how to protect yourself. I want you to think long and hard about what might have happened in this parking lot if I hadn't been here."

Maggie's heart tightened so fiercely in her chest that she couldn't breathe. Her sister was right. If Deidre hadn't been here, she would have seriously been hurt, or worse. She opened her mouth to say thank you, but Deidre had turned her attention on Micah.

"My sister hired you to protect her," she snarled. "And let me tell you, mister, you fucked up big-time. I saved her ass today but you're going to step up to the plate and do your job right, or I promise you right now, you won't be fucking her anymore."

"Deidre!" Maggie yelled, having about enough of this bossy-older-sister crap. "You've made your point clear enough."

"That's your problem." Deidre pointed at Maggie but then turned that same finger on Micah. "That's her problem. You see, there is something about my sister you need to know."

"What's that?"

Maggie looked at Micah. Deidre even paused for a moment as if Micah speaking somehow yanked her out of this insane frenzy that had suddenly hit her. Micah's expression was serious, but she swore when he looked down at her, his gaze softened.

"She's an idiot," Deidre yelled.

"I am not an idiot. I'll compare my GPA to yours any day, big sis."

"That's my point exactly." Deidre waved her hand in Maggie's direction. "My little sister is as smart as they come in a classroom. Straight A's all the way. I don't think she ever brought home a B. Even in college. Everyone loved bragging about how smart little Mags was. She aced her way through school and made Mom and Dad look so smart. It was disgusting. But nonetheless, the damage was done." Deidre exhaled, shook her head, and continued. "The damage is done," she said in a softer, almost deflated tone. "She wasn't out of school a week when our mother was damn near prancing around in her kitchen bragging to the entire family about how her Mags was now a college graduate and had a job doing the books for a nightclub." Again Deidre shook her head. "So you see, she is as book-smart as they come. But she is more street-stupid than I realized. The way it's going to be is this. From this moment forward, you're in basic training." Deidre crossed her arms and gave Micah an appraising once-over. "You're going to give my little sister that street education. Think you can handle that?"

"Yup," Micah said, not hesitating.

"Good." Deidre turned and for a moment looked dizzy.

Maggie was more than a little put out but reached for her sister anyway.

"I'm fine," Deidre said, waving her off.

"Yeah, right," Maggie whispered.

"Go with him to see Dad," her sister told her, and started running her fingers through her hair. "Give me a moment to put myself back together."

Maggie pulled the keys to her car out and handed them over. "You put as much as a dent on my car."

"I won't hurt your car."

"You do and you'll learn real fast all the street smarts this math geek actually has."

Chapter Nine

"Set me up, Don," Maggie said, and slapped her hand down on the smooth wooden bar.

The bartender, a man in his mid-fifties with a slight pudgy build, looked at her, then glanced past her at Micah.

"I mean it, Don. Make it whiskey."

"Okay," Don said and finished drying the glass he had in his hand. He wiped his hands on the bar towel then poured Maggie a shot of whiskey.

She downed it and put the shot glass on the counter. "Again."

"Maggie," Don complained.

"I said again."

This time the bartender looked over at a table where a group of people sat. Micah immediately noticed Maggie's brother, who'd brought her to the lawyer downtown. Damn good thing she never made that appointment.

"Don," Maggie said.

Don sighed and poured another shot. Maggie tilted her head back and downed the second shot.

"Again," she demanded.

"I don't—"

"Again," Maggie insisted.

Don poured the shot. Maggie downed it.

Micah leaned into the bar next to her. "What are you doing?" he whispered in her ear.

Maggie placed both elbows on the counter and turned her

head so she was looking at him over her bare shoulder. "My sister believes I'm an idiot and someone tried to kill me. What would you suggest I do?"

"I can think of one or two things."

Maggie's eyes narrowed and she hummed as she lowered her gaze, then took her time raising it to look at his face. "Want to fuck me?" she whispered.

"Why are we at this bar?"

"Oh yeah." Maggie straightened and held a finger in the air. "Don, where is my shot?" she demanded. This time she reached in her pocket and pulled out a twenty. Slapping it next to her empty shot glass, she yelled, "Take care of me, bartender, and one for my friend here, too."

Don seemed to take her request more seriously after looking at Micah. He put two shot glasses down on the counter and filled them both three-quarters of the way with whiskey. Maggie grabbed hers and downed it with one swallow.

"Drink up, dear," she encouraged, nudging Micah. "They have only the best at my father's pub."

Micah saw the label on the bottle the bartender was pouring from, definitely not the best whiskey there was. On the other hand, it wasn't the worst whiskey a bar could serve, either. A quick glance around showed proof this was a workingman's bar, a neighborhood pub. It wouldn't surprise him if most of the people who came into this bar had been coming here a very long time. There was no pool table, no darts, no jukebox. Something from before Micah's time played through speakers behind the bar. This was a place where folks came to drink off their worries, which appeared to be what Maggie was doing right now.

"One more round," Maggie announced, sticking her finger in the air. "Hell, make it one for the family."

She turned her back on Micah and the three people at the table in the corner of the bar looked at her. Her brother was already standing, but the old man with him stopped him.

"Bring your whiskey and your man over here," the old man said. "If you're going to have him, you're going to introduce him properly."

"And what exactly is properly, Daddy?" Maggie asked. She left the bar but before reaching their table turned again and pointed to Don behind the bar. "Five shots, Don. Let's see, at three dollars a shot, that is fifteen dollars." She pulled a couple of bills out of her purse. Then, waving the bills in the air, she returned to the bar and slapped them down. "I'm good at math. That's what I'm good at. If I suck at everything else in life, like keeping myself alive, at least I am fucking good with numbers! Because I so rock at doing math, I will definitely get your tip on the next round, Don. Don't worry. You know an O'Malley is good for it."

Don came around the bar with the shot glasses filled to the rim this time with the dark amber alcohol. Maggie looked at Micah and held out her hand. "Come on, we're going to learn what proper is."

Micah had endured many situations that he'd rather not be in. He didn't mind meeting her family. But these circumstances definitely qualified as not proper in his book. He moved in behind Maggie but watched her father and brother over the top of her head. The young lady with them didn't look up at him. She had to be another one of Maggie's sisters. He wondered if she had any more.

This sister wasn't all done up the way Deidre was. Her hair was the same color as Maggie's yet by her choice in clothing he'd guess her younger and not style-conscious like Deidre, nor into expensive clothing like Maggie was.

"Father, this is Micah Jones."

Micah flashed his attention to the old man, who didn't bother standing. Micah had no problem taking the initiative and walked around Maggie to shake the old man's hand.

"And Micah, this is John O'Malley. You may call him John, everyone does."

The old man's hand was leathery, smooth, and cool, yet his grip firm. He summed Micah up with blue eyes sunken in his pale wrinkled face. His white hair was slicked back and receded a fair bit from his forehead. He released Micah's hand to take the tray from Don. Micah caught John's change in expression when he made eye contact with the bartender. His features relaxed as he gave the man a swift nod and moved his lips, mouthing something Micah didn't catch. More than likely, he'd just cut his daughter off.

Maggie tapped her sister's shoulder, and the young lady looked up. There wasn't the eager-to-know-life happiness that helped make up Maggie's features on this sister. Nor was her face done up with makeup like Deidre's. Micah saw something in this sister's eyes as she stared up at Maggie—fear, possibly unhappiness. She nodded in understanding, then moved over to free up two chairs at the table. Micah waited for Maggie to choose the one she wanted then took the chair next to her.

"There," Maggie said, scooting her chair in and reaching for one of the shot glasses. She handed one to her sister, one to Micah, then took one for herself. "You all think all I can do is math. But see, not only do I know how to be proper, I can buy a round of shots for my family." She held her glass up in the air. "And maybe I don't know how to run away from a crazy driver but who the hell does? Do they teach that in Street Smarts One-oh-one?"

"What the hell are you rambling on about?" her father demanded. "And where is your sister?"

"A toast!" Maggie announced, ignoring her father.

The door opened from the street and Micah shifted his attention from Maggie long enough to see Deidre enter. She hesitated only long enough for the door to close behind her then marched up to the table.

"A toast to my older sister," Maggie continued, holding her shot glass higher. "She is perfect in every way. Always had the boyfriends. She has her own apartment and makes her mama so damn proud working as an LPN at the county hospital. Since she only had to go to school for one God-damn year to get her piece of paper that said she can stick a thermometer in someone's mouth or wrap a blood pressure belt around their arm, she had plenty of time to become street-smart. Let's all drink to perfect Miss Deidre O'Malley." Maggie shot the drink back, gulping it down but this time dribbling a bit out and choking slightly.

"Fuck you, Mags," Deidre hissed, grabbing a chair from another table and dragging it loudly around the table. She made her father and brother move so she could sit between them. "You didn't go to some Ivy League university."

"I stayed here for the family," Maggie yelled, slamming her shot glass on the table. "I went to UCLA and graduated in three years instead of four."

"I'm so proud of you," Deidre shot back drily. "Oh, and you're welcome for me saving your ever-so-important life!"

"What are you two fighting about?" their father yelled.

"What do you mean, saved her life?" her brother demanded at the same time.

Maggie reached for her brother's drink. Micah grabbed her wrist just as her fingers tried wrapping around the glass. Ice clinked together and her brother took the drink, bringing it to his lips as he stared hard at Micah over the rim.

"What happened?" he demanded in a low growl, staring at Micah.

Micah doubted he'd get a word in at this table, and he was right.

"Did you know Deidre carries a gun in her purse?" Maggie demanded, not pulling her hand back but instead moving it and pointing at Deidre.

"Some crazy tried running Mags over before we could leave the motel," Deidre said at the same time.

"What?" her father, brother, and other sister all exclaimed at the same time.

"God, are you all right?" Annalisa asked, turning and putting her hand on Maggie's arm.

"Someone tried running you over? Is that why you come into my bar like a crazy woman?" her father demanded.

"A crazy woman with no street smarts," Maggie corrected. This time when she took her sister's drink next to her, no one stopped her in time before she tilted it back and downed it. "Holy crap," she gasped, and shoved her chair back as she began coughing and choking. "What the fuck was in that?" she gasped.

Micah moved his chair, too, as everyone began talking at

once. He leaned into Maggie and rested his hand on her leg as she slowly caught her breath. Her eyes were bloodshot when she looked up at him.

"I have street smarts," she mumbled.

Micah would argue that she or her sisters would have a clue what to do in a truly dangerous situation. He prayed none of them would ever have to find out.

"Yes," he agreed softly. She smiled.

"If I weren't there she would have gotten herself killed," Deidre announced over everyone else.

"You don't know that," Maggie yelled, coming to life and leaping out of her chair.

She would have fallen on to the table if Micah didn't move quickly and wrap his arm around her waist. He intended to stabilize her, but Maggie collapsed backward against his body.

"How in the hell can you say what would have happened if you weren't there?" Maggie questioned, waving her finger in the air as she forced Micah to place her back in her chair.

"Don't be an idiot," Deidre snapped.

"You forget. That's the one thing I have going for me. I'm a fucking genius!" Maggie tried again coming to her feet. This time Annalisa was faster and pushed her back into her chair.

"Someone, and not you, Mags, better tell me what is going on right now," their brother demanded. When Deidre began talking he glared at her. "Shut up," he growled. Then he turned and looked at Micah, his glare cold and angry. "What happened?" he asked.

"He wasn't even there," Deidre complained, excusing Micah with a wave of her hand. "Mags hires him to protect her and he shows up after I saved her life. She froze like a pathetic puppy." Deidre leaned forward in her chair and looked at Maggie with wide eyes, outlined with black and bordered with lashes thick with mascara. "That's right. I said it. Don't you ever cut down what I do for a living again. I work my ass off and have a respectable job. At least I don't work with crooks who get my ass landed in jail."

"I didn't go to jail!" Maggie yelled. "And I worked my ass off, too. Goddamn, Deidre! You are such a bitch! I babysat Mom's fucking perfect baby brother day in and day out. Then I come home and make sure Mom is doing well that day, and if not I take care of her, too. Where the hell were you? Don't you or any of you," Maggie hissed, waving her finger around the table at her family. "None of you has a clue what my life is like. And why not? I'll tell you. Because all of you moved out. All of you spend your money on you. I get paid and make sure Mom and Dad's bills are covered. If something breaks in the house, I pay to have it fixed. I can't move out because then who would take care of them?"

"Is that how you feel?" Her father tilted his head, his blue eyes filled with more love than anger or disdain at hearing his daughter complain about her existence.

Micah felt a stab to his gut when Maggie looked at her father in horror, then dropped her head in her hands and began sobbing.

"I'm ready to go home and face Mom now," her sister said.

Micah didn't know what she was talking about, but Maggie raised her head and cried louder then lunged at her sister, wrapping her arms around her.

"Annalisa, I'm a stupid selfish bitch," Maggie wailed, her arms so tight around her sister it was easy to see how identical their hair color was. Maggie said something else but it was impossible to hear.

Her brother stood from the table and walked around, gesturing for Micah to follow him. Maggie didn't look as if she would know if he got up and left her for a minute. Standing, he caught the old man watching the two of them but made no effort to follow. Micah had learned a lot about Maggie in that minute-long visit with her and her family. There was strong jealousy and competitiveness between Maggie and her sisters. As well, she might drive a brand-new car, but she probably didn't pay rent or a mortgage. Whatever Larry Santinos had decided was a good amount to pay Maggie, it had been used to take care of her parents. One of whom was Santinos's sister. Apparently this sister, Maggie's mom, adored

Santinos. Her mother probably encouraged Maggie to stick to the job, since Maggie referred to having to babysit her uncle. It was possible Maggie grew frustrated with her uncle and might have overlooked some of his actions or behaviors. Micah followed Maggie's brother out of the bar and made a mental note to go over her routine at work and what her uncle did once she'd sobered up.

"My sisters don't usually go at it like that," Aiden began. "Maggie doesn't drink and not once in the three years she's been living with Mom and Dad has she ever complained about it. Deidre adores Maggie and thinks the world of her for getting a college degree. They are shouting insults at each other that they are both going to seriously regret later."

Micah faced him, waiting to hear what the man wanted.

"What happened to upset them like this?"

Apparently he didn't put a lot of faith in his sister's rundown of what had happened at the motel. That said something about his opinion of Deidre, which more or less concurred with what Micah had surmised from her personality.

Micah focused on Aiden's determined features. He guessed the man was about his age, if not older. Despite his apparent dislike of Micah, the way he searched Micah's face and pulled him outside to hear what had happened to his sisters spoke volumes. Micah couldn't relate to the bond between siblings, but there was a mound of education here for the taking. Maggie's family might be screaming and yelling at one another, but he'd done his fair share of yelling at his father and uncle. The O'Malleys loved and cared for one another. They didn't hide their emotions, and they vented their anger when they had it. Right now, Aiden O'Malley had two sisters in there who'd just experienced something terrible. Aiden wanted the facts. Then he'd probably want blood. Micah could only relay what he'd seen.

"When I showed up to meet Maggie, she and her sister were terrified, incredibly upset, and Deidre was holding a gun so tight I worried she'd shoot something."

"Deidre has taken several self-defense classes and knows

how to shoot," Aiden informed him, immediately defending his sister.

Micah nodded once. "Good to know."

"Why were they so upset?"

"They told me an old car with no muffler had entered the parking lot and tried running over Maggie."

"It wasn't an accident?"

He'd just defended his sister yet now questioned their judgment in reacting to the situation.

"I believe the car came at Maggie more than once."

Aiden noticeably stiffened. His dark eyes narrowed on Micah. "Do you think this is related to this mess with her uncle?" he asked, lowering his voice.

Micah was fairly certain it was. The fact that someone might want Maggie dead, or so scared she would run from her life as she knew it, confirmed his suspicion that more than one person believed she knew about the *other* book-keeping done at Club Paradise.

"There is no way to say right now."

Aiden's exasperated sigh matched Micah's view on the matter. "Did you see the car?"

"Apparently your sister successfully shot out both of its back tires. I showed up right after it left. They both told me what happened and I left to search for the car. It was parked, abandoned, just around the corner. There was no one with it."

"What about the tags?"

Micah didn't like revealing the extent of his connections. Aiden wasn't biting Micah's head off the way Deidre had. He wasn't trying to threaten him or order him away from his sister. The man wanted facts. He needed to know everything there was to know to rationalize the nightmare unfolding around his sister. Micah never felt compassion toward anyone he worked with. This was Maggie's family, though. And this wasn't an assassination job. He had no rules for how he should behave around clients he was protecting instead of killing.

"They were fake."

Aiden raised one eyebrow.

"The car was an old junker that looked like it barely ran before it had two flats."

"What does that mean to you?"

"My guess is it was only being used to scare Maggie, or worse," he added, letting his words trail off.

The door to the bar flew open and Maggie stumbled outside toward both of them. Micah instinctively moved to reach for her, as did her brother. Aiden clasped his hands behind his back and pressed his mouth into a thin line when Maggie fell against Micah.

"What are you two talking about?" she demanded, her words slurred. Her eyes were large, glassy, and bloodshot. Her hair was tousled and parted in a zigzag as some strands were stuck behind her ears and others fell around her face.

She looked up at Micah then twisted in his arms to point a finger at her brother. "You better not be telling him all your secrets about me."

When she tried twisting again, she stumbled over her feet and started to fall. "Whoa!" she cried out, flinging her arms in the air. "Alcohol makes it very hard to balance everything around you," she announced, her voice still too loud.

"I think it's time you went home." Micah adjusted his grip on her until he was holding her firmly against him with both of her arms confined within his.

She leaned her head back against his arm. "Will you take me home and put me to bed, darling?"

Aiden cleared his throat. Maggie didn't appear to notice.

"I think we should go to your house instead."

Micah looked over at Aiden, whose pained expression might have been comical if circumstances were different. "You said she doesn't drink?"

"I don't drink," Maggie announced. "Who wants to feel drunk all the time?"

Aiden rubbed his chin and studied his sister. "Our youngest sister is with us for the first time in two years. We were all going to go home with her. She and our mom had a falling-out of sorts."

"Mom is a prude!" Maggie announced and tried raising her arm but couldn't move it with Micah holding her so tightly. "I wouldn't love my sister any less if she were straight."

"Maggie," Aiden hissed. "Let's not tell the world about family business."

"What world?" Since she couldn't move, Maggie let her head roll on Micah's arm to stare at her brother. "It's just you, me, and Micah. And Micah is wonderful, Aiden. You should really like him as much as I do." She rolled her head back to focus on Micah. "I think you're wonderful, Micah."

"Okay, darling," Micah grumbled. "Let's get you sobered up."

When he glanced at the businesses around him and across the street, Aiden stepped closer. He reached for Maggie. "Might as well just take her back inside. Don makes the strongest coffee in the neighborhood."

It was mighty convenient for the local bartender to have the means to sober up his customers after aiding in getting them plowed. Unsure if it would be a good idea if he went back inside or not, Micah tried handing Maggie to Aiden. Her brother reached for her but Maggie looked up at Micah, a mixture of confusion and hurt on her face.

"Am I ugly when I'm drunk?" she whispered. "Do you not want to be around me?"

"No, you're not ugly," Micah told her, staring down at her tormented expression. Her full lips curved slightly. He doubted she could ever be ugly. "But you did too many shots way too fast. You're not accustomed to drinking, and strong coffee will help sober you up."

"I can't imagine you drunk," she whispered, searching his face with her glassy eyes.

Micah tried giving her a relaxed grin, hoping it would keep her calm so she wouldn't yell out her feelings or thoughts spontaneously. Those things she'd already said would be what she regretted the most here in a few hours.

"You were entitled to a good drunk after what you've just been through."

"I wish my family held the same sentiment," she murmured, slurring her words and relaxing completely against him.

Her legs went out and Micah was forced to adjust his hold on her so she wouldn't slump to her knees in front of him.

"Whoa, girl," Aiden piped up, coming forward and trying to take her from Micah. "I promise no one is going to hate you in the morning. Micah explained what happened and I agree with him. No one deserves to get drunk more than you do. But now we need to sober you up, for Annalisa's sake. Okay, Mags?"

Her lids were heavy when she lazily looked at her brother. "For Annalisa's sake," she repeated. "Crap," she hissed. "I was selfish to do this to her."

"She won't feel that way. Promise." Again Aiden tried taking her.

"Maggie, go with your brother," Micah instructed, handing her over to him.

"Are you leaving?" Maggie came to full alert quickly and managed to stand on her own two feet when Aiden put his arm around her.

"I think it would be better if you handled your family affairs with just your family," he told her.

"Don't leave yet." She pressed her hand to her forehead. "Damn, everything is spinning."

"Let's get you that coffee." Aiden turned to Micah. "I'd appreciate it if you came inside and explained everything to my father. It would make him feel better if he was informed. I'll have her sisters pump coffee down her and we'll sit alone so we aren't interrupted."

"Man talk," Maggie announced and whipped her finger in the air in a circular motion. "God forbid the women are around."

"Shut up, Mags. It's not like that and you know it."

"Damn right, it's not."

"You and your sisters as well as Mom would never stay quiet long enough for it ever to be like that," Aiden complained. He gave her a playful punch but held on to her as he led her back into the bar.

It was dark when Micah pulled his bike into his garage. He entered his house just as he had with Maggie the other night. Micah jerked his attention to his security wire that this time was taped to the wall at the corner of the top of the door frame. It didn't look tampered with. Then, closing his kitchen door, he walked over to flip on the kitchen light and glanced into his living room. All was just as he'd left it.

"Whew," he breathed, letting out a heavy sigh and heading for his refrigerator.

He stared at the meager selection of food items inside as he leaned against the open door. The time he'd spent with Maggie's family had left his head spinning. Even the ride home hadn't been enough to get his head back on straight. Maggie had a tight-knit family. They were dysfunctional as hell but somehow that worked best for them. He wasn't sure if he envied them or not. In the end, he simply was trying to return to his realm of indifference.

"You'll have a harder time learning who is trying to hurt her if you get too close," he instructed himself.

Deciding he wasn't hungry, Micah closed the refrigerator door and walked through his house, turning on lights as he went. There was work to do. He had an agenda to follow.

"Get the wiretaps for Haley," he began. "Somehow I need to find out if there are dirty cops out there. If they are, are they somehow connected to what is going on with Maggie?"

As he spoke he headed to his bathroom trash can where he'd thrown them away after destroying them. Micah flipped on his bathroom light and picked up the small trash can. Resting it on his bathroom counter, he stared at its contents. The condom wrapper from the other night was in there, nothing else.

"What the . . . ," he grumbled. He was positive this was where he'd thrown them away.

Micah looked away from the trash can and toward the

hallway, replaying in his mind how he'd found the small listening devices, smashed them until he was convinced they were inoperable, then thrown them away. He had put them in the bathroom trash can.

"I'm not remembering wrong." He looked down again, this time picking up the condom wrapper. The used condom was underneath it. There wasn't anything else in the can.

Just staring at the contents sent his mind whirling back to Maggie here with him. He ached to be inside her again. Even when she'd been drunk and staring up at him, she'd stirred emotions inside him he'd managed never to feel for another woman.

Somehow Maggie had the ability to cruise right past the impermeable wall that had been part of his being as long as he could remember. That wall had allowed Micah to run through job after job. No matter the intensity of it, or the level of danger involved, Micah had always performed like a machine. There was a code he'd always followed, and his method had kept him alive and effective in pulling off any type of job.

Until Maggie.

He dropped the trash can to the floor and stood there as it toppled but managed not to tip over. The sooner he found his code again, wrestled with these new emotions until they were conquered and dissipated, the sooner he could properly protect Maggie.

Micah stalked out of the bathroom into his bedroom then stood there looking around the room. The instant he tried not feeling what he was already feeling for Maggie, his mood soured. He didn't want to let go of his feelings for her, and it pissed him off.

"You don't care about her," he growled, saying the words out loud to help put feeling behind them.

Damn it! Yes, he did!

"Where the fuck are those listening devices?" he howled, suddenly wanting to hit something really hard. He fisted his hands, turning around in the room.

There wasn't a trash can in here. There was no possibility of him having destroyed the devices and leaving them in his room. Micah stalked out of the bedroom, paused outside his bathroom, then stomped into his living room. Even as he was unable to squash all emotions building inside him, a specific truth surfaced.

Micah walked over to his living room door, studied it, then squinted at the barely visible wire taped to the door frame. He moved closer, then reached up and ran his finger along it. It appeared to be in position and hooked up just as he'd placed it.

"Those listening devices aren't in the trash can," he voiced out loud, pointing out to himself the obvious. Now all he needed to figure out was why.

Micah listed the facts. He'd found them. He'd destroyed them. He'd thrown them away. He hadn't emptied the trash. They should be in the trash. They weren't. Therefore, they'd been removed. He hadn't removed them.

"How the fuck did you get in here this time?" he whispered, and stepped closer to his front door. "And why are you fucking with me in the first place?"

After examining, and testing, his security system around his house, Micah determined that it was working properly. Nonetheless, the fact remained that the smashed listening devices were no longer here. Somehow, someone had successfully entered and taken them out of his house.

"Removed all evidence that might suggest a dirty cop," Micah mumbled.

Micah returned to the back door and scrutinized the wires in place there. They appeared to be just as he'd left them. And they were working.

"What if someone were good enough to disengage them and put them back as if they'd never been tampered with?"

He dragged his kitchen chair out and shoved it up against his back door. Then, standing, he took a closer look at the small wires that ran from his back door and across his wall until they disappeared into the tiny hole he'd drilled.

"The receptor box," he hissed. He jumped off the chair backward, maintained his balance, and shoved the chair back under the table.

Micah grabbed his flashlight and headed outside. His backyard was unkempt and weeds grew everywhere. He let the beam of light travel across the yard before entering it. There were plants that were common to this area that probably had a name, although he didn't know what it was. They were abundant in his backyard, though, and their thick round leaves were trampled up against his house. Someone had been back here.

"Son of a bitch," Micah snapped, hating the feeling of someone going one-up on him. He always covered his tracks, made sure his plans were foolproof, and above all always made sure he was 100 percent safe wherever he was. Apparently just because he was a master at killing people, that didn't make him just as good at keeping them alive. "That's bullshit," he grumbled, refusing to accept that he couldn't pull off this job.

Stomping through the yard, he didn't care what damage he did to the undergrowth. It wasn't as if he'd pull someone back here to observe and confirm he'd had company today while he'd been gone. Micah walked up to the wall behind his house, held up his flashlight, and stared at the wires coming out of the house to the small box that relayed information to the main security system. This wasn't the average home security system. Whoever had come out here and tampered with it understood which wires to cut to let themselves inside unannounced.

And that was exactly what happened. The wires leading to the box had been cut here and not inside his house. Someone had entered his home then fused the wires back together when they'd left. They'd entered with a specific intention. Micah held the flashlight so the circular light aimed directly at where the person had disabled his system. Whoever had been here not only had skills in wiring and handling complicated security systems, they now knew Micah required such a system. He guessed they were now wondering why.

It was one thing working for Maggie and fighting to prevent people from following her. Micah wasn't sure if those same people were following him. He was sure that someone, and his first guess was the Osborne detective, had made quite the effort to learn how to enter his house. They'd studied his security, then breached it.

A gross unsettling feeling sunk deep in Micah's gut. This was now not only about Maggie, it was also about him. He'd been compromised. His brain went on autopilot. When compromised, relocation was required.

Chapter Ten

Someone knocked on Micah's front door. His heart hit hard against his chest as he slowly straightened from the squatting position he'd been in for too long. His muscles were strained, but he ignored the sharp pain. He'd sat hunched in more peculiar positions for longer in his past.

Micah shot a quick glance at the digital clock on his microwave visible in his kitchen. It was one o'clock in the morning. He rubbed his lower back. Whoever it was knocked again. Micah scowled at his front door. They weren't pounding as if some life-threatening emergency had just occurred. It was a soft knock. He doubted he would have heard it if he hadn't already been in his living room.

Stepping around his coffee table, Micah began cleaning up the place. There were heavy curtains drawn over the blinds on his front window. No one outside would know there was a light on inside. There was that knock again. They were persistent, if not determined.

What if Maggie was out there?

He picked up wire cutters and scooped fragments of wires into his hand. Micah shoved his electrical kit under his arm and took the contents to his kitchen then dropped them all in one of the kitchen drawers. It had taken him just under three hours to devise several traps that should do the trick. If his security system were breached again, he now had backup in place. Any intruder would be in for a very unpleasant surprise if they tried entering his home.

It had been the only solution he'd been able to come up with to justify not packing up and leaving. Micah moved across his living room to his front door and lowered his head to his peephole.

Maggie stood with her back to the door. As he watched she began walking away. He straightened, immediately turning the locks to unlock his front door.

Let her go. You know what will happen if you let her in.

He moved faster, unlocking the door. Micah ignored the argument that feelings for Maggie would destroy everything he'd worked so hard to become. It was a dangerous neighborhood and not a place for her to be at this hour.

Maggie was in the middle of his yard and turned around when he opened the door. She was dressed down quite a bit and still looked hot as hell. Pale yellow sweats were pushed up her legs and bunched together just under her knees. She wore cloth tennis shoes with no socks. Her bare legs from knee to ankle looked smooth as silk. Her tank top was the same color as her sweats, and she was definitely not wearing a bra. Her nipples were hard and pointy and instantly he wanted them in his mouth.

"I thought I'd see if you were still up," she offered, her tone flat. She raised one shoulder as she spoke then dropped it. "If I'm bothering you, it's no big deal, I can come back later."

Micah imagined she'd probably gotten herself wired on coffee while sobering up. More than likely she had then dealt with the humiliation from her family for getting drunk. None of this was his problem and he shouldn't care how any of these events affected her. They weren't part of finding who was behind the Club Paradise ordeal.

Maggie fidgeted as he stared at her, shifting her weight from one leg to the other. His brain was instantly full of ideas on how to help her burn off all that energy.

Micah stepped to the side, opening his door farther. "Come in."

Her relief was noticeable as she hurried to him and into his house.

"I'm sorry, Micah. I know it's way too late," she began as she entered. Maggie turned in his living room, not looking around at anything but focusing on him. "Tonight was a nightmare. Getting drunk didn't fix a thing. Sobering up sucked. I had to be there for my younger sister as she faced Mom for the first time in two years. I fought with my older sister until finally she left for work. My dad and older brother confronted me about you and everything that has happened with Club Paradise. I sat with Annalisa after she tried for a couple hours to get Mom to talk to her. Mom announced her youngest daughter would always be able to stay in her home but until she went to confession Mom had nothing to say to her. It really tore Annalisa up. Nothing any of us said would convince Mom otherwise. She's the most stubborn—"

Maggie took a breath then threw her hands up in the air. Exhaustion created lines around her eyes, which were still bloodshot but much more coherent than earlier.

"I'm sorry, Micah. This is hell," she continued, then without warning ran into his arms.

Micah wrapped his arms around her. His hands easily slipped under her tank top. She didn't stiffen or straighten when he began caressing her bare back. He rested his cheek on the top of her head as she clung to him.

"It's all just too much, Micah, you know? There are too many emotions going around in my brain and I just can't handle it anymore. If I could just quit feeling, I know it would be so much easier to cope with all of this." She sobbed and sucked in a choked breath. "Part of my brain says the smart thing would be to just get the hell out of here and start over. If I left town and moved far away to some small town no one has ever heard of, then nothing going on here could touch me. I'd be just fine."

God, she was voicing his thoughts.

"Is that what you want to do?"

Maggie raised her head. "No, yes, hell, I don't know."

She let go of him and backed out of his arms. "But I just can't deal with all of my family's drama and having people try to kill me. It's too much."

Micah noticed she didn't mention trying to cope with any feelings toward him. Maybe these new feelings for her were one-sided. Or maybe she already understood what it felt like to care for someone so it didn't bother her. He watched her walk away from him and over to his kitchen table. She ran her finger along the edge of the table. Part of her was shrouded in darkness but it only helped accentuate his view.

Sweatpants had never made a woman's ass look better. The elastic was snug against her waist. Her sweatpants weren't tight on her but were far from baggy. The material was thick but still hugged her just enough that her curves and firm, tight ass were nicely displayed. Micah found himself staring between the top of her legs and imagining the many things he could do to her right there.

Her straight auburn hair hid her face as she continued focusing on the edge of his table. Something deep in his gut encouraged him to walk over to her, assure her everything would be okay, because he would see to it. He couldn't make promises to her that he didn't know if he could keep. He dug himself in where he was standing and stuffed his hands in his jean pockets. His fingers still itched to touch her again.

"There's something I don't understand." She spoke so softly she was hard to hear.

Micah remained rooted where he was. He didn't say a word. There was a hell of a lot he didn't understand. Making his feelings for her go away would solve everything. Then it wouldn't matter if he understood or not.

Maggie turned her head and swatted hair from her face. Her hazel eyes burned into his soul, calling him out despite his efforts to remain immune to her.

"Why is it so easy to come over here and talk to you?" she asked him.

Micah was a pro when it came to plotting out a kill. There had been times when acting fast on his feet and coming up with a smooth, convincing argument had been necessary. He told himself this was just one more of those times.

He opened his mouth, certain a convincing, noncommittal

answer would put her mind at ease. "Because you've hired me to find whoever wants you dead."

"Wants me dead?" Her expression turned horrified.

Micah had surmised that the person, or people, behind the money laundering at Club Paradise were convinced Maggie knew more than she did. They'd rather kill her than risk her taking the knowledge they believed she had somewhere where it would cause them more damage.

Her laughter sounded more like a choking sound. "You aren't helping me forget all my problems," she said shakily.

Micah cleared the distance between them before he realized what he'd done. Grabbing her by each side of her head, he tangled his fingers in her hair and forced her head back. She stared up at him but didn't fight him.

"Do you want to forget all of your problems?" he asked, his voice a rough whisper.

"Yes," she said.

He pulled her into his arms then lifted her, stepping forward until her back hit the wall. Maggie gasped and looked up at him wide-eyed. Micah didn't wait for understanding to appear on her face. He attacked her mouth as a fever exploded inside him.

All of his efforts to convince himself he was better off getting her out of his system backfired. Instead of clearing his head of Maggie, he wanted her more than ever. If there was any turning back he wasn't sure which direction that would be at the moment.

"Is this why you came over?" he asked when he ended the kiss. He still had her pinned to the wall, but she was relaxed. She trusted him. *God, she trusted him.* No one trusted the assassin. They needed him but they never trusted him.

"Well, I—"

"What do you want, Maggie?"

He started a trail of kisses from her cheekbone to her neck, loving how she tasted. When she opened her eyes and stared at him instead of answering right away, Micah swore he saw the same turmoil eating her alive that was in him.

His dick was hard as steel. Blood burned in his veins.

Throughout the evening he'd used every argument imaginable as to how his life would be better off if he left Maggie alone. Now he couldn't get enough of her.

Micah would argue women were a complicated species. Now he was a firm advocate that they made a man insane. He was out of his head with need for her, built up by trying not to need her.

"Do you not know what you want?" he asked. Micah needed to hear her admit she came running over here because of this. He might not know anything about relationships, but he knew a thing or two about women. Maggie's breath was coming hard; her nipples were puckered points torturing his chest. He would bet she was thoroughly soaked.

He understood physical need. Hell, he had it all the time. If she said she came over to fuck him and not because she needed *him,* maybe that would help stop the annoying desire he had to be with her all the time.

"I came over to see you, but—" Again she didn't finish her sentence.

Maybe he was better off forcing Maggie out of his system. Micah took a step backward. His body screamed in protest. The anguish that raked over his flesh, tightened his balls so he could barely move, and left his dick swollen and throbbing was worse than any pain he'd ever endured in the past.

"But what?" he growled.

"No," she whimpered, leaning against his wall yet reaching for him.

More than anything he wanted to take her back in his arms. "No, what?"

She had to give him something. If Micah was this close to the edge he wanted to know Maggie was right there with him.

"Don't stop," she pleaded.

If he was too rough, he was beyond controlling his actions. Micah had never been blind with lust before. Not once had a woman spun something so intense inside him that not even he could unweave it. He grabbed her tank top, bunching it in his fist between her breasts. Then, pulling her closer by her shirt, he lifted it at the same time. Micah yanked it off her and tossed it somewhere in his living room before she could put her arms down.

"I won't stop, darling," he promised her and took her by the waist.

He didn't have a plan. His brain was on fire. Micah turned her around, tugged down her sweatpants, and exposed that adorable ass of hers. He thrust his hand between her legs and his eyes rolled back in his head.

"You're soaked." His voice was raspy, and he wasn't seeing straight.

Maggie moaned and twisted in front of him when she tried looking at him over her shoulder.

"Don't move," he ordered, pressing one hand into the small of her back while he undid his jeans with his other.

The moment his cock sprang free her body was like a magnet, pulling him into her heat. Micah didn't remember closing his eyes any more than he did entering her. But when her velvety flesh constricted around his dick, pulling him into the depths of her heat, everything around him faded so that there was only Maggie. He plummeted deep inside her pussy, grabbing her hips and holding her in place so he could fuck her hard and fast.

"Micah!" Maggie cried his name and he heard her pleasure at the same time he felt her explode around him. "God, yes! Fuck me as hard as you can."

"What my lady wants," he growled, and tightened his grip on her soft, smooth flesh.

His dick slid deep inside her until he filled her with every inch he had. Already his balls were too tight. The pressure had built up to a boiling point too fast. Slowing down wouldn't change matters.

The moment Micah realized he was going to come, it also hit him with frightening clarity that he wasn't wearing a condom. If it had hurt him trying to make himself believe Maggie didn't mean anything to him, it hurt ten times as much pulling out of her soaked heat before he emptied himself inside her.

He watched his come drip over her rear end and wished he could enjoy the sight better. "I'll get you a towel," he said, and heard the bitter edge to his words.

Maggie kicked off her shoes, pushed her sweatpants to her ankles, and stepped out of them. His come still clung to her ass when she faced him, stark naked.

"How about a shower instead?" she asked, and the glow on her face soothed some of the shame he felt. "I guess we overdid it a bit, huh?"

He wasn't sure exactly what she meant and wasn't going to guess. When she smiled and touched his chest, Micah could almost believe he had no reason to be ashamed. Maggie looked up at him as if it were perfectly normal for a man who was almost thirty to come after a lousy fucking minute of sex.

"We're not done," he informed her and led her to his bathroom.

"Oh my God!" Maggie cried out when Micah stripped out of his shirt.

He turned and caught a glimpse of himself in the small mirror over the medicine cabinet. "Oh, that."

"Oh, that?" Already she was at him, her fingers nimbly working around the adhesive tape Haley had secured the gauze bandage with. "What happened? Why didn't you tell me you were hurt?"

"Honestly, I forgot." He'd had a hell of a lot more important matters on his mind.

"You forgot you were hurt?" she asked, disbelieving.

"I guess I should take it off to shower." He looked from her fingers to her face as Maggie began peeling away the bandages.

Maggie glanced up, and there was sincere concern in her eyes. "What happened? Will you tell me?" she asked softly.

Micah shrugged. "Taking down a client at work," he told her without hesitating. There was no reason to keep any aspect of this life a secret from her. "I don't think he took too kindly to being caught. He thought he had a pretty good hiding place. And it was pretty damn crafty." He'd seen some doozeys in his time. Those were stories he could never share with Maggie.

"What did he do to you?" she asked, and removed the bandage. She had to tiptoe to see the top of his arm by his shoulder where the bullet had grazed over his skin. "What happened?" she whispered.

"I was shot."

Her jaw dropped and she stared up at him, wide-eyed. Her expression was comical.

"With a gun," he added, and fought a smirk.

"You were shot?" she gasped. "With a gun?"

Micah watched the color drain out of her face and caught her before she fell backward into the shower curtain. "Maggie, it's what I do." He got her to sit on the toilet lid and waited for her color to return.

She was slapping at him before he backed away from her. Maggie's breasts bounced and her nipples were hardened beacons as she punched at his chest and arms.

"What the hell?" he complained, dodging almost all of her swings although she managed to make contact once or twice. Maggie had a good arm on her. "You're hitting a man who got shot?"

She froze, took one look at his face, and made a fist. "How dare you make fun of me, Micah Jones!" she cried out and the fist came at his jaw.

Micah cut her off mid-aim and held her fist in his. "Sweetheart, I wasn't making fun of you, and taking a bullet is never a laughing matter." There were quite a few exceptions to that rule but in Maggie's life there never would be.

"Don't change your tune now, mister. A second ago you were doing your best not to bust a gut when I asked if you were shot with a gun."

Now wasn't the time to ask her what else she thought he might have been shot with. Maggie had been through a day she probably never dreamed would happen in her lifetime. And by all odds, it shouldn't have. In Maggie's world, the only gun might be the one her father had stashed away to protect the family. It would never be loaded, and her mother would never allow bullets in the house because of the children.

His life as Micah Jones was more than Maggie could handle. It should have been his wake-up call. He shouldn't have pulled her into his arms and cradled her until she calmed down.

"Forgive me for worrying," she mumbled once she'd relaxed against him.

"Nothing wrong with worrying."

"It only means I care." She added quickly, "as a friend."

Micah put her at arm's length. "I like you caring as a friend."

Maggie's smile lit up his world. She shouldn't be affecting him this way. After all, she'd just given him firsthand knowledge of what she'd think if she knew what he really did. More than likely, she'd turn tail and run.

Showering not only invigorated his body, but cleared his head as well. His fears before Maggie had arrived might have come close to paranoid, but they'd also been accurate. The way she looked at him, her comfort level around him naked, and her desire to see to his needs right down to soaping and rinsing his back, and washing him very carefully around his wound, were all indications that she was falling for him. If he allowed it, he would fall hard for her, too.

Maggie would never love you if she knew who you really were.

What if he retired? He had a fair amount of cash on him. There were bank accounts with enough money in them to set him up for life. Micah could give Maggie anything and everything she had ever dreamed of having. She would never have to know about his past.

"I'll grab a second towel." Micah stepped out of the shower after they'd both rinsed and wrapped the only towel in the bathroom around his waist. He didn't have to go far to the small closet outside his bathroom door, where there were a couple more folded towels.

Maggie turned off the water and moved the shower curtain. He held the towel but just stared at her.

"I almost hate to dry you off," he growled.

"You brute." She laughed.

The wholesome glow in her eyes and her cheeks and her easy smile made his heart constrict. There wasn't any denying it. He was another Mulligan, gone hook, line, and sinker. Maggie had stolen his heart and she didn't even know whose heart she'd stolen.

He wasn't just another Mulligan, though. Micah had surpassed every Mulligan before him. He'd accomplished what each of them had yearned for but never succeeded in doing. Micah was the ultimate killer, respected for who he was and what he did.

His heart constricted even farther when he realized what he had to do. He might hurt Maggie but hopefully she wasn't as far gone as he was and she'd simply be grateful for the wake-up call. Micah had to chase her away. Which he would figure out how to do—tomorrow.

Micah took his time loving her body while Maggie lay stretched out on his bed. He kissed every inch of her, enjoying the odd patterns of freckles scattered across her arms, legs, and belly. She was soft yet firm in the right places. When he settled between her legs and breathed in her rich, enticing scent, her smooth shaved flesh was a vision of perfection.

He stroked his finger down the creases of her entrance. She was instantly wet again. "You're absolutely perfect, darling," he rumbled, his voice rough with need.

"That feels so good." Maggie's eyes were closed and her head on one of his pillows. Her hair was straight silky strands falling away from her face. The worry and uncertainty were gone. Instead her face glowed. Her lips were puckered and her breath came quickly in short, tight pants.

Micah stretched her legs apart and moved closer to taste her.

"Oh God!" she cried out, her body jerking.

Micah chuckled and held her where he wanted her as he began feasting. This was going to be harder than he thought. He'd killed people when others hadn't been able to do the job. Micah had maneuvered positions in order to keep his presence a secret during a hit. He'd pulled the trigger and ended lives of young and old alike. Micah had made a hell of a lot of money killing people others didn't want around. Having done all of that, it should be child's play to get a little rough, push Maggie into submission, and demand she adhere to his sexual desires. She would never know who he truly was, but he could be what she didn't want so she'd push him away.

There weren't many people on the planet capable of doing what Micah did. He had skill levels far beyond any trained military specialist. Once those few elite were trained, the government seldom wanted to let them go. No one would ever control or have any power over him. He was capable of killing anyone on the planet then disappearing without a trace. He was more than a mechanical killer. He was a monster. He had lived his life without any deep emotions or concerns for anyone. If he allowed his feelings for Maggie to grow, they would destroy who he was.

Micah had always accepted the dark side in him, the monster as he'd labeled it. That monster wasn't worthy of a woman like Maggie. Once this mess with Club Paradise and the assholes creating hell in her life were gone, she might want to settle down with a good man. They would have a family, raise them in a warm, cozy house, and be incredibly happy. That life would never be for him. He was honor-bound to the Mulligan tradition.

Maggie's breathing grew more ragged and her perfectly shaped breasts moved as she inhaled and exhaled. This was what he had to do. He would push her sexually, demanding what she'd probably never given to a man. He would make her give it to him, and later she'd hate him for it.

His tongue dipped inside her pussy, moved lower, and ran circles around her tight, puckered ass. She jerked when he pressed into her asshole. His stomach tightened and he forced all remorse over what he was about to do to her out of his mind. All he had to do was clear his head. Stay grounded and his movements mechanical. Micah kept feelings out of actions all the time. That's all he had to do here.

"Have you ever been fucked here?" he whispered.

Micah watched for her reaction. For a moment she didn't move or respond. It was as if he'd sent her into some erotic trance. He circled her tight ass again with his tongue, drew moisture from her pussy lower and dipped her cream from the tip of his tongue into her ass. All the while he kept his eyes on her face.

"Maggie," he whispered.

"Umm."

"Open your eyes. Look at me. Feel what I'm doing."

"I'm feeling what you're doing," she said as a sly grin crossed her face.

Micah moved his hand and pressed his finger against her tight entrance. Maggie's eyes flew open and she came almost to a sitting position.

"Mother Mary, Christ!" she exploded.

Micah couldn't stop himself. He broke out laughing. Maggie's expression stilled and she watched him, not appearing offended or put out.

"I swear sparks just shot through my entire body," she gasped. "I'm soaked," she added and moved her fingers between her legs then stroked her pussy. "That was definitely different," she told him. Her focus on him was hidden by her eyelashes stuck at half-mast.

"I guess that answers my question." But it definitely wasn't the reaction he'd expected from her. Micah watched Maggie closely, making sure he understood. No lady enjoyed anal sex. They endured it for the man, and most men only ever had it when they paid dearly for it.

What if what he had just done to her truly got Maggie off? He'd barely pressed against the entrance of her ass. That was a lot different from penetration. Micah was still staring at her when she finally focused on him and smiled.

"I didn't realize you'd asked me a question," she said and fell back with a sigh.

Maggie had lost herself in fantasies of Micah adoring her as he promised his never-ending love. She'd imagined him bringing her to orgasm after orgasm as he whispered all the right words she needed to hear.

Micah might not ever have a chivalrous nature. But he had one hell of a skilled tongue. He knew how to touch her. And he most definitely could make her come.

There were no promises or commitment between them. The only agreement they did have was Micah saying he'd try to find out who'd allowed her to take the rap over the money-laundering deal at Club Paradise. Maggie saw interest in his eyes, though. Maybe she didn't want something to build between them. But whatever was simmering, it was doing so in him as well as her. He didn't have to open his door for her when she'd first come over. Hell, with those thick, heavy dark curtains in his living room, Maggie never would have known if he had been awake or asleep.

This was exactly where she wanted to be. No one had ever made her feel as good as Micah did right now. He took control of her body and made her feel he was the only one who truly knew how to give her the perfect orgasm. But was it the fantasy of forbidden sex that had just gotten her off so much? After all, she was damn near having erotic, kinky sex with a complete stranger.

She was growing more concerned about the "complete stranger" part. Micah had been so indifferent about his gunshot wound, she'd thought he was making fun of her. After the day she'd had—some stranger trying to run her over, then her sister pulling out a gun and acting as if she were a super-cop or something—she didn't need Micah flipping her shit. So she'd lost it on him. Once her temper had cooled she'd seen that he hadn't been teasing her after all.

When he'd pulled off his shirt in the bathroom, he'd acted as if he'd forgotten about the bandage on his upper arm. More than likely he really had forgotten about it. That should have been her wake-up call. Micah lived a life where he was shot at on a regular basis. That would never be a life for her.

Maggie tried raising her head. Every inch of her was relaxed—but then without notice Micah would do something to create tingles of pleasure rushing over her body. She fought to clear her blurry vision and stared at dark tousled hair that fell around Micah's focused, brooding expression. Knotted muscles bulged in his shoulders, and corded roped muscle stretched down his arms. Micah was ripped. Every inch of him perfect beyond belief. His body was so beautiful, she could damn near cry at the sight of such intense masculinity.

But then there were the puckered scars. At first when she'd noticed them on his body, she'd thought they had added to his bad boy good looks. That just showed how naive she'd been. The cut under his bandage had scabbed over but was red compared to the other scars. Soon it would be another war wound on his body. She began imagining where he might have received the other wounds that were now scar tissue puckered against his otherwise smooth, taut flesh.

Then he did it again. This time Maggie managed not to leap off the bed and blurt out her aunt's favorite form of cursing. Micah pressed his finger into her ass. Sensations she'd never known before tripped over one another. This wasn't the same as an orgasm after mind-blowing sex. It was different, more eruptive, definitely taboo and dangerous. Micah looked up at her, pushing his finger just inside her. He was watching for her reaction and making some determination accordingly. Did he want to know how much kink she would indulge in?

Maggie had spent the entire evening listening to Aiden berate Micah. It was so incredibly fitting that Micah would silently suggest, with the slightest pressure from his finger, that they indulge in something more extreme than she'd ever done before. Aiden had run several searches and had announced the results he found loud enough that the entire family heard. Micah Jones didn't exist. Aiden wouldn't let it go and had continually questioned her judgment on how she was handling matters. This was how she was handling matters. She was managing not to come flying off his bed and crying out every saint's name she could think of as he pushed her toward a sexual peak she hadn't known existed before tonight.

Aiden had convinced the entire O'Malley household that Maggie was mixed up with a man who was more than likely not who he said he was and had a questionable past. Correction, according to Aiden, no past. Maggie had finally lost it once again in front of her family. She'd yelled at Aiden, telling him in no uncertain terms that his searches could very well be wrong and that she knew for a fact he worked for KFA. Micah Jones most definitely existed.

Aiden had been able to confirm Micah worked for KFA, the bounty hunters. But there wasn't any other information on the man. Aiden had made it very clear, using each family member as an example as he'd plugged her parents, himself, and even Maggie into his different search programs, that normal people had a history, many often going back more than a decade. Sometimes they only went back five years or so, as Maggie's did, since she'd signed for her first loan, put her name on a lease, and had bank accounts as most adults did.

Micah had nothing. There were no credit cards under his name. His name had never appeared on a lease. He had no bank accounts, lines of credits or loans, outstanding or paid off. Micah Jones didn't exist.

"Hey, sweetheart, are you lost in a fantasy world?" Micah asked, kissing the inside of her thigh.

"Oh, yes." She raised her head and stared at the good-looking man between her legs. "Most definitely a fantasy world," she purred and made a humming sound. Micah was making her feel so damn good and it just pissed her off that her family would think the worst of him. So what if he got shot at on a regular basis.

Her brother was wrong. That was all there was to it. How could Micah not exist?

Who are you? she wanted to ask.

Micah lowered his mouth, sucked on her clit, and every inch of her trembled. Maggie gripped the blankets, bit her lower lip, and refused to look away from his sexy eyes. To hell with her brother and the rest of her family for doubting her judgment in men. She would figure out Micah Jones on her own time.

His head lowered and his tongue moved over her entrance, then soaked her asshole. Every time he licked or thrust his tongue inside her ass, sensations rippled through her unlike any she'd ever known.

"Have you ever been fucked here?" he asked.

She swallowed, his understanding sinking in. "No," she whispered. His next question was on his lips and she beat him to the punch. "Not yet."

Maggie swore his gaze fogged over. Something in his expression changed. She watched as his eyes rolled back in his head and he adored her puckered, tight entrance.

It was the forbidden sex, the ultimate taboo. Bad girls gave blow jobs in alleys or fucked more than one guy at once. No one ever mentioned anal sex. The thought of it should terrify her. Maybe it was proof that everything she'd endured recently had truly sent her off her rocker. But Micah fucking her ass sounded hot.

The pressure that swelled inside her when his tongue flicked around her ass, then dipped inside sent her places she'd never known existed. Would she be able to handle the pressure if his dick entered her there?

As if he could read her mind, Micah opened his eyes and moved to his hands and knees over her. His incredibly muscular chest, with dark tight curls spanning across it, was in her face as he reached for the drawer next to his bed. Her attention riveted from one small scar to the next. He pulled out a condom and a small bottle of lubricant. She counted four scars before he moved again.

"If the sensations grow too intense let me know," he whispered. "The gel should ease any pain. If this isn't good for both of us, I don't want to do it."

Maggie simply watched him put on the condom then coat it with the lubricant without commenting. She didn't know what to say. Her body was tingling with nervous anticipation. Her pussy throbbed and she was acutely aware of her ass from the sensual torture he'd administered so far.

From the moment she'd entered his home everything had been different than before. Their rough spontaneous sex up against his wall was so hot. She hadn't minded that it hadn't lasted long. It had been as if Micah couldn't wait to see her. He'd been so excited he couldn't hold out. Knowing she did that to him made her want him even more. And it hadn't surprised her a bit that he'd still been hard. The entire time in the shower his cock had poked her with silent promises of what would come.

Micah adjusted his body over hers, and his cock immediately found her asshole. She stiffened when his swollen tip pressed against the tight hole.

"Relax," Micah whispered.

"Easy for you to say," she whispered back. "You don't have to relax."

He laughed again. Maggie had hardly ever seen him smile. Now twice since lying here with him he'd laughed out loud. The sound of it did something to her heart she couldn't explain. She stared up at him, stretching her legs as his large body hovered over hers.

Micah didn't put any of his weight on her. There were inches between their bodies, allowing her to look down between them and see his thick hard cock pressed between the curves of her ass. The view was so damn hot she sucked in a deep breath, filling her lungs, and stared past her breasts at the closeness of their bodies.

Micah's body was powerful, dark, and covered with sprays of coiled black hairs. Her gaze lifted and she spotted more tiny puckered scars on various places on his body. She wanted to kiss each one, experience the adventure and pain he'd known as he had received each one. By studying his body it was as if she got a peek into the story behind the man who was such a mystery. At the same time he was crawling into her heart. She lifted her gaze up his body and studied his face.

The moment she looked into his eyes Micah thrust inside her.

"Oh fuck!" Maggie latched on to Micah, possibly creating new scars he could stare at in the future to help him remember this moment. She dug in deep with her nails as too many nerves ignited in a fiery protest over the initial invasion.

"Breathe," Micah whispered over her lips, then kissed her softly. "Kiss me back," he instructed.

His voice hovered in a dark, lust-filled cloud stretching past her line of sight. He penetrated her, and a heat unlike any she'd ever known spread over her body. She took that breath and suddenly remembered how to move her body. When she latched her legs around his and wrapped her arms around his neck, he sank deeper inside her. Heat so intense it would boil her alive consumed her. When she focused, Micah was watching her.

He was a predator, a man above most men. Maggie saw something in his eyes she hadn't seen before. For a moment she thought of him as a conqueror; she'd been captured by the dark soul she saw deep inside him. That wasn't quite right, though. His soul was dark and filled with more scars than his body. Maggie stared at Micah as if she were seeing him for the first time. Exposed, vulnerable, conflicted, and very much hers. The scars on his body were mended. But his soul still bore open wounds.

She wrapped her arms around his neck tighter. "Make love to me," she whispered.

Micah growled into her mouth. Her heart opened wide enough to wrap around his tormented soul. He began moving inside her, and the fiery heat she'd first experienced exploded again. The pressure was more intense than it ever could have been fucking her pussy.

As his momentum built, that pressure erupted with more force than she knew possible in an orgasm. Her world blew up with a mixture of pain and pleasure so acute and tightly intertwined it was hard to tell one from the other. And the heat—volcanic—burnt her alive. She wanted him to fuck her harder. She wanted it slower. She wanted him to stop. She wanted him to keep going. Her brain was a whirlwind of emotions as mind-boggling as the sensations that tore through her body.

"Oh my God, Micah!" she howled, unable to handle it any longer and at the same time wanting more.

"Maggie." He rumbled her name over her lips.

Micah kissed her as deeply as he fucked her.

She couldn't take it. This was nothing like anything she'd ever imagined. Her body convulsed and she came so hard a flood of dark colors blew up and erupted before her eyes. Lavender, cobalt, and emerald green, yellow and orange, splashed and blended as her orgasm ripped through her at a velocity too fast for her to grab ahold of.

There wasn't time for her to enjoy the afterglow when the next round of sensations grew and erupted. Maggie cried out again, no longer able to relax or prevent her body from convulsing around his cock. She was vaguely aware of Micah stiffening over her. His growls turned to protests. His words rumbled and floated over her, but she wasn't able to grasp their meaning.

Maggie's world had turned into a series of convulsions and intense orgasms. She spasmed with each one, fighting to bask in the moment before they ebbed and the next one hit her. But they were too strong. There were too many of them.

Micah tried to penetrate and recede at a pace he would control. Maggie sensed his frustration when her body took over, constricting around him. Her tight muscles, unaccustomed to surrendering to such elasticity, tightened and convulsed around his dick.

His sharp breaths each time her body tried pushing him out became hard, uncontrolled pants. Maggie thought such a dark, forbidden type of sex had meant surrendering and turning her body over to his ultimate pleasure. She never dreamed that after coming harder than she ever had in her life she would experience an overwhelming sense of control.

She tightened around him with a fierceness that prevented him from moving. His initial thrusts had slowed until Maggie bound his cock with her ass muscles. She held him deep inside her and endured the burning heat until it became a warmth enveloping her with erotic pleasure.

When she blinked and focused on his face, she saw that battle-torn soul and all of Micah's open wounds deep inside that had never healed. Here was a man hovering between one life and another. He'd entered her world and become something to her. She sensed his yearning to latch on to her world. But there was something dark, something unknown and dangerous buried deep inside him. It was the cause of his tormented expression. It created the hard lines and sharp angles etched deep in his brooding expression.

"Come inside me," she whispered, and felt the sting in her throat from screaming through each orgasm.

Maggie watched that dark abyss in his soul disappear when Micah focused on her. He secured those secrets he hid from the world and had briefly exposed to her. Possibly he hadn't realized that fucking her like this would force open all well-kept hidden parts of his nature he didn't want the world to see.

She wondered if he had the same revelation. Had he stared into her eyes and seen her exposed and vulnerable? Did the scared, uncertain part of her nature reach out to him as his had to her? Had he seen how terrified she'd been when she'd learned he'd been shot? Did he see how she knew she couldn't live a life with guns and gunshot wounds in it on a regular basis?

Then he fucked her hard. He moved fast and with skills that left no doubt nothing she had could hold on to this man if he didn't wish it. Maggie might have glimpsed at a part of him too raw and battle-torn to prevent her from guiding him where she wanted him. Micah stared down at her with powerful intent. Nothing would hold this man at bay unless he allowed it.

Her heart retreated from the pain, knowing she had nothing strong enough to handle the dark, almost terrifying side of him she'd just seen. But at the same time she exulted in the fact that she was here. When he raised his head and stared straight ahead, veins bulged in his neck as a fierce growl erupted from deep inside him.

Micah's body tightened. Her fingers brushed over muscles so solid and hard she relished in the incredible strength emanating from them.

"Now," he roared and his body convulsed.

He lowered himself onto her and continued trembling. Maggie kissed each muscle that had been well trained to become part of this perfectly polished machine. Micah was a mystery but part of him had opened up to her, albeit briefly. The dark abyss inside him was terrifying—but at the same time, it didn't scare her.

"Are you okay?" he whispered.

A fresh sensation of fire scorched her flesh when he slowly receded and pulled out of her. Maggie gasped despite herself.

Okay? She was better than she'd ever been in her life. When he rolled to his side she curled into him and ran her hand over the fierce, intense man who lay next to her. Sweat made his flesh glow around his gunshot wound, but he didn't seem bothered by it.

"I'm fine," she whispered, and continued stroking his warm flesh. She wanted to add, *and you will be, too.*

Maggie didn't say anything else. Instead she stretched out next to him. The smooth sheen of perspiration on both their bodies allowed them to mold against each other. Micah wrapped a heavy, muscular arm around her and pulled her closer.

"You amaze me, Maggie."

"Why is that?" she asked.

He turned his head and stared at her, his lashes preventing her from seeing beyond the surface of the man. Micah was once again a mystery, the overwhelming protector, strong and invincible. He looked at her with the expression he offered the world. She refused to be hurt knowing he had no intention of letting her see beyond the persona he offered everyone else. Somehow she would show him that revealing all he was wouldn't scare her away.

"You came really hard." The look on his face showed he had considered saying something else. Micah was holding back. "Get some sleep, sweetheart. Morning will be here before you know it."

She closed her eyes, instantly aware of how exhausted she was. Her dreams came quickly and she wasn't sure if she heard him say, *I never knew a woman like you existed.* Maybe she just dreamed him revealing his thoughts.

Chapter Eleven

Micah spoke his name into the small speakerphone built into a cream-colored brick wall.

"And who are you here to see, Mr. Jones?" the crisp voice asked.

Micah hated country clubs with every fiber of his bones. "Mr. Perry Ramone," he said, using the last name Perry had instructed him to use over the phone.

Silence lingered on as Micah relaxed against the handlebars of his bike. He squinted against the glare of the early-morning sun over the rolling hills on the other side of the tall, black rod iron gate. A brick road that had to be hell on all of those Mercedes-Benzes wove through the hills and disappeared around the bend. Micah was sure the landscape had been designed that way to prevent any outsiders from seeing the actual country club. Like anyone out here would care what it looked like.

The lock connecting the two gates clicked, and there was a buzzing sound as the gates opened inward. Micah watched and waited until they were all the way open before entering. As anxious as he'd been for Perry to call him with any information he'd unearthed, the man's timing couldn't have been worse.

Maggie had been sound asleep, breathing heavily and peacefully when he'd slowly moved his arm out from underneath her to answer his phone. He had crawled out of bed

over an hour ago. That had been at six in the morning. Never
enough sleep for the wicked.

Micah's bike rumbled over the brick road as it curved
around the landscaped grounds and finally opened into a
large parking lot. There were a surprising amount of cars
there for it just being eight o'clock on a weekday morning.
Either a lot of rich people were out of work, in which case
their membership here would probably have been terminated, or there were a fair number of housewives leaving the
maid to tend to their family while they escaped to the club.
Micah took a choice parking place, then walked up a path to
the large glass doors that opened automatically when he approached. So much for the days of the doorman.

There was a bar to his right with the lights dimmed, giving privacy to the rich barflies. Micah continued walking to
a quiet, spacious dining area. A young cute thing blushed
when he approached and batted long, thick lashes at him.

"May I help you, sir?" she asked, looking too damn innocent for her own good.

Micah pictured Maggie tangled in his sheets back at his
house and, once again, ached to be back there with her.
Hopefully he'd be able to return before she woke up.

"I'm here to meet Mr. Ramone."

"Yes." She nodded and turned to look at something on
the podium next to her. "He's this way, sir."

Micah followed her, letting his attention drop to the sensual sway of her very round ass in tight white slacks. Like
most girls her age, she had a deep golden tan, and her sun-
drenched blonde hair fell straight down her back. He'd put
her somewhere around eighteen. By the time she was forty
she'd be as dried up and wrinkled as a raisin.

They didn't enter the spacious dining area; instead Micah
followed the girl around a corner. She paused as they headed
down a wide hallway and tapped on a door that was barely
noticeable in the wall. That's when Micah noticed there
were doors lining the hallway on both sides. The young girl
opened the door and gestured for Micah to enter.

"Bring us more coffee, Lacey," Perry said cheerily. He sat at a large round table reading a newspaper and sporting a hideous yellow polo shirt and pale yellow slacks that were just as ugly. The color choice did nothing for his already pale complexion. "And Mr. Jones will prefer a more traditional breakfast. Sausage, bacon, eggs, toast, pancakes," Perry rambled and waved his hand in the air. "Did I forget anything?" Perry asked Micah.

Micah took a chair facing Perry. He looked at Lacey, who remained at the door. "No pancakes," he told her and gave her a wink.

There would always be some warped pleasure in making young girls blush. She was out of his mind before she'd closed the door, though. Micah sat with his back to a glass wall. On the other side of it an indoor tropical rain forest provided one hell of a view.

"The crime rate in this town is terrifying," Perry said and made a tsking sound as he turned the page in the newspaper.

"Maybe LAPD should focus harder on lowering the crime rate." Micah didn't look at Perry but played with the corner of his cloth napkin.

Perry put down the paper. "Right there is the gross misperception of so many people in this town," he said, leaning forward in his chair and sounding excited about the topic of conversation. "Something goes wrong and we're so quick to blame our men and women in blue." He wagged a long, thin finger at Micah. "The LAPD takes a bad rap for so much. Quite often they aren't at fault."

Micah leaned back in his chair and crossed his arms, willing to hear Perry out. The man would always paint a lavish story in which he would give Micah the information he wanted. Micah had never asked why but he guessed it was in case someone was listening in on their conversation. They'd have one hell of a time figuring out what Perry was talking about.

"Now I say lay blame where blame is due." Perry narrowed his gaze on Micah, and lines appeared around his eyes. The man was looking a bit more weathered lately. Maybe his job was taking its toll on him. "I was just reading this article in the paper." He stabbed the newspaper that he'd put down on the table with his finger. "Some money-laundering racket is baffling the local police. But they are giving it their all. I read between the lines, my friend. I have heard the rumors of how some think the police might be letting information slide. Not true!"

"What do you think is going on?" Micah asked.

He paused when there was a knock on their door and Lacey appeared with more coffee. She refilled Perry's cup, poured Micah a cup, and left a carafe in the middle of the table. She then disappeared without a word. Micah saw why Perry chose this country club. These private rooms were ideal for conversation.

"There is an inside source," Perry said, leaning forward as he lowered his voice. "But it's not the police."

Micah lifted his cup and blew on the hot coffee. "Interesting theory," he murmured, truly wishing that Detective Osborne had been dirty. He'd love taking the asshole down.

"The cops believe the same thing, so they are sticking real close to anyone who might have been connected with that nightclub."

Micah studied Perry over his cup. Steam lingered in front of his face, and the rich smell of the expensive brew helped wake him up. He drank, enduring the hot liquid as it sank inside him. He had more than a few sore muscles today and hoped Maggie didn't wake up any worse for wear than he had.

"Now, my friend, my theory is this," Perry said, and paused, also sipping, then leaned back in his chair, letting out a satisfied sigh. "Good coffee," he murmured. "But anyway, I think the police believed they had arrested their man until the laundering didn't stop."

"It didn't?"

"Nope." Perry shook his head. "Recent developments revealed new activity coming across the border. So do they have the right man in jail?" Perry nodded. "He was most definitely in on it. But someone has taken his place and kept the ball rolling. That person isn't as important as whoever put that replacement person where he is."

"Who did?" Micah willed Perry to get to the point.

Perry leaned forward again and whispered, "I believe a city official is involved. I haven't narrowed it down to which one."

So that was the news. Perry had called him in to let him know the detective was clean. The culprit had yet to be named, though. Micah couldn't wait to put whoever it was who had let Maggie take the rap for his crimes out of his miserable existence.

"Oh yeah, and why do you make me waste my time on people who are so Goddamn squeaky-clean?" Perry complained. "Your employers were beyond boring and I really do think I'm going to charge you an annoyance fee. My skills aren't to be wasted."

Micah nodded once. "Sometimes we need to know who the good people are."

"A bit of common sense always worked for me."

Micah seriously doubted Perry took anyone at face value. Their young hostess appeared, again tapping gently on the door, then opening it without waiting for anyone to give her permission to enter. Two waiters carrying trays entered and breakfast items were spread out on the table. There was enough food to feed ten people, if not more, steaming before them with mixed aromas that quickly woke up Micah's stomach.

He suddenly wished he was sharing a breakfast like this with Maggie. Micah imagined her sitting across from him, her hair unbrushed and tousled around her face. Her cheeks would be pink still from sleep and her smile sheepish as they stared at each other and remembered the sex from the night before.

Micah never knew a lady would enjoy anal sex as much as Maggie had. She wasn't putting on an act to impress him, either. He doubted thoughts like that even entered Maggie's brain. She was honest and sincere to a fault, the exact opposite of him. Maybe that was the reason for the strong attraction. Micah had finally found a woman who was the yin to his yang. Maggie worked her books honestly at the club. She believed there was good in everyone and approached them as if there were. When she had a new thought, she wanted to share it. If she liked someone, she told them. And if someone pissed her off, Maggie had a temper to take on the best of them.

Micah pulled himself out of his thoughts, worried for a moment that dwelling on Maggie might have actually made him smile. Some of her comments the night before had been so spontaneous, so open and humorous, she'd made him laugh. Micah didn't laugh. He didn't smile. But then, he didn't get lost in thought during breakfast over the woman he'd been with the night before.

His phone hadn't received a text message telling him someone had left his house. Maggie was still there. Micah had a hard time fighting off the urge to hurry this meeting up and race back home. Climbing back into bed with Maggie sounded a lot more pleasurable than listening to Perry rant and pulling out the information he needed from the man.

So far, he'd learned the Kings were clean, something he'd pretty much already concluded. But with the suspicious behavior around that detective, Micah needed proof. He'd also learned that Perry was inclined to believe whoever was behind the Club Paradise money laundering was right here in the city, in LA. Micah might have guessed a drug lord in Mexico. He also suspected that a few cops might be padding their measly paychecks with some serious bucks. Neither appeared to be the case. Perry hadn't clarified but Micah would love to know why he believed the backbone of the operation was a city official.

"Micah," Perry said softly, but firmly.

Micah realized he was poking his fork into the yolk of his eggs while his thoughts got the best of him. He raised his head slowly, unwilling to give Perry the satisfaction of snapping him out of his thoughts.

"I have a message for you."

"What?" He picked up a sausage link and put the whole thing in his mouth.

"You're going to take a trip today."

"Oh yeah?" The only place he planned on heading was back to his house and to Maggie.

"Yes," Perry said firmly. He dug into his pants pocket and pulled out a business card. "You're going to Santa Clarita. It's not too far north, shouldn't take you more than an hour to get there. Here is the address. You can thank me later."

Micah took the card and Perry leaned back, studying his fingernails. He didn't show any interest in the many serving dishes between them, all full of delicious-looking food.

"What's this?" he demanded, turning the card over and staring at the address. There was a street address, then Room 212. It looked like the address to a hotel.

"There aren't many people who know how to reach me directly." Perry gave Micah a pointed look. "Those who do know how much I appreciate discretion. I offer the same to everyone I spend time with."

Micah tried making sense out of what the man was saying.

"Therefore, if someone contacts me and asks if I've spoken with someone else, I wouldn't tell them. It's a courtesy, and one I appreciate in return."

"Okay," Micah said slowly.

Perry nodded at the card in Micah's hand. "You should probably head out soon. If I understand right, they will only be at that address for the rest of today."

"They?" Micah asked.

"Yes."

Micah studied the card. Someone had asked Perry if they could reach him. Someone who knew how to contact Perry the same way Micah did. Perry wouldn't tell this person if he had spoken with Micah or not, but had apparently taken down information from this person in case he did speak with Micah. He was now passing this information on.

"Now understand," Perry said, using his gentle, friendly

tone. "I'm not an answering service. I don't make it a habit of relaying messages. But I am privy to some information that most might not know. Such as the reason you're here in LA by yourself."

Micah looked up at him, his appetite suddenly gone. "What are you saying?"

"I'm saying go to that address. Leave soon. Enjoy your reunion on me but know I don't make a habit of bringing people together."

"People together," Micah murmured. He suddenly got it. Staring at the card for another moment, he then looked across the table at Perry. "My dad and uncle."

Perry nodded. "Get going."

There would be no heading back to the house to crawl into bed with Maggie. Micah had considered for a moment stopping there to let her know he might be gone for a while. He refused to give himself the privilege. It would have sounded too much like they were a couple. Micah needed to clear his head. The drive up to Santa Clarita would do him good. Micah would help Maggie figure out who was really doing the money laundering, clear her name, then he would have to move on. Helping her had compromised his location and the entire reason he'd come to LA. Micah would have to find another town to hide out in for the remaining months until he could seek out the men who'd ordered the hit on that CIA agent.

The address was to a nice hotel in Santa Clarita, which appeared to be a clean, laid-back community, so unlike the fast-paced lifestyle of LA. Micah parked his bike in the parking lot, then entered the lavish hotel and walked through the lobby. The employees behind the front desk smiled at him, but didn't question what he was doing there. He found the signs indicating where the rooms were and took a glass elevator to the second floor. The hallway opened to the fancy lobby below, but Micah focused on the room numbers until he reached Room 212. He knocked twice.

The door opened almost immediately and Micah stared

at his father's solemn expression. Micah got the overwhelming impression he'd done something wrong and entered the room, not turning around when his father closed the door and followed him.

"Micah," his uncle Joe said, standing from where he'd been sitting at a round table with a laptop on it. His uncle tapped the mouse, probably closing out whatever he'd been doing, then approached Micah with open arms. "It is so good to see you."

Jacob Mulligan, Micah's father, came up behind the two of them and patted Micah on the back. Jacob and Joseph Mulligan, twins, weren't identical, but there were times when their actions matched. Jacob, who seldom hugged anyone, took his turn wrapping his arms around Micah just as his uncle Joe had.

"How are you doing, boy?" his father asked quietly.

Micah straightened after the warm greeting and tugged his shirt. Both his father and uncle were studying him, drawing their own conclusions. Micah wondered what they might already know. He never thought for a moment either one of them would be ignorant of his actions. They never were.

"It's been a long three months so far," he told them truthfully.

"Almost four," his father pointed out, then walked around Micah to stand behind the laptop where his uncle had been sitting. He focused on the screen. "Tell us about Maggie O'Malley."

Micah sighed. They would, of course, know everything about what he'd been doing. Someday Micah would spend all of his time tracking their every move just to show them how it felt.

"She approached me after being questioned by the police."

"We already know about her and Club Paradise," Uncle Joe said, returning to his seat at the laptop.

"We want to know why you're spending so much time with her," his father concluded, finishing Uncle Joe's thought.

He remained standing behind his brother and stared at Micah with that hard look that used to scare the crap out of him as a kid. He wasn't a kid anymore.

"Because I want to," he told both of them, not caring if his tone was a bit harsh.

"What are you going to do once you solve her problems?" Uncle Joe asked.

Micah refused to sigh. He'd already accepted the truth and knew what his father and uncle needed to hear. "I already know I need to relocate again once this is all over with Maggie."

"Good." His father walked around Uncle Joe and slapped his hand on his thigh. "Good enough," he added, nodding once. "As long as you don't let her get under your skin. Fuck her all you want, boy. But remember who you are, and what your real intentions are while you're here."

"I've never forgotten who I am," Micah told his father, meeting his hard gaze. His dad didn't intimidate him anymore. He respected the hell out of him, and gave him credit for everything Micah knew today. But he had no problem facing him, man-to-man, and letting him know exactly how things were. "I will help Maggie. And I'm going to enjoy the time I'm with her. But if you think for a second that I would reveal to her anything more than what she believes I am right now, then you underestimate me."

Micah raised his hand, stopping any reprimand his father might have given. "Not for one minute have I ever let my guard down. I won't give in during pillow talk and reveal to anyone who, or what, I really am."

Micah would have loved to have had that pillow talk. His phone beeped, and he looked away from his father. Grabbing his phone, he stared at the screen for only a moment. He'd received the text message telling him someone had just left his house. Micah closed down the emotions that might have stirred thinking about Maggie. His uncle and father were on his ass, already thinking Maggie might compromise all of them. Micah didn't want to think about what either of them might do if they debriefed him and found her to be a liability.

"What are you doing?" his father asked, coming closer and staring at the phone.

Micah pulled up the particular app he'd installed and activated his alarm system. He glanced at his father, who was still staring at his phone.

"I'm activating the alarm system at my house."

"Why didn't you do that before you left?"

Micah told them what they wanted to hear. "Because I needed to wait for my house to be empty before doing it."

"That beep we just heard told you that your house was now empty?"

"Yup."

His father sighed and walked away from him. Micah finished what he was doing and looked up as his dad rubbed the back of his head.

"I want to show you something," Uncle Joe said, and reached for the chair next to him at the table. "Come over here, boy."

Micah would be fifty and his father and uncle would still be calling him boy. Micah took the chair his uncle offered.

"Look at this."

Micah stared at the screen. "What am I seeing?"

Uncle Joe had been the one who was quick with the computers. Micah tended to be more like his old man. He got the basics, but computers had never been his specialty. Micah worked better face-to-face with people. Chatting on computers took away the ability to read the face and emotion behind the words spoken.

"This is Micah Jones's background history. There isn't much there."

"I didn't think an elaborate background was necessary."

"No. I agree." His uncle glanced over at him and smiled. "Keep it simple. Nothing wrong with that." He nodded at the screen. "This is a simple people search program. It's pretty much idiot-proof. But look at this." He tapped the screen.

"What?" Micah leaned closer.

"This is a special program I have running on the side."
He smiled as he explained. Uncle Joe loved manipulating
any program and was always proud of himself when he
managed to gather inside information the three of them
wouldn't have had otherwise. He had that look on his face
now. "It's showing me who has checked out your background."

"It is?"

"And it shows where they were when they were checking
you out," his father announced.

Micah looked over his shoulder at his dad. He didn't have
the same satisfied grin Micah's uncle did. Micah looked
back at the computer screen.

"Who checked me out?" he asked.

"It appears your girl did some investigating."

Micah looked closer. Uncle Joe's program was pulled up
in a small box next to the people search website. It displayed
an address and then offered a street view of where this address was.

So, Maggie was more than a bit curious about him. She'd
done a search and had come up with nothing. Micah's background was a lot more blank than most people's, but that
was explainable. He leaned back, laced his fingers behind
his head, and looked from his uncle to his father.

"This isn't something to be concerned about."

"Finish up your job with her," his father instructed. "There
is a town up in Utah. Logden is a good, quiet community. I
can get you a job up there without any problem. There are
several houses that rent by the month outside the city. It's
quiet, uneventful. We'll shack up together for a while. I think
that will be best for all of us."

Micah understood he was the bread and butter for his dad
and uncle. It made sense they would keep a close eye on him
wherever he went. And he'd planned on heading out once
everything was resolved with Maggie. For some reason,
hearing how his father already had it set up for him to leave
didn't sit well with him.

He looked at both of them again. "Is that where the two of you have been this whole time?"

"Nope. I found you and sought out your dad," Uncle Joe said.

"I thought we were going to stay separated for a year," Micah said.

"All of that changed when the announcement came out about Sylvester Neice."

Micah's attention shot to his uncle at the mention of the CIA agent Micah had killed. "What announcement?" he demanded.

His father smiled for the first time since Micah had entered the room. "It appears our year has been cut short."

Chapter Twelve

"Why are you following me around the house? Just leave me alone, Aiden." Maggie tried closing her bedroom door in her brother's face.

He proved the stronger. "You're going to listen to me. It's for your own good," he insisted, entering her room and following her across it to her bathroom. "He has a prepaid cell phone."

"So . . ."

"So, it's a TracFone. Which means," he continued, raising his voice as if anticipating her interruption, "no one can track his cell phone records. No one, not the police or anyone."

Maggie sighed. Her brother had become obsessed by this. "I'm going to take a shower, Aiden. Go spend your time doing something productive for a change."

"Protecting my little sister is productive," he roared.

Maggie almost jumped from his sudden explosive anger. She wanted to say she had Micah to protect her. That wouldn't have gone over well at the moment. She leaned against her bathroom door, took a deep breath and counted to three.

It didn't work. Aiden still had her pissed off. She tried to sound cool when she made one last effort to get him off the Micah subject.

"Aiden," she began. "Has it ever occurred to you that Micah may live the way he lives for a reason?"

"Yes, because he's a bad person," he barked.

"Only bad people try to stay off the government's radar? And that of every other snoopy person on the planet?" she added, and gave him a look that let him know he was at the top of the snoop list.

"What are you saying? What do you know about him that you aren't telling me?"

"A lot," she snapped. "All of which is none of your business. Now back off and let me shower."

This time she did manage to shut the door in her brother's face. For good measure she locked it, then sagged against it. She pressed her back against the door and let her feet slide forward.

"Shit," she hissed, not sure how much longer she'd be able to hold together.

It was going on day two since she'd seen Micah. There were guys she'd dated in the past that she would see one, maybe two nights a week. They would talk over the phone occasionally, usually to set up the next date. The rest of the time she lived her own life. Maybe it was different this time because she had no life.

Or maybe it was different this time because she and Micah weren't dating.

"I'm going to go nuts," she wailed, although she kept her voice down in case Aiden hadn't left her room. Just to be sure, she yanked open her bathroom door. Aiden had gone so far off the deep end on this Micah thing that she wouldn't have put it past him to try snooping around her bedroom. He wasn't there.

"Yup, definitely going nuts." She walked over to close and lock her bedroom door then returned to her bathroom for a shower.

By early evening, Maggie had her parents fed and was cleaning up the dishes when her phone rang. She all but yanked it out of her pocket with damp, sudsy hands. It wasn't Micah. He was at work. She had no pride. She'd driven by earlier that day and his motorcycle had been parked alongside the

Kings' house, next to the KFA office. After waking up alone at his house and waiting a couple of hours for him to come home, she'd finally left; she hadn't heard from him since.

"Hello," Annalisa said. "What are you doing?"

Maggie stared at bubbles of soap popping in the kitchen sink. "Getting dishpan hands," she grumbled.

Annalisa laughed. She definitely seemed a lot happier than she had the first day Maggie had talked to her. Either talking to her mom for the first time in two years had really helped bring some peace to her, or Annalisa had been happy all along with her girlfriend and tried sorting things out with Mom out of family loyalty.

"I thought I'd give you a call and see if you'd like to go see a movie with us. We're in town tonight seeing friends, and—well . . ." She hesitated. "I thought I'd see if you wanted to go with us."

"You thought you'd check in on the family loon."

"It's not like that."

She held her phone between her shoulder and ear as she dried her hands. Maggie really should buy her mother a dishwasher, especially since she would be the one using it.

"You went to bat for me, big sis," Annalisa said, her soft relaxed tone sounding as if she didn't have a worry in the world. "And Goddamn, with all the issues going on in your life, you were there to help me out? All I want to do is take you to a movie and say thank you."

Maggie wasn't convinced Aiden didn't put their younger sister up to this. Thank God he'd finally left, since he had used up what vacation time he had and needed to be at work the next day. Deidre would still drop in when she felt like it but otherwise the O'Malley home was back to normal, an empty nest shy of Maggie. And since she'd opened her big mouth after slamming shots and announced how persecuted she was to have to stay home and care for her parents, both her mom and dad now wanted her to move out.

"I'm not sure I'm up to a movie, but thanks," Maggie said, pulling her thoughts together. Lately she'd drifted from thought to thought with no apparent ground to hold her mind on any one topic for too long. Unless of course it was Micah; then she'd be lost in thought on him all day. "I'll probably call it an early night."

"Do you want us to come hang out with you for a bit?"

Now she knew Aiden had put Annalisa up to this.

"I'll be fine," she insisted.

"Okay," Annalisa said in a more determined voice. "It's just that I'm worried about you, Mags. So sue me."

Maggie blinked at Annalisa's outburst.

"You've always been the rock, the stable one. You always have your act together, and if any of us ever fall apart—and with this family it's always one of us, if not all of us—you are always there to calmly help us out. So who is helping you out, huh? That is all I'm trying to do."

Maybe Maggie had been a bit premature in guessing Aiden had put Annalisa up to calling her. "I'm sorry, Annalisa. I really am."

"Forget it. I just wanted to help take your mind off things."

"No. I was wrong. I'm sorry," she mumbled again. "And you're right. Lately my mind is off the charts thinking about too many things. I honestly couldn't concentrate on a movie, or company. But soon, okay? Love you, little sis."

"Love you, too," Annalisa mumbled. "And apology accepted."

Maggie smiled and hung up. That had been a close call. She was getting paranoid over her brother hounding her about Micah. And she had to admit, some of it was because she didn't want to think he might be right, even about some of it. Maggie knew in her heart Micah was a good man. That wasn't open to discussion. She wanted Micah to be on her shit list since he hadn't talked to her in—she looked at the clock on the microwave—over forty-eight hours. It sucked that she couldn't add him to that list since he was under no obligation to call her, even if she had given him her ass virginity.

Maggie finished up the dishes and pouted. Annalisa was right. She was going nuts and needed time away from it all. But until her life was in order, she couldn't escape from any of it. Maybe another person could, but Maggie didn't leave without her affairs in order. Still, once they were, she had half a mind to get the hell away from her family.

By eight her mother was sleeping and her father was sitting in bed next to his wife reading. Maggie checked on them one last time then wished them good night. Her mother looked so small cuddled under her blankets. And her father looked old when he glanced at her over his reading glasses and whispered good night to her. How would they make it without her?

Maggie pulled her phone out the moment she was in her car. She called Micah's phone. It went straight to voicemail. She hung up. Aiden had told her that Micah had a prepaid cell phone. Maybe he'd run out of minutes. Maybe that was why he wasn't calling her.

It wasn't as if she had anything to say to him, other than to scream at him. She thought back since they'd met each other. Had he gone a day without talking to her? She was pretty sure they hadn't gone a day without seeing each other. Maggie was having serious Micah withdrawal.

She'd already decided that she needed to put her life in order. Call it her fixation with numbers, but Maggie knew she was losing control of her mind and her temper so often because her life was in complete chaos. The sooner things were all neat and organized again, the happier she'd be.

It would make her nuts sitting around waiting for Micah to call her. Maggie might not be a wiz with firearms the way he was—or the way Deidre was. But so be it. She would just have to do her best to not go anywhere dangerous.

A small voice in the back of her head pointed out that Club Paradise obviously wasn't the safe place she'd once believed it was. But the place was closed down. No one would be there. If her key didn't work, she would turn around and leave. She needed answers. Maybe no one else understood.

Maggie had to find out who was behind all of this now, or she'd go nuts.

By the time she pulled into Club Paradise's parking lot, Maggie wasn't positive that she wasn't already nuts. What had made her think the place would be safe because it was closed for business?

The usual floodlights that had lit up the parking lot at night weren't on. The many lights along the building were off. The neon light at the edge of the parking lot that flashed CLUB PARADISE was off. The building was barely visible from the road. Her headlights glowed along the side of the building as she pulled around back. But when she turned off her car, she was cloaked in the thick, inky blackness that the building she had once considered a home away from home had now become.

Her heart thumped against her ribs when she got out of the car. For a moment she couldn't catch her breath. Maybe this wasn't a good idea. She could hop back in her car, leave, and be safely home in half an hour. Then she could cuddle up in her bed with a good book and forget about all her worries.

Like that had worked for her so far. She hadn't been able to enjoy her books, or even solve some of the tougher math problems in her *Math Wizards* magazine. Going home was not an option.

"It's just the dark," she mumbled to herself and forced her feet to move.

Maggie walked across the parking lot to the back door then cursed her stupidity for not picking out the right key while still in her car. She couldn't see a thing.

"Damn it," she cursed when she dropped her keys on the ground.

She bent down to feel for them when the sound of someone approaching made her freeze. Maggie pulled her hand off the ground but remained where she was, frozen, squatted in front of the back door to the kitchen. She couldn't swallow from fear when footsteps came closer. Someone was walking alongside the building, and they were almost to the back.

Maggie turned her head just as a tall figure came into view. A bloodcurdling scream burned her throat at the sight of the gun in the man's hand. Maggie ran. She ran harder than she'd ever run in her life. Her shoe lost traction over the gravel parking lot and she went down, burning the crap out of her knee when she scraped the flesh off it.

She scrambled to her feet and hurried to her car. Just as she rounded the driver's side, she remembered that she didn't have her keys. Despite her heart thumping too loudly in her chest and a ringing sound filling her ears, Maggie could hear the loud thumping of shoes on the gravel lot as whoever it was gained speed on her.

What should she do? All she could do was run around her car and toward the street. She didn't have her keys. Not that there would be time to unlock her car and get in before they gained on her. Even if she pushed the button on her keychain to unlock her car, by the time she opened her door they would be on her.

Why did she think coming here was a good idea?

A thick arm wrapped around her waist and yanked her off her feet. Maggie wouldn't go down without a fight. Maybe if she kicked and fought hard enough they might drop their gun. She had a slight chance of living through this. Maggie would take any chance she had.

"Forget the keys to your car again?" a familiar voice whispered in her ear.

Maggie took her time slowing down her kicking and struggling. Recognition seeped into her brain, and she finally stilled. Micah took just as long releasing his hold on her. When he let her go, then turned her around and gently stroked her hair out of her face, she didn't know whether to cry or scream. His hand lingered on the side of her face.

"What are you doing here?" he asked.

Even in the darkness Maggie saw concern in his eyes. Or was it something else? Had he missed her? His hand moved to the back of her neck and he pulled her face closer to his, then tugged on her hair to make her lean her head back. She should have pride. She should demand to know why he hadn't called or sought her out for two days. This wasn't her imagination. Maggie had too practical a brain to create some kind of love story in her brain that didn't really exist. Micah had feelings for her. They might be as confused and as tormented as her feelings for him were, but nonetheless they existed.

His kiss began soft, gentle, and hesitant. She wasn't sure if she demanded more or if he did. Her arms went up and around his broad shoulders at the same time his hands moved to her back and crushed her against him. Their mouths opened and their tongues intertwined. He tasted like coffee and possibly beer. She couldn't tell.

There wasn't any questioning his quickly aroused state, or how much he wanted her when he crushed her against that incredibly strong body of his and growled fiercely into her mouth. She moaned in return and arched her back, feeling her breasts swell and her crotch grow soaked.

Maggie was no longer scared. The dark night didn't bother her. Her world didn't seem grossly out of order. It was amazing how being with Micah seemed to put everything in order.

That part was the fairy tale. Maggie didn't buy into cheesy romance. Those paperback novels that made love out to be some formula that, if followed properly, always turned into happily ever after made her sick. Primarily because that wasn't how it was. If it were, she would have plugged the right numbers into that formula long ago. Happily ever after couldn't be solved by some equation.

Maggie broke off the kiss, lowered her head, and pushed against that virile chest.

"Stop," she whispered, then licked her now swollen lips and tasted him on them. She had a logical brain. It was time to use it. "Don't do this."

"You're right."

Her heart sank. Despite how rational she prided herself on being, hearing him agree with her stung. She looked up at his handsome face. It was dark enough that even standing this close to each other, she might not be seeing his face accurately.

Shadows made his cheekbones appear higher. His dark hazel eyes were shielded by his black lashes, and his mouth closed as she stared at him. He definitely wasn't smiling.

"I can't take this," she informed him and turned around then marched around the back side of her car and to the back door to the club, where her keys were somewhere on the ground.

For a moment she had thought she'd once again seen into Micah's soul. This time she had sworn she'd seen love, and a desire for her so strong that he'd lost his head and had kissed her behind the club, which wasn't the safest place in the world. Maggie didn't want to know where he'd put his gun, although she knew that what she had felt pressing against her during their kiss was no gun. But Micah had a gun. She knew what she saw when he came around the building.

She spun around in her tracks and Micah ran into her.

"Damn," she cried out when his chin hit the top of her head and her body smacked against his rock-hard body. All wind flew out of her lungs.

"Crap, sweetheart," Micah growled, grabbing her arms. "What the hell are you doing?"

"I was about to demand the same of you." She stepped backward and he let go of her, which was what she wanted. Just his hands on her seemed to do odd things to her body, which in turn caused her brain to forget how to be sensible. "What are you doing here?"

"What am I doing here?" he bellowed, grabbing her by the arm. "What are you doing here?" This time he whispered.

They stood at the back door and he pulled out his cell phone, then used the light from it to move over the ground in front of the door until he spotted her keys. Maggie reached down and grabbed them, embarrassed and pissed that she hadn't thought to do that same thing when she'd first dropped them.

"I work here," she snapped, her frustration mounting.

Micah kept the light from his phone on her keys while she searched for the one she needed. She held it up then

yanked it back when he tried taking it from her. When he
cocked one eyebrow at her she gave him a smug look.

"And you're here because?" she prompted, unable to keep
her temper in line. "And don't feed me some bullshit about
following me, because I would have noticed."

"You didn't notice me parked across the street when you
pulled in here."

"I wasn't looking on that side of the street. I was looking
on this side of the street since this was the side of the street
I was turning toward." She looked away from him first and
slid the key into the lock. "Son of a bitch. No one changed
the locks."

"Why would they? The police aren't going to change the
locks. The owner of the building is in jail."

She almost corrected him but remembered that Uncle
Larry's name was still on the deed to the building. She had
finished paperwork to turn the ownership of the building
over to some corporation. Uncle Larry had insisted Maggie
take his name off as owner. She had argued that they
couldn't just turn ownership over. But when she'd insisted
on checking out the corporation, her uncle had lost his temper and demanded that for once she just do as he said without second-guessing his every word. Maggie wondered why
she'd forgotten about that until now.

"What are you doing?" Micah asked when she reached
for the light switch.

"No one can tell these lights are on from the outside."

"They'll know they are on if they come inside."

Maggie had her hand on the light switch just inside the
back door and stared at Micah. He must have seen the question on her face because he answered before she asked.

"I've been driving by several times a day, watching this
building. Sooner or later whoever is in on this with your
uncle will show up here. I really think this is truly the scene
of the crime. I was parked across the street." He paused as if
he changed his mind about what he was going to say next.
"Imagine my surprise to see you pull into the lot."

"So you came at me with a gun?" she demanded. "If you'd simply said it was you, I wouldn't have screamed and run for my life."

"I don't walk into darkness where my surroundings are unfamiliar without being armed," he told her flatly.

She accepted the answer. That was Micah. And she'd be smart to hear his words and convince herself that they were truly not compatible.

"So how would someone get into the building?" she demanded, shifting her thoughts. She didn't want to think about how she and Micah weren't right for each other. He was here, next to her, and as pissed as she was that he'd scared the crap out of her, she was also exhilarated to be with him. Not that she was ready to let him know that. "I'm the only one with the key. Uncle Larry didn't even have a key. He always lost it."

"Are you sure he always lost it?"

"Of course I'm sure," she hissed, suddenly not sure at all.

"Well okay."

Micah closed the back door. This time it was even darker than it had been outside. Maggie was proud of herself for not jumping when he touched her arm. His body moved closer until his front was pressed against her backside.

"Do you have a flashlight?" he asked, changing the subject.

What was it about him and whispering into her ear from behind? Chills rushed over her flesh. He was touching her arm. He had to feel her goose bumps spread, which meant he knew what he was doing to her. Maggie shook her head instead of answering him.

He sighed, and she waited out the silence that followed. So help him, if he tried doing anything to her right now she would not miss her aim despite how dark it was.

"Turn on the light."

Maggie flipped the switch and stepped away from him, praying he didn't hear her sigh with relief.

"Why did you come here?" he asked.

Out of habit she headed toward her office. "I was going to search, look for anything that would prove my innocence."

"Okay," he said slowly. "Where are the best places to search?"

Maggie stared at her office. She had turned on the light but remained in the doorway when Micah came up behind her. She was a strong woman. There was a lot she could handle. But damn if one blow after another hadn't been sent her way. She stepped inside and squatted in front of the statuette that she had kept on her filing cabinet.

The small statue of the Mother Mary holding baby Jesus had been a gift from her grandmother O'Malley on Maggie's confirmation. It was shattered, most of it dust, but she picked up one of the remaining larger pieces and her eyes filled with tears.

"This was a gift," she murmured.

"Who gave it to you?"

"My grandmother during confirmation. It's one of the Catholic sacraments where we become adults in the Catholic Church." She wasn't sure why she was telling him this. Micah remained silent behind her. She stood slowly and spotted the rosary and small octagonal container that it had been in. Maggie reached down and picked them up. "These were on top of my filing cabinet, too. Mrs. Hope, our religion teacher, gave each of us our own rosary in the eighth grade. The rosary was in this," she told him, and returned the beads to the case that had held them. "They're made out of crushed rose petals and have been blessed by the pope." She held the beads up to her nose. They still smelled of roses. One small thing in her office that wasn't ruined.

Otherwise it looked as if a major earthquake had destroyed the place. The filing cabinets were on the floor. Her desk drawers were on their side next to her desk. All of their contents had been spilled onto her desk. And as if ransacking every inch of her office hadn't been enough, the walls had major holes in them. She guessed whoever had searched in here got pissed when they couldn't find anything and decided to look in the walls, too. Her home away from home had been destroyed.

Maggie dropped the piece of the statue of Mother Mary and baby Jesus on the floor and put the rosary in her purse. "I guess there's no reason to search anywhere in here," she said. She took one last look at her office and turned to the door.

Micah still stood in the doorway. "I'm sorry."

She lifted her gaze to his face. He sincerely looked as if he meant it. Maggie wasn't sure why that surprised her. She'd seen quite a few emotions replace his usual stony expression. Usually they were only visible during sex.

"Thank you," she murmured.

He stepped out of her way and turned his back to her. "Let's focus on the kitchen. The lights are only on back here, right?"

"Right. There is a light switch on the other side of that door." She pointed at the closed door that led out into the club—the same door Micah had hauled her through the first day she'd met him. Little had she known that would be the last day of her life as she'd known it. Granted, she'd only worked at Club Paradise since she had finished college, but up until the day Micah had sauntered into her life, Maggie had existed in a world of numbers and sensibility. Everything had its place. There were never surprises. Her schedule never varied.

God! She'd been boring as hell. This life she had now was a bit too extreme for her liking, but maybe once this was all over she would put some effort into being a bit less dull. *If Micah stays in your life there will never be a dull moment.*

And how often would she see gunshot wounds? Maggie shivered at the thought.

"Are you cold?" Micah asked, coming up next to her and running his hand down the back of her head.

"No. Just nerves," she admitted and tried smiling up at him.

"You're safe."

He didn't elaborate. Not that he had to. Micah would protect her to the death. She walked toward the first row of tall shelves where cooking utensils were still stacked. This time when she shivered, Micah didn't notice. Which was a good thing, since it was not nerves that twisted her tummy in knots, but a scary premonition. Would Micah kill to protect her?

"Are there gloves in here?" he asked.

"Gloves?"

"So that we don't leave fingerprints."

"Oh." She looked around the kitchen then snapped her fingers. "There might be."

Micah followed her, his solid footsteps as powerful sounding as the rest of him. Maggie moved to stand where Max usually started his day, in his personal space. The counter had been wiped clean, and she imagined that on the last day he had worked here he'd cleaned everything before he had left. She wondered where he was now. Hers wasn't the only life that had changed that day.

She started to open one of the drawers in Max's workstation and hesitated. "How do I search for gloves and not leave fingerprints?" she asked, looking over her shoulder at Micah.

"Where were you going to look?"

She pointed. "In these drawers."

Micah reached around her and opened the first drawer. As Maggie suspected, it was full of odds and ends, everything from paintbrushes to rulers to random-sized measuring cups and flour sifters. Micah closed that drawer and opened the next.

"Bingo," Maggie exclaimed and pulled out the kind of gloves doctors wore before giving an exam. "Don't ask what these are doing here. I don't know. I just remembered having seen them in here months ago when you just now asked about them." She pulled out two pairs and handed one of them to him. "Hope they fit."

"I'm more concerned about you."

She gave him an odd look. "Why aren't you worried

about you? Wouldn't it be just as damaging if the police found your fingerprints here?"

"The cops aren't going to dust this place for prints again."

"Then why are we doing this?" she asked, pausing after pulling one glove over her hand.

"Because if whoever is laundering money comes back here and believes things aren't as they left them, they could check for prints. I'd be less worried about them finding my prints. We don't want anyone else after you."

"Good point." She was relieved to hear him say that he had fingerprints and immediately was mad at her brother all over again for putting the thought in her head that Micah might not have fingerprints. "So, do you know what you're looking for?"

Micah stared at her, his solemn expression unreadable. "What were you going to look for?"

"Another accounting book," she said immediately. "I think I'm not the first person who thinks it exists and that it might be here," she added pointedly, nodding toward her office.

They spent the next half an hour working in silence. Maggie worked her way down one of the tall shelves stocked with kitchen utensils. Micah's back was to her as he went through the items on the shelves opposite her. She picked up every kitchen product on each shelf, turning it over, examining it, then returning it to where it was. The shelves were taller than she was and lined up next to each other in rows. She never realized how much stuff was in the kitchen until they'd finished the first row.

The next row of shelves were full of pots and pans of every size imaginable. They made quite the racket picking up pots to look underneath and checking stacks of pans.

"Hold on," Micah said, sticking out his hand.

"What?" They were halfway down the row, and Maggie held a large soup pot in her hands when she looked at him.

"Put that down, quietly."

She stared at him a moment, but Micah wasn't looking at her. His head was tilted as if he was listening for something. Then Maggie heard it, too.

"Oh crap," she whispered. "Who could be out there?"

Micah took the large soup pot from her and placed it on the shelf. Taking her hand, he moved fast toward the back of the kitchen. She thought they were leaving, but Micah turned off the lights and pulled her against him.

"Don't say a word," he whispered.

Maggie nodded, her eyes wide open in the pitch blackness surrounding them. In the silence she could hear men talking up front. How did they get in? Only she had keys to the place.

The voices grew louder, and Maggie felt a wave of panic hit her when a key sounded in the door leading from the club to the kitchen.

"Is there a light switch at that door for the kitchen?" Micah whispered.

She shook her head.

"We need a good hiding place."

Micah was telling her to suggest a place for them to hide. Her brain was whirling with fear at the thought of being caught in here by men who quite possibly had ordered someone to frame her for money laundering, and arranged for someone to try to run her over. She heard the key turn the lock in the door.

"Sweetheart, now isn't the time to panic," Micah whispered.

"Right." She gave herself a firm shake.

"We're going to take down the assholes who have made your life hell. We can do that if they don't know we're here."

"This way." Maggie grabbed his hand and moved through the darkness. She knew the kitchen pretty well and led them to the supply closet, or where she was pretty sure it was.

"Where are we going?" Micah whispered.

The door opened and two men entered. They hadn't turned on the lights in the club. Thank God for small miracles!

"Who the fuck designed this place and didn't put light switches at both doors?" a man growled.

Maggie frantically ran her hand along the far wall, searching for the doorknob. When she found it, Micah's hand covered hers. He helped her turn it slowly then open the door, which thankfully didn't squeak. Maggie would eternally be grateful for how neat and orderly Max was. Brooms and mops were hanging on the wall, and buckets were underneath them. The floor in the middle of the closet was clear, and there was enough room for the two of them to stand, closely. Micah pulled her inside with him and closed the door.

He pulled his gloves off and tossed them somewhere on the floor. Maggie did the same and heard hers hit something against the wall. She froze for a moment, afraid she'd knocked something over, but nothing moved. Maggie exhaled and almost hiccuped. She was terrified.

When Micah's arms went around her Maggie blinked, then opened her eyes. She'd had them squeezed shut. Her eyes slowly adjusted to their surroundings when she noticed Micah hadn't closed the closet door all the way. She started to reach for it but it was too late. The kitchen light came on and the men started moving around. Maggie yanked her hand back and clutched Micah's forearm.

"How soon will they be here?" the man who had complained about the light switch asked.

"We shouldn't have to wait too long."

Maggie stiffened. Micah's face lowered until he pressed it next to hers.

"The man who just spoke sounds familiar," she whispered, barely making a sound.

Micah adjusted his arms around her, holding her close. His strong, powerful body touched her everywhere. There was no reason for her heart to be pounding a mile a minute. She was probably in the safest place in the entire city. There were plenty of tall, well-built men, and Maggie had met her fair share over the years. Something about Micah made him seem more a weapon then simply an in-shape good-looking guy.

"Everything is ready?"

The man whose voice she recognized laughed. "Why do you stay in this business if you get so nervous right before the excitement happens? I promise, Frank, we're good to go."

"I'm not nervous. I just like being prepared," Frank complained, defending himself. "You were vague on the phone."

"For obvious reasons. You never can be too careful."

"No one is going to tap your phone, Ryan."

Maggie straightened. That was how she knew his voice. Ryan Stabler was a judge. Not too long ago, a serial killer was tried in his courtroom. Judge Stabler sent the man away for life. He was quite the hero. Stabler was young for a judge, good looking, and the press loved him. There was talk of him having his own column in the paper and even a talk show. He was a local celebrity. Maggie's head started spinning when she remembered that he'd met with her uncle several times earlier that year.

"The moment you start thinking you're invincible is the same moment you can be beaten. Always remember that."

"Save your words of wisdom for your courtroom. This is a different job, and we're partners."

"What do you have ready for these guys?"

"Fine." There were footsteps; it sounded as if Ryan left the kitchen. "Everything is right here."

"Damn, Ryan," Frank said after a minute. His voice was calmer, almost sedated. "You had everything already stored here?"

"I can't carry it around on me." Stabler laughed again. "It wouldn't look good for my image."

Apparently Frank didn't see the need to comment. "This looks like pure shit," he said instead.

"They'll be satisfied." Ryan sounded confident.

"Did you have it delivered here? How did you pull it off when they were expecting Santinos?"

"Yes, and I have a way with people."

Maggie could almost see the judge flashing his broad, toothy smile. Who would have thought that the all-American judge, with his perfect teeth and hair, his flashy car and charming demeanor, was a big-time drug dealer? Maggie couldn't get it to sink in. They'd just implied her uncle had been doing the judge's dirty work before going to jail.

"What about Santinos's daughter or cousin or whatever she is?"

"She's his niece, although close in age from what I've learned," Stabler said, his tone as smooth as satin. "And I'm working on it. Little bitch has had a stroke of good luck but it will run out. If I can't take her out one way, I will find another."

"The good judge speaks," Frank said, chuckling.

"There can be no liabilities, not anymore. Santinos getting busted was the best thing that could have happened to us."

"He did make some mistakes." Frank almost sounded regretful, as if possibly he had liked her uncle.

Nonetheless, a cold sweat broke out over Maggie's body. Judge Stabler was an evil, cruel man. She didn't know him, had never met him, and yet for some reason he was the one trying to have her killed. But why?

"Some mistakes aren't allowed in this line of work. They aren't cost-effective. Santinos had his niece making his travel arrangements when he traveled south. I won't risk her knowing anything else about his business."

"Why didn't the charges stick when they hauled her in?"

"She did too good of a job hiding Santinos's books."

"Santinos said there aren't any books."

Stabler made a scoffing sound. "Can you picture Santinos keeping track of all this in his head? The man isn't that smart. There are ledgers, and the cops were idiots not to find them before questioning her."

"So now we kill her?"

"That's the plan."

"What about that Jones guy?"

"He's not Jones," Stabler hissed, a sneer in his voice.

"What do you mean he's not Jones? Isn't that his name?"

"Who he is, is on a need-to-know basis, and if you know he'll kill you."

"I know nothing," Frank smirked.

"Keep it that way."

Maggie's head was spinning. All the answers and information put her brain on overload. Despite her uncle swearing Maggie didn't keep records of whatever it was he'd been doing on the side, not even his partners believed him. She'd been hauled in for questioning on Judge Stabler's orders, or so it sounded. Then when they couldn't charge her with anything, people were following her and trying to kill her simply because they didn't believe her uncle and thought she knew too much. If that weren't too much to take in, Stabler had just suggested that Micah wasn't who he claimed to be. What the hell was that supposed to mean? Micah hadn't even flinched when they'd mentioned him. He remained the calm, sturdy rock with his muscular arms wrapped around her protectively.

Silence followed, and Maggie heard one of them pacing. They were waiting for someone to show up. Judge Stabler was doing a drug deal in her club. But why here? Was it because the club was closed down? It was probably a great location. No one would think to come here to look for drug dealers. But who had the key to the club and how did they get it? Had her uncle lied about losing his key? He'd told her not to bother making another one and had laughed it off at the time, telling her he'd probably just lose it. Uncle Larry always showed up after she'd opened the club for the day. She was always the last person to leave, after she'd finished all the paperwork. Anyone watching would think she ran the club, which she had. Did her Uncle Larry set her up? Apparently he hadn't really lost his key. Somehow he'd given the key to Stabler.

Micah adjusted his arms around her and Maggie found herself sagging against him. In the dark, just the two of them, there was plenty of room for all this insanity to roll around in her head. How long ago had her uncle *lost* his key? Months ago; she couldn't remember. How long had she been running a club that was a cover for a huge drug operation? From the beginning? Maggie felt sick.

Also, Micah might be more dangerous than she'd imagined. He wouldn't hurt her, though. Maybe that's why she'd been pissed and hurt when he hadn't talked to her in over forty-eight hours. There was a connection between the two of them. If he tried denying it she would kick his ass no matter how dangerous he was supposed to be.

As if he read her thoughts, Micah ran his fingers up and down her arm. Her hand moved to his and she locked fingers with hers. They held hands, waiting out the silence in anticipation of act two.

It sounded like a chair scraped over the bare kitchen floor. The high-pitched sound made Maggie jump, and she almost shrieked. Micah's hand moved to her mouth, and she covered his hand with hers. Once again their fingers interlocked and he moved their hands together down her body to her waist. There were hurried footsteps, a door opening and closing, then two men began speaking in Spanish. Their conversation was in low, soft baritones; they spoke very quickly. Maggie barely managed to pick out a few words here and there. Other than hearing mention of them being in a hurry, she wasn't sure what was said.

"Señores, you'll have to forgive me but I'm not bilingual like you are. I'm afraid this transaction will have to take place in English."

"Why isn't Larry Santinos here?" a man asked. He didn't speak with an accent although he was one of the men who had just been speaking in Spanish.

"Eric, you remember he went to jail," Frank said. "This is Judge Ryan Stabler. He's here with everything as we agreed. Judge, this is Eric Torres. He is a good friend of mine and Larry's."

"Santinos is still in jail?" Eric repeated everything in Spanish and ended his conversation with his partner with, "And if you agree, senor, we'll speak in English for Senor Joe and Senor Ryan."

"So Senor Santinos remains in jail?" the second man, who had yet to be identified, asked with a thick Spanish accent. "If you are a judge, then why do you leave our friend behind bars?"

"I'm not the judge who can release Santinos," Ryan said in his professional and too-friendly tone. "If I understand his case correctly, it will be a while before he'll be released. Santinos worked for me, though. Everything he told you, I approved."

"I see. Then you are now doing the work of your laborers."

Ryan Stabler's laugh was as fake as the rest of him. It made Maggie sick thinking her uncle was the fall guy for this creep. Stabler would never spend a minute behind bars, let alone be arrested for any crime.

"I don't mind the work when it will make us all incredibly rich men." Stabler said. "But we haven't been properly introduced."

"Forgive me," Torres jumped in. "Judge Stabler, this is Senor Gomez."

"Gomez," Stabler said.

Maggie wondered if they all noticed that Stabler didn't say Senor Gomez but simply used the man's last name. It was a subtle insult and one she wished they would all call him on—even call the drug deal off based on the judge being a rude and pretentious jerk.

"Since Santinos won't be joining us tonight, or anytime soon, I'll conduct all future business transactions with you."

"I will have to see if the quality holds up to what Santinos provided me. He will be missed."

"I guess if you want you could always wait until Santinos can meet with you again. Of course that could be in twenty years, if not longer," Stabler said, then laughed.

Micah's hands moved to her arms. He moved her to the side of the closet and she looked at him through the darkness, her eyes wide and burning.

"Stay here and don't come out," he mouthed.

"What?" Maggie started shaking her head.

Micah stepped around her, left her standing there without him, and walked out of the closet. Was he insane?

"Who the—?"

"Who are you?"

"I'll be damned," Stabler said in a frosty, menacing tone. It was all that was said. Micah didn't speak. But Maggie screamed when she heard gunshots fired. The gun went off again and again. Why the hell had Micah gone out there? Was he dead?

She sunk to the floor of the closet and pushed herself as far from the door as she could manage. When her back hit the wall, she pulled her knees to her chest and wrapped her arms around her legs. They would check the closet. It was where Micah had been hiding. They would check it and she would be dead, too.

The shots ended and an eerie silence followed. The echo of the gun going off still rang in her head. Maggie looked down, resting her forehead on her knees. There wasn't anything she could do. Even if she pulled out her cell phone and called 911, she would be heard and they would kill her before help arrived.

Maggie hugged herself tighter when she heard footsteps. One of them was still alive. *Please be Micah. Please be Micah.*

The closet door opened and light flooded over her. Maggie didn't dare look up.

"Come on, let's go," Micah said calmly and reached down to pick her up.

"What? What happened?"

"Put your face against my chest and walk with me."

She stood, her legs shaking so badly that Micah lifted her off her feet and pressed her head against his chest as he backed out of the closet.

"We'll be out of here in a second," he whispered.

"Mulligan."

Maggie stiffened at the strained voice calling out to them. "Oh God," she whispered and twisted against Micah, although for the life of her she had no idea where to run. She was probably the only one not armed. "Run, Micah. We've got to run."

"You won't get away with this. You've messed with the wrong judge."

Maggie's ears were ringing again. She was shaking terribly and it took a minute before she realized her feet were dangling in the air. That was, until Micah lowered her so her feet touched the floor.

"Walk to the back door. Don't look back." Micah sounded strained.

"You're coming with me," she insisted.

It was one time she wished she had blindly followed instructions. Maggie was standing on her own two feet and Micah pressed his hand into the middle of her back, pushing her toward the back door. She turned, her insistence he come with her on her lips.

No sound came out. Maggie looked in horror at blood splattered against the shelves and kitchen utensils. Four men were lying on the floor, sprawled in strange positions.

"Maggie!" Micah snapped.

She shot her attention to his face. Micah looked frustrated. There was something else, too. Was it pain? Maybe sadness? He blew out a loud, exasperated sigh at the same time that one of the men behind him said something else. Micah turned around and Maggie thought he was going to answer the man. Instead, Micah raised a gun and fired.

"Let's go," he insisted. When he turned toward her, his hand disappeared behind his back. Then the gun was gone.

As easily as someone might pull their wallet out of their back pocket and put it back again, Micah had his gun in his hand and then he didn't.

She was shaking her head, her jaw hanging open, when Micah began pushing her backward.

"Out of here now, sweetheart."

"But wait . . . I mean . . . Are they?" She stammered with every sentence she began and finally gave up.

Later Maggie would remember Micah tugging on his shirt to cover his hand when he turned the doorknob on the back door. That was about all she clearly remembered. They were parked in a very nicely lit-up shopping mall. There was a Bed Bath & Beyond, an American Vintage clothing store, and a Barnes & Noble bookstore, all with bright lights and normal people entering and leaving. Where they were parked, in her car, with her in the passenger seat, the parking lot was empty. There were plenty of vacant stalls on either side of them. At the edge of the parking lot, on the corner of a fairly busy intersection, a Mexican restaurant was doing a fair amount of business.

Everyone's life was in order. People got out of their cars talking with one another or hurrying children to the sidewalk. None of these people knew four men were dead. Holy crap! One of them was Judge Ryan Stabler.

"Are you okay?" Micah looked too big to be sitting behind the wheel of her car.

Maggie looked at him. She didn't remember them driving here. She didn't remember giving him her keys. Micah was so damn sexy. He stared at her, watching her closely.

"You just killed four men." Her voice was trembling. She looked down at her hands. They were trembling, too.

"We had all of our answers," he said simply, as if it had been the plan to kill them all along.

Maybe it had been Micah's plan. Maggie couldn't wrap her brain around any of it and get it to make sense. "But you killed them," she stressed. That was the big hurdle. Once she understood why she'd seen four men lying on Club Paradise's kitchen floor, covered in blood and dead, maybe she would probably understand the rest of it.

"You said he was a judge. You remember overhearing their conversation, right?"

She nodded and at the same time forced her brain to replay facts it would much rather shut out. "Stabler is—was," she corrected herself, "a drug dealer and an asshole." Maggie looked over at Micah. "He thought I knew what my uncle was doing."

"And was having you followed and tried having you run over." Micah covered her trembling hands with his hand. It was cool and felt good holding her. He wasn't shaking. He didn't look bothered at all about having killed the four of them. "Think about it, sweetheart. If we had taken what we'd learned to the police and tried proving your innocence, it would have been our word against a judge."

He had a point. "But now you're going to be charged with murder."

Micah looked very confident when he shook his head. "A judge will be found dead in a nightclub closed down because it was involved in money laundering. He is lying dead among drug dealers and a lot of drugs. Trust me, they are going to keep this very quiet. I'm not going to be charged with anything."

She wished she was as sure about that as he was. Good people weren't accused of crimes. Maggie had been hauled in for a crime she didn't commit. It would be just as terrible if Micah was hauled in for the death of despicable lowlifes. And it was a crime he had committed.

"What did the judge say before he died?" she asked.

"Nothing." He nodded toward the steering wheel. "I'll drive us back to my motorcycle if you're ready. But then I think you should follow me to my house."

"Why?" She suddenly remembered how upset she'd been that Micah hadn't called her for over two days. "I'm not going to come over and have sex with you then be ignored until you are in the mood again," she snapped.

He let go of her hands and brushed his knuckles over her breasts before reaching her face. Micah stroked her jawbone with his fingers.

"You're right. I didn't get ahold of you." He didn't say anything for a minute and stared into her eyes. Then he gripped her chin. "I usually keep things casual with any woman I spend time with."

"I'm not going to be a casual fuck partner." Maybe with someone else. But with Micah . . . Maggie shook her head. They'd crossed over some line that existed between casual and not casual.

"I know," he whispered, his voice turning gravelly. "I didn't call you because I was taking time to sort things out. I needed to figure out what was going on between you and me."

"What did you figure out?"

"I haven't," he admitted.

She couldn't condemn him for that since she hadn't figured out what was happening with them, either. "I won't come home with you if you aren't going to talk to me afterward."

"You are coming home with me and I will talk to you afterward."

Chapter Thirteen

The next couple of days didn't help Micah understand what was happening between him and Maggie. She came over to his house the night they left Club Paradise. Each night after that she met him there once he was done working for the day. When he left for work the following morning, Maggie drove back to her house.

No matter how he tried twisting around how things might be in his head, he couldn't come up with a plausible resolution. Maggie's problems were solved. That morning she'd mentioned that she needed to start job hunting. After lunch she had called him excited that her accounts were no longer frozen. She'd laughed and asked how much she owed him for solving her case. Micah had been a sap and told her he'd have to get back to her on that one.

His father and uncle wanted him to drive up to Utah and join them. The investigation over the CIA agent Micah had killed, Sylvester Neice, had been closed. Uncle Joe had obtained a few files that revealed Neice had in fact not been working undercover but had gone rogue. He had the names that Micah had wanted. His father had been excited when he'd handed the file over to Micah.

"They're yours for the taking, son," he'd said with pride.

Four months ago Micah would have been on the next plane to Washington. The men who had wanted Neice's killer were now his. He'd split up with his father and uncle for the first time in his life. They'd shut down Mulligan's

Stew. Micah could have his revenge and return to his old life. His old life didn't sound as appealing as it had four weeks ago.

"I still don't know how you shoot like that." Ben had been quiet most of the drive back to the KFA office but now started back up again on their last case. "He had a gun pointing right at you. Yet you drew and fired so fast I didn't even see it happen."

"Got lucky," Micah mumbled. Luck had very little to do with it. The guy they'd been chasing for more than two hours had been cornered, was nervous, and screamed empty threats at all of them. The guy never had planned on pulling his trigger.

Ben laughed. "Don't be modest, man. You're an amazing shot. I wish you'd teach me how to be as good as you." He looked out his passenger window. "That is, if I get to stay on here."

Micah didn't mind focusing on someone else's problems for a while. "Why wouldn't you stay with KFA?"

"A bounty hunter has to be licensed in the state of California. I can't get licensed with this felony on my record and it's taking longer to get expunged than I thought it would. I don't know how much longer the Kings are willing to wait. They don't need me manning the radios in the trucks or making sure no one sneaks up behind any of you when you're tracking people."

"But you're so good at it," Micah teased and tried grinning when Ben moaned. "I'm sure you'll get that felony wiped off your record soon enough. King is investing time in training you how to do the job. He isn't going to write off that time just because the courts are dragging their heels."

"My lawyer has the paperwork drawn up." Ben didn't say anything when they pulled into the circular drive in front of the Kings' home. "Man, don't say anything but it hasn't been filed yet. It's going to cost me two grand and I haven't saved up that much money yet."

"I won't say anything." Micah parked the truck and got out on his side.

Ben hurried into the KFA office but Micah dragged his feet, pulling his cell phone out to check messages. He had a text from Maggie.

How about a candlelit dinner tonight? My treat, your house, and I have a new outfit I think you'll love. A little devil emoticon followed the end of her text.

His father had also texted him. *We're in town. Time to talk.*

Micah shoved his phone into his back pocket. His father and uncle were going to confront him about why he was procrastinating. More than likely they wouldn't do that much. They would lecture him about allowing a woman to get in the way of his work.

"Greg wants to see you," Patty said when Micah entered the KFA office. She nodded toward the door leading into the Kings' home.

Ben sat on the couch against the wall and Patty looked at him as Micah headed to the door. She slid her finger across her throat and grinned at Ben, thinking Micah didn't see her do it. He ignored her and entered the Kings' living room, closing the office door behind him.

"In here," King called out when their security system beeped, letting them know someone had entered their home.

Micah entered their kitchen where Greg and Haley sat at the kitchen table.

"Have a seat," King offered.

Micah pulled out a chair and sat, facing the two of them. King had a laptop opened in front of him and moved his finger over the mouse then looked up at Micah.

"Hell of a shot today," he began, his expression grave.

"Thanks." Micah knew King didn't hand out compliments easily, especially when he hadn't appeared too pleased with Micah lately.

"You're welcome. I was on the force twenty years before opening KFA. Not many men could have pulled off a shot like that."

"I got lucky."

King scowled. Haley spoke before he could.

"Luck had little to do with it, wouldn't you say, Micah?"

She was using that gentle tone of hers again and put her hand over her husband's as she spoke.

Micah nodded, leaned back in his chair, and relaxed. It didn't surprise him that they would probe for information about him. This was one argument he would give his father. It was time to leave KFA. King wasn't an idiot, and they were becoming more and more suspicious about him.

"I knew the guy wouldn't shoot," he conceded.

"He could have," King snapped. "And if that was your logic then you're an idiot."

Micah didn't say anything. Neither of them seemed surprised when he remained quiet. He watched them look at the laptop screen then glance at each other. They wouldn't have found anything on him, but something had them bugged.

"I'm sure you've heard the news about Judge Stabler being found shot to death at Club Paradise," King grumbled, not sounding pleased.

Micah had heard the news. He'd also reassured Maggie that they wouldn't investigate the case. Although yesterday's paper had announced the death of the four men and had mentioned that it appeared to be a drug deal gone bad, they hadn't speculated on why Stabler might have been there. This morning's paper hadn't said a word about it.

"Maggie O'Malley was pretty upset about it," he added, diverting the conversation in her direction. "I haven't been able to gather any details about what happened," he lied. "But she did call to tell me her bank accounts are no longer frozen."

"That's great," Haley said, smiling.

"None of the details are going to be revealed about the shooting," King stated and pushed the laptop to the side. He folded his large hands on the table and leaned forward, facing Micah. "There are a few reasons why they won't be. Care to guess what any of them are?"

Micah imagined King had been a decent interrogator during his days as a cop. Micah didn't change positions or break eye contact. "Judge Stabler was quite a celebrity. Dying in the heat of a drug deal isn't exactly how people would want to see him go."

"If the man was a criminal, he'll be painted that way. The press will show no mercy. In fact, they'll eat it up. I spoke with the officers who first responded to the scene. Apparently a vagrant happened to notice the back door wasn't locked and thought he'd found a good place to crash for the night. Hard to say how long those men would have lain there otherwise."

Micah had been curious how the bodies had been found. Normally after a kill he was long gone out of the state before anyone found the bodies. He seldom bothered to hear the details of his handiwork.

"The narcotics officers found it interesting that the back door was open. There was a hell of a lot of heroin in boxes with the bodies. Their guess is that Whithers and Stabler were going to sell the drugs to the other two men, who were both from Mexico. If they were, it would make sense that they would have locked the back door before conducting their business."

It wasn't hard to figure out where King was going with this. Micah continued listening, waiting to hear how King saw it playing out. Haley had grabbed a washcloth and was wiping the island in the middle of their kitchen. It was already spotless. Her hand moved methodically over the countertop, but her attention was on her husband. She looked nervous.

"Did you kill those four men?"

Micah blinked, sincerely surprised. He hadn't expected King to come out and ask. It would have been more King's style to build up his argument to where there was no backing out of his conclusion.

"No." Micah didn't hesitate. "If I'd known a drug deal was going down there I would have called the cops."

"There's something the public doesn't know," King continued. He continued staring at Micah.

The man was positive he had Micah figured out. Since all

he could do was speculate and there were no facts he could back any of it with, Micah remained leaning back in his chair, relaxed, and listened.

"Aren't you curious why the police have decided Maggie O'Malley is no longer a suspect in the Club Paradise gig?"

"I had planned on asking her."

"I doubt she knows," King said drily. "Frank Whithers was an undercover narcotics cop. He was wired and everything that was said leading up to those four men's deaths was recorded. I pulled a few strings and went into the station earlier to listen to the tapes."

Micah was positive his expression didn't waver. He had never killed a man, or a woman, and not checked them after. But this time he had been so concerned about getting Maggie out of there before she saw all of the dead bodies, he hadn't done anything more than make sure they were dead. And even at that, Stabler had been badly wounded and would have bled out but was stubborn enough of a prick to hold on and make his accusations.

His accusations. Fuck! Stabler had called him Mulligan. Maggie hadn't brought it up but she was pretty foggy on everything that had happened that night. King, on the other hand, looked like he had his kill in his mil dots and was ready to pull the trigger.

"Whithers had everything he needed on that recording to bring down Santinos's partner and nail a dirty judge to the wall," King stated. "Then someone shoots and kills him, the judge, and the two Mexican drug dealers. Enough was said to clear Maggie and point the finger in the right direction to show who was trying to frame her or—as the case proved— kill her. There was no doubt she was completely innocent. The shooter could have killed everyone after hearing enough to clear her name. That wasn't how it played out, though. Do you want to know why?"

"Why is that?" Micah asked. He wished King would get to the punch line already. Although he'd never sat through an interrogation before, his father and uncle had both raked him over the coals more than once. Micah had to rely on those experiences and sat and listened. Sweat trickled down the inside of his shirt. He was no longer calm.

"Because the shooter was good, really good. One shot to each man killed him." King paused and smiled. "Well, almost killed him. As good a shot as the shooter was, he should have been able to kill all four men easily. I'm thinking he might have been a bit distracted. I think the shooter wasn't alone."

"There was more than one shooter," Micah threw out, making it sound like he was into the story enough to throw out a guess. He was growing antsy. Saying something allowed him to shift positions and not appear nervous. Micah leaned forward and hoped he looked like he was anxious to hear the rundown of how it all happened.

King's smile didn't fade. "Nope. Just one gun, one shooter. There were four shots, then the shooter walked away. The recording didn't pick up what the shooter did next but I think he wasn't alone and he returned to whoever he was with. Fortunately for the two of them, they were far enough away from the wire not to reveal who they were. But, as Stabler spoke his last words, he was lying close enough to Whithers to be picked up clearly."

King leaned back, crossing his arms over his large chest, and looked away from Micah for the first time. Haley was now watching him, and Micah shifted his attention to her. She'd never been a cop and she'd never run an interrogation. Micah didn't underestimate her skills. She was watching him a bit too closely.

"So what were his dying words?" Micah asked, knowing that if he didn't ask it would confirm what they already thought they knew. King had left his story unfinished and Micah had to demand to know the ending.

"He said Mulligan," King replied. He was looking at his laptop again. "I think he was addressing the shooter. Earlier on tape he mentioned you."

"Mentioned me?"

King nodded once. "He said you weren't Jones. Stabler also said that if anyone knew who you were they would die.

Right before he died he said Mulligan," he repeated again, then turned his laptop so Micah could see it. "What is Mulligan's Stew?"

Micah stared at the laptop. King had an empty e-mail box pulled up. The address box had Mulligan's Stew in it, but with a Yahoo! account. They had quit using Yahoo! and switched over to Gmail.

"I don't know, why?"

King sighed, pushed his chair back and stood. Haley dropped her washcloth and watched her husband as he ran his hand over his short hair.

King gestured at the laptop. "You have to know what to look for, but if you type the right words into the search bar there's a fair number of articles." King dropped his hand to his side and faced Micah. At six and a half feet, with a barrel chest and a fierce look, the man was definitely intimidating. "MulliganStew appears to be an e-mail address if you put the two words together. It's how you reach the Mulligans, who are a multigenerational family of assassins. What's interesting is that the current generation is one man. His name is never mentioned, but there is one article stating that he is over six feet tall and muscular, with dark hair. Another article refers to him as a ladies' man. It's not easy to go through the archives of newspapers, especially when you don't know which paper to focus on," King added.

He leaned his rear against the counter and pressed both hands against it. Then, glancing from Haley to Micah, he continued explaining what he'd discovered.

"We dug pretty deep, which should tell you how sure we are of our findings." King looked at Micah for a long moment. He looked resolute when he stared at Micah.

"It appears that this young Mulligan first appeared on the scene before he was twenty. That was in Michigan. A drug lord was pissed that another drug lord was pushing in on his territory. He even narked the guy out, which of course pissed this new drug lord off. It said in that article that they had law enforcement up and down the street when they brought this guy in. Before they got him inside, though, this new drug lord was shot. Bullet straight to the heart. The gunman took out two other gang members brought in as well. Prosecution was ready to go, quite a few man-hours had already been billed to the state. And suddenly they had no one to prosecute.

"There are similar stories as the years go by. From city to city, and state to state. The dead men are con men, money launderers, murderers. There are hardly any reports describing the assassin who took out these people. In the past couple of years there were two mayors shot, one governor, and a senator. All of them were corrupt. Some of the articles speculate that private parties paid good money to bring someone in and have them clean up their town."

King was pacing now, tapping his finger against his lip. When he stopped he stood next to Micah, forcing him to lean to the side and look up to see King's face.

"Then finally," King whispered, looking down at Micah. "There is a report of a CIA agent being shot. This time the gunman was spotted, although the article says the witnesses refused to comment or go on record stating what they saw. Off record, the shooter was tall, well built, dark hair. And," King said, his voice low as he finally moved and stood behind his wife, "the CIA agent was killed by a single bullet going straight through his heart. Now, this CIA agent was bad news, abusing his power and authority. Quite a lot of people were interviewed and suspected of hiring the Mulligan assassin to do the job. But the Mulligan assassin has disappeared.

"Now, what is odd is that Mulligan was quite busy for a few years, busy enough to garner a reputation." King turned around and picked up a folder. When he faced Micah, he held it up in the air. "I managed to gain access to reports not released to the public. These are notes from detectives across the country who investigated the deaths probably long after the killer was far away, possibly even plotting his next hit." King opened the file but then handed it to Haley as he fished through a stack of papers. He held one up and looked at Micah over it, a grin appearing on his face. "This one is my favorite." He held the page up so Micah could see it, then began reading. " 'The black Irishman is at it again. It's always straight through the heart. This Irishman doesn't even take time to play with his target. He doesn't feed on fear. He's comfortable enough with himself that he doesn't need to hang around after his mark is dead. His confidence level must be off the charts. He's made an appearance more than once in my town but leaves before the blood runs cold in his prey. My guess is he's young and has had a weapon in his hand most of his life.' " King looked up from his paper, studied Micah for a moment, then flipped to another sheet. "Now this one," he began, then shook his head before reading. " 'The Mulligan assassin has returned. I'd bet a month's salary on it. His MO is always the same, straight through the heart, one shot, and never a clue where he stood when he made his shot. As with all the derelict gunmen in our history, he will go down. I would love to be the one to bring him to justice. The Mulligans have been at this for way too long. My father used to say, no one man should have the right or power to play judge, jury, and hangman. In this case, Mulligan believes he's omnipotent because all of his targets are dirty. That doesn't mean he won't pad his bank account with the exorbitant fee he charges to play God. I wonder if even he knows how many lives he's taken.' "

King lifted his gaze and watched Micah for a moment. "A murderer," he hissed. "Mulligan is a despicable killer who needs to be put away for life."

Micah barely managed to remain in his chair, let alone sit there and not shift his weight. King's words sliced through him like a sharp knife. Worse yet, he and Haley knew they had him. Micah wasn't sure what he was supposed to say. He could handle being flat-out accused of being Mulligan. But King had taken it a step farther. He'd finished accusing Micah and now was showing his outrage and disgust over who and what Micah was.

King looked away first and returned the pages to the file, sliding them neatly inside. He started talking before he'd finished his task. "Over the past few months there has been no sign of him. I guess he could have left the country after killing that CIA agent, but I don't think so. No one has ever reported having any contact with any of the Mulligans. I believe they're a tight family, and this young Mulligan has been taught to kill since he could first walk. He probably thinks the world of his family and believes he's not evil. Either way, I doubt he's delusional. My guess is deep down in his heart he knows what he's doing is wrong. He knows he's breaking the law. Nothing has ever been pinned on him so, for now, he's probably living the life of a normal, average American. Or at least he's trying to live that way." King put the file down and paced the length of the kitchen. He seemed into his depiction of how the Mulligan assassin would hide out. His face lit up as he continued with his speculating. "I bet he took off across the country, stopping in different towns until he found the one that fit. He would choose a city where he's never been hired to kill. And it would be a large city, because it's easier to get lost among the masses. I bet he was fairly decent at changing his identity and creating a background history that would be boring and not raise any flags. Then he'd get a job where no one would think to look."

The biting fury in King's tone came out with every word. "I bet he was quite pleased when he landed a job working for a well-known bounty hunter who used to be a cop," King sneered, his eyes glowing and his face red when he stopped and took loud, slow breaths.

After a few moments of silence, King leaned against his kitchen counter and turned his head to stare at Micah. "Are you simply going to sit there and say nothing?" He seriously seemed surprised that that was exactly what Micah was doing. "Micah, your background check goes back three months, which is normally as far as someone looks if they are hiring. Honestly, I didn't dig any deeper until those four men died over at Club Paradise. Prior to three months ago, you didn't exist. Your credit report is squeaky-clean, too clean. And I have spent the past two days trying to reach your landlord. He won't even answer my calls."

King sighed and shook his head, looking disgusted, and tired. "You fit the MO, son. You're one hell of a good shot, quite possibly the best I've ever seen. You've been here around four months now and I don't think either one of us has heard you say a word about your family, a girlfriend, kids, or anything about your personal life."

Micah had to say something. It had to be convincing and simple. Another part of him insisted he didn't have to say a word. Let King ramble on all he wanted. The old man knew he couldn't prove any of it. Micah could simply let him go on until he ran out of hot air then wish him a good night and leave.

Micah had to figure out what to say. He'd never rehearsed how to respond if anyone directly accused him of being an assassin. There were times when he and his father and uncle had discussed it in the past. He was sure of it. At the moment, though, his mind was blank on standard answers that might apply to direct questions. No one had ever asked him to his face if he were part of Mulligan's Stew.

Micah respected King yet he'd just described him as a horrific murderer who should be locked up and the key thrown away. Micah's uncle and dad believed they offered an exemplary service. He understood their thinking but also knew it curbed the appetite of the monster in him. He knew he could never lead a "normal" life. But having someone he liked, respected, and even looked up to stare him in the face with disgust and state they despised who he was made it damn near impossible to look him in the eye and feign innocence. Yet he had no choice. Micah had to ignore the sickening feeling in his gut, had to endure the dryness in his mouth and the lack of a quick response. He had to stare King back in the face and lie to him, knowing it would be clear to both of them that it was a lie.

An innocent man wouldn't sit there while King rambled on and not say a word. Micah cleared his throat and as he suspected, King's expression sharpened with impatience. He narrowed his eyes and waited to hear what Micah could possibly say.

"It's a good story," Micah said calmly. He didn't react when King puffed out his chest and straightened to his full height. "If I'm not doing my job the way you want me to, I swear, tell me what I'm doing wrong and I'll fix it."

"For crying out loud," Haley wailed, throwing her arms up in the air as she turned and looked at her husband.

"You're kidding me," King snarled at the same time.

Micah stood, moving to the back of his chair then holding on to it. "What do you want me to say?" he yelled at both of them.

"We're not going to let an assassin destroy what we have," Greg yelled back.

Micah didn't like how King stared at him as if he were trash. The way he spit out the word *assassin* turned Micah's stomach. They were both right, though. He was a trained killer. The CIA had stopped looking for him, and it was clear who the men were who had tried hunting him down. The plan was for Micah to fly to the other side of the country and kill the men before they said or did anything to implicate the Mulligans.

Greg King wanted nothing to do with someone who killed people on a regular basis. It was quite clear that a person like that was as much a lowlife as the four men Micah had killed at Club Paradise. And that stung.

Micah let out a slow breath as he took his time looking at each one of them. Part of him wanted to tell them the truth. A larger part of him knew he could never do that.

"I'm going to head home," he told them finally. There was nothing else to say.

"Micah," Haley said. Her motherly tone was gone. She sounded firmer than he'd ever heard her speak. "We think it best if you don't come back."

His protest was on his lips. Micah shouldn't have looked at both of them. He should have turned and walked away, grateful that part of his brief life while here in LA was now severed. He did look at Haley. When he met Greg King's knowing stare something closed up inside of him. King looked disappointed, as if he'd expected more out of Micah and he'd failed him.

"I'll miss working here," he said truthfully.

Neither one of their expressions changed. They were protecting what was theirs from a killer and a monster. This time he walked out of their house and didn't look back.

Chapter Fourteen

Maggie parked in front of Micah's house and stared at the nondescript place. His bike was in his garage. Heavy curtains covered all windows. It was hard to say if someone lived there or not. Apparently he liked it that way. It gave Maggie the eerie sensation that someone was hiding in that house. But Micah wouldn't hide from anyone or anything. He would stalk, attack, and kill.

He already had killed—four times. Had he killed prior to the other night? He'd been so cool and unemotional about it.

Everything had changed since the other night. Maggie would never be the same after seeing such a heinous crime. She reminded herself that she'd heard the terrible crime going down. Judge Stabler had been trying to kill her just because she *might* have had information that could jeopardize him. He was an evil person. He would definitely rot in hell for his crimes.

Maggie could only guess that the other three men were just as evil. The Frank person had seemed agreeable to Stabler's plans. They were partners. He'd been partners with her uncle. God! Was her uncle going to rot in hell, too? Maybe he would make amends while in jail, although that could be his hell.

In a way, Micah was giving evil men their justice. Believing that helped her wrap her mind around all of this. What she witnessed was Micah's reaction to a very large-scale drug deal about to go down. And he had stopped the man who was trying to kill her.

He didn't *stop*—he *killed*.

Maggie quit staring at his house. It would take her time to come to terms with what she'd seen, and there wasn't anyone she could talk to about it. If she said something to Micah, he would think she was no longer interested in him. That wasn't true. She was trying to understand him.

Grabbing the two bags she'd brought over with her, Maggie caught a glimpse of the silk outfit she'd planned on putting on while preparing dinner. The knee-length silk robe that came with it would come off after dinner. She'd been so excited about tonight she had almost raced through the grocery store buying everything she needed to make her mother's famous manicotti. Maggie had all the fresh greens for a salad and a bottle of wine. Now staring at everything, her stomach twisted in knots. What if Micah didn't want her playing house over here?

He'd agreed to it over the phone earlier. Maggie found her confidence, grabbed the bags, and got out of her car, making sure she locked it. Why had he chosen such a crappy neighborhood to live in? Micah didn't strike her as a poor person, and he certainly worked long hours. She hurried to the door and knocked.

The locks clicked immediately, as if Micah had been waiting for her on the other side. He unlocked his door and opened it, his gaze sweeping up and down her as she walked inside and past him.

"I'll take those," he offered, reaching for the bags in her hands.

Maggie thought she heard him growl as he looked down and caught a glimpse of the silk. She watched him stroll into his kitchen and put the bags on the table. His faded denim jeans hugged his muscular legs. He wore a bright blue tank top that was tucked into his jeans. Micah's shoulders were so broad, his chest muscles rippled and taut, and his waist slender, flat, and rock-hard. Maggie was almost drooling before he put the bags down, then turned around.

She almost didn't have time to react when Micah cleared the space between them and grabbed her. The air whooshed out of her lungs when he lifted and pressed her against his front door. Maggie forgot to inhale when she stared into his eyes. She'd never seen him look so tormented, so haunted.

"What's wrong?" she asked.

He didn't answer but instead attacked her mouth, his kiss greedy and hot. Maggie wrapped her arms and legs around his virile body and kissed him back. Maybe she'd misread what she'd just seen in his eyes. Her phone call earlier had definitely suggested they would have sex tonight. Apparently Micah had decided to do things in a different order than she'd suggested. And maybe he didn't care about lingerie.

Micah used his body to keep Maggie pinned against the wall while moving his hand between them. He undid her shorts. His hand moved to her breast, kneading it for only a moment before shoving her tube top up. The moment both breasts were exposed he shoved her harder against the door, growling into her mouth as he tweaked her nipple with skilled fingers.

Her world exploded from an array of concern, desire, and an unleashed need to have him inside her. Maggie was instantly soaked. Her pussy swelled and moisture coated her sensitive, smooth folds.

Micah was rough, almost animalistic, and it turned her on even more. Here was a man more intense than any she'd met before. As he devoured her mouth, sinking deep inside with his tongue until she almost gagged, Maggie didn't forget the tortured look he gave her before trapping her against his front door. Micah was strong, demanding, so incredibly confident in who he was and what he could do that he took on life with a fierceness most men didn't know.

Despite his collected, quiet, and protective nature, something simmered just underneath what he showed to the world. It was something others didn't see. Either he was trying to show her the tortured soul he hid so well, or it was coming out along with his feelings for her. If she learned what it was he barely managed to control inside, Maggie would know

Micah so much better. Possibly it would also relieve whatever was bothering him.

She held on to his rock-hard shoulders, pressing her fingers into warm flesh on either side of his tank top. There wasn't any way to yank his shirt up in their current position but she desperately wanted to feel his chest against her breasts. When she grabbed the top of his shirt and pulled, the rumbling in his throat turned fierce.

"Maggie," he said, growling her name.

She held on tight when he backed up from the door, turned, and almost threw her onto the couch. She landed on her rear end but immediately repositioned herself to her knees.

"Get out of your clothes," he ordered. "All of them."

Micah tugged off his tank top, kicked his shoes off, and was unzipping his jeans as he stared at her. He wasn't focusing on what he was doing but watching her while his hands moved mechanically at undressing him. Maggie drowned in the carnal, possessive way he focused on her. He looked so hungry.

Her fingers were damp as she kicked off her sandals, pulled her tube top over her head, and slid out of her shorts that he'd already unzipped. She jumped, but managed not to yelp when Micah shoved his coffee table out of the way. He cleared all the space between the two of them then reached for her. His hands were on fire when he grabbed her ankles and stretched her legs apart.

"Couldn't wait until after dinner?" she teased and reached for him when he moved between her legs.

"Nope." He knelt against the couch, and her pussy brushed against his taut stomach. Micah wasn't looking at her face any longer. His gaze traveled over her body, scanning every inch of her as if he couldn't decide where to start.

"I've been looking forward to this all day," she whispered.

Micah's attention jumped to her face. He stared at her a moment before placing his arms on either side of her. He lifted himself over her, arm muscles bulging. When he was inches from her face he stopped.

"Because you couldn't wait to fuck me?"

Maggie felt heat spread over her face, but she couldn't stop it. Maybe opening up, being honest, would help his demons surface as well.

She sucked in a breath. "That and I wanted to see you," she admitted. "You're starting to mean something to me. It's way past fucking and I think you know that."

Maggie wrapped her arms around his neck, feeling the chain from his Saint Michael pendant he never took off. When she couldn't forcibly lower his mouth to hers, she lifted her body up and pressed it against his. She was too close to focus on his face, or his eyes, but their lips brushed together.

"Kiss me," she whispered.

He obeyed. As rough and bruising as their first kiss was, this one was so gentle it almost made her cry. Micah shifted his weight and braced himself with one arm as he wrapped the other around her back and held her to him. She ran her hands down his back, up to his hair, wanting to touch him everywhere.

Their mouths moved together, their tongues stroked each other. The kiss was as hot as his body was against hers. Maggie could kiss him like this all night. She felt like a cat, craving to rub herself against him, get herself off just from the feel of his incredible body.

When she was sure she might come from the tension building between them, Micah ended the kiss. She collapsed down on the couch, panting and needing more.

She reached for him and he grabbed her hands. Then pushing them down by her sides, he let go and pushed himself to his feet.

"You deserve so much better," he muttered.

Maggie was off the couch when he turned from her. "Maybe I don't want better," she exclaimed, afraid he was walking away from her. "Maybe I worry I'm not good enough for you."

Micah grabbed a condom he'd apparently put on his kitchen table before she'd arrived. When he turned to face her, every inch of him was hard and flexed. Muscles rippled all over his body. The wound on his shoulder puckered as it healed. Soon it would look like the rest of the scars on his body. Were they all from gunshot wounds?

Maggie didn't want to think about other men he might have killed. She focused on his dick as he sheathed it with the condom. Even with the latex, it bulged like the rest of him. She stared as it stuck out from his body, swollen, long, and thick. Her pussy throbbed in pain as she ached for him to make love to her.

"Why would you think you aren't good enough for me?" Micah asked. That tortured soul was so visible in his hazel eyes.

Maggie didn't move as he approached but stayed rooted where she was until he was close enough that his cock pressed against her belly. She leaned her head back to look into his eyes.

"Because you might think I don't understand," she said. "You're a dangerous man, Micah, with so many secrets and so much turmoil inside you that maybe you think I'm not strong enough to handle it."

"Are you?" he asked, not skipping a beat before demanding to know. His expression didn't change as he stared at her, waiting for her to answer.

Had she nailed it on the head that easily? Was this the root of the demons inside him?

She opened her mouth to answer, closed it, then closed her eyes and let the truth out. "I want to be," she murmured, her heart pounding so fast it was hard to speak. "I don't want to lose you because I've witnessed a part of you I think you'd rather I'd not seen."

"You haven't seen that part of me yet, sweetheart," he informed her.

Maggie tried opening her eyes. There were so many questions she wanted to blurt out. Micah pulled her into his arms, lifting her off the ground as he kissed her again.

She was so torn inside, her stomach twisted in knots.

Micah must have viewed their conversation as over for now. He kept her lifted up against him as he stepped sideways. Then they were on the couch again. Micah didn't drop her but released her slowly so that her body slid down his.

"Turn around," he instructed, his voice gravelly.

Before she could respond he gripped her waist, flipped her around, then lifted her so her knees were on the couch. She held on to the back of it and lifted herself, arching her back and exposing her pussy.

"You're so beautiful," he whispered, running his finger along her entrance then dragging her moisture to her ass. "Did I hurt you here?"

"No," she told him. Every inch of her trembled, eager to feel him wherever he might touch her.

Micah hummed, then ran his finger back down to her pussy. He caressed her clit and she thought she might come right off the couch. Her body was electrified by his touch. Maggie wanted to cry out, to scream for him to fuck her.

"Don't move, darling." He continued running his finger over her pussy.

"God, Micah. I don't know how long I can take it."

"How about forever?"

When Maggie tried looking over her shoulder, wanting to see his face to understand his meaning, Micah shoved his dick deep inside her.

She howled. He thrust all of him inside her. Micah grabbed her hair, forcing herself to arch her back more. His cock hit a tender area that released all of her pent-up desires. Maggie howled again, crying out loud enough that her throat hurt. She didn't care. An orgasm tore through her so fast she could barely hold herself up. She came hard, every inch of her trembling from its impact.

"I love how I feel inside you." he growled over her shoulder.

Micah held her in place as he began fucking her. One hand pushed up against her chest. Long fingers stroked her swollen breasts while he impaled her again and again. He made sex seem like a drug. Maggie needed him more and more every time they fucked. And once he entered her, she was out of her head needing the next orgasm more than she did the last.

Sex shouldn't be this good. Maggie closed her eyes, feeling his chest glide up and down her back and his balls slap against her ass. He used his thick, strong legs to brace himself over her while he held the back of the couch with one hand and her body with his other.

Once again he brought her to her peak. She cried out again when she came. Micah never stopped the momentum, never stopped gliding as far inside her as he could go. The heat built, the pressure continued, and their bodies melded together, providing the perfect union. There was no way sex with anyone else would feel like this. Maggie honestly believed she'd found her soul mate. But he was so tattered and scarred that he was leery about them being compatible. If their lovemaking didn't convince him, she wasn't sure what would.

What words would soothe that savage beast inside him?

"Maggie," he grunted.

She swore his cock grew larger. Her pussy was on fire. He had her so stretched, so filled to extreme capacity that words at the moment were impossible. She grunted her response.

"I'm going to come."

Micah left her alone in the kitchen to cook while he disappeared at the other end of his house. Not that the place was that big. Maggie had managed to find a pot large enough for the pasta to boil in. She'd brought over her own personal sauce, and he had a skillet that worked for warming it up. The cheese was grated and his oven preheated for it to bake.

Once she reached the stage of stuffing the pasta, Maggie was stuck. She couldn't wander down his short hallway and find out what he was doing. Her fingers were messy but she felt sexy in her outfit. The silk robe brushed against her legs as she reached for more of the large, round noodles. As she stuffed each one with the cheese mixture, she slowly relaxed until she was getting into the repetitive steps of preparing the meal.

Maggie turned to reach for the last of her pasta in the straining bowl in the kitchen sink and shrieked.

"Damn it," she groaned, then started laughing. "How can a man your size manage to sneak up on me without me hearing you?"

Micah didn't smile but moved closer, then brushed her hair away from her shoulder and neck and kissed that sensitive spot at her nape. "I wasn't sneaking," he told her.

"Okay, I believe you." She smiled when she turned to look at his face. "Pour the wine?" she asked, and held up her cheese-covered fingers.

The man who'd seemed so upset and disturbed about something when she'd first arrived now appeared relaxed. Maggie liked watching how Micah moved, each step he took reminding her of a deadly creature, master of his lair, and prepared to stop anyone who might bring them harm. Her thoughts reminded her of the four men lying in their own blood at Club Paradise. Suddenly her stomach was in knots and she fought off an unpleasant tremble that shook through her body.

"Are you a wine connoisseur?" Micah asked, holding two glasses of wine.

Maggie finished washing her hands off and put the manicotti dish in Micah's oven. "I asked the guy at the store which bottle was best with an Italian dish," she confessed, and grinned up at him when he handed her glass to her.

"To complete honesty," he told her, and tipped his glass against hers before bringing the wine to his lips.

"To complete honesty," Maggie repeated and lost herself for a moment in how bright Micah's hazel eyes were. The tortured clouds of pain and primal aggression seemed to be gone. She sipped her wine but continued studying him. "What are we going to talk about?" she asked, knowing his toast to honesty meant he had a particular topic in mind.

"Us," he said without hesitating, then pulled her by the

silk tie holding her robe closed at her waist until she was up against him. Micah took her glass of wine and placed it with his on his counter. "I'm no longer working for KFA," he told her.

"What? Why? What happened?" she sputtered.

Micah had put his jeans back on but not his shirt. Her fingers stretched across his bare chest, and she felt the solid beat of his heart against her fingertips.

"Apparently the Kings were a bit upset about the four deaths at Club Paradise."

Maggie was acutely aware of how his heart maintained its solid thumping while hers picked up pace as she stared at his solemn expression.

"But how did they know it was you?" she whispered. She'd been convinced she was the only one who knew Micah had killed those four men, and she'd been prepared to take that secret to her grave.

"There aren't many men who can pull off such perfect shots. Four of them is almost unbelievable to most." Micah spoke calmly, sharing this with her as if it were as trivial as discussing a walk after dinner.

Her hands were glued to his chest. His heart didn't pick up pace. His Saint Michael pendant was cool against the side of her finger.

"That part of the night is a blur," she admitted. If she were to be completely honest, the reason was because she hadn't wanted to think about it.

"Why is that part a blur, Maggie?"

She stared up at him. "Because," she began, then balked. "I killed four men."

"They were drug dealers. You heard them say they would kill me if they had to," she blurted.

"So you're okay with me murdering those men."

Maggie took a step backward. She hadn't realized Micah still held the tie to her robe until he let it slide out of his fingers as she put distance between the two of them.

"They would have killed us," she stammered. It was the

first thing that came to her mind as she tried, this time under protest, to justify that terrible night.

"No," he said with conviction.

"No what?"

"They wouldn't have killed us."

"How can you be so sure?"

"Because none of them were as capable of killing as I am."

She stared at him, her mouth suddenly too dry. When she reached for her glass of wine, Micah picked it up and handed it to her. He was as sturdy as a rock, calm, in control, just as always.

"There's no way you knew that," she told him, and took a rather large gulp of her wine. It went down smoothly, and the alcohol vapors seeped up to her brain. "I've tried to justify that night, too, Micah," she told him. It dawned on her that this was where the honesty was needed. He was guilt-ridden, even more so now that it had caused him his job. "But if you're worried about it, no one knows we were there." She reached out for him again. "And no one will ever know. I promise."

"I believe you, but I wasn't worried about it. Cops can speculate all they want. They won't be able to pin any of the deaths on me."

"I hope you're right." Maggie drank more of the wine. She couldn't imagine Micah being charged with murder. But maybe that was because she wouldn't let herself think about that night. "I can't believe your boss would fire you over that."

"Greg King believes I'm too dangerous to work for him."

"Too dangerous?"

"Yes."

He had her cornered in the kitchen. Suddenly she felt claustrophobic. When Maggie moved past him, he stepped to the side and let her pass.

"You don't scare me. Not once have I thought you'd hurt me." She stood in the middle of his living room, facing him, and finished off her glass of wine. The alcohol gave her the strength to continue. "Even during rough sex, and knowing how incredibly strong you are, it's never crossed my mind that you'd hurt me."

"Good," he said, approaching. Micah stroked her cheek. There was an unmistakable sadness in his eyes. "I know I could never hurt you," he said, his voice suddenly rough.

"I told you we were moving far past just fucking," she whispered and went up on her tiptoes to kiss him.

"Maggie," he said gruffly as his lips brushed over hers. "We need to talk about this."

"About what?"

He sighed and took her wineglass from her. He didn't fill it up but left it on the counter, then came as far as the end of the hallway. Micah leaned against the wall and just looked at her, not saying anything. Her insides twisted with nerves.

"What do we need to talk about?" she demanded, her nerves turning to fear. "What do you want to say to me?"

"So much more than I can say, damn it," he let out. Micah didn't yell, but that calm reserve he'd been holding onto broke with a dam of frustration. He balled his fists at his side and stared at her. "Killing those men makes me a murderer. You're saying you're okay being with a murderer."

Maggie shook her head. "You had to do it," she whispered. "I know you feel terrible about it."

He sliced his hand through the air between them when she took a step in his direction. "Maggie, no, I don't."

"You don't feel terrible?"

"I did what seemed the logical next move at that moment. We'd gained all the information we needed to confirm that killing them would end your problems."

She stared at him. Why did it startle her when he said he had killed for her? Images of those men lying on the floor, of all the blood, and before that hiding in the closet, hearing those repeated gunshots. Five shots. No, four shots. Four shots then another shot. Micah had held her in his arms as he'd fired that last shot.

"He knew who you were," Maggie muttered.

Micah tilted his head. "Is it getting less blurry?"

"Thinking about it makes me sick. I don't see any reason to dwell on it. It was terrible. Maybe we will both go to hell for that night. But damn it, Micah, they were really evil men and they would have killed us. It was self-defense."

"So if someone is really bad and doing harm to others, you're okay with someone killing them?"

"You mean the death penalty?"

Micah shook his head. "Sweetheart, I mean someone aiming a gun and firing, ending someone's life because the community would be better off with them dead."

"Why are you asking me this?" she asked. She couldn't breathe. She didn't like the way he was looking at her. And this conversation didn't make sense at all.

A loud pounding on the front door damn near made Maggie's heart explode in her chest. She might have yelped. She wasn't sure. Micah had her so worked up that a pin dropping on the floor might have made her jump. Someone knocking loudly on the door behind her was enough to give her a heart attack.

"Stand over here," Micah said in a hushed tone. He did that movement thing again. It was as if he glided across the floor instead of taking steps the way a normal person would.

"Stay back," he instructed, and held his arm out, gesturing with his hand for her to move down the hallway. He lowered his head and looked through the peephole. "Damn it. Not right now," he snarled under his breath.

"What? Who is it?" Maggie whispered.

When Micah turned around his expression was harder than she'd ever seen it before. He looked at her without commenting but instead seemed to be deciding something.

"What?" she pressed.

She swore he cleared the distance between them again without taking more than one step. "I want you to know something and believe it in your heart no matter what you hear from here on out."

"Okay . . . ," she said slowly. He was acting so strange she didn't know what to think, other than something really awful was about to happen. Before she could demand to know who was at the door, or that Micah explain his bizarre behavior, whoever it was at the door pounded even louder.

Maggie jumped and Micah grabbed her arms. He bent over so their faces were close to each other. "I have never, in my entire life, loved another person the way I love you right now, Maggie O'Malley."

He straightened, leaving her stunned, and walked over to the front door.

Maggie watched the muscles move under his skin as he unlocked the dead bolts, then the lock in the doorknob. He took a step backward and opened the door. She noted instantly that he didn't open it far enough to look outside and demand what someone wanted but enough to allow whoever was on the other side to enter his home.

His words he'd just said to her floated around in her head as two men sauntered into Micah's house as if they lived there, too.

"Well, I'll be damned," the first one said the moment he spotted her standing at the end of the hallway.

"This explains a lot," the other grumbled, appearing to finish the first man's thought.

Maggie should have run down the hallway to Micah's bedroom before he'd opened the door. These two men were large, broad-shouldered, and tall, well built for their age, which she would guess was somewhere in their fifties. They also looked very much the same, like they might be twins. It wasn't often she saw adult twins together. Her mind was whirling from what Micah had just said to her. She gaped at the men, at Micah, and her heart beat too fast to catch her breath.

They stalked into the house, both of them moving as far as the entrance of the kitchen. Each one of them glanced around the corner. She saw their eyes shift to the wine-glasses on the counter. They sniffed the air and picked up on her cooking manicotti. Then they circled around, taking her in with a quick appraisal. Their gruff comments at her being there left her unnerved. Suddenly she felt grossly under-dressed.

She tugged at her robe, closing it around her tighter then pulling on the silk belt at her waist.

"Don't tell me this is why you're ignoring us," the man closest to Micah said, facing him but pointing at Maggie as he spoke.

"Who are these men?" Maggie asked, inching closer to Micah. Both of them made her terribly nervous.

"Yes, please tell us," the man farther from Micah stated.

"Who is this woman?" the man closest to Micah grunted.

Micah closed and locked the door, turning his back on all three of them for a moment longer than Maggie thought necessary. Was he fighting for control, or trying to figure out what to say? Her head was spinning. Micah just told her he loved her. Then he opened the door to these two men, whom he obviously knew well, and was taking his sweet time clearing the growing tension in the air.

"I'm Maggie O'Malley," she announced, turning away from Micah and extending her hand to the man closest to her. He was about as tall as Micah. "And you are?"

Was that amusement in the man's eyes? "Mulligan," he told her. "Joe Mulligan." He had a firm handshake, but his hand was cold and leathery feeling.

The second he let go of her hand, Maggie stuck it out to the other man. "I'm Maggie," she offered.

"Jacob Mulligan," the man said and shook her hand. It was weird how his hand felt just the same as Joe Mulligan's did. They were definitely twins.

"Mulligan," she whispered, and was suddenly swarmed with memories from the night at Club Paradise. Stadler had said "Mulligan" right before he died. Maggie looked over at Micah. Was the look he gave her begging for forgiveness?

Micah reached her side and slipped his arm around her, facing the two older men. "I'm not sure Maggie has made enough dinner for all four of us," he said, although he didn't sound too upset about the fact. "I won't ask how you figured out where I'm staying, but you could have called."

"By the looks of things I doubt you would have answered."

Jacob glanced down at the coffee table pushed to the side of the room at an angle, then stepped around it and sat on the couch. He stretched his long, thick legs out in front of him and draped one arm along the back of the couch. "So what have you told her, son?"

"Son?" Maggie asked.

"My only offspring," Jacob told her. "This here is his uncle Joe."

Stadler called him Mulligan.

"Do you have your mother's name?" Maggie asked, twisting in Micah's embrace to see his face. If she thought she saw an apology in his expression before, it was now void of all emotions. Micah's face was a blank mask.

And he waited a moment too long to answer.

His father started laughing. "That's a good sign. Maybe we barged in here a bit prematurely. We can leave you two alone." He started to stand. "Micah, be ready to leave in the morning."

"Leave? Wait a minute. Where are you going?"

"My last name isn't Jones," Micah told her.

"Don't," his uncle Joe barked.

"Maggie, I'm Micah Mulligan."

"You're making a mistake, Micah," his father warned him.

"Why is he making a mistake?" Maggie snapped at Jacob. "Is it wrong for him to tell the woman he loves what his real last name is?" she demanded, her voice rising. "Or are you saying that because he lied to her about his name that he might have lied to her about loving her?"

For the first time since the two men entered Micah's home, neither one of them said anything. Maggie glared at the man by the couch, then sent an equally hateful stare to the other man standing closer to the kitchen. For the first time she noticed how Micah looked a bit like both of them.

"Maggie," Micah said, but he didn't sound the least bit apologetic. Instead he spoke her name as if it were a warning.

She marched away from him and into the kitchen. Grabbing her glass and the bottle of wine, she walked around the corner and looked at the three men.

"Would anyone else like a glass of wine?"

"They aren't staying," Micah told her.

"What? Why not?" she asked Micah, her overly sweet tone causing him to narrow his gaze on her suspiciously. "Where I come from we care about family. We don't send them packing when they show up at the door."

"Good." Jacob slapped his hands against his legs, then stood up. "Then it's settled. We're in the city at a hotel. We'll leave you two alone so you can explain why you're leaving with your family." His father looked fiercer than Micah ever had when he focused on his son. "And Micah, don't say anything that will jeopardize her life."

"Jeopardize my . . ." Her words trailed off.

Micah did that moving thing again where he was next to her before she'd seen him take a step. He lifted the wine bottle and glass out of her hand.

"That wasn't necessary, Dad," he growled, moving behind her and putting the glass and bottle back on the counter, then coming up behind her. He slipped his arms around her waist and held her tightly against him. "I have no problem getting ahold of you in the morning. But I don't know if I'm going anywhere yet or not."

"I knew it," his uncle said under his breath.

"You don't know anything," Micah growled at him.

Maggie thought his uncle almost looked hurt when he shot Micah a pensive look. Micah's father looked pissed.

"That's right, damn it. You don't know shit." Jacob walked up to the two of them but stared over Maggie's head at Micah. "You know this isn't a choice, son," he said softly.

"There are always choices, Dad."

The anger and aggression faded from his father's face. "Not this time, Micah. Not with us. You can't change who you are. I think you've already learned that."

Micah tightened his hold on Maggie. "You think you know what you're talking about."

"I do know what I'm talking about," Jacob roared. "Do you seriously think your little stunt the other night didn't raise all kinds of questions? I know you acted instinctively. I know it never crossed your mind to do anything other than what you did. Now you need to understand the reason behind that is because of who you are. And you will always be who you are."

Maggie tried understanding what Micah's father had just said to him. Whatever the meaning behind his cryptic words, Micah didn't like them. He clung to her hard enough that her hand was over his, gently caressing the side of his hand before she'd realized her actions.

"Has your life really been that bad?" his uncle Joe asked.

His uncle looked at Micah with more fondness in his eyes. Maggie could imagine the two men raising the one son. The father would have been strict, determined to raise his son properly. The uncle, on the other hand, freed of that burden of responsibility, would have played with him more, joked with him, and possibly been the one Micah would have opened up to more.

"Of course not," Micah answered immediately. "But this isn't about how good or bad the past has been. This is about where I go from here. Why do I have to continue?"

Continue what? Maggie desperately wanted to know. She wasn't part of this conversation. And as easily as the two tall men looked over her head at Micah, she wouldn't be surprised if they forgot she was standing there, too.

"You've already answered that question for yourself." His father bit out the words. His hair, just like his twin's, was trimmed short and close to his head. Streaks of gray covered most of the black, but when they were younger both of them probably had the thick dark hair Micah had now. Micah definitely got his hardened, dominating, and harsh glares from his dad.

"What happens the next time you're cornered in a perilous situation?" Uncle Joe asked.

"I'll tell you what will happen," Jacob barked, his words as biting as Joe's had been coaxing. "You're going to do exactly what you did the other night. One shot straight through the heart. It's programmed in you, son."

"You can't change who you are," his uncle finished.

"Nor should you want to," his dad added.

"Enjoy the rest of your evening." Uncle Joe walked toward Jacob and slapped him on the shoulder. "We'll be out of your hair now."

"If she loves you the way you've told her that you love her, she'll be a good girl after you're gone." As threatening as Jacob's words sounded, this time his expression wasn't menacing. He turned and followed his twin to the door.

Micah didn't budge a muscle. He remained where he was, holding Maggie tight with her back pressed against his front.

"You know the only way you can truly break the Mulligan curse," Uncle Joe said at the door.

"Don't push the boy," Jacob snapped at Joe. "Let's go." He reached for the locks and began unlocking them.

"How's that?" Micah asked right before his father opened his front door.

"Be the first Mulligan to leave without getting her pregnant." His uncle looked at Maggie for the first time, nodding chivalrously. "You've got good taste in ladies, Micah. Maggie, it was a pleasure meeting you."

Maggie couldn't think of what to say in return. She got the uncanny sensation that Micah's uncle was putting her face to memory more than he was being polite by making eye contact and telling her good-bye.

The moment the door closed she spun out of Micah's arms. She'd half expected his cold persona to be hard in place and felt an ounce of her anger dissipate when he looked defeated, almost broken.

"Am I locking the doors, or are you marching out of here, too?"

"Don't you think for a moment, Mr. Micah Mulligan, that you're getting out of this without a good fight on your hands," she warned him.

"I'll lock the doors."

Maggie stepped out of his way and stalked into the kitchen, feeling her rage grow by the second as everything his father and uncle had said began repeating itself in her mind. She yanked open Micah's oven door, which almost caused one side to come off its hinge, and remembered the pot holders at the last minute before pulling the bubbly, delectable-smelling dish out of the oven. Too bad her appetite was gone. She placed one of the pot holders on Micah's worn-out countertop, then set the hot dish on top of it.

"Now where the hell do you get off toasting to me about honesty when you've been lying to me since the day you met me?" she shouted as she stormed into the living room.

Chapter Fifteen

Micah was sure he'd never felt more deflated in his entire life. Were his uncle's parting words said out of spite? His meaning had been clear. Uncle Joe had just told him the only way he could possibly break the Mulligan curse was by leaving a woman without her being pregnant. His mother had left him and his dad when Micah had been ten. Micah remembered her . . . vaguely. Maybe Uncle Joe said what he did to grab Micah's attention so he'd come running, demanding the truth, but at least he'd be with them. Or maybe what he'd said had been true. In which case Micah would demand to know the truth about what happened between his parents.

He sank onto his couch and looked over at Maggie. She had no idea how incredibly hot she looked. Her bright blue eyes were wild and her hair messed up just enough to show any attentive observer that she'd recently been well fucked. That sexy silk robe she wore had loosened at the waist and opened up so that the V-neck was low enough to offer one hell of a view of her cleavage. That hot little number she had on underneath it pressed her boobs together so that the swell of her breasts was even more enticing.

"I had planned on telling you everything before they showed up," he told her, knowing if he told her how beautiful she was right now he might get slapped for his efforts.

"Nice try at a save," she spit out, then turned on her heel and marched over to the wine.

Micah came off the couch and grabbed the bottle from her before she could pour any into her glass. "I already know how you are when you've had a few too many."

He was ready when she turned around swinging. Micah grabbed the fist that was meant for his jaw with his free hand. "I will answer any of your questions, tell you whatever you want to know, but no hitting and no drinking or the deal is off."

"You're in no position to lay out any ultimatums," she sneered and tried taking the bottle from his hand.

He could physically prevent her from taking it, but if Maggie wanted it badly enough the moment he put it down she would grab it. "Fine," he relented, and reached for her glass on the counter then filled it halfway. "You aren't driving if you get drunk and I won't budge on that one."

Maggie accepted the glass and took a small sip. "Why did you lie to me about your last name?" she demanded.

"I didn't know you," he explained, promising himself he would make sure everything he told her was as truthful as it could be. She'd been through enough, and so had he. Micah didn't want to lose her. He hadn't figured out yet how he would keep her, but somehow there had to be a way. "I'd been in LA for three months before meeting you and had been Micah Jones since moving here."

"Why did you change your last name?" Her eyes grew wide and she pointed a finger at his chest. "You're running from the law, aren't you? That's why Judge Stabler knew who you were. He knew you were on the run."

"No."

"Don't lie to me," she shouted in his face.

He'd known the moment she had remembered that Stabler had called him Mulligan. Part of him had hoped she would never remember that night. But if they were going to begin a relationship together, their foundation wouldn't be woven with lies.

"I'm not wanted for any crime, Maggie. I promise."

"My brother showed my father that Micah Jones had no

past," she informed him. "For two days before he left, Aiden followed me wherever I went in the house trying to get me to see I was spending time with a man who was bad news. He never raised an ounce of doubt in me. No matter how many times he showed me that you were a blank slate prior to a few months ago, I was able to explain to him simply and logically how that could be."

She stared at her wine, swooshed the blood-red alcohol around in the narrow, long glass but didn't take a sip. When she tilted her head, almost letting it fall back to stare into his eyes, the pain he saw there was staggering. Maggie cared about him, a lot. She quite possibly loved him, too. Suddenly Micah was more committed than he'd been a moment ago to making sure Maggie understood every bit of the morbid truth. He prayed she wouldn't walk out on him once she knew everything.

"When you showed up at my doorstep, I was bored, restless. Working for KFA was barely satisfying my craving for the hunt."

Maggie frowned but didn't say anything. He turned from her and paced across his living room, letting his memories trail back to the day the two of them had met.

"I remember entering your office at Club Paradise," he told her, taking his time turning around but only looking at her for a moment. The sooner he got all of this out, the better. "It only took a few minutes talking to you to doubt your guilt but I'd been told to find a bookkeeper, if there was one, and to bring him or her out to the police. As long as I've hunted, I've accepted the orders given to me and found whoever I was hunting without question. I did the same thing when I worked with my father and uncle."

He sighed. He was being vague but not lying. Micah didn't want to hurt her any more than she already was. This was a start. He would elaborate more as needed. But if the pain on her face increased, he wasn't sure he could bear it. He was experiencing emotions for the first time; his love for her, his need to protect her and keep her from harm. Until now, Micah had only worried about himself. He had worried for his father and uncle, of course, but had also known they were very skilled in taking care of themselves.

"I'd run down quite a few people who'd skipped out on their bail before meeting you, but not one of them stuck in my head like you did. So when you showed up here asking me to find out why they suspected you, and to find out who was truly behind the money laundering, the only thing that crossed my mind was how strong the physical reaction was between us."

"I was barely able to concentrate while talking to you," she murmured.

Maggie wasn't through being pissed off. He knew how deep her temper ran. Micah fought off the urge to go to her and instead focused on telling her what she needed to hear.

"None of this explains why you went by Jones," she reminded him, proving she was still angry.

"It was because of my life prior to moving here."

"I'd already gathered that," she said sardonically.

"My plans initially were to stay here a year then return to my father and uncle," he explained. "And to my old life. While I was here, I didn't want anyone knowing I was here. It never crossed my mind I would fall for a lady whose family would care enough to check on who their sister and daughter was spending time with. I believed I'd be able to keep a low-enough profile that my boss wouldn't have his suspicions confirmed after I killed four men and fire me because they'd worked too hard to build up their business to have someone like me come along and destroy what they had."

"How could you destroy what they have?"

"Because of who I am."

Maggie stared at him. Her breath came faster, causing her snug outfit under her robe to press her breasts together more. Micah didn't focus on them as much as how her face paled. She was imagining the worst. And whatever thoughts she conjured in her mind, none of them were as bad as the truth. She wanted to love the man she believed him to be right now. Maggie was scared that if she learned about the monster she had caught glimpses of already, she wouldn't be able to love that man. He saw it on her face and it tore at the monster inside him, who was already snarling and demanding it not be revealed. It created a fear inside him unlike anything he had ever known. No one had ever been able to look at him and read him as well as Maggie did. Not his father or uncle, not anyone.

She straightened, tugged at her robe, adjusted the tie around her waist, and lifted her head. That stubborn look he found so adorable appeared on her face. Maggie believed herself ready for the truth.

"Go on," she prompted, and kept her head held high.

"Those four men aren't the first four men I've killed."

"So you are wanted for murder."

"No, sweetheart. I promise there are no warrants for me anywhere." Micah reached for his pendant before he could stop himself. The chance existed King might turn the law on him. It would be a first for him. He would become a fugitive. Would Maggie run with him? A small cruel voice in the back of his head laughed at the absurdity of that thought. Maggie was too good a person to be an outlaw.

"You've never been caught but you didn't want to take any chances?" she asked weakly.

Maggie entered his kitchen and Micah followed. She put down the wineglass, picked up the wine bottle, tipped it to her lips, and drank. When she turned around her lips were wet. She burped quietly, pressed her fingers over her lips, and looked up at him.

"Who did you kill and why did you kill them?" she asked, and tilted the bottle back for more.

"I didn't know any of them."

Micah felt sick. Maggie would hate him when she knew the truth. Guzzling that entire bottle of wine wouldn't make her numb enough to accept the monster. There was no way he could erase his past, but he would do anything if she would be part of his future.

"They were men or women who had committed crimes."

"That's why you killed them?"

"I was paid to kill them," he said, barely managing to utter the words and terrified of the look of disgust and hatred that would cross Maggie's face once she understood.

Maggie slapped him across the face so hard and yet he barely felt the sting. Micah wasn't sure he'd ever be able to feel again.

"Get out of my way," she yelled, shoving at him.

Maggie rushed down his hallway to his bedroom, grabbed her clothes she'd put on his bed after they'd made love, then stormed into his bathroom and slammed the door hard enough to shake his house.

"Maggie," he said when she came out of the bathroom.

She was dressed and had her silk outfit he'd looked forward to taking off her later that night balled in her fist.

"Don't," she gulped, holding her hand up at him.

Micah spotted her tear-stained face when she grabbed her purse and pulled out her keys. Her sobs destroyed him as much as his front door slamming down on his heart as she stalked out of his life.

There was no point in trying to sleep. Maggie sent every call he made to her to voicemail. He considered going after her but didn't think he could handle her rejection twice. It took less than an hour grabbing his few possessions from the house. The furniture and kitchen utensils had come with the place. He washed up the dishes Maggie had used, then stared at the manicotti on his counter. It was probably really good. There was no way he could swallow a bite.

By the time he'd woken up his dad, found out where they were, then driven his bike to the hotel, the sun was rising. His uncle answered the door and let him into the dark, cold suite. Micah entered, feeling as if he were entering a tomb.

"Thought you didn't want to join us." His uncle followed him into the room wearing his boxers, then crawled back into one of the two double beds and pulled the blankets up to his waist. He propped pillows behind him and lit a cigarette.

"I don't," Micah told him, having no problem staying on his honesty kick.

"I see." Uncle Joe's cigarette lit up in the dark room as he took a long drag and stared straight ahead without saying anything.

Micah placed his duffel bag full of everything he owned on the round table alongside the closed curtains. He sat and leaned back in his chair, crossed his arms over his chest and straightened out his legs. Stiff muscles were setting in but he didn't care. All he saw was the overwhelming amount of pain on Maggie's tear-stained face when she stormed out of his life.

Micah pulled out his phone and stared at the glowing face in the dark. He opened up a new message page and stared at the blinking line in the empty text box. What could he say to her that would make a difference? He'd told her the truth and as he'd known already, it was more than she could handle.

"What did you tell her?" his father asked.

Micah shifted his attention to his dad's bare back. He lay sideways on the far bed, his head to the wall. The blankets draped over his bare waist. Even in the darkness Micah saw the thick white scar that ran down his dad's back like a lightning bolt. His dad had ripped his back open on barbed wire he hadn't seen in the dark while getting away from a bear. He'd been younger than Micah when it had happened. Micah thought of all the scars on his own body. Maggie had pressed her fingertips to a few of them but had never said anything. When they'd first had sex she'd been curious about him but hadn't asked any questions. From the beginning they'd both known the truth was more than she could handle. They'd also both known their relationship couldn't go anywhere without honesty. He and Maggie had been doomed from the start.

"Don't worry about it," Micah grunted.

"How much does she know?" his dad demanded, rolling over in his bed and propping himself up on his elbow. He stared his son down. "No fling is worth risking your life, boy," he growled.

"Maggie wasn't some fucking fling." Micah hopped out of his chair and stalked the length of the hotel room, turning hard before he reached the door. "This is what both of you wanted. I'm here. Get up. Let's go. I can't stay in this motel room any longer."

"Let's hit the road, Jacob." Uncle Joe climbed out of his bed again and turned on the lamp next to him. "It's smart to get on the road early."

"I need coffee, and a shower." His dad dropped his feet to the floor and scrubbed his head. "What time is it anyway?"

"Somewhere around five."

His dad squinted up at his son. "You get any sleep?"

"I don't want to sleep."

His father was smart enough not to play the parent at that moment. He found his jeans, climbed into them, then pulled them up to his slender waist and zipped the fly.

"Run downstairs and bring up a few coffees. It will be faster than room service and give you something to do." His dad pulled out a ten and handed it to Micah. "If she's cute give her a big tip and flirt with her, damn it. Nothing cures the pain better than jumping onto another saddle."

Micah glared at his dad, grabbed the ten, found a key card on the desk along the wall, then stalked out of the room without commenting. What his dad said was despicable. Micah didn't want another woman. He wanted Maggie.

The three of them barely finished half their cups of coffee before room service was ordered. Micah went through a pot of coffee on his own and tried eating a plain bagel. He tossed the thing down on the platter with just one bite out of it. His stomach was in too fierce a knot to put anything in it. Showering washed the grime off him but he still felt dirty inside. He walked out of the bathroom towel-drying his hair. He doubted he'd ever feel clean again.

"About ready?" Uncle Joe had his laptop set up at the table and had opened the curtains.

"Yup," Micah said. He dropped the towel on the floor by the first bed then sat on the edge of it. "Where are we headed?"

"I've routed us out of California this way," his dad began and moved to sit next to him with his atlas in hand.

"I'll send the directions to your cell phone," Uncle Joe said.

"We'll drive south of the Rockies," his father continued, drawing a line with his finger on the map.

"MapQuest shows we can get into Texas just after midnight."

"We're going to drive that far?" Micah asked.

"Your uncle and I agree that we need to put some good distance behind us today." His father gave him a pointed look. "Just in case."

"Okay. Whatever." Micah gulped down his lukewarm coffee, stood and stretched, then grabbed his duffel. "Ready?"

"Grab my suitcase, Micah," Uncle Joe said and began shutting down his laptop.

Micah followed his dad and uncle down to the SUV they were driving and helped load their luggage in the back. They were headed to DC, and although neither his dad nor uncle had mentioned it yet, he would kill two more men.

Since when did this start to bother him?

Immediately he was so sick to his stomach his coffee began rising to his throat. Micah gripped the side of the truck, bent over, and braced himself as all the coffee he'd consumed came up with a vengeance.

"Goddamn, boy," his father grunted behind him.

Micah endured the dry heaves that followed.

"Are you going to make it?" his uncle asked and opened one of the truck's doors.

Micah straightened slowly. He stared across the parking lot, toward the busy street, and the interstates twisting around one another. Half an hour in that direction would get him to Maggie's house. Turning slowly, he focused on the other interstate. That route would take him to his next murder.

When did you start thinking of them as murders?

Slowly the sludge in his brain began lifting. All his adult life he'd fired his gun or held his rifle to his shoulder and stared at the mil dots. It had been an incredible high securing his target, then watching the body slump after a perfect aim. He had never missed, never had to shoot twice. That was, never until he'd been with Maggie. Stabler had lived long enough to point out the truth to him. Micah was just now seeing it.

When he turned, still holding on to the back of the SUV, both his uncle and his dad were watching him. They already knew what he'd just figured out.

"You're right," he told both of them.

His dad exhaled loudly and squinted at the parking lot. "Don't do this, son."

"I've got to, Dad. I love her. Maggie was right. If I leave now I won't be good to either one of you."

"If you stay here you very well could get your ass arrested," Uncle Joe hissed, looking worried as hell as he gazed at Micah over his father's shoulder.

"It's a chance I'm going to take. I can't leave like this. You didn't see her crying." Micah felt sick again.

"We can head up to Santa Clarita," Uncle Joe said to the back of his brother's head. "Won't be so bad hanging out there for a few days. That waitress liked me."

"That waitress liked *us*," his father said, disgusted.

Some women really got off on the thought of being with Micah's father and uncle at the same time. It was the twin thing. Micah's father didn't like sharing his women. Micah felt the same way. He couldn't leave LA knowing some asshole might come sniffing around Maggie. She was unemployed. Her uncle was probably going to prison. Micah wasn't going to be the ultimate tragedy in her life.

Suddenly he was no longer light-headed, or sick to his stomach. "I've got to go," he said again. This time he touched his father's arm. "I don't regret anything you've taught me," he whispered.

He thought he saw understanding in his father's eyes. "You're the best there is. The best there probably ever will be."

"I want to try being the best at other things now."

"Like what?" Uncle Joe asked.

"Like being Maggie's man."

His father shook his head, disgust still lingering in his expression. "I'll give you a week."

"Thanks for the vote of confidence."

"He meant we'd give you a week before we hit the road," Uncle Joe elaborated.

Micah nodded at his uncle. His father's expression didn't change.

"Honor-bound is honor-solid," Micah told his father. "Grandpa Paul used to say that all the time."

"Yes, he did," his father acknowledged, although his hardened expression didn't change.

"He used to say find another who is the same and they will run by your side sure as Mulligan blood runs through our veins."

His father nodded once.

"I've found that, Dad," Micah said softly, not quite getting why he wanted his father to understand—but he did. He wanted that annoyed look to go away before he left. Emotions he'd never experienced before had surfaced with Maggie. He didn't want to risk feeling more unfamiliar emotions if the last looks he saw on his father's face were disappointment and anger. "Dad, I wasn't even looking. But the first time Maggie and I spoke the chemistry was so far off the charts neither one of us could pull off much of a conversation."

"Lust is a hell of a lot different from love," Uncle Joe told him.

"Love holds you through once that lust fades, son. You think you've got that?" his father asked.

"I won't know without giving it a shot."

His father's nod was barely noticeable.

"Dad."

His father stared at him, not grunting or nodding or doing anything to show he knew his son had a question. Maggie might have a deep-rooted temper, but those roots ran just as deep in Mulligans. Micah worried his father might be angry with him for a long time.

"Tell me something before I leave."

"You keep mentioning leaving but I see you standing

there not moving. There is always a reason for hesitation."
Of course when his father finally did speak, it was to point
out Micah might have even more issues to deal with.

Yesterday Micah was a man on top of the world, strong
and invincible, more powerful than any other man alive.
Today that world had toppled to the ground. There was no
strength. No matter how hard he tried pressing forward with
his dad and uncle, Micah didn't have the strength to keep
taking the next step. In fact, he'd never felt weaker in his
life. He wasn't powerful. He wasn't invincible. He was nothing without Maggie.

"I'm not hesitating, Dad." A trait he held on to now that
he had never embraced before was honesty. And he wasn't
going to let go and release the one redeeming quality he had
swarming in a world of death—yes, murder.

"I'm going after her, Dad. This life we've built together
isn't worth losing her. Not to me. You can tell me what this
Mulligan did, or what that Mulligan did, and I'm sure all of
them took the path best for them. This is what is right for me.
She walked out the door on me and I let her go. I have to try."

"Her world is one you don't know," Uncle Joe said, his
hazel eyes softening in a way Micah's dad's never did. "Your
father is worried it's not your world."

Jacob glared over his shoulder at his twin. "I know how
to fucking talk."

"Then tell him what he needs to hear. The sun is coming
up and it's getting hot. I'm not going to keep standing here
while you two stare at each other and pussyfoot around what
needs to be said."

"Suddenly you're a Goddamn counselor?" his father
snarled.

Uncle Joe threw his hands up in the air and walked away
from both of them to the driver's side. "I'm sitting in here
long enough to smoke a cigarette, then I'm fucking out of
here," he called out.

Micah wouldn't miss his father and uncle fighting. The
two of them could go at it worse than wild dogs.

Micah waited until Uncle Joe got situated inside the SUV

and closed the door. The vehicle started and Micah continued standing next to it. The motor helped keep their conversation private.

"What was Uncle Joe talking about last night?" Micah didn't hesitate with the one question he had to have an answer to. "He said I'd break the Mulligan curse if I left without getting her pregnant. I thought the Mulligan curse caused all women to leave us."

"Either way, it looks to me as if leaving us now will only bring you heartbreak."

"I have to stay and give it a shot. Dad, tell me," Micah insisted. He wouldn't focus on how his heritage suggested any relationship he might enter was doomed from the start. He couldn't go on with his life without giving love a chance. "What did Uncle Joe mean? You said Mom left when I was ten."

"She did."

Micah put it together. "You left her when she was pregnant with me."

"Our life wasn't conducive to raising a family."

Micah stared at his father. He didn't feel inclined to pass judgment. All he wanted was to understand. "She came back to you?"

"No. I found her."

"And she took you back?"

His father grumbled and sighed. Raking his fingers through his hair, he scowled and stared over Micah's shoulder. "I don't make apologies," he began gruffly. "I was told your mama had a son. She was living in a small town in Indiana and there were some rough people around her. When word got to me I was told she was struggling to feed you and keep a roof over your head. I didn't think about it for long. The right thing to do was pretty clear. We drove into town and I went to her house. What I heard had been true."

Jacob looked down, patted his pockets, then paused before straightening again. It was an act he did from time to time when he forgot he'd quit smoking. His dad glowered, once again, at some object over Micah's right shoulder.

"Your mom wasn't too thrilled to see me. But after an evening of conversation, we agreed that I would take you with me. She showed back up in our lives when you were seven, eight, something like that. Then when you were ten she left."

"Maybe that explains why I don't have clear memories of her," Micah mused.

His father looked at him. "I did a good job of raising you."

"Yes, you did." Micah didn't hesitate. "You taught me everything I know."

"Yup."

"You also gave me values."

"I tried."

"I need to do this, Dad."

"The law is going to come down on you, boy. I don't want that for you. You took that job with that bounty hunter. He was a cop before that. Once a cop, always a cop."

Micah didn't say anything. King might turn him in. Without asking, Micah stepped forward and gave his father a hug. Jacob hesitated a second but then wrapped his arms around his son and hugged him fiercely.

"I'll see you again, Dad."

"Keep Saint Michael with you."

Chapter Sixteen

"We have a few more people to interview but we have your application and résumé and we'll give you a call if we're interested."

It was what Maggie had heard for the last two days straight. She needed a job. Plunging into interviews and driving around town from one place to another, whether it was a place she thought she'd like working at or not, had seemed a smart idea two days ago. If she had stayed at home, she would have stayed in bed and cried all day.

Maggie glanced both ways before crossing the street from the courthouse. If she were crying right now no one would have noticed. She was dripping with sweat.

"Screw this," she complained, and tossed her thin leather attaché case, which had her appointment schedule and copies of her résumé in it, to her passenger seat.

Maggie didn't understand why leather seats were considered an extra in cars. She tugged on her skirt, fighting to get it to cover the back of her legs so she wouldn't burn them when she slid behind her steering wheel. No such luck.

"Ouch!" she howled then hit her steering wheel, hurting the side of her hand. "Life sucks," she complained out loud.

After turning her car on and blasting the AC, Maggie pulled her appointment book from the side pocket of her leather case. It was one thirty, and she had a two o'clock appointment written down.

"Where? Oh no! What was I thinking?" She hadn't been thinking.

Her two o'clock was with a fugitive apprehension business, which was how she'd written it down. When she looked at the address, she groaned. It was KFA. It had to be. Apparently they were looking for an office manager to answer the phones, schedule appointments, and do light filing as well as payroll. Maggie had scheduled interviews or dropped off résumés with anyone who had a job opening in her field. She'd gone to eight different companies since yesterday morning; this was her last appointment.

"I can't do it." She slammed her appointment book shut. It would be too hard knowing Micah had worked there. The owners would know she had history with him. Hell, they had fired him. It would be pointless to even try.

Which meant it was one thirty in the afternoon and she didn't have anything to do. She would not drive by Micah's house again. Correction, old house. She had stopped by there yesterday only to find he didn't live there anymore. Less than twenty-four hours after she'd walked out on him, he had disappeared. That knowledge had brought on a fresh round of tears. He told her he loved her but wouldn't even fight to have her.

"The hell with you, Micah *Mulligan*," she grumbled and scowled at the cars in front of her.

Maggie didn't want to think about going home. No one had the nerve to say I told you so to her face, but their looks when they saw her tearstains and puffy eyes were enough. Not even Deidre, who'd been there the night before eating brownies in the kitchen, said a word when Maggie had traipsed in, pulled a bottle of water out of the refrigerator, and shuffled back to the stairs and up to her room.

It didn't make her feel any better when she arrived home and no one was there. Maggie headed inside and dropped her purse on the kitchen counter.

"Mom, I haven't seen you cooking in quite a while." Maggie approached her mother, who was humming over a pot on the stove.

Lucy O'Malley was wearing her rosebud apron, a Christmas present from all of them when Maggie had been a child. Her mother had lived in it for years but hadn't put it on in ages. Nor had she hummed over a steaming pot of something that smelled delicious. Maggie inched closer trying to see what her mother was cooking.

"Your father was in the mood for his Irish stew. You know how I hate making those Irish dishes," she said, wrinkling her nose but then smiling at Maggie. "How did your job hunting go? Your father told me you had quite a few prospects lined up."

Maggie would have thought her mom would have made some comment about her youngest brother being wrongfully incarcerated, which had caused Maggie to lose her job in the first place. Instead her mom smiled at her before returning to her cooking.

"I went to a few places. Nothing yet." She'd left her attaché case in her car. Not that it mattered tonight. She wouldn't line up more places to apply until tomorrow, if she managed to get out of bed. Somehow she had to get her mind off Micah.

"I know you'll find the perfect job," her mother promised, then held up a wooden spoon that dripped with thick sauce and had chunks of potatoes and meat on it. "Now come here and tell me what you think."

Maggie wasn't sure her stomach could handle food. Still, seeing her mom in the kitchen, and cooking, was the best sight she'd seen since last seeing Micah. She stepped forward obediently and blew on the stew before taking a bite.

She barely tasted it when she chewed and swallowed. "Mom, it's delicious. Is there some kind of occasion?"

"I need an occasion to make my husband his favorite dish?" she asked, accusingly.

Her dad entered the kitchen from the hallway, wearing his forest-green vest and suspenders. He was dressed the way he always had when he went to work every day. These days he was usually in an undershirt and gray slacks, unless it was a day he claimed to go to the office and spent the day at the bar.

"Two of my favorite women," he announced, coming forward as he sniffed the air. "And what is this delectable dish I smell?"

John O'Malley grabbed his wife's rear end and she giggled, sounding worse than a flirting schoolgirl. He wrapped his arms around her waist and rested his head on her shoulder.

"Is it ready yet?"

"You're impossible," Maggie's mom declared, although she was still giggling.

Maggie didn't need this after the day she'd had. Her parents were in the Twilight Zone. They'd barely touched each other in the past ten years. She tried not to gawk, but her confused expression must have been apparent. The two of them looked at her and both started laughing.

"What are you two up to?" Maggie yelled, unable to keep her own miserable life in check and let her parents enjoy flirting with each other. "Cut it out, right now. You don't hug, or touch, or cook for him," she wailed.

"My poor girl," her mother said, resting the cooking spoon on the counter and coming up to Maggie.

Her mother was wearing perfume. Maggie was too confused to think. She couldn't remember when her mother hadn't last smelled like Bengay, or body sweat from sleeping for several days without bathing. That's when it dawned on her that her mother had bathed, and done her hair, and put on makeup.

"I'm going upstairs," she told both of them, too baffled to think. But if her parents were enjoying a romantic night together, the last thing they needed was their moping daughter bringing them down.

"Hold on a minute. Sit down here." Her father took her arm and led her to the table. "Your mother and I need to talk to you."

"Talk to me?"

"Listen to your father, sweetheart. This is important."

Maggie slid into one of the kitchen chairs, watching her parents warily. None of her brothers or sisters would believe her if she described John and Lucy O'Malley's behavior right now. Maybe they were doing drugs.

"Your mother and I have been talking," her father began, then reached out and took Maggie's hands. "It's not fair for you to have to live here instead of having a life of your own. Children take care of their parents when they are old and decrepit, but that is after they have a family of their own, not before. We both want you to be able to move out like your brothers and sisters and find that special man, get married, have a family."

"Wait!" Maggie leaped out of her chair. "Is that what this is about? No! I was drunk," she insisted, shaking her head and pointing at both of them. "And an idiot. And wrong," she insisted. "I'm not here under protest. I promise. I mean," she stumbled, looking at her mom. "Seeing you cooking and wearing your favorite apron is such a wonderful thing."

"Isn't it?" Her father looked at her mother with unadulterated love in his eyes.

Maggie was instantly jealous, and then she felt guilty. She wanted to be looked at the way her father looked at her mother, but only by one man. She couldn't handle his past life. In fact it still terrified her. But what if Micah really had changed? She was sick and terrified just imagining what it might have been like to be an assassin. Those demons in his eyes had started to go away. Was it because of her? Without her, had he run back to his old life? That thought turned her stomach even more.

"Tell her the good news," her mother prompted and picked up her wooden spoon.

"Yes. Right," her father said and cleared his throat. "Sit back down, Maggie. We've made a decision."

"I hope not based on what I said," she mumbled, and slumped in the chair.

She hadn't noticed the stack of brochures on the table until her father slid them in front of her.

"We're moving."

"You're what?" she cried out.

"Your mother and I are moving into these condominiums.

They have a special hospice center that will help your mother.
There are all kinds of activities."

Maggie flipped through the brochures. "Mom, Dad, how
are you going to afford this?" she whispered, her heart sinking. Why did she always have to be the one to explain to
them what they could and couldn't afford? She just didn't
have the strength to do it right now. "They seem very nice,"
she added flatly, but didn't have a clue how to take the sting
out of the reality she would have to break to them.

"Your brother Bernie is going to buy this house. He's already started the paperwork with the banker. The check
from selling this house will cover all our expenses there."
Her father beamed at her.

Maggie stared at him dumbfounded.

"It looks like you'll have to move out," her mother told
her, grinning broadly.

Micah parked his motorcycle in the circular drive in front of
KFA. Two of the three black trucks were gone. The truck he
had driven when he still had a job was parked in the driveway. There wasn't any reason to go inside. King wouldn't be
here. Micah didn't know if he'd be chased off the property
or not. But at least with only Patty in the office, he might be
chased, but not with a shotgun aimed at his back.

Micah reached the door to the office but didn't enter. Instead he held on to the screen door handle and listened to
Patty inside. It sounded as if she were on the phone.

"Yes, they fired me. Can you believe that? After all I've
done for them," she wailed, sounding like the snooty pain in
the ass she'd always been. "Haley tells me my services are
no longer needed, then not five minutes later decides she's
going with her husband to chase down some creep by Old
Shumba Creek. The bitch has the audacity to tell me she
needs me to man the phones until she returns. I have half a
mind to walk out of here and leave the place unlocked."

Micah didn't wait to hear what else Patty might complain
about. She loved to pout but Micah seriously doubted she
would actually leave the office unattended. She wasn't daring

enough. Instead he hurried back to his bike, started it, then pulled a quick U-turn in the driveway. Old Shumba Creek wasn't too far from there.

It wasn't actually a creek. From what the Kings had told Micah the last time they chased a fugitive there, Old Shumba Creek was once a stream, but today there was no water. There were high cement walls running along either side for a good portion of the old creekbed. Tunnels that had once been used to drain water were now stomping grounds for a lot of the homeless. And if someone needed a place to hide out, Old Shumba Creek was an ideal location. It had been a bitch chasing down their last guy, especially with no cell phone signal in the tunnels.

Micah found the black Avalanches easily enough. He parked not too far from them, then hoofed it over the hill and down into the creekbed. Micah stopped at the first three tunnels and listened. They were ideal hiding places if no one said anything. If someone in the tunnel talked, it was another story. The echo that carried made it easy for anyone standing outside to hear a lot of what was said inside. Deciphering it remained a problem, though, since three or four conversations could travel to the entrance of the tunnel at the same time.

At the fourth tunnel, Micah wondered what he was doing there. He'd thought catching King right after he'd made a bust and the man was high on victory would be the best time to try to get his job back. Ben was a felon, although wrongly accused, and King had given the kid a chance. Micah wasn't anything. King had his strong assumptions, but Micah was willing to challenge those assumptions. The monster was now part of his past. If he could convince King, without admitting his guilt, to give him another chance, he would prove to him and Haley that he was a changed man. Then he would get a place over on Maggie's side of town. It had all sounded like the perfect way to win her back. Now he wasn't so sure.

And what if his dad's and uncle's fears were proven true? His uncle had pointed out that Micah hadn't lived in this world as everyone else had. Granted, Micah had worked for

KFA and they hadn't thought him strange—just a mass murderer. But what if Micah hadn't read King right and he
would turn Micah in to the cops? Maybe he already had
called and given the police the heads-up.

Micah had the money to buy a nice home. He could set
up house and wine and dine Maggie until she wasn't pissed
at him any longer. Or at least it had been a thought. If Micah
truly wanted Maggie's heart, he needed to show her he
wasn't going to be the man he had been before any longer.
He desperately wanted Maggie's heart. He was doing all of
this just for her.

Wasn't he?

The echoes from the fourth tunnel were inaudible. Anyone in that tunnel was far enough back that their voices
weren't carrying well to the entrance. Micah looked over his
shoulder. He'd hiked a fair distance. He looked ahead of
him. If he remembered right, there were three more tunnels
to go.

When Micah reached the last tunnel he stood in front of
it quite a while before giving up and hiking up and out of the
man-made creekbed. He must have missed them. Micah
wasn't worried about Patty having seen him at the office. The
girl was dense. But if King saw Micah's bike, he would know
something was up. It would be easier to talk to the man if he
didn't know Micah was coming. He didn't want King having
time to prepare all the arguments he would spit out.

Or time to call the police. Why hadn't that ever bothered
him before?

Micah stared across the street and began walking. Part of
him wanted to run back to his bike. The other part of him
wanted to take his time. For all he knew King might have
returned to his truck, spotted Micah's bike, and called the
police—and now all of them were waiting for Micah to return. He really didn't want to go to jail.

It almost seemed a crime for him to be arrested now. No
pun intended, he thought morbidly. Maybe he would have
laughed but the thought soured his stomach instead. He had
finally reached a point when he'd seen how the first twenty

years or so of his life—as far back as when he first held a gun in his hand—had been wrong and misguided.

Micah could have blamed his father, and his uncle. They taught him to shoot. They fine-tuned him until no creature was safe from his bullet. Then, as a teenager, he'd perfected his aim, found pride in where he shot, and not just that he killed. But it was in his late teens that he'd first announced it was no longer enough.

Micah had no one to blame but himself. He stared down at his feet as he walked slowly along the paved road. His dad and uncle did everything but beat him to a bloody pulp the night he insisted he could kill a man. Micah wasn't going to hear anyone's argument. His mind had been set.

Staring ahead, there was still a distance before he reached his bike. Large trees cast their shadows from across the road. He walked in and out of the shadows, barely feeling the sun when it glared down at him. The next tree would send down its shade.

A chill rushed over him. Micah didn't remember the exact day, or moment, when he and his dad and uncle became the tight unit they were for the next ten years. His father made connections. Anyone interested in Micah's services contacted Mulligan's Stew. His uncle worked the computer side of it. He researched, validated sources, and did background checks on all requests. Uncle Joe and his dad often showed Micah new models of guns, accessories to fine-tune his craft. Micah left the hotel room of whatever city they were in and found the ideal spot. He never used equipment for that; he used his own intuition and how it all felt to him once he was where he needed to be. Then the moment would arrive when he would raise his rifle to his shoulder, stare through the viewfinder, line up mil dots on his target. Or other times Micah would use a handgun, taking pride in his aim and his ability to disappear in a crowd or deserted field the moment that trigger was pulled.

The moment the trigger was pulled.

A fierce shiver attacked him as he walked through an exceptionally dark patch of shade. Micah looked at the trees across the street. Every time he pulled that trigger he'd murdered someone. There was no way he could count the endless numbers of lives he'd taken. It was something King had read to him in one of those cop's personal notes. It returned to him now. Micah and his dad and uncle had become judge, jury, and hangman each time they agreed to an assassination.

He blew out a breath, overwhelmed by his thoughts. Somehow he would move forward. And hopefully not behind bars. Even as he tried coping with the numbers of deaths tallied resulting from the pull of his finger, Maggie came to mind. Was there any way he could get her to forgive him for who he'd been? Was there even enough time left in both of their lives for him to show her he was a new man?

And he was. He felt it in his bones, in his brain, and in the incredible pressure in his heart.

Something caught Micah's eye across the street. The trees went on forever adjacent to Old Shumba Creek, although it looked more like a mowed forest to Micah. Closer to where he had parked his bike there was playground equipment and a Frisbee golf course. But at this end it was just trees and grass. And there was someone standing next to a tree about halfway into the park from the street.

They weren't looking in his direction. Micah recognized the stance, the fold of the arms, and the way the person continued to look over his shoulder at something on the other side of the tree. The person was holding a gun in both hands. It was held up close to his face. He leaned with his back to the tree but glanced repeatedly away from Micah, and at something beyond his tree.

Micah trotted across the road and to the nearest tree. His back was to the road, but this time he didn't need to shield himself from the world. He wasn't a criminal, an assassin hired to kill someone. This time he was an innocent bystander who just happened to know how a person looked when they were getting ready to shoot someone.

There were several nearby trees close enough to hopefully keep Micah from being spotted. He ran the distance from the tree, where he stood farther away from the street and closer to the man. Micah stopped at a tree large enough to shield his body and inched around it until the man was in view again.

The guy was too far away to accurately judge his age. By the way he turned his neck repeatedly, remained relaxed with his back against the tree trunk, and kept his gun pointed up with both hands holding it, Micah guessed him to be thirty or younger. Age mattered. He'd learned that from King. A younger person was more agile, more daring, and more prone to spontaneous and often stupid acts. Older people weren't as agile so they wouldn't put themselves in positions where they had to run long distances, climb fences, or perform acts of idiocy as King called them. But they would think things through better than a young person would and wait in a hiding place longer. They had more patience. King had made it clear, though: Age didn't matter when it came to how well a person aimed. Micah would have to agree. He'd mastered his aim by the age of eighteen.

Another person stood by a tree not too far from where Micah had spotted the first person. Micah glanced at the ground around him. Thanks to the city's expenditures maintaining its park, the ground wasn't covered with lots of twigs that might make noise if he stepped on them. He made it to the next tree without either person spotting him.

That's when he spotted the third person, a man. Two of the three people were wearing black vests . . . bulletproof vests. All three of them were still too far away to distinguish faces, but by the build of the second and third people they were a man and a woman. Neither of them was looking over their shoulders, or pressed to the tree the way the first person was. The man and woman were searching, looking around them cautiously. They were looking for the man with the gun.

It was clear why they couldn't see him and Micah could. They were positioned all wrong. Then the woman held a black box up to her mouth. She looked in the direction of the

large man for a moment, then slipped the black box, a walkie-
talkie, against her pants. Micah watched her run to another
nearby tree.

The man with the gun spotted her, too.

Micah understood what he was witnessing. The man and
woman were Greg and Haley King. The third man had to be
who they were hunting.

The man moved so he didn't have his back to the tree any
longer. He aimed his gun straight at Haley. Micah placed his
hand on his own gun. Everything he owned was packed on
the side of his bike. But his own gun, the one he had often
chosen for kills in the past, was hidden under his shirt. Micah had owned many weapons, had used all different types
of handguns or rifles, but this small gun, best used for closer
contact when he needed to draw fast, had always been one
of his favorites. It slid into his hand without thought.

Too many years of training kicked in. Micah didn't have
to plot out his next move. He didn't need mounds of information from his father and uncle. The monster in him roared
to life. That man would not kill Haley!

Micah aimed and fired, adjusting his target at the last
minute. This bullet wouldn't go through the heart.

He didn't have a silencer this time. Micah wasn't used to
the loud bang sounding off in his face. It wasn't the first time
he'd fired a gun like this, but nonetheless it startled him, especially when he heard another shot that sounded almost as
loud.

The guy had fired his gun and Micah watched in horror
for a second. He knew he hadn't missed. But had he fired too
late? The man he had aimed at slumped to the ground. At
the same time a large branch high in the tree above Haley
came crashing to the ground.

Haley screamed and pulled her gun, looking around her
frantically. King raced over to her, his agility amazing for a
man so tall and muscular. Their guy lay on the ground,
howling in pain. King didn't look at his fugitive. He wrapped
his arms around his wife and looked over her head directly
at Micah.

God damn it! Reality came crashing in around Micah so hard and fast it almost suffocated him. What the fuck had he just done? This wasn't how he had wanted to talk to King. All the man's suspicions were probably just confirmed.

He looked down at his gun that he still held in his hands. His father, his uncle, even Greg King had all been right. Micah was a monster. He had been brought up and trained to do one thing, and one thing only—kill.

But he hadn't killed. Not this time. The guy would have shot Haley. It could be her cries of pain sounding through all the trees right now. Micah had saved her from that gunshot wound, which might have been fatal. Maybe she wouldn't have been howling in pain. She might have been silent and lifeless. King was holding her in his arms, standing, instead of slumped over her lifeless corpse.

There was no guarantee anyone else would see it that way. King probably saw, or he would hear soon, how tough a shot Micah had just pulled off. Micah had only seen half of the man's body when he'd fired. The man was turning toward the other side of the tree when Micah took his shot. Micah had aimed at the lower side of the man's torso. He'd intentionally shot to keep the man alive.

His head still spun with the inevitable repercussions of his instinctive action. Damn it. He wouldn't go to prison.

Micah hurried to the edge of Old Shumba Creek. His first thought was to toss his gun down there and run. But the gun would be found. It would be too simple to match his gun to the bullet that was in the man screaming in pain across the street. Micah had never left his gun near a kill before. All of Micah's weapons stayed with him. When he did a kill, though, Micah took the time to survey his surroundings and always had a foolproof escape route devised before he fired his gun.

So what would his foolproof escape route be here? If he were stuck being this monster, even if he had fired to save Haley's life, then he needed to use his training to get out of this predicament.

Micah hurried to the edge of the old creek. No, climbing

back down would be a bad move. He'd be easily spotted from where he stood. Micah could see quite a distance going in both directions. That left one option. Micah picked up his pace and continued walking toward his bike, which would also mean passing the black Avalanches.

King had spotted him. But would he call Micah in or console his wife and stay with his fugitive until an ambulance showed up? More than likely either he or Haley had already called in a man down. Micah wasn't sure how far away the nearest first-response vehicles were, but he wouldn't take any chances. Micah picked up his pace and stared at his bike. He had to get out of there before authorities showed up.

Someone took off from the trucks and raced through the trees across the street. It was Ben Mercy. He ran at full speed, not looking in Micah's direction. A car drove up from behind and Micah leaped to the side of the road. His heart damn near lodged in his throat. A mother with children drove past him in a minivan not once looking at him. No one was paying any attention to him. Maybe he was in the clear. His bike was just up ahead.

"Jones!"

Micah was almost to his bike.

"Jones! Wait!"

King was yelling for him. He wasn't yelling Mulligan, but Jones. After all his accurate accusations, had King and his wife decided to let it drop when Micah left their house? They had fired him because they believed he was Mulligan. Micah had never confirmed it, but King's evidence was damning. Had the Kings decided without his confession that maybe they were wrong?

"Jones!" King yelled louder. "Quit walking away from me!"

Micah stopped and turned around. The giant of a man moved at a fast-paced walk toward Micah.

"You didn't kill him," King said in a voice so soft it was completely opposite his harsh warning to quit walking just a moment before.

Greg King stopped when he was an arm's length from

Micah. He stared him straight in the face. "Thank you for saving my wife's life," he said, and sounded sincere.

Micah shrugged. He had to be more uncomfortable receiving the gratitude than King had been giving it.

"I had the shot," he said nonchalantly, as if that would explain his reason for being there at the same time the Kings were chasing down a fugitive. Micah added for good measure, having every desire in the world to delay the inevitable conversation that would follow, "And KFA doesn't bring them in dead. They bring them in alive so they can be tried and convicted in a courtroom where so much of the taxpayers' money is spent on a daily basis." Micah repeated what King had told him shortly after he'd started working there.

"Yup," Greg said nodding, then started walking, this time much slower than either of them had been before.

Micah fell into stride alongside him. When King didn't say anything right off, Micah understood the man was giving him the chance to come clean as to why he was at Old Shumba Creek. There were several ways he could play this, but only one that mattered to him. Micah had to come clean. His days of lying and killing were over.

"I didn't kill him on purpose."

"I know," King said immediately. He didn't quit walking when they came up alongside the rear of the first black Avalanche. "He'll be hospitalized but he might live."

"He had a gun pointed at Haley," Micah pointed out. "From where I was I saw him with his back against the tree. Then I saw both of you. When Haley ran to the next tree, he turned and aimed. I acted on instinct."

"You saved her life."

Micah didn't comment. He hadn't planned on gloating over the shot and wouldn't start doing so now. They reached Micah's bike and both men stopped. King faced him, his expression grave.

"Why are you here?"

"I want my job back." Micah looked at the older man.

King's face was weathered, and wrinkles were at the edges of both of his eyes. He stared Micah in the eye with his

bright blue eyes that weren't laced with anger and damna-
tion as they'd been the last time Micah had talked to him.

"Why would that be a good idea?"

It wasn't the response Micah had expected. He'd thought
King might say no. Micah had a rebuttal prepared for that.
King could have thrown in his accusations that Micah was a
Mulligan and an assassin, who would inevitably bring trou-
ble to their business. Micah would deny it. But King didn't
tell him no and he didn't bring up his damning proof.

"Because I want to be a bounty hunter." Micah straightened and stared him in the eye. "I think I would be a really
good one if you give me the chance to learn."

"You want to be a bounty hunter?"

"Yes."

"Nothing else?"

"No," Micah told him, and meant it. There was no turning back. "If you turn me down I'll search for another way
to be in this line of work. I'm good at it, and . . ." He faltered
for the first time. Although he looked away, Micah was
acutely aware of King looking at him. Micah knew the answer. He looked at Greg King. "It's rewarding doing the right
thing," he said. He had to clear his throat when his voice
cracked.

"Yes, it is, son," King said quietly. "You've got a lot to
learn. Any training you've had before won't apply to this line
of work."

"Then I'd like to learn from the best."

King grunted but didn't smile. "Think you can be the
best at everything you do?"

Micah stared at the man. King hadn't decided to disre-
gard the evidence he'd found simply because Micah hadn't
confirmed it. The sun suddenly seemed to be burning his
back through his shirt. A layer of sweat broke out over his
flesh. He stared at King and understood. King had never
doubted who Micah was. He'd gathered the information to
prove to Micah that he knew.

"I think learning from you would help me in many ways."

"How is that?"

Micah looked away from him. He circled his bike and gripped his handlebar. Suddenly it wasn't hard to say what he'd always known had to be said. "You've always worked to uphold the law. Your family is solid in your community. I'm sure you have enemies, but you know who they are. And I'm willing to bet that you have never intentionally wronged anyone."

"Don't paint me out to be a saint. Because I'm not."

"I have skills I have applied to this job and I think they would be put to good use being a bounty hunter," Micah pressed, not letting King's comment stop him now that his thoughts were rolling. He spoke from his heart, knowing everything he said was the truth. If that weren't enough for King, Micah would do as he had just said. He would keep looking until someone would hire him. "I only know how to do one thing."

Micah stopped talking. He hadn't meant to say that. There was no way he could look up. His shirt clung to his torso, and the pendant hanging around his neck burned his flesh just below his collarbone. When he tried to think of something to add to his confession, there weren't any more words.

"Will that be your fallback if being a bounty hunter doesn't work out for you?"

Micah was shaking his head adamantly before he looked up at King. "No. There is no looking back. I'm only pushing forward and hoping to . . ." He'd almost done it again. Micah pressed his mouth shut before this telling-the-truth kick he was on got out of hand.

"And hoping to what?" King asked.

Micah searched for something that would make sense other than what he had almost let slip out. "Obviously I'm hoping to be good enough that you don't regret hiring me back."

"I might give you your job back," King said.

"I'd appreciate it," Micah managed, and kept control as he nodded once. It was all he could do not to grin like a damn fool and shake King's hand vigorously.

"Tell me what you were about to say."

Micah looked at him. Sirens sounded nearby. More than one emergency vehicle was approaching. He would not look over his shoulder and confirm how nervous that sound was making him.

"I'm going to have to talk to them. Better tell me now so no one else overhears."

King didn't need to say it out loud for Micah to understand getting his job back meant telling the full truth.

"I really hope never to go to prison." His mouth was so dry when he spoke, he almost choked on the words.

King nodded, his expression not changing. "It's a rare blessing when a man is given a second chance."

"Get on out of here." King started toward the ambulance and police car that arrived simultaneously. He looked over his shoulder. "And Jones?"

"Yes?"

"It's Haley's call. You can show up in the morning and kiss her ass if you want your job back."

Micah's feelings were torn when he drove away from Old Shumba Creek. King told him he would possibly give him his job back, if his wife agreed. Micah would have to beg Haley to return as a bounty hunter. He didn't like the thought of begging anyone for anything.

But it had come to this. In order to live his new life, to completely forget about Micah Mulligan, he would have to get down on his knees and humble himself. This life could have come at a much higher price.

Was having a new life worth it without Maggie? Every inch of him constricted in pain over the thought of not being with her again, never seeing her smile, or watching her moods change, or dealing with her fiery temper. Could he press forward without her? He didn't know that answer but wouldn't go back with his father and uncle.

Micah hoped he would see both of them again. He wanted them out of their family business, too. Right now he barely had the strength to pull himself through.

He'd left the interstate and realized he was in Maggie's

part of town. More than anything he wanted to drive to her house and demand she talk to him. Micah slowed, taking a scenic side street, and searched for inner strength to convince Maggie she belonged with him.

A large church was up on the left. Next to it was a school with children playing in a playground outside. Micah wondered how different his life would have been if he'd gone to regular schools with other children. He shifted his attention to the church, which looked as if it was being refurbished. A few men were on ladders outside each of the stained-glass windows.

Micah had been born Catholic. Possibly he'd been baptized. It wasn't like he remembered. His father and uncle had made reference to the Bible occasionally, and had prayed to the saints whenever Micah had acted out as a kid.

He'd pulled into an empty stall outside the church before he'd realized he had done so. Micah climbed off the bike and walked up to the stairs. He stared into the vestibule on the other side of two large doors that were propped open. It was as if someone believed he should enter. The doors were already open.

Micah took it for a sign—although he didn't know of what—and entered the large church. Immediately he smelled incense. When he paused at the entrance and stared down the long aisle to the altar at the other end of the many rows of pews, something shifted inside him. He'd never been in a church, but he knew what he needed to do.

"Excuse me," he said, lowering his voice just above a whisper and staring at the back side of an older man wearing all black. "Are you the priest here?"

The man turned around, and the white collar around his neck answered Micah's question for him.

"I'm Father Charles." The older man smiled warmly at Micah, as if he'd been expecting him.

At least Micah felt a little better thinking about it that way. His clothes were suddenly not fitting him right, and it seemed he was itchy everywhere. He tugged at his T-shirt and cleared his throat.

"Um, Father, sir," he began. God, he should turn around and leave. He didn't belong here. "I thought I wanted . . ." His words broke off. "There are things I need for you . . ." Again he stopped talking. "Damn it, forget it."

Micah hurried as fast as he could to the doors.

"Wait. Young man." Father Charles didn't yell. His voice was still calm and there was a smile in it that gave promise he wouldn't condemn or be mortified by what anyone told him.

Micah turned around. He looked at the statues in the church, at the fancy altar at the other end, and at all the pews that were probably filled with people who would be sick if they thought a monster like him had entered their building.

"Come here." Father Charles gestured. "We can talk over here," he said as if Micah had already agreed to speak to him.

Micah found himself moving up the aisle toward pews at the front of the church. He continually looked from statue to statue and felt all the saints looking down at him, waiting to hear what he would say. Then judgment would be given.

He swallowed a lump of fear in his throat and stared at the pew where Father Charles was already sitting. The older man in black with the white collar patted the space next to him. Micah knew he'd never known fear as he did right now.

"I'm an assassin," he began, deciding he'd dump it all in the priest's lap at once.

Father Charles's expression sobered, but then he nodded. "Sit down and tell me about it," he said softly.

The church building didn't crumble on top of him. All the statues of the saints didn't explode and shred his skin with pieces of stone. There were no lightning bolts or furious rushes of water through the open doors facing the street. As Micah spoke, he realized it was still sunny outdoors. The sound of hammering continued. Everything went on just as it had before he entered the church.

Once Micah started talking, he couldn't stop. Father Charles listened intently, nodding, patting Micah's hand more than once, and asking very few questions, but never looking away. Micah started from the beginning. He admitted he couldn't remember all the names, or places, but he listed off every name of each person he'd killed that he did remember. And as he did a weight he'd been carrying around with him for years began to lift.

Maggie didn't know where she was going. After hearing her parents out she'd called her younger brother, Bernie. They had a good talk, and fortunately he didn't ask for her to catch him up on her life since they'd last seen each other, which had been last Christmas. He was too excited telling her how he was buying Mom and Dad's house. He didn't seem too concerned about the fact that these life-changing decisions he and her parents had made rendered her homeless.

You've been wanting to move out forever. You're the one who announced it. Got to love your family for giving you what you want.

Maggie knew her outlook on the whole thing was bitter. Her parents were happier than she'd seen them in years. Her brother had sounded very excited on the phone. She needed a change, too. Now just to figure out what to do with her life.

Her jaw dropped as she drove past Holy Name. "What the—?" she stammered.

A car honked at her when she slowed down, her attention focused on her rearview mirror. There was no way she'd just seen Micah's motorcycle parked in front of the school she'd gone to and the church where she and her family had attended Mass all her life.

Maggie drove around the block at dangerous speeds and barely managed to stop at the stop sign. She stared down at the church and at the motorcycle. Was it just wishful thinking?

"It seriously has to be," she informed herself. Like Micah would be parked in front of her family's church.

Maggie searched up and down the street. There was an empty stall at the end of the playground close to the church. She cut out into traffic, endured being honked at again, and swung into the stall.

Old memories should have come flooding back to her. This was where she'd gone to grade school and high school.

Any other time she might have taken a minute to watch the
children play. She would have stared up at the beautiful old
church and smiled when she saw them redoing the old
stained-glass windows.

Maggie did notice the men working on the church and
opted for the side door, the one she'd entered twice a week
all her growing-up life to attend Mass with her class and the
rest of the school.

Maggie opened the door on the side of the church just as
she had when she was a child, carefully and quietly. As a
young girl she'd always been afraid of interrupting God doing something important, like keeping people alive during a
hurricane, or making sure children didn't starve to death in
Africa. Today she opened the door quietly because she was
scared to death what she'd find inside.

She closed it just as carefully behind her, letting it hit her
back before she stepped into the side vestibule and let the
doorknob click back into place without making a sound.

There were voices. Maggie worried that she willed it to
be Micah. But who would he be talking to? And why? As she
tried convincing herself how insane this was and that she
would probably end up trapped by one of the nuns, or Father
Charles, who always seemed to know what was on her mind
before she told him, she heard the man's voice again.

"Five months ago I flew into DC for one of the largest
assignments we'd ever accepted," Micah was saying. "The
men who contacted my father through the MulliganStew
e-mail address had set up the necessary appointment just as
all the rest did. Dad was extremely cautious about this meeting. My uncle was all over his computer and all of his techno
devices making sure the meeting my dad had with these men
was secure as hell. Oh, sorry, Father."

"It's okay, Micah." That was Father Charles's voice.

Maggie tiptoed forward, not sure why she wasn't letting
her presence be known. There was probably no number of
Hail Marys that would get her out of the sin of hearing someone else's confession. And that was what she was hearing.
Micah was confessing his sins, and to her priest!

She wanted to jump with joy. She wanted to throw her hands up in the air and scream Hallelujah! She wanted to do a jig right there on the thick red carpet in the most sanctified place she'd known her entire life.

"I didn't know about this meeting until it was over. That's how it always was. I told you that already."

"Yes, you did. Your dad and uncle didn't tell you anything until it was time to go wherever you had to go to kill whoever it was you had to kill."

"That's right, Father."

She wasn't able to comprehend what she was hearing. Father Charles was the best man on the planet. She and her brothers and sisters all had stories they could share about their priest. Maggie had always thought him open-minded. Father had forgiven all her sins her entire life—or better yet, God had forgiven them. But Father Charles was the best stand-in on the planet. Now that she thought about it, it made perfect sense that Micah would rid himself of so many demons to the coolest priest there ever was.

"The kill went down just the same as the rest of them did. Just like every other person I had killed in the past, this CIA agent was crooked. He was doing terrible things. That's why I was always brought in, to get rid of really bad people who had found a way to be above the law. I was the last-resort assassin. When I made my kill, families and communities lived better without some scumbag making their life hell."

Micah cleared his voice and mumbled something, probably another apology for cursing, then he continued. "It wasn't until after—about a week, maybe less after I had returned home—that my dad came home and was in a serious panic. I had assassinated a CIA agent. They were looking for me and we all knew they had the connections to find me."

"So that is when you became Micah Jones?"

"At first I had no regrets. I was proud of who I was and convinced no one would find me. But when I met Maggie my past became more of an annoyance than anything else."

"She's a beautiful girl."

"The best," Micah agreed. "I love her, Father."

Maggie's jaw dropped. Father Charles knew about her
and Micah. If she hadn't just witnessed her parents in the
Twilight Zone, Maggie might not have been able to accept
hearing her priest talking with the man she loved, the assassin, in her church. But it was fitting, just another event in the
most insane day of her life.

"After Maggie walked out on me, I cleared out the house
I'd been staying in and left to join my father and uncle. I
didn't sleep but worked all night. I woke them up when I got
to their hotel but they were happy to see me and ready to go.
Listening to them talk, hearing the same routine I'd heard so
many times before, helped me see the truth. I was a murderer. And I was preparing to murder again. I left the hotel
and my father and uncle. I was going to quit for Maggie.

"I wanted my job back first; then I would get a nice little
home in the same neighborhood as Maggie's, so she'd feel
safe. Father, I know it's blood money, but I figured I could
pay cash for a house. I have quite a few bank accounts with
quite a bit of money in them. Maggie and I wouldn't have
money problems and would always be happy."

Micah was sitting in the pew facing Father Charles. Maggie could see him behind the statue of Mother Mary, who
was hiding her from them. Maggie wasn't positive the statue
wouldn't fall over and reveal she was there. She really
shouldn't keep eavesdropping.

"It wasn't hard finding my boss. They were hunting down
a fugitive and chasing him through Old Shumba Creek."

Father Charles shook his head and clucked his tongue.
Maggie had no idea what he was thinking at the moment,
but he sat sideways in the pew, his back to Maggie, and listened intently as Micah continued.

"When I saw that the guy was going to shoot Haley King,
Greg King's wife—they own KFA together," Micah explained.

"Ahh," Father Charles said.

"Old instincts kicked in. They aren't even really old.
They are part of who I am. I shot the guy. I couldn't let him
shoot Haley. As I was aiming the gun, I adjusted my kill spot

slightly so my bullet wouldn't go through the guy's heart. King had repeated many times how we always brought them in alive. But that is when the revelation hit me. I was a murderer. I know it's clear to you that I am. Maggie knows I am. But I was obviously in denial. Not only was I a murderer but I had been the instigator the first time I killed a man. No one made me do it. I insisted on it. It wasn't until I left Old Shumba Creek that I knew I would have to conform with or without Maggie in my life. I couldn't change who I was just for her. I had to change for me."

"You've already changed, son."

"Huh?"

Father Charles put his hands over Micah's and squeezed. Micah looked down at the priest's hand over his.

"In the name of the Father, and of the Son."

Micah looked up at Father Charles, his eyes wide.

"And of the Holy Spirit."

The side door at the opposite end of the church opened and a uniformed police officer entered.

"You are absolved of your sins," Father Charles said.

The door behind her in the vestibule opened. Maggie spun around to see another cop enter. Through the space between the back of the statue of Mother Mary and the wall, Maggie spotted a third cop walking down the far aisle.

Father Charles stood. Micah did as well, backing out of the pew where the two of them had been sitting.

She heard the main doors facing the street close, causing a dull echo in the church. Others had just entered the church. Her heart sank. There was only one reason so many police officers would enter all at the same time.

She looked around frantically when a young priest appeared in the doorway alongside the altar. Father Charles walked to the front of the pews. She'd never seen her priest's face look so strained. Maggie swore he appeared torn. He had liked Micah. She was sure of it. And Micah's confession had been so heartfelt and so real.

Maggie only imagined how much better Micah had probably felt talking about all the terrible things he'd done. He had been an assassin. Micah had come to God, to her priest and in her church, to reveal his tainted and bloodstained past. He had voiced out loud his many crimes. They were things he probably would never share with her.

Now he was forgiven. There wasn't any bringing back the people he'd killed. Most towns where the people Micah had assassinated lived were probably happier now with whoever it was dead. That didn't excuse Micah's crimes, but he had known that. He hadn't asked for forgiveness and decided to walk away from his old life for her. He'd changed his ways so he could truly be happy.

Maggie had every intent of being happy with him.

She didn't have a plan. There was only one thought on her mind. She would not lose the man she loved.

Maggie marched out from behind the statue hoping no one would notice she'd been standing there. "Thank you, Father Charles," she said in a hushed tone just as the officer who'd entered from the school entrance vestibule walked up behind her.

Maggie tried for an indifferent look when she glanced over her shoulder, then walked up to Micah. He looked as confused as Father Charles did when she draped her arm around Micah's. Maggie immediately felt Micah's strength, the hard corded muscles in his arm where she touched him. There was also a sheen of sweat coating his skin, and it dampened hers.

"Thank you for showing us all the stained-glass windows," she told her priest, who to his credit was pulling off a wonderful sober expression. She smiled at him and squeezed Micah's arm. "We both agree they need major renovation and will most definitely contribute whatever amount is necessary to complete the project."

Father Charles looked at her and Micah and smiled. "That would be wonderful. Now apparently I have other matters to attend to," he said, nodding to the police officer who was standing close enough to hear their conversation.

Maggie glanced around the church at the other officers,

who weren't approaching but standing in the aisles on opposite sides of the pews. "Something terrible must have happened," she said, amazed at how calm she was. But she had to be to pull this off, and they weren't going to take Micah, not now. Not ever!

"It doesn't look good," Father Charles nodded soberly and cast worried looks at all of the cops around them. "May God bless you both. Just send the check to the church's main address. It will be a much-appreciated donation."

"Come on, dear, the kiddos are waiting," she said, then genuflected toward the altar.

"I got a phone call from the LAPD dispatch advising us to be on the alert for a man—" the young priest began.

"Excuse me." The police officer behind Maggie interrupted the younger priest. "We're looking for a single white male about six feet tall, an assassin."

Maggie walked down the aisle, her legs trembling badly as panic rose in her. If they could get out of the church and to her car they would be safe. She had to believe that. Micah had all kinds of skills. The trapped look on his face when she first spotted the two officers had left by the time she'd walked up to him. Micah was confused to see her but she had seen how quickly he'd managed to change his expression. His strong, confident walk alongside her and his firm grip on her arm helped her believe.

Micah's arm was no longer damp. He didn't hurry down the aisle. Maggie prayed he would never use any of the skills he'd learned to kill ever again for the rest of his life. But she was all for him using them to get the two of them out of the church.

"The bullet used to shoot a man over at Old Shumba Creek came from the same gun used to kill a CIA agent in Washington, DC. This man is armed and very dangerous," the officer was telling Father Charles and the young priest. "He was spotted leaving Old Shumba Creek on a motorcycle. We've confirmed it's the same motorcycle that is parked out front. We need to search your church, Father."

They were at the front vestibule. There were two officers at the front doors; another disappeared up the stairs to her right.

"Oh my," she gasped when they walked past the officers at the entrance and stared at the police cars in the street. "My car," she continued, and her heart sank into her stomach, which was already so twisted in knots she thought she might be sick.

"It's okay," Micah told her calmly. "Hopefully they will move so we can leave, sweetheart."

He fell right into her unplanned means of escape.

"I hope you're right. The sitter always gets upset if I get the children late."

Another officer on the sidewalk was informing two women that there was no cause for concern but to please take all children off the playground. One of the women turned and waved her hand wildly in the air. Immediately a whistle started blowing and teachers began rounding the children up into multiple lines to go inside.

Maggie fumbled with her purse, trying to get her keys out to unlock her door. Micah lifted her purse from her hands, reached into her purse, and pulled out her keys as naturally as if he did it every day. Handing her purse back to her, he pointed the keychain at her car and pushed the unlock button. Her back lights blinked as the car beeped once.

It was enough to alert the officer on the sidewalk. He turned, giving both of them his attention as Micah opened Maggie's passenger door for her.

"Hey, Frank," he yelled. "Let these two out, okay?"

Maggie wasn't sure if she trembled with relief or the sinking knowledge that if Micah were arrested, she could easily go down with him. She doubted any of the cops would let her go after questioning her a second time. Pushing her leather attaché case that had all of her résumés in it to the floor by her feet, she fell into the seat. Her legs began trembling uncontrollably.

"My wife complains about the same thing with our baby-sitter," the officer said.

Maggie looked up at him just as Micah closed her door and walked around to the driver's side. The officer gave her a small nod. Maggie smiled, then looked down at her hands in her lap. Already her knuckles were turning white from being clasped together so tightly.

Micah slid in next to her. The motor started. The air conditioner blasted in her face and against her blouse. They didn't move. Micah didn't say a word. Maggie glanced at him and saw how tightly he held the gearshift between them.

It seemed an eternity that they sat there. Maggie wanted to reach to lock the doors but was scared any movement she made would draw attention to them. When Micah finally put the car into drive and pulled out from her parking spot, Maggie let out a cry, her entire body imploding as she dropped her head into her hands.

All her fear and panic rushed out of her. But the relief seeped in a lot slower. Were they safe? She dared look up and out the windshield. Micah was driving through the normal amount of traffic. No cop cars were around them. She looked behind them. The police cars in front of Holy Name were still there. No one was coming after them.

Micah turned a corner sharply enough that she fell against him. Maggie grabbed her seat belt when she realized she hadn't put it on. In her panic to do nothing that might draw attention to them, she'd forgotten her seat belt while surrounded by police.

"Oh my God," she wailed as laughter and tears hit her at the same time. "I don't believe it."

"I don't, either."

Maggie looked at Micah. The unreadable mask was gone. Beads of sweat lined his forehead. When he glanced over at her, all the demons she'd glimpsed since meeting him were gone. His eyes were so clear, they were beautiful.

"I told that priest about every murder I've ever committed."

"Your past crimes are forgiven," she told him and reached out to touch his face. "You walked out of that church with a clean slate, Micah."

"Maggie, why were you there?"

"My parents are selling our house. I was out driving. I didn't know what I was going to do with my life. I have no job and soon no place to live. Then I saw your bike at the church."

"I was cursing my stupidity for parking it on the street where anyone could see it, but now I see it was the best place I could have parked."

"It's how I found you."

"I love you, Maggie," he said, those clear beautiful eyes warming as he stared at her before turning his attention to the road.

"I love you, too," she whispered. Her heart damn near exploded when a lone tear slid down his cheek and he smiled at her. "We have a clean slate to write on. Where do we go to create this new life?"

"Anywhere you say as long as we're together."

"Somehow you have to send a check to the church. I don't even have an idea how much you should send."

"I have another matter I'm going to take care of once we get where we're going."

"What's that?" Maggie put her hand to his cheek to wipe away his tear.

"There's a kid working at KFA who wants to be a bounty hunter. There are a few obstacles in his way I'm going to take care of for him."

"Bad obstacles?"

He shot a concerned look at her then nuzzled his face against her hand. "I promise, Maggie, there will never be bad obstacles in our life ever again."

"Well, I have a full tank of gas," she said and the fear that had enveloped her disappeared and was replaced with an overwhelming amount of love for the man sitting next to her.

"Where to, my lady?"

"Let's see how far a tank of gas will get us," she said, adjusting herself in the seat so she was closer to him. All she wanted was to climb into his arms, but that would have to wait.

"How do the mountains sound to you?"

When she smiled Micah grinned at her again. The visible difference between the man she'd left in that small, broken-down house and the man sitting next to her now made her ache for them to get wherever they were going as soon as possible.

"They sound perfect as long as we're together."

"One thing," he said, glancing at her again as he drove through traffic toward the interstate. "The next time we walk down an aisle in a church it will be after we've both said I do."

"I do," she whispered, and cuddled into him as he accelerated on to the interstate.

"I love you," he told her and reached over to take her hand.

"I love you, too, Micah Mulligan."

Read on for an excerpt
from Lorie O'Clare's next book

Hot Pursuit

Coming soon from St. Martin's Paperbacks

Zoey was glad to leave the bookstore before Angelina read whatever was in the envelope from her father. It wouldn't be good news. With her father, it never was. He was a tyrant and an evil, vindictive man who got pure pleasure out of making others suffer, her in particular. If he mentioned Hector Isley to her one more time, Zoey would scream. Her father had ranted all of her life about how she would marry in the church, which was his way of saying a Catholic Mexican. He and Hector's father had both decided that their children marrying would create an unbreakable financial dynasty.

Zoey got sick every time her father brought it up. Not to mention, he hadn't stepped foot inside a church her entire life. Well he might have once they moved to Zounds, but then it was only to inform the poor priests that he now owned their church and all tithings would now go to him. Which was fitting. Her father did think he was God.

She walked with her head high down the street, knowing anyone who noticed her hated her instantly for being Cortez's daughter. She wanted to scream to everyone who looked away when they saw her that she hated him, too.

Especially now. Her father would not shut up about how once she married Hector their marriage would merge two of the largest families and make all of them incredibly rich and unbelievably powerful. He would then pat her on the shoulder and remind her that she would be secure for life. As if she cared a bit for any of his bloodstained money or manipulative power.

Zoey knew what her father did. She knew he was sucking this town dry. And that was simply because it entertained him. Emilio Cortez moved to Zounds ten years ago because it was directly in between San Francisco and Seattle, two cities he held onto by the balls, as he would put it. Zounds was the perfect place for him to hide from all of the criminal activity he oversaw in both of the large cities.

When she reached the other end of downtown, Zoey turned toward the library where she'd parked her car. Zounds wasn't big enough for her to entertain herself that well. But since her father ruled over her as cruelly as he did the town, his staff, and the many other employees underneath him, Zoey wasn't allowed to leave town. She seriously jonesed for a large shopping mall or a movie theater that showed more than two movies at any given time. Or a classy restaurant with a classy man at her side.

Images of the man on the motorcycle, the Harley Davidson, popped into her mind. He had looked tall, which meant he probably wouldn't look twice at someone as short as her. She'd reached five feet and two inches by the eighth grade and had never grown another inch. Even in her three-inch heels that clicked against the paved sidewalk, Zoey barely hit five feet and five inches.

The man on the Harley had to be at least six feet tall. He'd ridden around the courtyard in front of the bookstore long enough for Zoey to get a pretty good look at him. His helmet had covered his face, but she had almost hyperventilated over all of that packed muscle under his T-shirt. He might have been riding for a while because his shirt clung to him, as did his faded jeans.

She slowed when she reached the library, which was on the opposite side of the street. Zoey didn't cross the street though, but stared straight ahead. The bed and breakfast was on the corner in one of the town's historical Victorian homes. A blond man relaxed on the front steps that led up to the wide, long front porch. Zoey came to a complete stop when she was sure he was looking right at her.

The man was too far away to see the color of his eyes but they were light. And they pierced right through her. Zoey wasn't sure she could have moved if she'd tried. At the moment though, she wasn't thinking about walking. She was trying to remember how to breathe.

He was gorgeous, absolutely sinfully perfect. Her mouth went dry staring at him. Her heart began pounding too hard in her chest. She felt her breasts swell and her nipples harden. They pressed against her low-cut silk bra and itched painfully. It was all she could do not to twist, or fidget, anything to relieve the sudden pressure that built inside her until it sank deep between her legs.

Suddenly the man stood. It was a lazy movement, and Zoey caught herself tilting her head and admiring his lethal body as he pushed away from the steps and straightened. He tugged on his T-shirt, making it stretch over too many rippling muscles. Then he was walking toward her.

Zoey suddenly came to her senses. She couldn't be talking to some stranger passing through town. There were eyes everywhere. She knew this to be true. If she even had a polite conversation with this man, her father would hear about it. If not tonight, soon. He would chastise her, lock her in her room, or force one of his thugs to escort her around town until she remembered how to behave as a Cortez should.

"How's it going?" he asked before he reached her.

Why did he have to speak to her? Her pride and self-esteem had been thrashed by this town as long as she'd lived here. Damn her father! She wouldn't be rude.

"Fine," she said, glancing at him, and then caught herself staring at a rippling six-pack as it pressed against his shirt.

Polite or not, she wouldn't stand and gawk and pray he continued to speak to her. She turned to cross the street. He held out his hand and for a moment it looked like he would grab her arm.

"Don't walk away now." He didn't touch her but simply raised his hand to detain her, then dropped it to his side. "You noticed me staring at you and I couldn't help seeing that you were staring back at me."

"Of course I was," she said curtly, and didn't look up so he wouldn't see her burning cheeks. "You were looking right at me and I thought maybe I knew you."

She again tried crossing the street. This time Zoey walked into a rock-hard muscular arm. She looked at the taut, well-formed muscles in his forearm and bicep as she took a step backward, and almost began drooling. Zoey bet every inch of him was packed as hard as steel. Every inch of him.

"My name is Ben," he said hurriedly. "Don't run off. I don't know anyone here."

A thought hit her and she almost choked from the truth that might be in it.

"Why are you here?" she demanded, facing him and this time looking up at him. "Why do you want to talk to me?"

If he even indirectly mentioned her father, she was bolting across the street. It would be just her luck for the sexiest man alive to be talking to her because she was Emilio Cortez's daughter.

"Looking for work." His light blue eyes were clear and alert as he stared down at her.

"What kind of work?" Zoey asked, not yet convinced that he wasn't here because her father had brought him here. Or worse yet, because he was after her father.

"I can do anything, pretty much. But hunting, trapping," he told her, his eyes lowering and taking in her body as he spoke. They were back on her face when he finished. "I'm at home doing those sorts of things. But like I said, any kind of work as long as it pays a fair wage."

"Good luck with your job hunting," she said, smiling. Zoey didn't want to tell him that finding a job in Zounds would be hard as hell to do, unless the job was with her father.

"I was sitting on those porch steps thinking about wandering around, getting a feel of the town. It would be perfect if someone who lived here gave me a tour."

"It's just about dark," she pointed out. "You wouldn't get a good view of the town."

Ben was by far the best-looking man she'd ever laid eyes on. There wasn't a man in Zounds, single or otherwise, who compared to him. Zoey hastily pointed out to herself that he probably would have asked anyone who came along to give him advice on the town. If they talked to him as she had, he might have asked for a tour. He was a man, just like her father's thugs, his accountants, his business partners, and gave her an appraising once-over like all the rest. None of the men on her dad's payroll looked like this, though.

"You're right, of course," he said.

For a moment she thought he'd responded to her thoughts, which was ridiculous.

"How about a ride?" he asked.

"A ride?" Zoey looked up at him, and a slow, lazy smile appeared on his lips. She wasn't convinced yet that Ben wasn't on her father's payroll, or trying to be. But wouldn't it be scandalously wonderful to spend time with someone who had absolutely no ties, voluntary or otherwise, to her dad?

"Stay right here," he ordered, pointing at her before turning and jogging back toward the bed and breakfast.

Every inch of her demanded she march across the street to the library and get in her car. She might have actually done that, but she was mesmerized staring after Ben as he jogged away from her. He didn't look like any jogger she'd ever seen. His legs were thick with muscles that pressed against his blue jeans. And his ass, holy crap! Buns of steel was just too cliché—an overused expression. There wasn't anything cliché about his ass.

For the most part guys' asses had never been her favorite part of the male anatomy. Zoey would have to say a hard cock was her favorite part of a man's body. But while dressed, and if she hadn't had the pleasure of seeing that guy's dick, she definitely wouldn't think of his ass as being the part of him she would drool over. If asked, Zoey would have to say the chest appealed to her the most. If a guy had a broad, muscular chest, it caught her eye every time.

She continued staring, lost in the perfect formation of his body. Ben didn't really jog, she decided. He ran slowly, like a dangerous beast, content with his surroundings already, and satisfied that anything in his way would move so he could reach his destination. That level of raw, carnal confidence appealed to her as much as his perfect body did.

"Shit!" she hissed.

When he disappeared from sight, Zoey scowled at the sidewalk, trying to shake sense back into her head. No way would she be allured by a man she didn't know. And in spite of physical perfection and an incredible awareness of self-confidence, she didn't know anything about this man. Her attention shot to the bed and breakfast when the sound of a motorcycle starting up grabbed her attention. She couldn't go riding with Ben on a motorcycle. Why hadn't she been thinking? When he said a ride, of course he had meant on a bike. She'd seen him on it earlier.

The thought of being on that large, rumbling bike that she'd seen Ben on when she'd been at the bookstore immediately had her trembling with need. Not just wet between her legs. And not just feeling her breasts swell as lust created a feverish desire inside her. But a full-blown tsunami-strength wave of passion that ripped her entire body open.

Ben revved his bike and she swore she felt the vibration in the sidewalk as it seared up her body. There was no way she could do this. Even if she wanted to, and God, she wanted to, taking off with a strange man on his motorcycle was absolutely insane. Beyond the obvious, her father would have her head if she were seen in the company of another man when she was supposedly engaged.

Zoey darted across the street. Her car was one of only a few left in the library parking lot. She slowed when she neared it, but her timing was off. Ben entered the parking lot and slowed his bike, then came to a stop in front of Zoey.

"Get on," he instructed.

"I don't think so." She shook her head. "I don't think this is a good idea."

"I do." He did sound sure of himself. "I only have one problem."

"What's that?"

"I don't know your name."

"Zoey Cortez." Zoey watched for his reaction.

"Well, Miss Cortez," Ben began and pushed down the kickstand to the large, rumbling bike and climbed off it.

Zoey was entranced by his long, powerful-looking legs. There were roped muscles pressing against his blue jeans and they flexed in his thighs and just above his knees as he agilely slipped off the bike and faced her. She bet if he weren't wearing his jeans, his legs would be covered with a thin spread of hair. A man as rough and tough-looking as Ben probably would have a scar, or two. Her gaze raised slightly when she tried picturing his flat stomach. But she didn't look that high up his body. Her view got locked on the slight bulge in his pants.

Before she let her mind wander down dangerous territory, Ben grabbed her by the waist and lifted her into the air.

"Oh God!" Zoey cried out, immediately clutching his tan arms.

"Spread your legs," Ben instructed, his voice soft and so calm-sounding.

"What?" she gasped. It was more like a yelp—a very unladylike yelp.

Ben didn't ask but gripped her under her arms.

"Wait! Oh my God!" Zoey would have screamed. It was right there in her throat ready to come out. But instead she clipped out an, "Oh!" when he placed her on the back half of the long, wide leather seat on his motorcycle.

Instantly, she felt the vibration of the motor between her legs. Then Ben raised his leg and straddled his bike once again. He situated himself in front of her, which basically meant her crotch was pressed against his ass and her inner thighs rubbed against his outer thighs.

"Put this on," he instructed, handing her a black helmet.

Zoey took the helmet. She slipped it over her head just as he pulled the bike around and left the parking lot.

"This is kidnapping," she yelled over the loud motor.

"Oh?" Ben slowed instantly and began crawling down Summer Street, the main street running downtown. "Want me to go back?"

Zoey wanted to bury her head in his back. It wouldn't do any good. Most shoppers had headed home for the evening. But the slower he drove, the easier it was for anyone to glance up, check out the new guy in town, and wonder what the hell Zoey Cortez was doing on the back of his bike. Her father might very well already be getting a call.

There was a mixed blessing in that. He would be pissed, beyond livid. And there wouldn't be a damn thing he could do about it. At the same time, his temper was nothing to take lightly. He'd never physically hit her. It wouldn't do to bruise her body. But her father had many other ways to make her feel just as beaten.

"No," she yelled over his shoulder, which she was able to do only because her part of the seat was noticeably higher than his. "Just keep in mind everyone knows me in this town and you just paraded us through downtown. So don't even think . . ."

His laughter cut her off. "You're in the most trustworthy hands in the state of California."

She prayed he was right. For once, she would take a walk on the wild side, or make that a ride on the wild side. She was doing something because she wanted to do it. It was daring, spontaneous, and dangerous. And she prayed she wasn't making the worst decision of her life.